DELICIOUS TORMENT

"Travis!" Shaina felt her face color hotly. "Let me go . . ."

"Don't be a fool." Travis caught and pinned her wrists against the wall, his lips hovering tantalizingly over hers.

"Damn you!" Shaina heaved herself against him, but it was useless to fight against his superior strength.

"You don't seem to understand," Travis murmured. "I know you want me as much as I want you."

The pressure of his lips against her white throat expressed his desire, and fiery sensations flamed up within her in response.

"Are you afraid, Shaina?"

"Yes," she whispered. "Of what you do to me."

"Let me teach you how to be a woman."

Gently Travis popped the buttons of her bodice with one hand while the other kept her imprisoned against the wall.

Her heart pounding wildly, Shaina swam in a torment of delicious anticipation . . .

Captive Chains

Sonya T. Pelton

ZEBRA BOOKS
KENSINGTON PUBLISHING CORP.

ZEBRA BOOKS

are published by

Kensington Publishing Corp.
475 Park Avenue South
New York, NY 10016

Copyright © Sonya Pelton

First printing: March, 1988

Printed in the United States of America

If we don't have mountains to conquer,
we are not conquerors.

For the real Shaina. And her "helper."

Chapter One

WASHINGTON TERRITORY, 1887

In the stillness of a misty early morning the shrill cry of the steam whistle could be heard to echo for miles around. Long-haired white men and Indians, wearing faded blue jeans, labored on the deck of the riverboat working industriously to stuff the boiler with pieces of wood. One and all stood back as, with a mighty cough, the big engine started. Soon the mighty paddle wheel would begin to turn, the glow of its freshly painted paddles casting flickers of whiteness onto the rippling water of the river.

Wooooh! Wooooh! Wooooooh!

A young, handsome man stepped out of a tiny cabin and grimaced. He'd never liked the shrill cry of a riverboat, but he should have gotten used to it by now. His father was the captain of the *Clementine* and he'd spend enough time around ships. He joined his father now, watching for late boarders.

Captain Wilson and his son Giles stood among all the many items: wooden orange crates, bedrolls, picks and shovels, some new items of furnishings from the East, and livestock that crowded the *Clementine*'s deck. "Any more coming?" he asked his son as the younger man stared back toward the town.

"Looks like a pile of them today, Father." Giles was tall and slim, with a fine-boned face, thin mouth, highly arched nose, and pale-brown eyes—so light in color they resembled pieces of polished topaz. His jawline was the only feature that gave strength to his otherwise weak face. He was so different from his big, robust father.

The riverboat captain, like both the long-haired Indian men who were laboring on deck and the white men approaching along the rutted roads, was as solid and as rough as a lumberjack. He was built with plenty of meat, and no excess potatoes.

The whistle shrilled again.

Wooooh! Wooooh! Wooooooh!

In reply to the echoing hoot, an assortment of mountain men and miners moved toward the river-boat. There were no women this trip—or so everyone thought. The mountain men were garbed as every other man—white, red, and tan—was dressed in this forested valley. Rough work clothes, big boots, and hats pulled low over the forehead. No weaklings here.

At the gangplank, Captain Wilson called, "Single file now, lads."

When everyone had come aboard, Carl took hold of the plank and the captain headed for the wheel. Just then one of the laboring Indians gave a grunt, pointing toward the end of the rutted wagon road.

Collectively, they turned to look at what the Indian had pointed out. "Well now, ain't *that* a damn sight," the captain chortled.

A young woman, having heard the riverboat's loud cry, hurried along the narrow path, hoping she was not too late to catch it. She pinned the big floppy hat to her head with one hand while her other lugged her overstuffed carpetbag. Since she had packed in darkness, she hadn't noticed the sheer white stocking that now peeked out of the bag.

Shaina Hill raised a slender hand to flick a heavy strand of fiery gold from her brow with pink-tipped fingers. The full, soft curves of her breasts were displayed as the material across her bodice pulled taut. Primly she adjusted the lavender scarf knotted loosely between her breasts. She'd decided to wear it at the last minute, thinking it might make her look older, more mature.

All those men, Shaina thought, *and not another woman in sight.*

Shaina tightened her lips so no one would notice her nervousness . . . if anyone was looking her way, she wanted them to see confidence. She would not show them a silly little coward! Besides, when she puckered her lips at the corners slightly, this motion, like the scarf, made her feel less the young girl.

Watching his son's mouth drop, the captain called to him, "Giles, it must be *her*. A ha—" He rubbed his large, calloused hands together—"a pretty sight for sore eyes." Not for himself, no, but the captain was looking at his son, thinking it was time he found himself a proper little lady and settled down. And what could be more proper than a schoolteacher.

"Who is *her?*" a huge Indian who spoke a little English wanted to know. He was the father of Johnny

Wing, one of Wild Mountain's school-age children.

"She the schoolteacher?" someone cried out. "Oh, yeah. Wild Mountain's supposed to be waiting for one. But they's usually homely and scrawny spinsters. This one 'pears good enough to eat!"

The huge Indian took a better look at the young woman approaching, her slender ankles kicking up froths of creamy patched petticoat as she came. "She nothing but a pretty mouse." He guffawed loudly. "Wild Mountain eats schoolteachers for breakfast. Boss man Travis make them shiver and fill pants. None stay long. Always go away." He chuckled deep. "Scaredy chickens."

"Yeah, but this 'un looks a lot younger."

"And a sight more tender than them old hens used to come to Wild Mountain!" someone guffawed raucously.

In the whole crowd of gawking men on the *Clementine,* only Giles Wilson thought of going to the gangplank to meet the slim girl with the fiery blond hair who was wearing a dress that was all worn out to a shiny cotton and clinging to a body that Giles thought might not be too skinny after all. And the closer she got, the better she looked. Her age was hard to determine. Twenty-one. Maybe older. Cordell wasn't going to like this. He hated schoolteachers to begin with, so he couldn't understand why he kept hiring and firing them. The man was too picky for his own good. He was going to get in trouble someday. At least Giles hoped so.

"Hah!" someone cracked, seeing where Giles's interest lay. "Giles will make the little lady feel right at home . . . he knows just how to sweet-talk wimmen.

Shoot, he done learnt how in Seeattle and Californ-i-ay."

Shaina shivered, and it was not from cold. Panic rose in her as she decided she didn't fit in here at all. It wasn't far to the gangplank, but whether she really wanted to reach it or not was the question. *I have to do this,* Shaina told herself stubbornly. *I need that teaching job!*

Go back, part of Shaina commanded. But she couldn't, not now! If she wasn't careful, the relative dignity of her arrival could be lost in the haste of an ignominious departure. Her limbs shook and her dainty frame bent forward, tensed with awareness of movement. *That's right, step onto the gangplank.* The other passengers had all walked across the gangplank and were gawking back at her now. "What're you all staring at?" she wanted to shout, but she just stood there and stared back at them.

Oh . . . God. Too late now. One of them, a tall, slim man with light hair and a serious face, was coming toward her. He doesn't look as rugged as the others, she told herself placatingly.

He hadn't taken his eyes from her for one moment. Then he halted immediately in front of her and looked her up and down . . . down and up. Shaina sharply lifted her fair head but still felt his pale-brown eyes flickering over her. Sheer calculating interest was alive in the topaz depths of them.

She looked *him* over now, all of a sudden not feeling so timid any longer. Although he was wearing high boots and rough work clothes he had a close-to-gentlemanly manner and he obviously wasn't a logger.

"Hello, miss," he said pleasantly, inclining his head

11

in a gesture that was somehow gallant. "You must be Miss —"

"Shaina Hill." She didn't stand on ceremony.

"I'm Giles Wilson, the captain's son." He gave her a brief, warm smile that made him look almost boyish. "The captain sent me out to see if I could give aid for you to come aboard. You *are* the new schoolteacher, I presume."

"I am," she answered with a lift of her chin and a quick squaring of her slim shoulders.

The blond man smiled again. All the ruthlessness she'd seen in him at first glance vanished as his topaz-brown eyes admired her at close quarters. His gaze dropped to the rose-pink curve of her tempting lips.

Men on deck were watching. The captain's young son, so close she could detect the shadow of tomorrow's beard on his handsome cheek, was waiting. Again she fiddled with the lavender scarf, and when she looked up again she found those beguiling brown eyes lifting slyly to her face. This, she thought amusedly, was beginning to be quite an adventure. With a smile of her own, Shaina announced, "I will follow you," and quickly snatched up her carpetbag so he wouldn't think she expected him to carry it.

Head high, Shaina walked sedately past the lusty grinning men and sat down as gracefully as possible on the wooden bench nailed to the bulkhead of the cabin.

Giles Wilson, his eyes warm upon the new passenger, could not know how close Shaina Hill had come to running back to where she'd come from. Nor could Giles know Shaina's other secrets: that the new schoolteacher had never attended school herself longer than two months at any one time and that she had lied about her age in order to get the teaching job at Wild Mountain.

But neither would Giles Wilson have worried about all that rubbish. He wanted Shaina Hill, that's all he knew.

Chapter Two

The *Clementine,* bathed in the delicate pink glow of morning, shuddered along her wet path upstream as the dense, green, timbered hills hugged close at one side and became thinner, grayer shadows at the other. Assorted trees and conifers tangled with ocher weeds and verdant brush and concealed what could be on the slopes above — *like Indians,* Shaina thought.

She felt the hair rise on her arm as the captain came to stand by her, startling Shaina for a moment. "You surprised me," she said, then relaxed as he joined her in admiring the river country.

"Used to be wilder here," he was saying. "Ain't so bad now, not so many wild Injuns . . . but they're still poking about. Now there are new settlers coming in all the time to the valley."

"I've spotted a few cabins in the clearings above the river," she said, wondering about those who lived in them and what kind of lives they led.

The captain smiled, eager to tell the interesting young woman more. "See there." He directed a finger toward a homestead, its doors and windows opening onto the waterway. "The river is their only road."

"Umm, it's rather romantic when you think about it." Shaina felt her trepidation falling away as she studied the beauty of the river valley. The dark silver river flowed deep and sluggish and here and there, cedar canoes were moored to long logs or an overhanging branch. Children, laughing and skipping stones into the river, waved as they waited for the mail on muddy landings. Shaina smiled, waving back with slim, ivory arms. The sun felt good now.

The way became darker the farther upstream they went. They were slowly pushing into the very wilderness of the valley. Shaina was sitting quietly upon a bench, enjoying the savage beauty of the river country, her hands resting easily in her lap. She had no idea the men were watching her, staring blatantly from a respectful distance when they thought she did not see them. She rested her head on the bulkhead, relaxing and soaking up the warm rays of sunshine.

Shaina cared not what the men thought, or anyone else she might meet in Wild Mountain for that matter. She was here with one purpose in mind. But now every smack and deep gurgle of the paddle wheel snatched her farther from the nice, secure world she'd dreamed of once finding in the big city. She made a promise to herself, here and now. "I'll be back in the city," she murmured, her eyes closed, not caring if anyone heard, "before long!"

"Miss Hill?" A throat cleared, the voice went on. "Are you comfortable?"

"Hello, Mr. Wilson," Shaina said, opening her eyes to the pleasant sight of his handsome face bending over her in concern. "I am very comfortable, thank you. The sun feels so good."

"Lovely, isn't it?" Giles smiled into the dark-blue eyes, fringed by thick, spiked lashes.

For long moments Shaina sat in the glow of his gaze. She wanted to ask him so many questions and she wanted to tell him how grateful she was he'd come to her rescue—otherwise she might have never boarded the *Clementine* on her own. For some reason, however, she could not break the tranquility of her relaxed mood. It was nice to have him smiling at her . . . as if he knew her plight and understood.

For several minutes more she basked in the peacefulness of the deep afternoon, then shielding her eyes from the sun, asked, "Do you work on the *Clementine?*" She smiled. "I mean, are you following in your father's footsteps?"

He smiled back at Shaina. "I don't intend on doing this—" he gestured around the deck"—the rest of my life. Really, I'm at my best when I'm studying law in Seattle."

"Oh, then you're an attorney?"

"Yes." A tawny wave fell over his forehead, and Shaina again realized how handsome he was.

"Then," she went on, desiring to have him continue this conversation with her, "you plan to be an attorney right here in the valley?"

"No. My plans are to live in town . . . I don't much care for Wild Mountain. I never will. Before long," he said softly, watching her beautiful blue eyes closely, "I will be practising law in Seattle."

"Oh, in a few years I'll be teaching in Seattle, too!"

He stared at her for long moments, looking as if he would like to kiss her. "You will?"

"Yes. At least I hope so."

16

"I'm glad."

The softness of the air, the savageness of the land, drew Shaina's attention once again, and she breathed deeply and feasted her eyes on the riverbanks. When she looked at Giles again, he was smiling that boyishly wicked grin that went clear to her toes. She hadn't thought much of love or marriage, but she hoped that there was a man waiting for her somewhere. Someday. Right now all she could think of was making her way in life.

Giles's voice broke her reverie. "I am needed . . . I'll speak to you again later, Miss Shaina Hill."

With that, the handsome, fair-haired man strode to another part of the riverboat. Shaina leaned back, resting her head against the bulkhead while the challenging mountain ahead drew closer and closer.

Shaina was conscious of her heartbeats and of the eyes, green, hard glittering green. As the man looked at her, she had the strangest sensation that he was wishing he'd never met her. She trembled with an emotion she couldn't fathom. Then his face came nearer. Now his mouth lowered and his lips were on hers. Violently Shaina's heart pounded against her chest, and her body was suddenly limp, completely helpless as the stranger's mouth crushed Shaina's into submission . . . arms tightening as they slipped all the way around her . . . and the kiss continued. Shaina felt encompassed by a fiery cloak. Arms . . . a man's virile arms. Whirling her around in a dizzying spiral were multicolored sensations . . . whirling while the lips plundered hers, whirling until the blood seemed

17

to be rushing madly through her very veins . . .
·"Miss Hill!"

Warm hands were pulling her up from the spiral she'd fallen into, and when she opened her eyes Shaina found her shoulders being held in Gile Wilson's secure grip. Looking down over herself, with her feet flat on the floor, Shaina realized she'd fallen asleep on the bench, and had been apparently rolling off the thing.

Shaina confusedly stared up into Giles's handsome face. She had been dreaming. He had kissed her hard and brutally until a million stars had burst in her head. Dear Lord, and she was telling herself only moments before falling asleep that romance was impossible, even *stupid* for her to think of at this point in her life. Swallowing hard, gazing into Giles's face as he asked her if she was all right, Shaina discovered the man kissing her had not been Giles at all, as she'd first thought upon awakening, but someone else . . . a stranger with disturbing jade-green eyes.

The Indians on deck stirred, sat up, sleepily scratching themselves, stretched, and then pulled their bandannas back into place. Shaina stood, too, giving a small smile to those who were smiling at her . . . as if they shared a secret she was left out on. One Indian, one she'd heard called Red Wing, was gaping and grinning hugely. With icy calm, she stared back. *How dare he grin so wickedly!* she was thinking. She had a good mind to tell him to jump in the river! And yet what could she do? She was a mere woman, alone with all these men. She hoped that the gentler sex at

18

Wild Mountain would greet her with kindness and some respect, but here on the boat she hadn't met any women at all.

She knew she was going to have to fight all those against her . . . no matter how difficult. And she would win, too, she'd show them. Even the man with the green eyes . . . if such a one existed!

It was right before shadows lengthened in the afternoon that Giles Wilson paused at her elbow to say, "Wild Mountain River is just up ahead. Around the bend . . . and we'll be there." His eyes seemed say, Don't be afraid . . . everyone will like you.

"Thank you" was all she said.

Again he paused, turning back to face her when he would have walked away. "Are you expected at the Cordell ranch?"

"Cordell?" Shaina was startled by the name for a moment. "Oh, yes, Travis Cordell." Why did the mention of the domineering man — for surely he was that — why did it cause her nerves to become frayed?

"That's him." Giles Wilson frowned. "And Noah Starr."

"Yes, those were the names in the letter I received." She looked at Giles strangely. How was it that he knew everything?

Giles nodded slowly, again giving her the warm smile that lit up his thin face.

"You'll need a horse."

"A horse? Why?"

"You wouldn't want to walk from the boat landing, would you?"

"Is it that far to the ranch?" Somehow she'd pictured Cordell's ranch situated at the foot of Wild

Mountain a mere hop from the river's edge.

"Wait for me at the hotel," Giles was saying. "I'll get two horses and accompany you to the ranch."

Relief washed over her. It was only momentary, however, as he added, "The country can be . . . difficult."

Before he strode away, she added, "Thank you again, Giles . . . I mean, *Mr. Wilson!*" Furiously she blushed.

"No," he corrected. "Call me Giles." That devastating smile again. "It feels better."

Shaina's uneasiness stayed with her in spite of Giles's encouraging manner toward her, and as they approached the settlement, she saw the muddy bank crowded with lots of people. They stood in a clearing so wide and long, Shaina could only think of it as having been man-made. The blue-gray sky was deepening to amethyst and the big trees beyond were sighing as the *Clementine* pushed closer. Now Shaina could actually make out faces of the people who stood there.

So many children—of all sizes and color, some barefoot, and even bronze-skin lads with hair so long it was pulled behind and braided—children who, Shaina knew, were Indians. So many men with beards, dark shirts open at the throat, their women dressed in calico and colorful shawls.

If you counted the Indians, Shaina thought, they would outnumber the whites. The older Indians were dressed only in breech clouts, and Shaina shivered at the mere thought of such scanty dress. Blankets of gray, turquoise, and red were wrapped around some, their hair, which was long and hanging, loose about their shoulders. The younger Indians—some, at least—were wearing trousers, shirts, and boots of the white man's dress. For the most part, the Indians were silent, while the whites shouted greetings across the strip of water separating them from the riverboat. From the bronze faces stared night-black eyes, and Shaina felt a cold knot form in her stomach. She had never been even this close to one Indian . . . let alone half a tribe!

As the riverboat crept up to the landing, Shaina saw the town come into view and her heart fell in disappointment. The sun had been swallowed by the darkening sky and the structures up ahead appeared deep purple in the encroaching shadows of evening. She could make out a weatherbeaten sign bearing one word: Hotel. There looked to be a store, a warehouse, and . . . not much more.

The *Clementine* chugged and gasped to a halt. Men elbowed forward to the gangplank. Giles Wilson strode past, a huge mailbag over his shoulder. "See you at the hotel," he said, and then disappeared into the blankets and children and noisy dogs.

"Well," Shaina said, hoisting her carpetbag, "how do you like that?"

Trying to act calmer than she felt, Shaina walked down the plank to the landing and up the muddy slope, her strawberry-blond hair bouncing down her back. Some voices came to a halt as she walked by; others grew louder, boisterous, voices owning leering eyes. Once or twice her overcautious steps made her stumble and, unbeknownst to her, the lavender scarf had become loose from all the fiddling and slithered to the ground. Heedless of its loss, she continued on her way, heading directly for the creaking sign at the hotel.

Shaina heard a voice at the river's edge shout and her heart picked up its beat. She had heard every word distinctly. "Where's that shipment for Travis Cordell? Travis is getting impatient. Been waiting a long time!"

"Shoot!" a voice answered back. "Tell Cordell to send his own crew down to unload if he can't keep his pants on!"

The first man let loose a string of swear words. Shaina felt her cheeks burn, not from the cursing, but in remembrance of the disturbing dream.

Shaina and Giles shared an early supper of venison steaks smothered in gravy, hot bread, and apple pie. Giles, with a surprisingly hearty appetite for one so thin, mopped up every last bit, down to a speck of potato in a dollop of gravy. She was only halfway through when he sat back, patted his flat stomach, and sighed in repletion of the meal.

"My," Shaina said, "you do eat well here!"

Giles smiled contentedly and then went to fetch the horses the hotel proprietor had arranged for them to use — a black horse for Shaina and a big roan for himself. The black was a little frisky, and Giles asked if she wanted to trade.

"No thank you," Shaina said a little shakily. "Adriane will do . . . just fine."

Giles looked back at the hotel owner and hunched his shoulders. "Be sure to have the horses back by morning," the man said with a mischevous grin.

"That I will," Giles called back over his lowered shoulder.

The pair rode slow and easy. The trail from the river to the Cordell ranch cut east along a beaten path in the prairie between the woods and the river. To their left the river flowed swift and shallow over the ripples, sparkling from the slanting moonbeams as the silvery orb rose in the sky.

"Oh . . . !" Shaina found herself exclaiming softly.

They had rounded a bend in the trail, and directly above the trail's horizon loomed a great mountain, dome-shaped and majestic, the moon rising beside it making it a startlingly breathtaking scene.

Giles smiled at Shaina's reaction. "Big Blue," he informed her. "Cordell's ranch is located on the prairie right at the foot of the mountain."

At the bitter note in Giles's voice, Shaina turned sharply to look at him. His thin, almost aristocratic face was like a hard mask gilded by the light of the ever-mounting moon. Dark shadows pressed into the hollow areas of his face, making him appear almost cruel. Had she really heard a voice hoarse with envy? Was she mistaken . . . or could there be bad blood between him and this Travis Cordell?

Shaina looked at Giles curiously as he said, "He's got the biggest flax ranch in the world."

"Really . . . the biggest?" She could not read his expression now, for he'd tipped his hat low over his forehead. But his voice was cold and the tone made Shaina uneasy.

"Yup."

Her boss! Cordell had signed the letter granting her the teaching position in Wild Mountain, but that's all she knew of him — a signature. It was plain as day Giles did not like him much, and Shaina wondered if she would share his feelings.

Gilded in moonlight pouring down, three Indians — two men, one woman — were standing knee-deep in the river.

"What are they doing?" Shaina asked with a slight shiver. "Aren't they cold?"

"Fishing . . . can't you see their spears?"

"Yes," she answered, her voice carrying more strength, "now that you mention it, I can."

They rode in hushed silence for a time, and then Giles suddenly asked out of the blue, "How old are you, Shaina? Nineteen? Twenty?" His smile was gilded by moonbeams. "Older, maybe?"

"I can't tell you my age, Giles."

"Why?" He peered over at her closely, intently. "You can tell me. Cross my heart I won't let your secret out. I'm your only friend here, right?"

That was true enough — so far. "Promise to God?"

"Swear on the Bible." He chuckled, "If I had one."

"I am almost nineteen."

He whistled. "Never had a teacher that young here." Giles snickered. "Travis hires only old ladies!"

Shaina thought Giles's tone seemed to imply she might be in for trouble in Wild Mountain. "Well," she said with a laugh, "there's a first time for everything!" Would boss man Cordell see it the same way, though? She was curious what his reaction would be, but she would have to wait.

Up ahead a sawmill became visible in a little clearing of moonlight and Giles said tersely, "Ralton's mill . . . used to be. I just heard Travis Cordell bought him out."

Cordell again! Travis Cordell must own the valley, kit and caboodle.

All of a sudden Giles came to a halt, holding up one hand in a military fashion. "We'd better go back to the mill and spend the night there."

"Why?" Shaina's horse stopped, backed a few steps, and came forward again, alongside Giles's roan.

Adriane, Shaina's black mount, snorted through her nostrils and stamped as if impatient to keep on moving toward the wooded foothills. Shaina stared first at the full, rounded moon lighting the landscape and then in the direction Giles was pointing.

"See those woods up ahead?"

Shaina nodded, seeing where the trail bent toward the woods, seeing trees so tall and thick and foliage so interlaced that there wasn't a space of light between. She didn't think she'd care to go through them at night, yet what Giles told her next made her believe he was exaggerating just a little.

"It's so dark in there in the daytime you can hardly see your mount's head, so you can guess what it's like at night. You can't see your hand in front of your face."

Shaina looked back at the mill; the place intrigued her. "Can we really stay there?"

"Sure. Travis always keeps a bed in his buildings . . ." As he said this, his head swiveled around to her, and he added, "Just in case he should need one."

Giles gallantly sacrificed the large bed with over-stuffed mattress to Shaina. While she slept, he stared out the window of the musty office, surrounded by mounds of papers and other items of the industry that had been piled neatly in corners, giving evidence that someone had come to clean up the place not too long ago.

"She is a temptress," Giles spoke softly into the night, "and an angel at the same time."

Desire for the strawberry-blond rode Giles hard and it was an effort to restrain himself from going into the other room and having his way with the new schoolteacher. Schoolteacher? That was a laugh . . . she was hardly the prim and proper kind. And he couldn't wait much longer to have her. She was just too tempting . . .

Giles walked softly into the adjoining room and stood quietly over the sleeping figure in the bed. The moon, wind, and stars seemed to have collected themselves in her hair. In her sweetly seductive pose on the clean linen sheet, with the moon falling across her, Shaina's loosened hair appeared indeed to be blowing in the wind. One pink-tipped hand was curled above her head and the blanket he'd found for her clearly outlined the lush curves displayed without the many layers of her daytime wear.

Giles stood perfectly still while Shaina stirred and her honey-sweet lips moved in her sleep, amazingly forming the name this man hated most . . . *Travis*.

Chapter Three

Giles Wilson sat his horse staring moodily along the trail that bent toward the woods. Shaina was just as quiet, for she couldn't understand Giles's gloomy mood. The trail was now plunging them from sunshine into inky darkness, darkness that closed in like a drawstring. Shaina looked up, searching for light. The trees were so tall and the foliage so wildly interlaced that except for the skinny crack of light directly overhead, what was left of the blue sky of day had completely disappeared.

Here among the great timber it was damp, and the smell of cedar was cold in Shaina's nostrils. The splendid forest closed in on either side of the road and, wherever a log had toppled across the trail, that section of trail had been hacked away to the width of a wagon bed. Breathing heavily, the horses lowered their heads as the trail grew suddenly steeper.

Now the way grew even denser, the horses' muscles bunching and straining with every step. Shaina's ears perked. Muffled by distance and the heavy timber was the steady, thundering roar of a waterfall. When they reached a clearing, Giles motioned for Shaina to rein in.

"How very beautiful," Shaina said in breathless awe, for below her the river crashed over a precipice for several hundred feet to pound and spew into a rocky basin below. Shaina held her breath as its force beat the water to a frothy white, raised billows of foam which blew upward into a soft, rainbow-hued mist. Rocks and logs tangled in the froth of white water below.

"Thunder Falls," Giles shouted. "The flax ranch is about one mile ahead. We'll be there in no time now."

Shaina said nothing. For some reason, Giles had seemed cold ever since they had awakened that morning. As she had prepared the coffee he'd brought along, she had pondered on this man whose peculiar moods she found so difficult to understand. She still couldn't get any closer to figuring him out.

As they continued along the tangled trail once again, Shaina felt goose bumps rise along her arms, coming only partially from the cool mist of the waterfall. She knew that soon she would come face to face with Travis Cordell.

Then there was Noah Starr, the man to whom she'd addressed her letter. They were going to look her over, she thought now, and judge the new schoolteacher. Lord, how she dreaded that meeting!

Suddenly the trail widened and Giles pointed directly ahead and explained. "That's Stampede Pass, and it leads to the dry, piney land of the eastern Territory."

"Is that where we are going?"

28

"No." He gave her a lukewarm smile. "The ranch is only up ahead and you'll see it before long."

Shaina hoped so. She was getting hungry and saddle-weary. Besides, she couldn't wait to get this meeting with Travis Cordell into motion.

The forest crept down off the hills but ended abruptly in an open prairie that was very grassy. Shaina knew that at this time of year in Oklahoma the prairies were still brown, but here in Washington Territory the grass was verdant as new leaves, as if winter never came to the valley. Thunder Mountain range was closer now, dotted with dark timber and pinkish-gray rock.

Shaina grimaced as she looked down at the faded dress she wore. She'd had to don the blue again, for she wanted to save her best for Sunday . . . that is, if the people here went to church at all. Maybe there wasn't even a church. And what about a school? Maybe class was merely held outside in someone's backyard!

"Shaina?"

"Oh . . . I'm sorry, I was deep in thought."

"The Cordell ranch is right up ahead," Giles announced, watching her closely.

Transferring her attention to the grouping of buildings, Shaina's heart began to pound and dark fright swept through her. She gripped the saddle horn, and realized then what frightened her. It was the rancher, Travis Cordell. His word had the power to bring her here . . . and so could get rid of her if he so wished it.

Buildings came into sight — a barn, cabins, lean-tos, some tents, and out back of these, an odd kind of shed that seemed to go on forever into the field.

People were all over the place, working in the barnyard, and they stopped to watch the riders approach.

"This is only the first 'working ranch,'" Giles informed her. "There are several more, like Travis's 'home ranch,' the Lazy C."

And then Shaina saw the Indians. There were so many! Hundreds, it seemed. There were white men, too, but they were far outnumbered by the Indians. All of the workers noticed the pair's arrival, and Shaina felt a little nervous having so many men looking at her at one time.

"Smile, Shaina," Giles was saying. "Don't forget to smile or they will think you don't like them."

She did as he bade, but the smile she turned on the workers ahead felt more like a grimace. A pulse beat a wild rhythm in her throat and her hands were like ice. *How*, she wondered, *am I going to get through this day* . . . and she had yet to meet the boss!

A youngster, detaching himself from the group of men, began running down the road toward the pair. He was carrying a slingshot.

"He wouldn't . . ." Shaina was whispering to herself. "Oh, yes, he would . . . !"

First came the whine of the stone heading her way. Then, when she felt the horse buck with a jerk to gather strength, she knew the mare would go plunging forward wildly.

"Oh . . . *no!*"

Gasping, Shaina felt herself lurch out of the saddle, and when she made a frantic grab for the horn, she missed it completely. The frisky black, gone wild with shock, bucked again and Shaina, too frightened to cry out, keeled over the side.

30

"Help!" she cried weakly, one foot caught in the stirrup as the crazed horse thundered onward. "I'm getting killed . . . *help!*"

Oh, the hooves . . . Oh, my God . . . I'm going to be trampled!

Then, when her skirt was thrown humiliatingly over her face, the dangerous hooves did not seem to matter so much and she fought with all the strength in her to keep her petticoats from lifting, too. She could seen the grins of rough-faced men as she passed them, riding almost upside down.

All of a sudden the frightened black stopped abruptly—so abruptly that Shaina's hold on her petticoats was cut loose. Someone had grabbed up the reins of her horse and she had felt the warm brush of flesh, very solid flesh.

"Shaina . . . are you all right?"

It was Giles's voice, but when she finally righted herself and looked up, it was into a pair of laughing green eyes.

Green eyes . . . jade-green eyes.

All of a sudden a hundred men were milling and forming an impenetrable circle about her. A large Indian wearing a red lumberjack shirt said nothing, just handed her lavender shawl over to her and then stepped back. He was still grinning.

Giles helped Shaina down, supporting her with a strong arm about her waist. She looked up, and saw that Giles looked more embarrassed than she herself felt, his face red, his eyes . . . well, sort of hot, she thought.

Disappointedly she realized there was now no man with green eyes in sight. She was certain she'd looked into a pair of jade-green eyes, eyes with a hundred specks of amber floating in them.

"Shaina?" Giles asked with concern. "You all right?"

"Fine, I'm just fine," Shaina said, although she hardly felt fine. She'd been almost killed by sharp hooves, bounced like a sack of flour through the dirt . . . *dirt!* Her face must really be a mess. No wonder the green eyes had been laughing. Shaina Hill, the new schoolteacher was always worth a good laugh.

Dubiously Giles's light-brown eyebrows rose. Shaina's hair hung loosely down her back in a wild tangle of fiery yellow waves and every pin that had held it in a prim knot at her nape was sticking out every which way from her waist-long hair. She tugged at her sleeves and skirts, trying to bring some semblance of order to herself.

A man laughed, a deep, velvety laugh, and Shaina's head swiveled.

The first thing she caught sight of were the man's pants. They were faded jeans and his thumbs were hooked casually in the edges of the well-worn pockets. Shaina didn't know where to look first. Her gaze slid down slightly and her eyes widened, then flew away. Upward they then traveled, then away again. She felt so disoriented. The man was standing but a few feet away. He was big, a very big man. Held erect with such easy pride, inches above those of the tallest, was a head with black, unruly hair — or maybe it was just wavy, she couldn't be certain of anything at this time. Sun had burnished the hair in places, and his skin was as dark as an Indian's. He was, all in all, devastatingly attractive.

His eyes were green . . . laughing green.

But the man had stopped laughing and there was mockery in the way he looked her over . . . most thoroughly. He smiled and inclined his head.

Shaina stood alone in a sea of men. The green-eyed man was Travis Cordell, no one had to tell her that! He was measuring her, and his look seemed to say he'd ordered a Thoroughbred and got a jackass. Featherlike lines crinkled at the corners of his eyes. But he wasn't laughing now; his eyes were hooded like those of a hawk. Here was a man bigger than life itself, she thought, a man who could do anything he wanted.

Her temper flared as he held his silence, staring impertinently at her. Memory of a day in the fifth grade came to her, the time when, shaking with anger, she'd faced the school rowdy, sobbing, "If I were only bigger, oh . . . I'd beat you up, you, you bully!" Instead of yanking on her pigtails, he'd grabbed her and kissed her thoroughly. Oh, how she'd despised Junior after that!

"Those Wildbloods'll have hell filled by the time we boys'll be ready to go down! Slingshots and all!"

Shaina looked at the man who had spoken of the bad boy who had struck her horse with the stone, while Giles's voice cut the air like a knife through warm butter.

"Miss Hill, may I introduce you to—"

"Never mind." Travis interrupted the introduction rudely, his voice grating on Shaina's nerves. "I know who she is already, you don't have to trouble yourself, Giles."

"But she doesn't know you."

Like a live thing, Shaina could feel the antagonism

33

curl about Giles's words.

"Lady," Travis Cordell said with a boredom in his deep voice, "do you know who I am?"

With a hellcat's fury in her eyes, Shaina said, "The only person I care to know is Noah Starr. It is he I am to meet here."

"You'll find him in his rocking chair . . . as usual this time of day."

"Rocking chair?" Shaina wondered just how old this Starr man was.

Taking hold of Shaina's arm, Giles said to her, "I know where to find him." He threw a dirty look to Cordell.

"Wait a minute," Shaina said, pulling out of Giles's grip, and, leaving his side, she went a little closer to the raven-haired man. "You laugh a lot, Mr. Cordell. But tell me this, would you have done the same if that black devil had trampled me under her hooves?"

He laughed again. "No . . . little one, I would have *buried* you."

Chapter Four

Shaina turned her head on Cordell and walked over to Giles, asking him to please take her to find Noah Starr immediately. "I don't care who he is," she hissed when Giles told her to hold her temper, that Travis was not a man to be making angry.

They walked toward a cabin, and the boss man was following at a more relaxed pace. The crowd of men had dispersed, going back to their individual chores. Shaina was grateful for that — at least the whole crew of men were not coming along, too, and gawking at her some more!

"Noah! Noah Starr!" Travis shouted from behind their backs, causing Shaina to start a little. "Like to talk to you, come on over."

Shaina looked across the dusty ranch yard, seeing an old man shuffling across the area, angling toward them. Long, hoarfrost hair hung in twirls around his face, a face that was wrinkled and hawklike. He could very well be over a hundred, for all she knew. She was beginning to believe nothing could be impossible here in Wild Mountain.

"The new schoolteacher, Miss Shaina Hill, would

like to meet you, old man," Travis was saying, smiling as he watched the old-timer's mouth moving as if he were grumbling to himself about something very important.

"He's Noah Starr? The very same man who wrote me the letter to come to Wild Mountain?" Shaina asked Giles.

"That is him, believe it or not," Giles told her. "He might be old, but he's not in any way senile." Then Giles's eyes grew brittle as he looked to Travis, saying to her, "He's been bending and scraping to *King* Travis for the past seven years . . . One thing he can do is write like he's just in his twenties and fresh out of school."

"He can?" Shaina said, mildly surprised.

"Yes, in his clear spells."

Finally the old man shuffled to Travis's side and was narrowing his eyes toward Shaina, asking the younger man, "Is she really going to stay here?" He looked at the boss out of the corner of his eye.

Brusquely Travis replied, "Not at my house she's not." Then, gesturing to Shaina, he ordered, "Come here and let Noah Starr have a good look at you."

"Excuse me?"

"Come here, and give us a turn, Miss Shaina Hill," Travis said, mocking laughter glittering in his eyes.

"Shaina," Giles said, trying to gain her attention while she stared at the man Giles obviously hated with a passion, "you can leave here in the morning with me, you don't have to take this. The riverboat goes back to Seattle in the morning."

"No, Giles," she replied. "I am not going back . . . I'm staying here." Realizing that Travis was listening, she said in a lowered voice, "I won't give up without a fight. And don't look at me like that."

"Shaina, don't be a fool, you don't understand all the ramifications of your predicament. If Travis Cordell decides you won't do, he'll send you packing anyway."

"Giles, don't play lawyer with me, please. I said I'm staying, and that's the end of it!"

"You don't understand," he gritted out, "there have been ten different teachers in Wild Mountain in the past year. Shaina, no one stays here . . . it's just too dangerous."

"Please, Giles, don't argue. I thought we were friends."

His amber-brown eyes told her he'd like to be more than just friends with her. "We are friends, Shaina, but it's not healthy here." As he said this, he noticed angrily the smiling curve of Travis's full bottom lip. For a moment he stared at Travis in lofty disdain, but he didn't want to hold the look too long, not wanting Shaina to notice his intense dislike of the influential man.

"Why did you bring me this far if you didn't think I'd go through with the rigors of being a schoolteacher at Wild Mountain, in the first place?"

"I thought I'd let you give it a try," Giles told her, "but to tell the truth, I've never seen Travis so—"

"So *what,* Giles?"

"Never mind. Let's just go, huh?"

"No!" Though her voice shook, she felt confident inside. "Is there a hotel somewhere near?"

With a jerk of his chin, Giles said, "There is, but it's a little ways from here."

37

"Take me there . . . please?"

He nodded, trying not to let her see his inner turmoil and feeling of defeat.

Head high, beginning to walk away, she said over her shoulder with a toss of rare defiance, "And I am going to ride that she-devil again!"

Noah Starr closely surveyed Travis's reaction and kept watching while the younger man's eyes trailed after her. Noah had to smile, for she was quite a slip of a girl. Hell! she was almost a full growed woman. But did Travis think so? And where did that fire come from in the man's eyes all of a sudden? Must be from the fiery arrival of that feisty Miss Hill, he thought, twirling the ends of his beard between two fingers. And what would Travis's woman, Miah, think of all those interested looks going to the pretty new schoolteacher?

Travis was watching, and he couldn't drag his eyes away to save his soul. Wild strawberry waves tumbled down the ramrod-straight back, blowing and tangling like yellow-red tentacles in the rising wind. The lavender scarf, the silly Miss Schoolteacher scarf, it was caked with mountain mud. Travis watched as one of the Indian lumberjacks held it out to her, but she shook her head in a gesture saying she didn't want it anymore, it wasn't good enough for her now.

Miss-la-dee-da, Travis Cordell was thinking.

Shaina walked past them all, heading straight for the black mare. With a strong grip on the saddle horn, and with the strength of anger and desperate determination, she flung herself up onto the big horse's back . . . without a hand from anyone, thank you!

38

Rumbling laughter coiled with a heavy insult about her as she kicked the horse into a gallop. Oh yes, she knew just who had been the one to save her, and it irked her that her true hero had actually been Travis Cordell and not Giles!

Then Shaina smiled against the boiling rage inside. She'd show Travis Cordell what kind of stuff she was really made of . . . or her name wasn't Shaina Hill!

Travis Cordell watched until Miss Hill and Giles were out of sight. "So the schoolteacher's a little spitfire with a hellcat's fury!"

"Yeah," said Noah Starr, "she sure told you off."

"What are you talking about, old man?"

"Her eyes were spittin' damnation fire at you all the while you stood there undressing 'er with your eyes."

"She sure took an immediate dislike to me." Travis's green eyes twinkled disarmingly as he recalled the sparkling eyes flashing his way.

"You didn't like her any too well either, lad."

"She'll pass."

"More'n that."

"Keep to your business, Noah Starr. Which is what you do best. Paper work."

"Paper work," he echoed with a grunt. "You got more of that than you got mountain gnats."

Travis chuckled warmly. Then he said matter-of-factly, "What is it about schoolteachers that makes them all get under my skin? Either they're pimple-faced, skinny, too smart for their skirts, or too damned skittish."

"Most of 'em have been old and anemic, you mean."

"You didn't seem to mind them all that much. But this one seems too young and inexpérienced for my liking. Or maybe she just *looks* young. I don't know."

"You sent for her." Noah tried to hide his face in his long hair by turning just a little away from Travis. He didn't want the younger man to see the smiling smirk etched there.

"So I did . . . with your help." He smiled at Noah, and then out of the blue returned the picture of lovely Miss Hill bouncing in the dust like a travois gone mad while clutching at her petticoats in preservation of her dignity. Jesus, what a sight!

"She's got some pretty legs, sure," Noah said, sucking at his front teeth . . . what there was left of them.

"Yeah" was all Travis said. He gazed out over his spring-raked fields strung out across the valley. "I've got some work needs taken care of before noon. Why don't you go take your nap, old man." He had a feeling, ever since the feisty teacher had arrived, that they were all going to need a lot of rest.

"Too excited to snooze."

Travis snorted. "Because of the new schoolteacher?"

"You really got something 'gainst learning. Shoot, Cordell, your own daughter needs to go to school."

"Roux has the Indians, her mother's people, to teach her."

"Lord, you want that girl growing up like a savage?"

With a shrug, Travis protested seriously, "Doesn't really matter all that much, not around here." The muscles tightened in his face, giving him a lean, dark, dangerous look.

"You went to school once, whippersnapper!"

A look of irritation crossed Travis's eyes, making his

full eyebrows look even thicker. He shook his head, lowering it a little.

"Maybe school is important to some. I'm not much concerned . . . I have got a growing ranch to think about. Miah will take care of Roux . . ." he said of his estranged mistress, looking displeased just by mentioning the woman's name. She was always running off somewhere . . . like the savage that she was. Miah had needed always to prove that she was beautiful and desirable to men, and he had gotten damn tired of her going off at night, using the excuse that to hunt by the moon was the best way to catch your prey. Two-legged prey, no doubt! Over the years, she had spent less and less time at the ranch and it had reached the point that she was hardly ever there at all anymore.

That dark cloud had passed, Travis thought to himself, and there was no happy horizon in sight for him and the woman any longer.

"You gonna let Roux go to school or not?" Noah said with a little anger in his yet steady voice.

"Go take your snooze, old man."

Travis turned on his booted heel and went in the direction of the field. Noah Starr watched him. What was wrong with Travis? He should have invited the pretty schoolteacher to bunk in at the ranch. Most men would have shown a little courtesy, heck, whether he liked schoolteachers or not. But Noah had held his tongue, and he was wise to do this. White folks, especially women, did not stay in the sprawling house. Travis was ashamed of his Indian mistress and child. Still more ashamed, Noah guessed, because Miah was rarely home to act the proper role of a mother. She was a shameless, flirting hussy, and it was sad to see

41

Travis take it like he did, and even sadder that the little girl, Roux, watched her mother rip her father's heart out. Travis never should have kept the Indian woman in the first place, was his way of thinking, and better yet that he had never made Miah his wife.

After all his business was accomplished, Travis slowly walked the dusty road strung out between the dwellings of his largest flax ranch. The land was purpling . . . it would be dark soon. The big mountain towered above the fields, looking like a sentinel over the buildings grouped near the river, the long sheds in which most of the Indians slept at night. Indians served as the work force in this section of his ranch, while up in the higher reaches, where he made his home, the cowboys took care of the animals, like cattle and broke wild grullas — those strong, free horses he loved so well. The boys saw that his ranch was run like the fine movements of a big clock.

Travis was too restless to go "up home," and, besides, who would be there to welcome him? His wife? He didn't have one. His daughter? He hardly ever spoke to her anymore, either, and if he did he always allowed his temper to show. They were hardly ever there anymore, Miah and Roux. Time had pulled him and Miah in opposite directions . . . but she was still the mother of his child. And not even the change that had come over her could alter that fact. And Roux, she really was important to him. He loved her. In fact, she was the only female he could say he did in truth love. He had been promising himself, that he was going to pay more attention to his daughter, for he knew she desperately needed him—especially with a mother like Miah. The only outstanding problem was, how was he to get close to her now after so long?

What he really needed was a woman. A *good* woman, one who would come to love him and his lonely daughter.

Travis thought that Miah had gone to stay with her own people, for the Indian camp was only five miles away, below Thunder Falls. Travis could not entirely blame Miah for leaving, since he himself had done things to help the situation. At first he hadn't resented her leaving. He should have missed her . . . Travis swore softly. If he kept thinking about it, the evening would be spoiled, and it was too nice out to be brooding . . . or looking toward his bed just yet.

Travis walked faster. After a few steps, he could see a short squat figure up ahead detach itself from the shadows. That would be Indian Joe. He was a doctor of sorts, not quite as old as Noah Starr but hardly any youngster. Indian Joe was scrawny, not well rounded like Noah Starr or Big Doc up at the home ranch. Poor Joe was a perennial refugee from his own kind, and when one of his people died they desired for him to go along to the great beyond. Joe knew more hiding places than Travis did himself about his own ranch!

"Well, Doctor Joe, run out of hiding places?" Travis chuckled; it was one of their running jokes.

Brown eyes and a thousand wrinkles stared back at Travis, and all together they pulled themselves up into a happy smile. Joe might be emaciated, but he was sure a happy bag of bones. He owned a funny head of silver hair, sticking out all over like porcupine quills.

Just looking at him always made Travis want to laugh and he had often punched the nose of someone who did poke fun at the beloved Indian.

"Green Eyes," Joe called to Travis Cordell holding something soft in his hands, "I have something for you . . . I think you will be grateful that I have brought this to you." He grinned, thinking how pleased Travis would be with the pretty purple scarf he had found on the ground near where the *Clementine* had docked.

The moon gave enough illumination for Travis to see what it was the old Indian was handing over to him.

Travis's eyes seemed haunted as he reached out to take the big lavender scarf from Indian Joe. Then, on second thought, he shrugged and withdrew his hand.

"You keep it," he said, and after a moment, added, "What will I do with it, Joe."

Grinning from ear to ear, he announced, "Give it to Roux!" He tried to place it into the younger man's hands again.

"Roux?" Travis said, looking at the Indian as if he'd metamorphosed into a chicken hawk. "My daughter will not wear that thing . . . it's too fancy. Roux is simple . . . and wild. She's at home in doeskin and moccasins . . . not white women's fancy trappings."

"Who should I give it to then?" Joe wanted to know.

"Give it to the man who was wearing his heart on his sleeve."

"Oh? Who was that?" Travis suddenly shivered, from his wide shoulders down to narrow hips and long, muscularly powerful thighs.

Nodding this time, Joe thrust the lavender scarf back at Travis Cordell. But Travis shoved the thing

44

away with the back of his hand, as if it held contamination.

"Not me, man. Giles Wilson . . . that's who should have it."

"Ah!" Joe exclaimed. "That one is like a buck — always it is mating season for Wilson. He has collected enough of them. You take this one."

"The scarf or the woman?" Travis questioned with glistening bitterness in his eyes.

"Wilson does not want a woman who has feelings."

"Miss Shaina Hill does not have any feelings, you're saying?" Travis was confused.

"He wants one who behaves well at the tea party. You, Green Eyes, want a woman with fire in her soul."

"Well . . . I've already had one too many. Give the scarf to Giles Wilson and be done with it. Shaina Hill is the one with manners."

"No, you are wrong," Indian Joe grinned, and slapping the scarf over the white man's shoulder, he informed, "She is Shining Fire and you are her beautiful jewel."

"Jewel? Hell!" Travis sputtered as the old man walked happily back to the forested hill. Indian Joe's been drinking too much firewater, he thought, and muttered to himself that he'd rather bleed to death than have that Indian treat one of his wounds!

Chapter Five

Shaina and Giles rode into Wild Mountain late in the afternoon. Mist curled off the ground and floated about a cluster of buildings that hugged the brown ribbon of road. As they drew closer, Shaina could see the smoky flame of a kerosene lamp through the windows of the general store and heard loud voices hurtling through the open door of a saloon down the street. In some houses windows were still dark . . . or had been darkened as they rode in.

"Here's Selby's Trading Post," Giles announced as he halted in front of a peeled log fence that had been sanded down to raw wood.

While Giles was dismounting, Shaina frowned and asked, "What will we do here?"

Nodding toward the building, Giles informed her, "It serves as the hotel, too."

"Oh." Shaina nodded wearily, her blue eyes clouded.

A high level of anger had carried Shaina all the way from the flax ranch to here, but it had also exhausted her. She looked over at Giles as he dismounted and loosely tied the reins of each horse about the log. Now he looked up at her, his gaze wondering. Why did she not feel the same vibrant thrill as when Travis Cordell had looked at her? Although she knew Cordell's character was fierce and his nature arrogant, she had felt an intense physical attraction to the man. What was it about him?

Giles was staring up at her, but Shaina seemed to be a thousand miles away. What was keeping her so entranced? With her red-gold hair hanging down her back over his hide jacket he'd loaned her when the chill came on, she looked like an angel, her blue eyes sleepily blurred.

"I'll help you down," he said, already reaching for the tiny waist.

With a tired sigh, Shaina slid toward Giles, allowing him to lift her from the horse and put her on her feet.

"Thank you, Giles. You have been very kind."

Smiling down into her face, Giles took her hand gently and led her into the trading post. Shaina started when a funny-looking man popped up from behind a rough-hewn counter where he'd been unpacking a box of cloudy green bottles. The man sported foggy eyeglasses which slid down a very long nose. He looked up and blinked, as if he couldn't see very well. Then, squinting, he removed the glasses, blew on them, first one side then the other, and, after cleaning them with a nearby rag, he looked down his long nose at the young woman.

"Abner Selby," Giles announced to Shaina. Then, "Abner, this is Shaina Hill—ah, Wild Mountain's new schoolteacher."

"Howdee."

Shaina smiled weakly as the storekeeper narrowed his small eyes in speculation and Giles continued to speak. "She needs a room for a few days, Abner. Just until she finds permanent lodging in a boarding-house."

"Well, then, come on and follow me, young lady. The new schoolteacher, you say?"

"That's right," Giles answered for Shaina while Abner snatched a lamp from a table. Giles smiled as Shaina hesitated, then indicated with a jerk of his head for her to go ahead and follow.

"Good-bye, Miss Shaina Hill." He stared at her pink lips for a moment, then added, "Good-bye . . . for now."

Shaina's eyes clouded with uneasiness, and she hesitated. The *Clementine* would be leaving in the morning, with Giles on board. He had been her only friend. Now she knew no one.

Now Shaina noticed there were other people in the store . . . men at the other side. They were watching her, silently surveying her every move from their tilted-back chairs that rubbed against the wall, big boots caught in the lower rungs, thumbs hooked under leather belts. Big men . . . just like Travis Cordell. Mountain-bred men.

Fortifying her confidence with the hoisting of her chin, Shaina smiled across the room at Giles once more, then followed Abner Selby up the creeking stairs.

Shaina looked down at the clear-cut lines of Giles's profile, and she stood there on the landing just staring at him, until he turned as if he'd felt her eyes burning into him.

"I'll be back Friday, Shaina."

"I'll look for you, Giles," she said in a strangely hollow voice.

Shaina's room was directly above the trading post, the windows opening on Wild Mountain's rutted, dusty street. There, she stared into the large, wavy mirror. Deep-blue eyes looked back at her. Touching her mouth, she wondered what Giles's kiss would be like. Would he kiss her slowly, thoughtfully, and leave her cold? Or would his kiss leave her mouth burning with fire? And would she return his kiss with reckless abandon?

Then, staring at her blurred lips, Shaina thought of another kiss . . . what *his* would be like. Him. Travis Cordell. Even thinking the name made her feel shivery all over. His kiss . . .

Travis would crush her to him, she knew. His eyes would smolder with fire before he claimed her lips. Then his lips would move against her neck, and the heady sensations would make her dizzy. Shaina would throw back her head and the man would open his hand to rake his long fingers through the spilling mass of bright gold. His lips would recapture hers, much more demanding and coaxingly this time. His tongue would thrust deep to send the blood pounding through to her nerve endings . . .

Shaina's closed eyes flew open and she found herself staring down. A tall, shadowy figure stood there. Even though she could not recognize the individual, could not make out his features, she knew he was gazing up at her dark window . . . a still, dark

49

shadow in the night. She sighed and closed her eyes again.

When the first pink color streaked the sky in the lower parts of the mountain range and filtered some color into the room, Shaina stirred and flung one arm above her head in a restless movement. Her hair was unruly and spread about her like a golden mist.

Blue slits showed as she began to open her eyes, then, as the disoriented feeling left, Shaina looked at the room with a slow perusal.

The bed she was lying in was covered with a thick, multicolored quilt, like the ones her mother used to make sewing together different scraps of material from items of clothing that had seen much better days.

There was a chair with a hand-hewn back and a seat of scraped doeskin. A washstand with a big pitcher, hand-painted with green vines twisted in and out of misty roses was accompanied by a cracked bowl of white porcelain. Surprisingly, for such a modest establishment, there was a bar of soap, smelling curiously of wood violets. Provided for her luxury, too, were several bleached linens.

An unwelcome surge of resentment had come over her when Abner Selby had shown her room to her. She'd felt the need to question him, wanting to know a little more about the people she was going to be seeing almost every day in the valley. Asking him if this was his hotel, he answered with, "I only run the place, miss, this hotel belongs to Travis Cordell." Then he'd left her with the warning, "Lock your door,

Miss Hill."

Slowly now, Shaina pulled herself erect, placed her feet on the floor, and got up, the straw mattress crackling behind her. While she washed with the wood violet soap, she reflected back to younger days . . . a little girl in a sod house. Her mother was crying again, and her father was promising Eleanora a better house, one with the white picket fence she'd always desired. But it had always been the same with each house they had moved into across the country — first Missouri, then Oklahoma, Texas, California, then back to Oklahoma once again, and finally settling in a small town below Seattle — from where she had run away.

It had always been so cold in the houses in the winter, but her father had promised over and over her mother a "palace." Her mother hadn't wanted that . . . she'd only wanted a nice house with a picket fence. "We'll get another place, Ma," her father had promised. And then, "I'll tell you what I'll do" . . . But father never did anything toward his promises.

Like Indians they'd ground corn into coarse meal, which most of the time arrived to the table as thick, hot gruel. Molasses, pork fat, and yet more corn. After the graces had been said, Abbie, Shaina's youngest sister, would cry out in a tinkling voice, "And damn the gruel!"

"Abbie!" Mama had gasped. Eleanora would shoot her turquoise eyes to her husband. "Don't swear around the children anymore . . ." And he returned, "They are only hungry . . . don't get angry, El."

"I understand, Graham," Eleanora would say. "Things might be better someday." She looked at

51

Shaina's father hopefully.

"I *promise* they will be."

Shaina recalled the weary patience on Eleanora's pinched face as she said, "Of course, Graham. We'll have new clothes, a real wood house made from boards . . . and a white picket fence."

White picket fence! Oh, sure, Shaina had thought back then, tasting the full potency of her bitterness. Only rich folks had fences all around their houses . . . and Mama was going to have another baby. What would one more matter, she already has three, Shaina thought angrily.

"When I grow up," Shaina had vowed as she stood in her mother's weedy garden, "I am going to be somebody . . . not just a mother who's always barefoot and pregnant!"

Then Eleanora had died . . . had gone away . . . and Shaina had felt completely alone. She had grown up wanting the things Eleanora dreamed of. All her yearnings had been Shaina's, and the things Eleanora hated, Shaina hated also.

Eleanora's education had been full, and Shaina wanted that for herself, too, but Graham had taken his family far from the civilized places where his children could have gotten a good education. Once Eleanora had owned the finest dresses, ones that had been fashioned in the French Quarter of New Orleans. She had been a fine young lady. So fine and beautiful. Then she'd married penniless Graham, and Mama's family disowned her.

Then, after Mama was gone, the relatives showed up. Her brothers and sisters had needed her, their big sister, but Shaina had been fed up . . . Papa was still promising. Now, even after Mama was gone. From the moment her relatives walked in, Shaina resented them. She had studied them, her aunts looking prim and high-browed, her uncles wearing well-tailored suits and polished shoes, symbols of prosperity, all four disagreeable faces turning toward Shaina's father. Shaina had felt a warning rolling in the pit of her stomach. The aunts and uncles wanted the family to move down to Texas with them. "You poor, poor dears," Aunt Charity had said, her beady brown eyes alive with disapproval when they came to rest on the thin bodice of Shaina's best dress. "Ah just can't be lettin' you all go on without your mama." Her eyes riveted on Shaina's ankles, her beady orbs glaring as she whined, "For shame, so much ankles showin', it just ain't right . . . and you comin' into womanhood any time now." Shaina had so wanted to tell her she was a woman by now, and thank you to mind your own business, Aunt Charity, these are my legs and I will display them any way I wish!

Shaina's brother Will, the Hills' first child, broke in with, "Shoot, I ain't goin' nowhere with you folks!" He was standing as tall as his reed thin body would allow. His auburn hair seemed to bristle right before Shaina's bewildered eyes.

"Now, children," Graham had pleaded. "Be good. Some of you will go with Aunt Charity and some with my other sister, Katie. William, behave now!"

"No, I won't, damn it!" He had always defied his father, who he thought was very weak and never kept his promises, never even tried. He also hated the name Graham had given him. "Will Hill, you come on and do your chores now!" he'd always shout at the boy.

Now Will defied him and his aunts and uncles further. "I'm going to ship out on a boat in San Francisco. I can get on the boat now as cabin boy and work myself up. I ain't going to Texas or any other place, hear? I'm old enough to leave and that's just what I'm going to do!" He whirled on a startled Shaina. "You leave too, Sis, don't go with them old fuds—" His voice lowered. "You'll never amount to anything. Go and teach school now, like you always wanted to do . . . you're old enough. Go, Shainy, go, before they—" he indicated their arrogant relatives "—turn you into one of their own kind." He grabbed his sister and hugged and kissed her. Then, after whispering in her ear he'd see her again someday, he'd find her not matter what, he went his way under the glare of his father's eyes drilling in his back.

Graham Hill turned to the younger children, his eyes skimming past a stiff-backed Shaina. "I'm going to work and save up for a new home, kids, and soon as I have enough, we'll all be back together again. Things are going to be better, you'll see. I promise."

Shaina had set her teeth. There it was again . . . the promise. Her father had been smiling cajolingly at the other children—Abbie, Charlie, and Robert—but their faces hadn't moved, they'd remained solemn as church mice. "Why won't you kids talk to me?" he'd asked them. "Shainy? You going to go with me and help, so we can get the kids back? Together, Shainy, we can make enough to build that new house."

"No." Shaina's words had fallen into a sea of silence. "No, I won't go with you, Pa."

"Oh, Shainy, you can't leave your pa go alone.

What'll I do without you? I need someone to stand by me, just like Ma did."

You ruined Mother's life, she wanted to shout back at him. And, she told herself, he wasn't going to ruin hers. All Graham could think about was, who was going to take care of *him.* Well, she wouldn't. Her mother had enslaved herself to him, but she sure wouldn't . . . She had to live her own life now, and his promises be damned . . .

Aunt Charity clucked, "My, my, just like her mama. Yes, she favors Eleanora." With a snicker, Aunt Charity peered through her round glasses in firm disapproval . . . always disapproval in her eyes. And in Charity's husband's eyes . . . there, too. When she was a child, Shaina had thought Robert had been a nice man, but as she grew up, she realized he was no kinder than Charity. He looked at her as if she belonged to another world, hot fit to walk the same ground his feet trod upon. And Aunt Katie, no help there, that one would just stick her arrogant nose in the air as if she was too good for the likes of the Hills. But she wasn't. None of them were any better . . . and she would show them one day.

She'd made the break, at last, while her father and his uppity sisters watched her go. Katie had had the impropriety to giggle out loud, and then Aunt Charity had joined Katie's laughter. Actually, Shaina had thought then as she did now how filled with envy and spite they were. They knew she was going to be happier than both of them one day, and they hated her for the fact.

And now she had another demon to contend with, a man by the name of Travis Cordell. He didn't want her here. She knew it. He would do everything he could to thwart her every effort here at the Wild Mountain school.

Dressing quickly in a lavender dress that had seen better days, Shaina then drew her brush down through her long hair and tossed the strawberry-blond hank back behind her shoulder. She stared through the window of the hotel. Travis Cordell owns this, she thought, and almost everything else in the valley. Her papa had owned her mother's emotions, and she'd been a victim of his weakness, too. Never again would she be owned by another person . . . and she was going to show those aunts one day that no one laughed behind Shaina Hill's back. She set her jaw in firm determination and her tears choked her voice as she promised herself. "I am going to be a lady someday. I will shine, as God as my witness, I *will* . . . and let no one stop me. Not even big shot Travis Cordell!"

Chapter Six

Shadowed by deep purple, Travis stood below the window of the room he knew Shaina Hill occupied. Shivers racked his tall frame, but they were not from the crisp mountain air . . . he was used to that. It was an emotion that shook Travis as he clenched his big hands into fists of steel.

Travis had been out riding his black and white stallion, Dice, so named because he'd won the fiery horse in a game while aboard the *River Queen* out of St. Louis. He had felt compelled to go to the hotel. He was lonely. Miah was not there in his home, and Roux had gone to visit her mother's people.

Now Travis mounted Dice again and rode slowly back to the ranch house that sat midway between the town and the mountain range. He liked it that way, is home a ways from his working ranch. The trip didn't take long either way and he could think while he rode. Think about things other than the disturbing presence of Shaina Hill in the valley.

It had all been so long ago, before Roux had been born. He was Jase Cordell's heir, had been nineteen when his father fell and broke his damn fool neck while mountain climbing. At such a young age he'd had all the land a much older man could ever hope for, land so remote that only three dozen families had registered claims in the valley. He wanted the ranch to be bigger and better than Jase had seen it, something gigantic, something that would set him above everyone else for hundreds of miles around. He not only wanted to be rich and strong, he wanted to be the best. He wanted to show everybody there was nothing Travis Cordell couldn't do!

And show them he had. The old settlers had thought he was young and crazy, but their blood hadn't run as hot as Travis's. He had planted and planted and planted. Besides the cereals such as wheat, oats, barley, and flax, he grew grapes, apples, cherries, peaches, prunes, potatoes, both white and sweet, cotton, broom corn, sorghum, peanuts, egg plants. Thank God the rainfall was sufficient.

Soon Travis's flax ranch and cotton plantation were the largest of all, and more than one visitor to Wild Mountain had gone back home with Cordell's methods of cultivation spinning dreams of wealth in his head.

That had been his love, the land. Then Miah had come along. How beautiful she'd seemed to a lovestruck young man. Ten years ago. Ten years that had made him hard and cynical concerning love. Love was merely a four-letter word to him now. He called Miah his mistress, but she'd ceased to be that long ago. She was his child's mother . . . nothing more. It had, however, not always been so. There had been a time . . .

How beautiful Miah had been. It was summer

when the Valley Indians collected into their long cedar canoes and paddled seventy miles downriver for the summer games. Travis had come down from the mountain range to the old sawmill, and the sound of happy voices attracted him to the sloping banks of the river. He'd watched idly, enjoying the warming sun on his back, while in a nearby field hundreds of crickets made their creaking sounds. The Indians were stepping into canoes, five or six to each, with the squaws readied in position to do the paddling. Many people, including children with their parents, crowded the bank. Pretty, doe-eyed Indian girls chattered as they loaded the canoes with baskets and thick bedrolls. They were dressed in the full elegance of beaded moccasins, colorful blankets, shiny black hair braided or left hanging loose. Many of the braves wore the work clothes of the white man. The Indians would be gone for several days, and there at the mouth of the river they would be met by tribes paddling in from every direction. The games would last, Travis had known, for almost a week. There would be canoe races, barbecues on the shore, ceremonials, dances, and many speeches.

Watching the Indians, Travis had suddenly felt lonely. The sound of their gaiety was a deep hum in his ear . . . and then the sound of a young woman's laughter rippled and rose above the others. He burned with eagerness to know to which girl the voice belonged, and his eyes searched, going from one bronze face to another. Then he saw her. Standing up in a canoe with the sparkle of mischief in her dark eyes, she laughed wickedly because she was rocking a canoe from side to side and upsetting those within who were trying to hold on to their belongings. Awareness should have come to him right then that this girl meant trouble, for it was alive in every inch of her, but he had not heeded the urgent message in his brain, only the pounding of his heart. The ache in his loins had meant everything that sunshiny day. She is beautiful, was all he could think, her body straight and slim, hair in heavy plaits down her back shining blue-black in the sun. The face was wild and sweet, with a narrow nose above a laughing mouth . . . a mouth he'd longed to taste from the first moment he heard her laughter ring out. He saw her move out of his life as she slid out into the water effortlessly to disappear soundlessly around the wide bend. He'd listened until the last ripple from the moving paddles and the happy laughter faded away downstream.

The old-timer standing next to him on the river-bank picked up on his interest in the woman and said in a coy voice, "You kin always marry if ye'r lonely, Mister Cordell. I mean . . . don't look at me like that. What I meant was there ain't too many white women, I mean 'available' white women in the valley . . . unless you go to Seattle."

"I do," Travis had informed him with a dangerous glint in his green eyes.

"I mean, if ye'r thinkin' of taking a woman, there ain't nothing like one of them Salish. You kin marry her without ceremony and always send her back to her own kind iffen you get tired of her, or find a white gal to take in a real proper ceremony."

Miah had returned and Travis had wooed and won her—in a way. "Yes I join with you, Travis Cordell," she had said in answer to his appeal. She hadn't even

60

taken a breath as she agreed to become his mistress. But it had to be her way, mistress or nothing. "No marriage," she'd insisted.

It hadn't been that Miah didn't know the difference between a legal, white man's ceremony with the vows "to love and to keep" for the rest of her life. Travis found out later to his profound disappointment that she just didn't care. To her, their bonding had been like playing house with Travis a toy she could toss away when she tired of him. "Legal ceremony" had frightened her, Travis realized later when they had argued heatedly.

Travis continued to ride slowly to his ranch house, thinking of Miah, remembering the dream that could have been. But the long-familiar nostalgia had disappeared. He used to ache for her, an aimless, hopeless longing that brought nothing to him but deeper pain. He used to dream of Miah running, slender, always laughing that musical sound. She would caress him and assure him that she was real. The dream had come to him every night in her absence and he'd awaken with hopeless despair tight in his chest and an ache in his loins that would not abate even when he sought release in the "Scarlets" of Seattle. It was somewhat like dreaming of a beloved one whose death one has been mourning. In the waking hours she was actually dead to him. Then she'd return at night to haunt his dreams, so beautiful and *alive*, the product of his heart's refusal to believe she was really gone. In the dream she proved she was alive. She kissed him, caressed him up and down his fiery body, she even spoke, laughed in his ear. Then he'd awaken feeling ashamed of his dreams.

61

In the first five months of their "marriage," Travis had lived with Miah like an Indian . . . and then the Indians had come to work for him. Sometimes the couple would stay at Travis's ranch house, but when that got to be too confining for Miah, they would, mostly in the summer months, move into a place she'd prepared of mats tied over a framework of fresh-cut willow poles . . . and they had made love like exuberant savages. Even though Miah was an enchantment for Travis, he did not forget his work and began cutting timber, which made him even more money. For pasture, he had cleared land, but his most pressing desire was to gobble up land . . . more land. Year after year he'd bought up homesteads others had given up, for there had always been the settlers who'd yanked up roots because of wanderlust. He had also been forced to be cold-hearted at times, confiscating the land of those who had borrowed money and refused to pay back. He and Miah had shot game for food when they were out on their frequent trysts in the wilderness and at night they roasted the meat over a campfire Miah had built. At night they wrapped their bodies together in a blanket and made love like wild beings to the river's gentle roar and the cry of the night owl. The nightmares had never come to him at those times. He had been twenty when he'd first met Miah.

Then the time had come when Miah had learned she was carrying his child. Travis had named the baby Roux, Red Fox, for she'd been born with dark red fire in her hair. Even as a baby, Roux's hair and skin had marked her all Indian, but her eyes had turned out a dark jade, almost like his own. All the time Miah had been carrying the child, Travis had been totally absorbed in his new business ventures and hardly thought of the baby's birth. From the first, however, it was Travis who cared for the child, always taking her with him in a specially made seat fastened with leather thongs to the front of his saddle.

When had Miah begun to change? Hardly had she ever looked into the face of the child she'd bore him, a child as different from herself as the color of her bright green eyes. Hardly ever did she seek her "husband's" warmth at night. She was always off to her village with a different brave each time, the brief periods she returned, the only times little Roux had a mother. Travis would not make a fool of himself and chase her. He adored his daughter, but Miah had died in his heart the instant he saw her with the first of a string of lovers, both running naked in the mountain stream.

Now Travis kicked Dice into a full run, pounding across the foothills toward his ranch. The sprawling house and outbuildings rose up like gray ghosts, seeming to come and meet him like the memories, always the memories. He was filled with hatred again, hatred for what Miah had done to him and the child. As he approached the main house, he could see cookfires spiraling upward from the kitchen, the sign that his housekeeper was waiting supper for him. Travis clenched his fist and vowed that he would never fall in love again. The only female in his life would be Roux. Only Roux.

Roux was her father's name for her, but the Indians

of her tribe called her Fox Fire an apt name for one with such a mane of thick hair so like the dark red fox and so filled with fiery glints when the sun struck the heavy mass. Her skin was a pale bronze, her eyes a startling green.

The young Indian girl was searching for spring herbs at the same time Jay Ridingbow saw her for the first time near the bank of the river. His breath caught as a young Indian girl of no more than ten summers stepped from the cover onto the bank. He was a lad of fifteen summers and had just begun to test his prowess on the more experienced of young women. This girl was too young for him, of course, a mere child, yet she looked familiar, and Jay wondered where he had seen her before. He lived in Wild Mountain with his half-breed father, Nick Ridingbow and his half-Spanish mother, Rosa. They all worked for Travis Cordell and lived on the small cotton plantation situated near the Skomish River. He didn't know too many people in Wild Mountain, so that could account for him not knowing if he'd seen her there or not.

Jay's golden eyes were sharp and assessing for one still so young. The young half-breed girl was very lovely, he thought, and was strangely pleased to notice that, like himself, she appeared to possess some white blood. She was slender, fine-boned, graceful even under the straight, unbelted folds of the fringed-and-beaded dress that hung from her shoulders to her knees. His eyes brightened with pleasure just watching her. Her wrists were thin and her hands small and dainty. Her hair was wet. He decided she must have just finished her toilet at some nearby pool.

64

Just then a frog hopped from under the girl's feet into the water and she paused to watch, a gentle smile curving her mouth as it swam away. Jay moved slightly to watch her as she began moving along the bank toward a spot opposite his hiding place.

Jay's fingers tightened on the trigger of the rifle when she turned toward him, but she was not looking at him, rather she was trying to peer over the aspen in the direction of the camp. He saw then that her eyes were a bright leaf green, in startling contrast to her fox-dark hair and the creamy bronze of her brow and cheeks. Where, Jay wondered, had he seen those green eyes before? If she was daughter to one of the mixed families in the valley, it was apparent she had been kept well hidden from the traders and riverboat men who came their way, and with whom Jay and his father had dealings.

The girl was directly across from him now, not a dozen feet away. Sweet spring-grass scent threaded her clean hair and garments and drifted his way.

Jay jumped when she cried an exclamation in Chinook as her dress hem snagged on a thorn. She turned to disentangle it. Her willowy thigh, revealed momentarily as the dress was rucked above the top of her leggings, was as flawless as any white girl's. But he had to remind himself she was not a woman but a mere child. Perhaps she would help him — he certainly needed a friend here to get the mare back that had been stolen by one of the young men of the Songish. All she'd have to do was to get up in the night and lead the mare out to where he was hiding.

Whatever the risk of accosting her, it was a far lesser risk than any other that faced him if he tried getting Sheba back by himself.

Now!

Jay sprang across the creek and ran up behind her, swiftly, silently, keeping hunkered down to make sure he could not be spotted from the camp between the fringe of brush.

Roux couldn't tell what had made her turn, for there hadn't been a sound. When she turned and saw the young man, her green eyes widened incredulously.

Jay smiled as pleasantly as he could as he kept on advancing toward her, praying she would not scream. She didn't. But she whirled and started to run. Jay was faster, however, and he lunged, grabbing her by her slim arm and spinning her about to face him.

"Shhh, pretty one," he warned in Chinook, putting a finger to his finely shaped lips. "I am not going to hurt you." When she began to struggle to break from him, he murmured close to her ear, "I tell you I will not hurt you. This is not a lie. I only want to talk to you, little fox." He was unaware he was saying the name that was so close to her real one.

"Stinking polecat," she cried in halting Chinook. "Let me go or I'll kick you where it counts!"

"Ohh-ohhh, little one," he said, slipping the strap of his rifle over his shoulder and then grabbing her other arm, "You are like the cat. I am not going to harm you. Promise. My only wish is to speak with you."

A cry of half rage coming from her, Roux peered up at the tall lad, her bright eyes filled with tears and anger. Then, in an instant, her face made an abrupt change, and Jay thought she might speak to him at last. Good, he thought, here was help at last.

Roux's lips did part, but it was not to address the

66

young man but to give the Indian alarm. Drawing a ragged breath of disappointment, Jay clapped a hand over her mouth and, dragging her straighter with him, he looked toward the Indian camp. The elderly Indians around the fires had not taken notice of the cry, but three squaws with baskets of water from a spring had heard enough to make them startle and run toward camp.

"You little fool!" Jay snarled, giving the girl a shake. "Don't you understand I wasn't planning to do you harm. I've white blood . . . just like you."

Jay had reason to howl low in pain next, for the girl sank her sharp little teeth into the hand held over her mouth. Instantly he thrust her away from him, but the look he gave her was a little sad. There was no hope now of his getting back Sheba.

A warning gleamed in his dark golden eyes as he pulled her close again, Jay said softly, "Make sure they don't get to me, little one, or else I'll come back for you. I will make you my captive, just as they have taken my Sheba from me." He watched as her eyes grew rounder, even greener—if that was possible—with stormy emotion threading through the flecks of yellow. "Yes, I see you know what I'm talking about."

Jay could hear the squaws giving the alarm and the sound of men excitedly snatching up their weapons. The place where she had bitten him in the hand began to throb. He gazed down at her, seeing a most enchanting face, pretty as a wild mountain flower. Someday she would be a beautiful, sensual woman. He'd met a few . . . but none even in their maturity as lovely as this pretty little fox. Then his mouth and eyes turned hard.

"Remember," he warned one last time, "you didn't notice which way I went. Tell them that." The girl's black lashes were so long that he could not be entirely certain he could trust her, eyes not withstanding. "I know you understand me . . . I heard you speak Chinook."

Nothing. No response. Only big green eyes peering between thick, spiked lashes. Finally she spoke, one word, "Go!"

Jay Ridingbow smiled, and then he was gone. When the braves came to her side, Roux turned on them her stoic Indian composure, stood, brushed herself off, then showed them the rent in her long skirt.

"You big fools," she said with a childish giggle, "I have only torn my dress!"

"Clever Dove and Lady Bird have said they heard a man cry out," Silver-White Fish said, looking up and down the river as he spoke.

"Hah! They do not know the cry of a girl from a man? Foolish women!"

Moon Dog watched the half-breed girl closely, and knew she spoke lies for someone . . . but who? Was it the lad from Wild Mountain whose horse he had stolen? He thought this was so. Moon Dog decided not to let the others know what he'd detected in Fox Fire's eyes . . . and the slightly bruised rings around her slim wrists where a man's hand had obviously encircled them. He would deal with young Ridingbow when the time came . . . and with Fox Fire someday. . . .

As the men were returning to the camp, Moon Dog narrowed his evil eyes at Fox Fire. She watched him as he mounted a beautiful golden mare she had never seen him ride before now. She looked again toward the lonely wilderness the tall lad had vanished into. The boy with eyes the same color as the beautiful mare. His horse! Moon dog was a thief, always stealing from the white settlers.

Suddenly there flashed before Roux's quick mind a wonderfully cunning scheme. She smiled widely as she thought of what she would do to Moon Dog . . . later that night.

Roux's plan had been to appear to be dozing off by the fire. But her scheme did not work so well, for the moment she saw Moon Dog go into his tipi, she'd let her head nod a couple of times, thinking sleepily this was going to work out according to her plans. As soon as she heard Moon Dog's snores filling the camp, she'd planned to take the big golden one back to the handsome lad. She would find him . . . somehow. Only one thing went wrong in her plans. In pretending to sleep when another passed by, Roux herself fell sound asleep . . . and slept on like a dead warrior.

Chapter Seven

The mountain air was crisp and clear in the morning, with the sharp fragrance of pine needles tickling Shaina's nostrils as she stepped out onto the low porch of the hotel. Her gaze swung upward, to summits blue with distance and white with snow. Her slim figure erect, feet planted solidly on the plank floor, she inhaled deeply and was filled with a sense of well-being.

Nothing, Shaina told herself, could subdue her spirits this day.

After Shaina had finished her breakfast of oatmeal, toast, and black tea—served by Elsa, the chubby, waddling cook now wearing a spanking clean apron—and was hanging her undergarments on the span of twine stretched from corner to wall near the basin, a knock sounded at the door.

Casting one last look at the line of thin, worn unmentionables, Shaina shrugged, and, tucking the straying tendrils of hair back into her long pony tail, went to answer the door.

It was Elsa, whose red cheeks wobbled in amusement as she spied the delicate garments on the line in the corner. "Got company, Miss Shainy Hill." The younger woman smiled at the use of her childhood nickname. "It's Noah Starr . . . better hide your pretties." She guffawed in a loud voice.

Smoothing her hands along her slightly damp skirt, Shaina checked her hair once by bobbing in front of the wavy mirror and then closing the door behind her, said to the friendly woman. "No that's not necessary. I'm coming down anyway, Elsa."

Elsa laughed heartily, her three chins wobbling as she snorted, "Need the exercisin' anyways." A substantial chuckle arose from her throat. "You sweet on Noah, huh?"

"What?" Shaina almost tripped on the last stair. "He must be a hundred years old!"

"So?" Elsa chortled. "All the gals is sweet on him —" She winked. "And o' course on Travis Cordell."

Deep chuckles from the hefty woman followed Shaina out the door and she experienced the first moment of irritation for the day. The next would be felt not long after she stepped outside.

"Mornin', Miss Hill." Noah Starr stood holding the reins of a huge Indian pony, and said, "This here cayuse is fer your convenience."

"Oh, thank you!" Shaina stepped to the black and white face, stroking the pony under the neck, making clucking sounds with her tongue. "He's very pretty. Where did you get him?"

"She's yours."

With a laugh, Shaina crooned to the huge pony, "I'm sorry, girl, you're so strong I naturally thought—" She caught the humor in the old man's eyes, and told him quite haughtily, "Well, Mr. Starr, girls are strong, too, it's just that—"

"Lady," Noah Starr said, holding up a long-fingered hand, "you don't need to be doin' any explainin' to this old man. I knowed what yer meanin' was." Still, he kept smiling as if he'd discovered gold in his pocket.

"Well, thank you anyway, Mr. Starr. You're very ki—"

"I'd like to be on the receivin' end of all the thanking, Miss Hill, but this here cayuse is from Travis Cordell himself."

"Oh . . ."

"What's wrong?" Noah peered at her closely.

"Nothing." Shaina tossed her head, flipping the long hank of strawberry-glinted blond hair around her shoulder. Quickly she inquired, "Where's the schoolhouse, Mr. Starr?"

"Shoot, wish you'd call me Noah . . . and I'll call you Shainy."

"I don't mind, Mr—ah, Noah. But it doesn't sound very proper for a schoolteacher. What will the children think?"

"That old Noah's sweet on the little schoolteacher." Noah blinked one eye and rounded the other one hugely.

Shaina smiled. "Where is the school? I'd really like to see it . . . I just don't know how to get there."

"Shoot, gal, you gotta take the bull by the tail here!"

"I'll take him by the horns!"

"Good, that's the sass. Now, the schoolhouse is on the edge of town, right before the first flax shed. It's

72

old Webberly's barn fixed up like a genuine school-house. Webberly was married to one of the Salish women, think she's dead now. Anyway, she was a cousin to Travis's woman Miah."

Going white, Shaina said, "Mr. Cordell has a . . . *wife?*"

Noah peered closely at Shaina. "Ahhh, she's more like a mistress. Miah's always gone to the Indian camp. Used to be she was home long stretches at a time . . . not anymore. Travis don't talk about her much, neither."

"Oh —" Then a sudden chill entered her words. "I'd like to find the schoolhouse . . . now."

"Sure . . . sure." He tugged at his long beard. "About where you're going to live. Deanna's people are going to put you up."

"Who's Deanna?"

"Mr. Cordell's housekeeper. She goes home on weekends."

"Oh. Who decided I'd be staying with *her* folks?"

"I think you know." Noah puckered his mouth. "Cordell, of course."

"Naturally."

"Travis Cordell is the power in the valley. You would be wise to show him some respect, Shainy."

"I'll show him respect when he's earned it!"

Noah shook his head in disappointment. "Oh . . . but my dear young lady, you're going to have to. See, it's Cordell who'll be paying the new schoolteacher . . . always has."

"Damn that Travis Cordell!"

With a shake of his head, Noah warned, "Careful, Shainy. There's a lot of kids in this valley . . . and if they hear the pretty schoolteacher cussin', they're gonna talk. Travis will be the first to hear and spank yer hand."

"Well you can give your *master* his stupid horse back. I won't accept her."

"She's a good mare . . . Spotted Bird." There was humor twinkling in Noah's eyes. "And she's a cayuse, Indian pony, Shainy."

"I don't want her. I mean it, Noah Starr!"

"I'd be behavin' if I were you, gal, and, besides, it's a good four miles to the schoolhouse from where you'll be stayin'. It'll take you a long time, through the woods—mighty scary even durin' the day. Screamin' or nothin' is gonna help you if you get attacked in them woods."

"Attacked?" Shaina cocked her bright head. "By who?"

"Oh . . . Indians mebbe. Sometimes river men hang out . . . lumberjacks." He began to lead Spotted Bird away, calling over his shoulder, "After a few days walkin' through them spooky devil woods, you'll be beggin' Travis Cordell for this here Indian pony."

"I'll take her."

Noah stopped, not turning, and, grinning, said over his shoulder, "Did I hear you say somethin'?"

"I said, *I'll take her!*"

"I thought you said that."

Shaina lay facing the open window that was propped wide by a stick of kindling wood. Moonlight spilled over her and cool night air stirred through the opening and blew softly against her warm cheek. The comforter came up to the points of her breasts and rose and fell with the gentle movement of her breathing.

The mountain, moonlit and splendid, reared up into the darkness of sky, the rocky dome over four thousand feet above the earth. In the day, the great mountain was black where the timber was dense and turned roseate when the setting sun colored the steep cliffs.

The Kingswells' cabin was made of cedar shakes that had been split by hand. There was a big kitchen with a fieldstone hearth, and a bedroom at each end of the kitchen. Shaina touched the rough wall with her fingertips, running them with the grain. There was the smell of new cedar, sweet and spicy.

The Kingswell children were all sleeping soundly . . . the night air was heavy with sleep.

But Shaina could not sleep. She wondered if Deanna was as pretty as her sisters, with solemn grace in their big violet-blue eyes, long, slender arms and legs, and thick, silken wheat-blond hair. Was Deanna Kingswell, the eldest of five, not only Travis Cordell's housekeeper but his mistress as well?

Shaina tossed and turned. Night-thoughts flew at her like bats in a belfry. She was paralyzed into the wakefulness that came to those who made worry a habit at night . . .

When she finally was half asleep, the dreams came of the man with the disturbing green eyes. At last, the rushing colors and erotic movements blurred with delicate vibrating quivers lulled Shaina to sleep.

Several miles away and closer to the foothills of the mountain, there in his ranch house, Travis, too, was finding sleep hard in coming. He had, in fact, slept for fifteen minutes or so — he couldn't be sure how long it had been — but he'd been dreaming of the schoolteacher; and now his body flared with desire so intense that it overwhelmed him with its throbbing heat.

What had she said in the dream?

"Oh, my, but you dance very well —" breathless she'd been "— you *are* full of surprises, Travis Cordell."

He'd grabbed her up and swung her around, holding her soft, gentle curves hard against his own rock-hardness and kept on whirling her until she had actually become breathless and panting. When finally he stopped whirling her, he continued to hold her just as closely and the cessation of rapid movement made their clinging together suddenly more intimate. Under her full skirts her slender thighs were against his. His breath rose and fell, his chest against the softness of her full, rounded breasts. Shaina's supple body seemed at once to yield and to resist. There was laughter and chatter in the fuzzy dream-room, and then the very room itself seemed to fall away into the distance, to leave Travis and Shaina entirely alone in the huge shadow of the mountain. The dance was no longer a dance but an embrace. They were lolling in sensation, willfully prolonging it . . . and the music ceased to be. Shaina leaned back to look at Travis and one bar of moonlight fell across her face. When he bent down her quivering lips parted for him, and he could feel the sudden rigidity of her fingertips digging in his shoulders. Her mouth was nectar, hot and sweet. Then she whirled around by herself, came to a standstill, stood staring at him with big smoky-blue eyes. She was standing near a doorway, and she said, "Now, Travis Cordell, you have something you can always wonder about . . ." And she went in the room and closed the door.

Travis awoke, his eyes blazing and feverish, but soon he felt cooled by the night air coming in his window. One way or another, he always got what he wanted. And suddenly Travis wanted Shaina Hill . . . for however many times it would take for him to exorcise her out of his blood.

Chapter Eight

Shaina's golden-bronze waves shimmered when the sun peeked through the leafy bowers in the woods touching her hair. She rode the Indian pony, Spotted Bird.

There was solitude here in the woods and she had to admit to feeling a little spooked.

Another horse was in the woods with his master, and they were closing in on Shaina and Spotted Bird. But she heard nothing, nothing but the haunting sounds of mountain creatures and the muffled beat of Spotted Bird's hooves.

She sighed, beginning to relax and enjoy the peaceful woods. It was so beautiful here. So green and deep . . . so hauntingly still.

She reflected back over the two weeks since she'd come here to Wild Mountain. The children already worshipped her — at least most of them. There were some boys — She had to sigh in frustration even thinking of them, they were such mischievous lads. Lovable just the same, though, as was every child in the valley, she'd come to know.

The schoolhouse was large enough, but sometimes it seemed very small with so many energetic children moving about. They were hard to keep still for very long.

The schoolhouse had been fixed up a bit. There was rough plank flooring and three windows with split-cedar shutters and four benches long enough to seat seven children apiece. A large slate board occupied a good amount of space on one wall. After school was out and the children were laughing their way home, Shaina often stood alone in the mote-filled barn with the sun shining peacefully into the window watching her Indian pony grazing in the clearing. She felt secure until the thought of Travis Cordell and his domineering, possessive attitude came to haunt her. It was a long arm that reached out to encompass the valley, with the spirit of Travis Cordell moving through, saying, I own it all, I am master here.

Well, this was one human being Travis Cordell did not own, Shaina thought as she rode slowly through the woods, but the fact still remained that Travis Cordell owned a big part of the valley and was a very powerful man who paid her wages out of his own pocket.

Shaina's heart thudded at the thought of seeing Travis Cordell again, but she quickly dismissed the hard, masculine image from her head.

Shaina heard a sound, and to her horror, she saw Travis come riding toward her like a dark, handsome lord of another place and time. Turning back to face the road, Shaina closed her eyes for a moment as though she could cancel out the vision of him riding

79

toward her, but it did nothing to make him disappear.

She had been at school all day and, as he rode up alongside her, she glanced at him with puzzlement. Fatigue and anxiety making her eyes appear huge and pale.

They rode side by side, their horses touching now and then due to the narrowness of the winding road. Why hadn't he said anything yet? Shaina wondered. A wild tremor shook through her body as she caught a glimpse of his manly, chiseled features, the strong jaw, the determined mouth. She would not, she told herself strongly, would not allow his virile attraction to affect her. Suddenly the woods felt like the most deserted place on earth to Shaina.

He finally spoke. "Good afternoon, Shaina Hill."

An odd fear leaping in her heart, Shaina answered, "And to you, Mr. Cordell."

"Travis," he said softly. "Call me Travis."

Noah Starr had not been wrong, she thought wildly, for the woods were indeed full of dangers!

"I have to talk to you, Shaina."

"I am listening, Mr. Cordell."

"Travis!"

"Please . . . I am tired. My only wish is to get to the Kingswells' so that I can lie down and rest. The children have been especially naughty."

"There are no naughty children, Shaina, only energetic ones."

"Well then," she laughed shortly, "mine were really full of it today."

"Were they?" His eyes smiled into hers as she glanced around at him. "Children are smart, too. They really don't need any schooling. But—" he

80

shrugged — "as long as you are here to instruct them, I suppose it can't hurt."

"Tell me, Travis Cordell, how did you get your instruction? Was it from your mother or your father?"

"Father."

"No schoolteacher?" Shaina raised a dubious eyebrow. "How did you get so smart? You practically own the entire valley, I'm told."

"From my father, I told you. My mother . . . she never spent any time with me." His eyes clouded. "I hardly knew her," he said tersely.

"My mother was very special to me," Shaina said. "She was a real lady."

"Yeah," Travis snorted, "so was mine."

Shaina's head spun about. "You say that with much bitterness."

"So I do, Miss Hill." He smiled into eyes that were much bluer now. "Come on," he said suddenly, "I'll race you to the mill."

With a new light in her eyes, Shaina called, "Ralton's mill?"

"Not Ralton's anymore, Shaina. It's mine. Come on!"

Though Shaina smiled, she shook her head at the man's arrogance. Spotted Bird could never keep up with Travis's thundering mount and he knew it. But she had underestimated the Indian pony's stamina, and soon was racing through the tunnel of trees, happy to see light at the end of the towering walls of wood.

Shaina laughed for the sheer joy of the wild ride on Spotted Bird's back; she hadn't had such fun in years. She was wild and free and so very alive!

81

Travis knew she was gaining on him, for he could hear the pony's swift, muffled beats pounding closer and closer all the time.

"Come on, Spotted Bird," Shaina shouted breathlessly, "you can do it!"

When Spotted Bird pulled alongside Dice, so close in the tunnel of trees that the horses' sides were almost touching and the legs of the humans were brushing, Shaina chanced a look at Travis. She lifted her eyes and her gaze encountered an appreciative smile — and the greenest eyes this side of paradise. Then, when Spotted Bird pulled forward, nosing past the huge Dice, Shaina laughed exultantly, and the glorious sound slapped Travis in his smiling face like a fresh cool wind.

She emerged from the woods into the dazzling orange blast of slanting sun and was momentarily blinded. In that moment, Travis's hand clamped on her arm and she could hear him laughing softly.

A faint smile touched Shaina's mouth as she said, "I won."

All Travis's attention was taken up by the wild, beautiful look of Shaina. For a second, Shaina thought he was going to lean forward and kiss her.

Travis did want to kiss her, but that could wait. For now he feasted his eyes on her face and the tempting rise and fall of her breasts as she tried to catch her breath after the wild ride. Travis had not been breathless, but now, staring into Shaina's face, he felt as if his very breath was being knocked out of him. Fighting down the urge to kiss her here and now, Travis dragged his eyes away from Shaina's wild beauty, let go of her arm, and when he spoke it was with an effort to calm.

"Yes, you're the winner," Travis said out loud, but thought to himself, I will win next time, little one. And the next, and the next round.

They dismounted at the huge doors of the sawmill, and Shaina was suddenly remembering the first night she'd spent here with Giles Wilson. Travis tied their mounts outside and then stepped inside the cool, dark barn behind Shaina.

Silence reigned. At the same moment, both still a little breathless—Shaina from the wild chase, Travis from her nearness—they turned as one and faced each other. Green eyes held blue ones.

"Shaina," Travis murmured, lifting a hand to lay it alongside her flushed cheek.

When he moved near and his head bent, Shaina's breathing quickened. First he murmured her name against her cheek, and when his mouth savagely took hers, the very floor beneath seemed to heave and buck under her. Shaina's first taste of ecstasy began flooding her, and then when she felt the hardness of man's desire pressing against her she became alarmed.

Travis took his lips from hers, and his eyes buried into hers as he said, "You make it very hard for a man to control his baser instincts, Shaina Hill."

"I—I don't know what you mean," she stammered, averting her gaze to avoid looking into his blazing green eyes.

"Yes you do, little one, and I don't think you are altogether indifferent to it, either."

"Travis!" Shaina was shocked, and pushed against his hard chest. "You have a mistress and I have—"

"—never been with a man." He smiled into her

83

eyes. "So surprised? You shouldn't be. It's written all over you, Shaina. But you want to, and you're afraid."

Terrified at the strange emotions coursing through her body, Shaina wrenched out of his arms, then realized she was not to be freed that easily and was immediately pulled back into the circle of his embrace.

"Don't turn away from me again, Shaina. I need you—"

Once again his mouth claimed hers, and once again the hard length of manhood was grinding against her. Shaina couldn't decide if it was torture or ecstasy this time as he kissed her deeply, his tongue learning the shape of her mouth and thrusting in a rhythm that made her knees go weak. She gasped when his hands slipped to her hips and pulled her fiercely against him . . . and her lips parted under his.

At the corner of her mouth he murmured her name, his body moving against hers hungrily. Seducing her with their touch, his big hands moved over her shoulders, down her arms, then dived in around her waist. A whirlwind of mindless desire washed over Shaina as she felt one hand move to her breast and cup it and tease it. She moaned against the wild pressure of his mouth, his langorous kiss.

Before she could drown and become unconscious of what she was doing, Shaina pulled back and was shocked by the hot, pinched look of Travis Cordell. He looked to be in pain, or else he was angry.

"Your body makes no secret of your feelings, Shaina, little miss schoolteacher." Tanned fingers reached out to tangle in the loosened strands of hair. He tugged a little and she flinched.

Shaina's slender frame was shaken to the core. She was totally unaware how sweetly seductive she looked after being so thoroughly kissed. She tossed her head in defiance.

"You think to possess me, too, just like you own everything else in this valley. I have news for you—" her eyes flashed up at him—"I can leave any time I choose—."

"Be my guest."

"I will!" She set her teeth and stepped back, just in case he had it in mind to grab her again. "As soon as Giles Wilson returns, I'll go back to Seattle with him. At least Giles is a gentleman!"

"Go, Shaina, run away. I could have the schoolhouse torn down tonight if I chose to order it be done."

"You leave me with little choice, Mr. Cordell." She smiled with a curled lip as he flinched at the unaffectionate twist in her voice. "I go and the children suffer because they won't have a school in which to attend classes. You are a heartless man, Travis Cordell!"

She could leave, yes, leave behind the sunny, wild, tree-shrouded valley with the dark-visaged mountains pressing down, leave all the poor children, too. The Wildbloods. Johnny Wing. Little Crystal Slade with her big, trusting brown eyes. And all the other lovely children she was with almost every day of the week. They adored her, and the feeling was mutual.

"Don't you have a daughter, Mr. Cordell? Where is she? Why hasn't she attended school?"

"That's none of your business!"

"You do have a daughter? It isn't just a rumor, is it?"

"She's half Indian."

"So? There are other Indian children in school, half-breeds and full Indian."

"Roux is no *breed!*" he snarled. "She's . . . Roux Cordell."

"Well," Shaina breezed past him, tossing over her shoulder, "Send her to school. I'd like to meet her."

"And fill her head full of nonsense!"

"No." Shaina poked her head back around the tall doors. "Just to give *instruction.* Good afternoon, *Mr. Cordell.*"

Outside, with big hands on slim hips, Travis watched her ride away with straight back, on the Indian pony, hair blowing back from her pinkened cheeks. Travis swore softly. The woman was like strong liquor . . . she went clear to a man's head.

At least, he thought as he mounted a dancing Dice, he was fortunate she hadn't gone to his heart.

Chapter Nine

The girl known as Fox Fire to the Salish Indians rode into the valley mounted astride the beautiful golden mare. She had ridden it through the dark hours before dawn, and now only a few, faint stars were dimly shining in the sky. The morning star hung big and bright, the others paling in the powdery blue-gray dawn.

She was known only to a handful of people as Roux Cordell. And so it was when Jay Ridingbow saw her, he didn't recognize the young Indian girl — and especially not as Travis Cordell's daughter.

One thing did stand out to Jay, however, and that was the fact that the golden mare was his own Sheba.

"Hellfire!" Jay swore, every muscle in his tall, lean length coming alive to do battle.

Creeping stealthily through the grass smelling of wild clover, Jay watched her coming along the mountain rode down from Stampede Pass.

The sun peeked its face over the lower mountain range.

Jay Ridingbow felt a surge of pride as he watched Sheba lift her forelegs high in a delicate prance, watched her tail form a golden, flowing arc, her curving neck rise like a cobra about to strike. And then Jay looked the girl over, and a vision of sharp clamping teeth alerted him as the wound in his hand began to ache in remembrance.

Little vixen . . . a thief no less!

Stepping bold as you please out into the road, Jay startled his horse for a moment, and then in the next Sheba had pranced to a halt and was giving her long nose into Jay's hand so that he could stroke the velvety length.

"My love, my beauty, I have missed you," he crooned into the twitching ear above the long, gentle face of the mare as she bowed her head even further to nudge his trouser pocket in search of a sweet.

Looking up at the surprised girl, Jay narrowed his eyes into hardened shards of glitter. "It was you who took my horse. Oh, little one, you should not have done that. I am very unhappy with you."

He spoke in Chinook and Roux understood every word.

"I should not have brought your horse back to you, tall one?" Roux blinked brilliant green eyes and cocked her auburn-dark head.

Trying to read her face, Jay studied her closely, but found nothing there but stoic Indian composure. To see this in such a young one was surprising, but then Jay remembered himself at a younger age. Still, this one was a girl . . . only a girl.

"If this were true," Jay began, "how did you know where to find me?"

"I did not know." Roux shrugged shoulders that were all bone and sinew and soft flesh. She reached down a hand, coming very close to his, and patted the mare's silvery-gold mane. "This one led me. She followed her heart. But first my task was to free her from the bastard called Moon Dog. That one is every inch the slimy, repulsive Dog, too! He had her tied!"

Flinching from the indelicate words, which were jarring coming from the mouth of one so pretty and dainty, Jay was shocked at first. Then he smiled to himself trying not to let her see how funny he thought she was.

"Where is your tongue, tall boy? You look to me and search with big wondering eyes but say nothing. Speak!"

"I believe you, little fox," Jay said with unusual gentleness in his deep, almost manly voice.

"Fox Fire."

"What?" Jay gave a short laugh.

The girl shook her head in exasperation and Jay had to fight down another chuckle.

"My name . . . What is yours?" she asked with big green eyes alive with curiosity.

"Uh—" Jay brushed his hand over the thick, coarse waves of his dark hair. "Mine is Ridingbow—Jay Ridingbow."

"Ah! I know who you are," Roux said with bright recognition on her face. "Your big man works for my big man."

"My . . big man? Who would that be?" There was a twinkle of humor in Jay's slanted golden eyes.

"The white man says Father, or Dah-dee, or Papa. My big man is Travis Cordell."

Jay gulped. "My *boss*?" he asked in a high-pitched voice. "Your pa is Mister Cordell?"

"Yaas."

Jay almost giggled as he corrected, "Yes!"

"Oh, yes. *Yes!*" She reached down, and for one so small and delicate her grip carried surprising strength. "Come and join me, Jay Ridingbow. I would like for you to ride with me."

Jay lifted both eyebrows as, at the same time, he said, "Me? Ride with you?" He caught her by the wrist, but gave most of his own force into the lift and sprang up behind her onto Sheba's backside. Scooting forward, he came closer to her.

She laughed, and said, "it is your horse. I am not so stupid. You must ask me to ride with you."

Tossing back his head, Jay shouted, "Ride with me, Fox Fire, ride with me into the wind!"

"My white name is Roux Cordell," she called back as Sheba lunged into a full gallop, whipping long strands of golden mane into the air. She laughed wildly. "Do you like Roux or Fox Fire . . . you must pick!" she said, serious about the matter.

When Sheba's stride lengthened, her muscles bunching and unrolling, Jay reached around the slim form and took hold of the thick rope. Smiling happily, with joy in her little heart, Roux wound slim fingers about Jay Ridingbow's wrists—they were so large her fingers barely touched.

"Sometimes I will call you Roux," Jay called, laughing into the morning sun and the wind, "and other times I will say, 'Fox Fire, bring me my horse.'"

Little Roux gasped. "You wish me to take care of the golden one for you?"

"When you can. If you can. Will you?"

"Oh yaas . . . *yes!*"

The boy in the third summer of his teens and the girl five summers younger than he rode through the valley with the fresh cool wind in their hair, happy to be young and alive, unaware it had been written in the wind that one day they would fall irrevocably in love.

Chapter Ten

"Good morning, children."

"Good morning, teacher."

Shaina smiled as she glanced out the window. It *was* a good morning . . . and it was going to be a good day too.

"We will begin the day with the Lord's Prayer."

To Shaina, several voices stood out as the class recited the prayer. Some were still puzzled, not having the words to the prayer down yet, and they turned their heads this way and that as their eyes lingered anxiously on the lips of others.

With heads bowed, the children mumbled dutifully, but the biggest boy in the class glared straight ahead with his arms crossed defiantly over his chest. The teacher hid a smile from this one, but oh how she remembered her first day in Wild Mountain . . . and this lad's expert hand with the slingshot!

The sun beamed into the room to touch the teacher's hair and turn it to soft fire. Many sighed at her loveliness, but the Wildblood lad set his mouth in a thin line and continued to glare straight ahead.

Shaina nodded, looking at her class with a seriousness born of her eagerness to teach . . . to *instruct*.

"Now," she said, "the roll call."

Marvin Wildblood tucked in a corner of his mouth in boredom and disgust. He looked around the class, over one shoulder, then the other, his look saying, Boy, what a bunch of dummies, listenin' to a silly teacher.

"We will start over here," Shaina went on, trying to ignore Marvin's surly look. "Each one stand in turn and give your name."

At last, a small, dainty girl stood up. Shaina was surprised she'd not noticed her before. As if mesmerized by the girl, Shaina came around her desk slowly, watching the perfect bow-shaped lips move.

"I am Roux—" she looked around shyly—"Cordell."

Shaina took in the delicate bronze of her skin, the gleaming mahogany of her thick shining braids. Her eyes were green. As green as her father's, Shaina thought.

"Roux Cordell . . . present," Shaina found herself repeating out loud automatically as the girl watched her with studied composure.

Roux . . . Travis's daughter. But she is so quiet, so watchful, and Shaina could at once feel the presence of the girl's father right there in the room with her, the green eyes compelling.

One morning several days later, Shaina came upon a most unusual scene. Before all the children arrived, she had been walking along a misty path, breathing in the exhilarating morning air, her gaze embracing the snowcapped purple of the mountain which sparkled after the morning's rain.

It was just a short time before the class was to gather at the tall doors, and Shaina was just making her way there when the sound of children arguing brought her up short.

Bending forward as she came to a halt, Shaina could see into the crevice of the trees that two of the taller children were engaged in a verbal battle — but she couldn't make out their faces. Then, wasn't that Roux's voice she heard above the other's?

Hurrying now, Shaina grasped a handful of her skirts to keep the hems from becoming too damp in the dew-laced grass that grew taller here between the path and the wooded area. She could go around, she told herself, and save her skirts from getting too wet, but by then, judging from the louder, angrier sounds she heard, there might be a full-scale battle in progress.

The thick lashes that shadowed Shaina's cheeks flew up as she stepped from the stand of pines into the pie-shaped clearing. She had heard the sound of a fist slamming into flesh and bone, then the deep, anguished groan following close behind the *thwack*.

Now she heard Roux Cordell's voice ring loud and clear as she spoke a warning to Marvin Wildblood, the boy who had received the full impact of her small driving fist.

". . . and if you ever say evil things about the teacher again, I will let you have it with both fists." Roux's voice sounded in the little clearing as an ominous warning to the lad. The half-Indian girl went on in her perfect English. "Bigger than Roux you might be, but not stronger . . . Good morning, teacher. I will walk with you to the schoolhouse."

Before Shaina took the small, bronze hand extended to her, she looked back at the big lad who carefully tested the fast-swelling area beneath his eyes that was beginning to purple. The only word that Marvin uttered was *"Ouch!"*, unable to look the teacher straight in the eye. Biting her lip to keep from smiling at the naughty lad's discomfort, Shaina turned to Roux who was gazing toward the mountain seemingly indifferent to all that went around her. Shaina regarded the girl's lovely profile quizzically for a moment. There was such strength and beauty all rolled together in the face. If Shaina didn't know better, she'd have thought somewhere in the girl's lineage there could be Spanish blood.

Then Roux was all smiles as she took the teacher's hand firmly this time and held it in a surprisingly strong grip.

"You pack some wallop, Miss Cordell," Shaina said, and then laughed. "You needn't hold my hand so tightly, Roux."

"I must," Roux insisted. "That bully might attack you. He hates teachers. All of them who came here before ran away . . . most because of that one! . . . I have never been to school before. My father has taught me. And Deanna has learned me many things, too."

Shaina smiled at the girl's grammar. "Well, you need to learn more, Roux. Do you mind if I call you that?"

"You can call me Fox Fire if you want. That is my

Indian name."

"That is a beautiful name, and it fits you." Shaina laughed delightfully. She was enjoying Travis's daughter's crude wit. "I shall call you Roux, as long as that is the name your white father gave to you."

The girl was smiling strangely at Shaina, and she wanted to continue the conversation, but they were nearing the school and most of the children were already waiting there restlessly at the tall doors.

"I'd like to talk more after school, Roux. Will you walk with me then?"

"You have a horse." Roux stated the fact. "I have one, too. My father has given me a small gray mare. She is very tame. Too quiet for me. I would rather have a swifter horse. We will ride after school, together."

And so Shaina and Travis Cordell's daughter rode through the woods with the afternoon sun slanting intermittently through the azure sky, gilding Shaina's pale complexion and adding more burnish to Roux's. Over the weeks, the rides became an after-school pattern for the two.

In several ways, with a cleverness belying her young years, Roux had been testing the teacher's mood and her interest in her. Finally, feeling sufficiently confident, she asked the question she had so wanted to ask. "You would hear about my mother. Is that not so?"

The boldness of this child! Shaina almost coughed in embarrassment. How perceptive! She had been thinking about just that subject before school and now again. Ever since she'd heard that Travis Cordell had a mistress, an Indian woman no less, she'd been interested, maybe too interested for her own good, to know what the woman was like. Was she pretty? Did she love Travis? Did he love her in return? Why didn't they live together? And how had she known this last fact?

Exactly how to put her thoughts into words Shaina wasn't sure, but she tried. "I'll bet your mother is as pretty as you are." Oh, how simple-minded that sounded!

Without pride, Roux answered, "Where I am like a plain yellow weed, Miah is like the wild mountain flower. She is beautiful. My father should never have looked at her with shining eyes and made her his woman."

Shaina was shocked, but she tried not to show it. When she spoke, her voice wavered. "You would not have come into this world if not for your mother . . . and your father." Shaina knew she was blushing and hoped the deep purple shadows of the forest hid the hot color of her skin.

"I hate Miah!" Roux cried out, jabbing the mare with her heels as she sent it into a jogging trot.

With a feeling of distress in the region of her heart, Shaina caught up with the girl. She looked over at the rigid countenance and said nothing. To speak at that moment would seem almost a sacrilege. But Shaina had to swallow hard at the little bronze face that tried so desperately not to reveal the sadness within her heart. What could have happened to cause a heavy heart in one so young? Was the woman mean? Did she beat the girl? She could see no signs pointing to abuse. What then?

"My father needs a new woman," Roux suddenly blurted, not looking at the schoolteacher. "Will you marry my father?"

Shaina coughed as if she had something caught in her throat. She had to swallow several times before answering.

"Your father already has a woman, Roux," Shaina said, her words slow and trying to sound comforting. "And he hasn't asked me." Shaina could almost laugh aloud. Travis asking her to marry him? The mere thought was incredible, to say the least.

"He does not have a woman. The Songish have said Miah disgraces the word *love*."

Shaina's eyes flared as she glanced at her little companion. "What are you saying?" Her heart was beating very fast.

Nonchalantly Roux shrugged a shoulder, baring its bronze smoothness where her shift had sagged to one side. Shaina looked at her, wondering how a child this lovely could think of herself as a common yellow weed.

"Miah and Travis have not lived together as mates ever since I was born. Miah is a camp woman. She is free with her favors."

Shaina tore her gaze from the girl's to stare straight ahead to the light at the end of the beautiful wooded tunnel. Her breath was caught somewhere in her pounding chest.

"You like my father." Roux tossed her braided hair with a flippant hand. "I can tell. He likes you, too. I have read his face. When Uncle Noah called you Shainy, Father smiled. He looked very happy."

"*Uncle* Noah?" was all Shaina could get out.

98

"Noah Starr." Roux giggled. "He is not my uncle true, I just call him that. He takes care of me when Travis is too busy." Roux studied the schoolteacher closely before she went on. "Tell me you will marry my father . . . please?"

Huge, slanted green eyes turned on Shaina with pleading in them, with her whole world there in them, in fact.

"Roux," Shaina began slowly. "There are many things which must be taken into consideration before a man and woman marry. They have to know each other—"

"You know my father Travis Cordell. He is very handsome and very rich. I have everything. But I like to wear my soft dresses I made in Witch Bear's camp. I will make you one someday if you like."

"Yes, Roux, that would be very nice . . . I'd like to wear a dress you made with your own hands."

"You could be like my mother. I would even call you Mother, would you like that?"

All stoic Indian composure gone, Roux gazed into Shaina's face with her heart and soul in the jade-green eyes. Shaina hated to say what she had to, but say it she must.

"Roux," she began tenderly, "I have come to like you very much—"

"And you make my heart glad too, teacher."

Shaina made to try again. "Roux . . . I won't always be here. You see, when this teaching post is fulfilled . . . I mean over, I will be returning to Seattle." How could you explain to a child that this wasn't all there was to life? "I can't stay here the rest of my life, Roux, I am needed elsewhere. I have

99

family, a sister, brothers—" She was going to say father, but thought better of it. "And I am surely not going to live in Wild Mountain the rest of my life!"

"Why? Do you not like it here, Shainy?"

"I like it here fine . . . for now."

"You are going to marry Travis," Roux insisted, "and you are to stay here the rest of your life."

Shaina calmly explained, "Two cannot be married if one does not ask the other first, Roux. And I doubt if your father will ask anyone to become his wife . . . especially me."

"Yes. He will."

"Roux, I do not *want* to marry your rich, powerful, handsome father. I—I have a man," she lied. "He . . . he has asked me to marry him."

"Who is he then?" Roux screwed up her face jealously.

"He is . . . Giles Wilson!" Shaina blurted. Then she blanched. "Oh, Lord! what had she gone and done now. Another lie!

"Ugh!" Roux grimaced. "That paleface?" Suspiciously Roux studied the woman's face for the truth. "He has asked you?"

"Well, no. But he will," Shaina ended on a cheerful note.

"That one is with women as much as Miah is with men."

Shaina frowned, and chided the girl. "Roux! I don't think we should be having this conversation. It is . . . too adult."

Roux shrugged. "If you say. You are the ah-dult. Look. There is my father!"

Shaina's eyes followed the pointing, tapered finger

100

and saw that Travis Cordell sat his huge horse at the end of the tunnel. He was a bronze god, set afire by the slanting rays of sun. Blood rushed in her veins — straight to her heart. The very sight of him stormed her senses, and as they drew closer, his stare was bold. She sensed there was something different about him . . . but what? There was a caressing light in his eyes, making Shaina's heart jolt. For a moment there was no reality in her fast-spinning world but Travis Cordell . . . and then like a dash of cold water he brought her back to earth.

"There's pox fever at the Kingswells'." His jade-green eyes flared and narrowed as he went on. "Deanna happened to be at home when the pox hit. She won't be coming back to the ranch. I know you won't like this, Miss Hill, but you'll have to come home with Roux and myself."

"But I—"

"Miss Hill!" Travis's temper flared. "No questions, just come." He turned his attention to his daughter. "Roux, you will have to stay at the ranch until this is over, do you hear?"

"Oh, yes, Father." She looked into his frowning eyes. "It will sweep through the camp along the river like woods' fire. The Songish will go into the sweat houses. Someday I will show you a sweat house, Shaina."

Travis looked from his daughter to the schoolteacher, wondering what had been going on between the two of them. They appeared too familiar with each other. Roux was getting too attached to the schoolteacher . . . and that he couldn't allow to happen. Roux was too eager to adopt a mother, he thought, unconsciously frowning at the girl as if she'd

101

done something naughty.

"I will have to stay at your ranch?" Shaina said, full of misgiving.

"Until this epidemic of smallpox passes, yes, and we can't be sure some of the hands haven't even come down with it already. So I want you and the girl to stay inside the house."

"But I could help . . . Wait a minute! Don't interrupt me this time, Mr. Cordell." Shaina held up her hand and Travis stared from it to her flushed face. "I am not going to sit back in a comfortable house while people are out here dying. I can help them."

"Do you know what to do?"

"No," Shaina answered honestly.

"In that case, you'd be more trouble than help, Miss Hill."

Deliberately Shaina said, *"Mr. Cordell* . . . I cannot stay at your home until this thing blows over. It might be *days*."

"No, *weeks*. And you *can* stay at the ranch, or are you afraid I'll bite?"

"I'm not afraid," Shaina said quickly and untruthfully.

"Good. Let's go home."

Roux nudged the gray mare with her knees and moved in behind the pair, a broad smile curving her sweetly molded lips.

Chapter Eleven

Down in the center of a vast bowl of green and tan lay the most natural setting for a homestead that Shaina had ever seen. The pastureland was moving, alive with grullas, well fed and sleek. Unlike most Indian ponies, the grullas were not at all wild, Travis had been telling her. There was pride and fire in the way these strong horses threw up their heads . . . savage, splendid, beautiful.

Just like these foothills. Awe possessed Shaina. All this belonged to one man and one child?

The ranch house itself was L-shaped, double-storied with a railed wooden porch and roofed over-hang. Several pots with trailing greenery squatted here and there on the porch, set between pieces of heavy outdoor furniture that consisted of rockers and padded chairs and one long table lined with benches that sat conveniently close to a smaller door Shaina guessed must lead to the kitchen.

Shaina was painfully reminded of her mother just then. Here at the ranch was a fence that went with the gently rolling terrain surrounding the house, a huge, fenced area designed to keep the animals out of the immediate yard. A gate and a plain board above announced the Lazy C Ranch.

The fence was not white but a weathered gray. Although not the picket fence of Eleanora's dream but a sturdy ranch-type fence, Eleanora would have liked it nonetheless.

What am I thinking, Shaina chided herself, I am not going to live here. I am only . . . visiting.

Upon closer observation, Shaina discovered the ranch house was larger than it had first appeared from the crest of the hill that sloped toward it.

When they dismounted before the gate — because Roux wanted to walk the short way to the porch — a young man with work-worn blue jeans came riding lickety split from the cluster of buildings set off to the right of the main house. In a dust-raising halt, he came down off his fat-bellied mount like a talented rodeo performer.

"Jack!" Roux giggled, making much of a coughing fit as she waved her hand before her face. Then she went on to speak to him in a guttural language that made Shaina's eyes blink from confusion at the Indian words coming with such rapidity.

"That's enough, Roux," Travis said. To Shaina he announced, "Miss Shaina Hill, this is my foreman, Jack Nolan . . . he's got some Salish blood. Takes care of the cattle business for me."

Sadly Roux looked at her father — he was always telling her to be quiet when she spoke Indian.

Jack Nolan turned to face Shaina Hill and smiled.

"Happy to meet you, ah, Miss Hill. Hope you'll like

your stay here." Dark-brown eyes slid down over her shapely figure almost shyly and the younger man regarded his boss with one squinting eye.

The two men exchanged a look that was lost on Shaina, but not so on Roux, it seemed. Sparkling happily, the green eyes flashed as she took in the manly looks of appreciation that were being washed over the schoolteacher. Roux's delight stemmed mostly from the thorough perusal her father was giving the woman — in fact had been giving her all the way out to the ranch. If he married Shaina, maybe he wouldn't always be so grumpy! Roux thought.

"I won't be staying too long," Shaina told Jack Nolan.

"Too bad," Nolan muttered under his breath, but Shaina caught the words with her sharply attuned ears.

Shaina's mouth curled up on one side, and the foreman looked aside with a sheepish grin.

"Oh, good!" Roux shouted into all three pairs of ears. "Here comes Uncle Noah. Ha ha ha . . . he's riding Quawpaw again."

The sight was hilarious, and Shaina looked Noah's way after she'd pulled her eyes from the eye-locking gaze Travis had had on her. Now he was frowning at his daughter again, and Shaina began to wonder about their strained relationship.

"Old carrot-lickin', sonofatootin', sidewindin' dumb jackass! Took me a good part of the day just to get here from Wild Mountain town."

Roux laughed even harder, her white teeth a startling contrast to her bronze skin. She hooted. "That is a good one, Uncle. I will remember it."

"Don't you dare, young'un!"

She sidled over to the old man, her little feet encased in silver-buttoned moccasins kicking up puffs of dust. Noah Starr was shaking a parchmentlike finger in her face, knowing she was up to something.

"We must of passed you a long ways back, Uncle." Roux giggled as Noah Starr tugged on her long, gleaming braid. "I can get that dumb jackass to move. Watch!"

As soon as Noah had slipped off the mule's back, Roux had leapt aboard. "Got carrot for you, Quawpaw," Roux enticed, holding her empty hand out in front of the long, fuzzy nose. "Go! Go! Go!" she shouted.

At once the fat mule began a quick-trotting walk, and to Shaina it appeared the long-eared creature was following her hand with the invisible carrot in it.

"Sure has a way with dumb beasts," Noah snorted, leaning forward to dust off his baggy overalls as if it pained him to do so. "I give him a real live treat and he just stands there ignorin' the dagblasted thing and won't move to save my soul."

"I would not move to save your soul, either, old man," Jack Nolan put in, covertly studying Travis who was in turn intently watching the schoolteacher's smiling face. "It was lost long ago."

"Well," Noah snorted. "I'm a goin' to get it back when that preacher fellow comes back in town."

"What's wrong with Hiram Nooner?"

"His wife is a black-haired witch. Don't trust a preacher with a nasty-minded woman at his side."

"She's a looker, Margarita is."

"Hell you say!" Noah argued. Then, "S'cuse me,

106

ma'am," to Shaina.

"Shaina. Like to go inside and see the house now?"

The words were softly spoken, and Shaina turned her face to find Travis standing close beside her. A shaft of dying sunlight caught his sexy eyes as he stared at her. "Yes, in a moment," she said. Shaina looked at the fence again and the memory of her mother and her desire for a white picket fence brought a wry, twisted smile to her lips. Maybe, she thought as she walked with him to the house, just maybe she could begin to make her own memories . . . maybe just a few.

Chapter Twelve

The black night was still studded with stars when Shaina awoke. The room was very dark and she felt forlorn and alone with only the twinkling stars for company. They seemed close enough to touch . . .

As she lay there staring out the window, her mind raced over the events of the previous day. Only her hard-won self-possession had gotten her through the day, but when evening had come on — so beautiful in these mountains it left her breathless with awe — she had relaxed with Roux in the living room. Travis had deserted the two females to see about his business.

It was magnificent living in the foothills. Nowhere she had ever lived could equal the feeling she got in Wild Mountain. It reminded her of a long, bulky book with so very many pages and so much to see and read, one was left dizzy just trying to get through it all. She had always loved books. Now she loved mountains.

What else did she love? Shaina wondered as she stared out into the shadowy coolness . . . Soon it would be getting light out.

Shaina shifted to the edge of the big bed, the golden cascade of her bright hair spilling almost to the floor. She sighed. Strange, she didn't miss her family. Well, maybe she did miss Will a little. More than that, for Will and she had been very close.

She loved Will.

She loved . . . Roux. Yes, that was true.

And she was falling . . . in . . . love with . . . Travis Cordell!

She had to get away. As soon as possible.

The kitchen was still dimly fuzzy with early-morning gray as Shaina crossed to the wood stove and, striking a match, she soon had a fire going. She was just looking for something to fix for breakfast when a deep voice came to her from the doorway and startled her.

"You don't have to do that. Silvanus is coming soon. He'll cook us breakfast."

With the surprised look on her face under control now, Shaina faced Travis, saying "I don't know who this Silvanus is, but I don't mind . . . really."

He asked with an amused smile, "Can you cook?"

"Of course!"

"Well," he drawled, "I wasn't so sure teachers were very domesticated. Thought you always had your noses in books and smudged with ink instead of flour.

"I can do both." She watched him saunter into the room like a big, lazy cat. He was unshaven and he looked tough and lean. Her body was quivering from his nearness, but the question of food still remained unanswered. "When will Silvanus be coming?" She couldn't trust herself to be alone with this man for too long.

Turning a lazy smile on her, Travis said, "Silvanus comes whenever he wants to. Why? You hungry?"

"Coffee would be nice," she managed to get out.

"I can do the coffee."

It was then Shaina realized his gaze was lingering too long on her face. There was an appreciative look in his eyes which caused mixed feelings to tumble through her.

"Please," Shaina said. "I would like to do something to earn my keep."

"All right." Travis stood with thumbs hooked in his blue jeans. "You make the coffee."

Before she turned away from him, Travis gazed longingly on the seductive curve of Shaina's breasts revealed by the tautness of the bodice of her worn, print dress. It was all he could do not to go to her and yank her into his strong arms.

"I guess Silvanus isn't coming." Shaina said after they had downed two cups of coffee apiece.

"Looks that way," Travis said, noticing the growing light outside the window. "He probably got stuck with those two sick cows . . . and one was ready to give birth. Guess you will have to make the breakfast, Shaina."

"That's fine with me," she said, beginning to look for the pans and the fixings.

"There's some bacon in the larder."

"Where is it?"

"Come here, I'll show you."

110

Shaina followed him around the corner, but as soon as she stepped into the darkened hall she found herself molded into the circle of his arms. Her knees were shaking as if she were cold all of a sudden.

She muttered a little. "Ohh."

Travis moved closer and cupped Shaina's chin in his big hand. Slowly her bright-blue eyes lifted and became locked with his in a gentle contest of wills. It was a contest that both would soon lose, as the brush of desire that swept them both became a torrent of driving need.

Suddenly Shaina's lips were begging to be kissed. They parted, very softly.

With a groan, Travis's fingers tilted her chin to bring her lips into contact with his. His mouth covered hers with passionate hunger that soon consumed them both. The clinging kiss became an exploratory one as Travis opened her mouth and his tongue thrust deep, taking on a more forceful form of lovemaking. Shaina was on fire from head to tingling feet.

Travis had never known such desire and such sweetness. He tenderly cupped the side of Shaina's face as he kissed her with eagerness. Then the fire that licked at his loins began to gnaw at his body with voracious hunger.

When Travis drew back, he was breathing heavily, and Shaina was secretly pleased that the kiss had been as devastating for him as for her.

"I want you, Shaina. But—" He turned away from her. "The price is too high."

"What do you mean?" She stared at the long, lean-waisted, broad-shouldered back he'd turned against

111

her.

"Marriage! A woman like you has to have that piece of paper before she can she can—"

Shaina blurted across his sentence, "—go to bed with him."

"Right."

Snatching open the larder door with a loud click that surprised Travis, Shaina said over her shoulder as she stepped inside, "Whoever said I wanted you to marry me?"

"Your body did."

"Oh, did it?" She shrugged. "It must know something that I don't know?"

He laughed easily, matter-of-factly, saying, "Maybe so," and started out the door.

She tried to shut the door on his face, but Travis stuck his booted toe in there. She stared at him for long moments. His eyes were doing a tantalizing rape on her person, stripping the faded print dress swiftly from her body. Hungrily his eyes stroked her small waist and gently swelling hips, returning to fasten on the round, firm breasts he had only fondled once before . . . in the sawmill. He should have taken her at that time, he told himself, instead of standing on ceremony.

The caress of Travis's eyes grew bolder and Shaina could feel the heat moving up from her breast to her throat to her cheeks. They all began to flame.

He walked away with a deep chuckle, leaving her staring at the hazy nimbus of light he'd just stepped into at the end of the hall. "Damn cowboy." She shook her head and pressed the fingers of one hand to her suddenly aching forehead. I don't want to marry

112

Travis Cordell. I don't want to marry *any* man! "I want to be a schoolteacher!" Shaina hissed as she lit the lantern beside the larder door. "Damn . . . *ouch!*" She burned her finger and sucked on the tip for a moment until the throbbing subsided.

Shaina shook her head in confusion. Sometimes she didn't know exactly what it was she wanted. She wondered why Travis and Miah had not gotten along. They really should have married, if not for themselves, then for the child. But Roux herself had said she didn't like her own mother. Could a woman be all that bad? Maybe there was a reason Miah was so free with her favors.

Shaina wanted to scream — or maybe just sit down and have a good cry. She could still feel Travis's kisses burn her lips. His touch lingered, even though he was gone. But she fought against the scorching memory with an instinct to save herself.

Leaning against the cool wall, Shaina relived the few minutes she'd spent in his arms. She could have escaped, but she might as well have tried her strength against an iron bar.

In her fight for independence Shaina had told herself that loving Travis would make her lost forever. There would be no independence with a man like that. He would possess her every waking moment. She sighed, remembering how she had been weakened by his kiss, by his mere touch — and just his physical size and strength were overpowering . . .

Travis was so strong, he was rich, he was invulnerable. He was everything. But Shaina had witnessed in Eleanora what love did to a woman and she was afraid of that.

There was a world of difference, however. Travis was everything her father had never been.

Shaina spent an uneventful first full day at the ranch. The morning had burst upon them with a beautiful sunrise, and then close to noon, when Roux was helping her with cleaning the kitchen and dusting the many rooms of heavy furniture, the rain that had begun to patter on the roof became a deluge. However, the uneventful day became one of joy and closeness as Shaina and Roux came to know each other better. School was out because of the pox fever, and there was plenty of time for everyone to do as they wished. Marvin Wildblood especially must be enjoying the quarantine, Shaina mentioned to little Roux, making her laugh. And Travis was in and out, saying the epidemic of smallpox was sweeping through the Indian camp along the river. For the first time in many days, Roux really looked worried for her friends in the camp. She told Shaina of the last epidemic she and her mother had survived, of the sadness of the widowed squaws who sobbed and wailed out their sorrow to the skies week after week, of the guttural chant of the doctor as he treated his patient, the sudden scream followed by a long moan when another one breathed his last.

"And always the whites shiver and pray to their God."

"Has there never been a cure?" Shaina asked the beautiful, willowy girl, meaning to speak to her later about God. It was apparent Travis hadn't taken her to church much or not at all.

114

"Valley Indians look for cure in the sweat houses, Shaina. They dig them into the mud of the riverbank. They become very busy, just like the ranchhands with the cattle and fences. Around the shallow hole the Indians pile fieldstones very high and lay rough boards across the top . . . like a roof. There is a big fire going close by, and they heat the big stones in it and roll them into the sweat house with long poles. Onto the red-hot stones they pour water and spread cedar branches over that. The sick Indian gets naked and crawls through the low door and pulls it shut behind him, very tight."

"How can he stand it?" Shaina wondered out loud, feeling hot and sweaty just thinking about it. "Does he just stay in there and roast?"

"Roast?" Roux laughed at the word. "Almost. When he can stand the heat and steam no more, he jumps through the door and into the river!"

Shaina's flesh prickled at the thought, just as it had when she read about the Finnish people across the ocean who leaped from the sauna into the snow.

"What do your people do for other diseases, Roux?"

"Diseases?" Roux wondered.

"You know . . . sicknesses."

"Do the same thing."

"From the steam into the river, right?"

As her black braids flew over her smooth shoulders, Roux nodded, giggling.

"Would you like to know how the Salish bury their dead?" Roux asked, laying her head against Shaina's shoulder. Her dark green eyes looked up into Shaina's and the blue ones misted with tears of caring.

"Yes, Roux. Tell me."

"We have got all day, huh?"

"All day."

"They bury their dead like the Catholic Father taught them."

"In graves made sacred by the cross?" Shaina wanted to know. This child is very knowledgeable, she thought, thinking she must have spent a lot of time with the Songish tribe.

"Yes," Roux answered. "They make the crosses with baby trees—"

"Saplings," Shaina supplied, smoothing the girl's glossy black hair with the back of her hand.

"Uhmm, saplings. The crosses made from saplings are planted in the middle of the burial grounds." Tears were misting Roux's eyes now and she blinked to hold them back. "Some Indians carry the bodies to the hill over the river. They are stretched out on the high limbs of tall trees. And some are buried on the high ground. When the whites of Thunder Valley see them walking Indian file to the high ground, they hurry away."

"Why?" Shaina continued to stroke the girl's hair.

"It is as if just looking at them, the whites might catch the fever. Last time of fever there were many and many Indians on the prairies above the falls. The whites did not know how fast the Indians died and no one cared anyway. The whites only pray the plague will not touch them."

"How sad," Shaina murmured. "The whites must flee like mice before a hungry hawk."

"Smallpox is bad," Roux said with a weary sigh. "It is not pretty what the sickness does to our people."

"Dear God, I wish there was something . . ."

116

Shaina bit off the rest of her sentence, for Roux was fast asleep against her shoulder, her silver-buttoned moccasins lying on the hearth rug below Shaina's tucked legs.

The ranchhands recognized Miah's ailment the moment she walked into the yard after sagging from her pinto into the dust. Cussing under their breath, most of the men began to flee like the bats from hell were giving chase. But Jack Nolan, with his brown fingers splayed over slim hips, shook his head and walked toward the feverish woman.

"Miah. Miah." Jack spoke to the sick woman in Indian. "You poor wild thing. What you going to do when you lose your looks?" He couldn't bring himself to voice out loud that what usually occurred from this sickness was—death. He took hold of the feverish woman and held her up as he whispered in her ear with familiarity. "What are you doing here, Miah? Thought you deserted Travis long ago."

"Travis kick me out," Miah muttered, her head lolling against the cowboy's round shoulder.

"Don't lie to me, Miah. You and I know each other better than that. Travis didn't kick you out. You left. You treated him like a dog—" here he winced as if in pain himself "—and a few others along with him. Now, eaten with pox fever, you turn to him." Miah was a very tall and big boned woman and Jack grunted as he half carried her to keep her moving toward the house. "Travis ought to send you packing. Should do it myself. Why don't you go back to your own people?"

Miah turned down her mouth. "They throw me away . . . like rubbish."

"Can't say I blame them. Your social conduct is something to be bitchin' over."

"You always bitch too much, half-breed."

Jack Nolan was not in a position to argue with a woman who could possibly be very near death's door.

"You are going to get fever, too," Miah said with a weak but cruel laugh.

"If you was so worried, Miah, why in hell did you come here?"

"To make all you paleface sick," she spat like a huge cougar riddled with death arrows and too weak to care.

"Even Roux?"

Miah's eyes narrowed and her beautiful face turned to ugly bitterness. Her long, dirty nails dug into Jacks' wrists and he bit down on his bottom lip to keep from yelping.

"You *are* a bitch, Indian woman."

"And you are no good on the mats, Jack Nolan."

"I shouldn't be bringing you here." Half dragging her onto the porch, he ground out, "Your daughter is here, and so is another woman."

Her teeth bared, Miah hissed, "Who is this woman? Travis has taken another mistress? I will scratch her eyes out!"

Jack sucked in his breath. "I *am* thinking you are crazy now. Or maybe it's just the pox."

"I will see this woman . . . now!" Miah hissed as if with her last dying breath, hanging on to a porch post and gasping for each breath.

"No need to holler," Jack said. "I see her coming

now."

Just then the door swung open and Shaina stepped onto the porch. Her eyes went first to Jack Nolan and then to the gorgeous Indian woman whose face, she could tell, even from a distance, was beginning to bloat. "Dear God," was all Shaina muttered while Roux clung to her arm from behind with huge green eyes of fear.

Chapter Thirteen

The moon had come over the mountain, and in the yard Travis unsaddled Dice, then led the big horse into the barn and to its stall. Streamers of misted moonlight entered the wide cracks here and there, lending a strange aura and quietude to the space.

About to walk back out into full moonlight, Travis halted when the low, anguished sound of a young person crying reached him.

"Who is there?" Travis called out carefully. "Roux, is that you?"

The sobbing only grew more intense. "Travis!" Roux cried, huddled in the dark corner of an unused stall. "Father—"

"Damn . . ." Travis fumbled around for a lantern and managed to light it as he calmed himself. Still he was worried, thinking maybe there was something wrong with Shaina. He had been gone most of the day, but had kept away from folks with the pox, concerned about Shaina and Roux . . . But now he could sense something was wrong. Terribly wrong.

Travis turned the flame up to see Roux's face, alarmed that she was crouched in the corner with her back against the wall. Going to her at once, Travis put his big hand on Roux's trembling shoulders, asking, "What's the matter?" He blinked in alarm at the disheveled, tear-streaked look of his daughter. "Darlin', what is going on? Is it Shaina, is she all right?"

"Shaina's all right . . . now . . . Father?"

"Yes. I am here, darlin'."

"I did not want to go into the house." She wiped the tear streaks with the back of one hand, sniffing loudly.

"Why?"

Travis knelt and touched both of Roux's shoulders with a gentleness he hadn't expressed in a long time. Roux was shivering.

"I am not so afraid now," Roux said, staring past the flickering lantern light and into the shadows beyond, "because you are here now. But, at the house—"

"Roux!" Travis shook her from her trance. "You must tell me what is wrong in the house!"

Roux groaned a word he couldn't understand, but it sounded like a distressed "oh" in Chinook. Then she blurted, "Miah is in the house and—"

Travis's voice cracked, "She's in the house? With Shaina? Sweet Jesus! Miah will tear her apart!"

Travis let go of Roux, and rose to his full six-foot four height.

"She is, Father. Wait. You have to listen. Miah is *sick*, too!"

121

"Oh, God." Travis went white, then softly said, "She's got the pox fever. You don't even have to say it."

"She has the pox," Roux echoed in a hollow tone. Then she grew alarmed. "Teacher is going to get it—"

"You stay put, Roux!"

"I want to see Shaina! Father, can I go with you?"

"No!"

"I am afraid, Father. Do not leave me alone."

Torn between his daughter and the woman—incredible though true—he knew he was beginning to deeply care for, Travis said, "I'll bring you something to make a bed—blankets. You can sleep in the hayloft. It's big up there."

"I'll see to her," came a voice from the midst of the moonlit swath laying across the chaff-covered floor.

"Hey! Jack Nolan!" Roux cried desperately, knowing her father had to leave her.

"No. It's Sam Carter. Jack won't come again, he was the one who brung Miah to the house." He watched Travis stiffen at the news. "He knows the girl's in here. He don't want to come, though, might infect her."

Running a rough hand through his hair, Travis asked Sam, "Has he scrubbed down?"

"Yep. He put himself in a tub of clean water, drunk some whiskey while he was a-soakin'. He hollered like a cat in heat when some of the guys offered to scrub his back. He's bunked down alone in the last bunkhouse in the row. Got himself some vittles and a few bottles of booze. He'll be all right, drunk a little maybe, but Jack Nolan'll pull through. Did many times before when he caught a whiff of the fever. Too bad Deanna ain't around."

Travis's eyes narrowed in curiosity, wondering what his lovely housekeeper had to do with Jack Nolan. "Deanna?" he echoed the name.

"She got it somethin' bad for good-lookin-Jack."

Sam's observation came as no surprise to Travis, for the pretty Deanna had had more eyes for Jack Nolan outside the window than for the dust on the many heavy pieces of furniture in his house. Deanna and Jack . . . Travis hadn't time to dwell on what the future held in store for the silver-haired girl and the wrangler foreman.

"I have to get to the house," Travis said quickly, brushing past the ranchhand hurriedly.

Sam Carter called to Travis's back going out the door, "I know Miah ain't gonna like this situation one bit. She be a jealous she-cat over any extra woman around. But then," Sam shrugged, "she ain't got nothin' to lose or gain either way you look at it."

Shaina had made the small bedroom as steaming hot as she could, securing all the windows and tying sheets together to make a tent around the bed by fastening the ends to the tall posts. To the steaming kettles she brought in and scattered about the bed, Shaina added drops of camphor oil she'd discovered in a kitchen cupboard. She'd tried to summon all the stored memories of the methods used to help cure pox-fevered folks that her mother and the neighbor women had used back when she was a little girl. Thinking of that time, seeming so long ago, Shaina realized with a jolt to her heart that Roux was missing. Then she calmed herself, recalling the frightened look in the girl's beautiful green eyes. Roux no doubt was afraid of catching the fever. Shaina searched her latest impressions of the girl—so sweet and peaceful and charming—and she came to the conclusion that Roux had not a fearful bone in her body—except where her mother Miah was concerned. It was so sad to think a child could so despise one of her own parents, yet this seemed to be the feeling. Even sadder was the fact that the strong feeling of dislike appeared mutual.

As she sat beside the bed of the feverish, tossing Indian woman, Shaina reflected back to the feelings she'd had for her own parents, her unconditional love for her mother and her desire to protect her from her weak-willed father. She had loved her mother whole-heartedly, wanted to protect her, but the situation had not been the same with her father. Yet, despite all his shortcomings, Eleanora had stayed with Graham and tried to make the best of her gray-colored life with him. Shaina wanted her own life to contain all the colors of the rainbow, and was determined to ride confidently into the best years of her life on that many-hued rainbow.

Shaina peeked in at the Indian woman who was Miah's mother, and at all the steaming kettles reeking of potent camphor. If she dies, maybe I will die, too, Shaina thought. Yes, I will die of the smallpox and never know the love of a man or the reason Eleanora stayed with Graham.

Shaina was dreaming. She had to be, she felt so warm and lovely in the strong arms of a man. In the dream she was being lifted gently from the chair beside Miah's bed and carried along a dark passageway that seemed to go on forever and ever. A voice came from far away at first, then seemed closer. It was the voice of the clean-smelling man bearing her in his tender, enfolding arms. Oh, so nice, he did smell so very good. Like a real flesh-and-blood man. Dark hair, he had to have loads of dark hair, for she could feel the delicious tingle in her fingers urging her to rake through that thick black hair . . .

"Shaina. *Shaina.*"

Travis went crazy with Shaina pressed intimately against his chest as he carried her to his own bedroom down the hall, for she had generously given her own room to Miah.

To make matters worse for Travis and his barely checked emotions, Shaina was in some wild dream, no doubt of an old lover, and pushing her slim fingers through his hair.

Sweet Lord! he couldn't take much more.

Am I insane? Travis asked himself as he strode across the carpeted floor and placed Shaina down in the middle of his big bed. *Miah could be breathing her last this very minute and all I can think of is making wild love to Shaina. Ah Shaina, Shaina, Shaina, you drive me wild with desire.*

"Mmmmm." Wrapping her arms about her dream lover's neck, not about to let go of this delicious male form so easily, Shaina sleepily purred, "Oh . . . kiss me, hold me."

Shaina clung to the dark-haired man, and the feeling of excitement racing in her blood intensified with every passing moment, until, with a jolt, she was

125

awakened by his tender kiss. Just like in the fairy tale *Snow White,* she thought as he hovered above her when her eyes at last opened.

With a fierce possessive need, Travis did as she'd asked. She must be crazy. Her body was responding while her mind fought this stunning assault on her senses. Now his kisses made her gasp with each breath he allowed her to take. The golden mantle of her hair was loosened to flow over his forearm and onto the bed he'd eased their bodies down upon, slowly, slowly pressing into her yielding softness.

"Travis . . . Travis," Shaina moaned, her lips, her breasts, her hips coming up to meet him, to greet his big body with the sweet fire building along her own lithe thighs.

Lifting his lips from hers, Travis's mellow voice held a challenge as he finally spoke to her, "Meet me half way, Shaina." He buried his face against her throat and licked the whiteness of the arch there.

Making love should be the furthest thing from her mind at this time—but oh! it wasn't. Shaina's cheeks were limned with flushes of desire, the heavy rise and fall of her breasts attesting to the eager passion raging within.

"We can't, Travis," she said in a tormented voice. "This is not the right time!"

Though he'd rather have had it otherwise, Travis listened with rising dismay knowing that her words carried sound wisdom and he would not have her this night. But when? Maybe never. Moving away from her, he was silent for a while, and then he said, "You are right, teacher." He went on. "But it is time we go see about Miah, right?" He kept his back to her as he sat on the edge of the bed.

"Yes. It is."

"I'll go get Roux, you see to Miah."

Shaina came up off the bed on the end of a bounce. "Let Roux stay where she is," she said. "That way maybe she won't become infected." She stood there staring at his dark silhouette against the moon-framed window.

"That's wise thinking," Travis said, then sighed deeply and reached to catch Shaina's hand. He murmured as he carried it to his lips, "Who are we kidding?" He whirled about, sliding a heavy hand along her arm to her shoulder. "Don't you know how much I want you?"

Laying her flushed cheek against his hand, Shaina replied, "Oh, Travis . . . I want you too!"

Suddenly Shaina tore away from him and fled from the room, running blindly along the hall with the back of her hand laid across her mouth.

Dear Lord! if she hung around Travis Cordell long enough she was going to fall in love with the man — if that hadn't happened already!

Shaina was exhausted and ached all over. Nodding her chin on her chest, she blinked several times to come fully awake. Going to splash some clean water on her face, she reflected back to a few hours ago . . . . when she'd almost succumbed to Travis's virile charms.

What am I going to do? Shaina asked herself, looking into the high, tilting mirror above the dresser. Her reflection stared dejectedly back at her.

Biting her lip that was slightly bruised from Travis's nibbling kisses, Shaina decided to go with the plans she'd made weeks before after the first stirring kiss she had shared with Travis. First kiss! She'd never forget its exciting impact. This night's stunning confrontation, however, had become the deciding factor — she couldn't allow these passionate scenes to go on. She must take control. Travis could only hurt her. He had a mistress. A child. He wanted her, but wanting was not the same as loving.

And she wanted a career in school-teaching. He wanted a thriving ranch . . . maybe a family. Well, he already had what he wanted. He had so much, she so little. No, Travis did not want her in the way she wanted to be wanted. Desired her, yes.

Miah moaned just then.

I have to get away from here! Shaina told herself in wild desperation! *I am going to perish if I stay. Dear God, make Giles Wilson return soon.* She would go away with him right after the epidemic was over.

"Travis!"

Miah's scream ripped through Shaina's already tormented emotions and set her nerves on edge.

Before Shaina could think of what to do, Travis barged into the room, his voice edged with alarm. "What's wrong?" He stared over at Shaina as if she was the cause of Miah's pain, then went to fling back the sheet on one side of the bed.

With every muscle in her body quivering, Shaina set off for the back door, having it in mind to saddle Spotted Bird and ride out of here, but only one thing hindered her. Where would she go? There was a smallpox epidemic sweeping the valley. What did it matter where she went? Only the strong would survive anyway. She'd been foolish to think Roux was safe from infection if she stayed away from the house.

Miah had been with Jack Nolan. Jack had been close to the other ranchhands. Travis had been riding the valley. They were fools to think anyone could be safe from the highly contagious disease that spread like wildfire and killed at will.

Travis gave Miah some water and gently laid her head back down. Once she'd been very beautiful, but that had been before she'd become a tarnished woman. Or had Miah always been that and only hid it from him so well? Would the pox eruptions on her face heal and return Miah to her former beauty? Beauty, though, was only skin deep with Miah, Travis thought as he turned around to say something to Shaina. But Shaina wasn't there, and after he searched the house, the barn, the yard, everywhere he could think of that she might go to hide, Travis still couldn't find her. Was she even hiding, he thought as he rode swiftly back to the barn to saddle up Dice to get a fresh mount. Shaina was not a coward. The pox hadn't frightened her. What had happened to her then?

She's run away, Travis thought angrily as he rode out on Dice under a full moon splashing the silvered mounds and midnight-blue rills of the foothills. She was riding Spotted Bird, he'd found that much out. But why in God's name was she running away? It couldn't be fear of the smallpox — not when he had seen her care for Miah as if she were her own sister.

Damn her, Travis thought with a feeling of vexation and some worry over where she might have gone. Eventually he came to the sawmill, eased down off his mount with a low creak of leather and, leaving Dice outside the door, Travis went inside. All he had to do

129

was follow the lantern light to the second floor to discover who was up there.

Shaina sat close to the lantern's warm glow, in the middle of the sagging daybed, her arms around her knees. Night was slowly enveloping the grounds surrounding the sawmill, and outside the window she could see the stars were already very bright. Shaina looked up at the ceiling in the corner, which was lost in darkness where the fuzzy circles of light did not reach. Remembering the feel of Travis's strong embrace, she shivered with longing.

Would Travis be angry with her?

Slow smoke arose from the lantern and Shaina followed its trail. Then her eyes flickered in delighted shock to see Travis standing just inside the door.

Torn between curiosity and fear, Shaina waited, her heart pounding savagely.

"Someday," Travis snarled softly, "I'm going to turn you over my knee, woman, and give you what you're asking for."

Chapter Fourteen

Shaina was off the bed in a shot.

"You wouldn't *dare!*" she hissed, unconsciously striking a dramatic pose with her hands on her hips.

"I do whatever I want." He walked into the pale circle of lamplight. "Always. One of the great pleasures in life, Shaina, is doing what people say you cannot do."

Shaina tossed her head. "Why don't you just go away and leave me alone."

"I wish I could." His nostrils flared.

Ignoring him, Shaina sat on a chair near the window, picked up her buff, high-laced shoes and began to put one on with fingers that couldn't stay calm. Watching her closely, with eyes brighter than a luminous mountain pool, Travis thought he had never witnessed a more fetching portrait of young womanhood. She moved her head ever so slightly and the long curls at the ends of her hair were like radiant bells dancing in the lamplight. How could he ever convince her that she was a woman grown, capable of loving a man?

"Do you always run away from life, Shaina?"

"No." She continued to ignore his changing expression as she finished with the laces of the second shoe. "Just from *wolves*, Mr. Cordell."

"Ah, so we're back to *Mr.* Cordell?"

"That's right."

"Shaina," he bit out, coming closer, "you began to nurse Miah and then ran away. Why?"

"No, sir! I did not leave her. *You* did." Shaina stood to face him, feeling weak from his compelling nearness. "You were there, too. She's your mistress. Why didn't you take over?"

Unwaveringly he stared at her. "You are evading the real matter here. Why did you run away?"

"Travis . . . *please* leave me be."

"Why?" he asked softly.

Her eyes glinting with a hostile look, Shaina snatched up the soft jacket she'd worn for the wind-chilling ride to the sawmill. She had prayed all the while she'd gone through the black tunnel of woods, patting Spotted Bird unceasingly, thankful the horse had known the way, for she'd been like a blindfolded rider the whole time.

"Shaina . . ." He positioned slightly shaking hands on either side of her shoulders. "Tell me!"

"Is it so important?"

"Yes!" He raked his long fingers through his hair, rearranging the deep black wave that had fallen over his forehead.

She peered up at him. He was so handsome, full of pride, strong. Oh, God, she couldn't tell him she was riddled with jealousy over Miah's arrival, envious of

132

his loving relationship with Roux . . . and that she was a little in love with him. Oh, yes, even that.

Breathlessly, Shaina lowered her eyes from the insolent green gaze. She had the fiercest urge to throw caution to the winds and allow Travis and the dream-like night of the full moon to take its willful course. No matter how much she wanted this, Shaina marshaled her courage to fight hard against his virile charms.

"Why are you fighting this, Shaina?" His voice was an easy drawl.

"I—I am not fighting . . . anything, Travis."

"You lie. Why don't we stop playing this cat-and-mouse game?"

"And get down to business?" She canted her head, raising finely arched eyebrows.

Travis gazed at her face that was tipped shyly downward and said feelingly, "Shaina, you can't cross a chasm in two small jumps. You have to give it all you have and leap. Oh, Shaina, there's nothing to be afraid of. I'm not going to hurt you."

Shaina smiled anxiously. "I'm only afraid of how I feel about you, Travis."

They stared at each other for long moments, the night closing them in together like an enveloping shroud, and Shaina, her curly eyelashes fluttering slightly, struggled hard to break free of that hypnotic gaze. When he spoke, it was abruptly.

"I can provide a remedy for that, Shaina."

Travis's expression grew suddenly serious as his hands traveled to rest upon her hips, pulling her ever so slowly to him. And this time Travis did not wait to kiss her. When the hot, bold lips claimed hers,

Shaina's pliant body surged up against his, making him groan into her mouth. His tongue probed her moist flesh insistently, and his hands possessively traveled down to her waist and then back up again. Shaina could not fight against the tantalizing sensations that his lover's mouth set aflame in the pit of her stomach. Her breasts began to ache for his touch, but before he could make contact with the throbbing globes, Shaina caught at his wrist and held on while he kissed her hungrily, demandingly, masterfully.

"Shaina," he muttered huskily, "don't push me away from you, I want to feel you all over."

Shaina fought the tenderness that tugged at her heart. She stepped out of his passionate embrace, backed away a few more steps, and began to move around him intending to walk out on him again. But before she could brush past him, Travis had gripped her forearm and whirled her back to face his chilling regard.

Travis swore softly. "Jesus, Shaina, are you made of ice?"

"No, Travis, I am not made of ice, but neither am I stupid!"

His eyes narrowed into green shards of suspiciousness. "I wonder if you can even know what it feels like to want someone so badly that you ache." He snatched up her hand and bringing the back of her hand to his thigh, rubbed it along the muscular length. "I ache for you, Shaina," he muttered thickly, inching her hand ever closer to his hardened desire.

"No!" Shaina cried, snatching her hand from his loose grasp.

The masculine tension in Travis's big, lean body

was ready to snap. "Shaina, is it the fear of the unknown?"

"Yes, it's that Travis, and also I don't know you that well yet!"

"You know me well enough. Give me half a chance tonight."

Remembering how strong her desire had been at the ranch when she'd awakened in Travis's arms, Shaina battened down all the hatches to her strongest emotions and challengingly stared back at him.

"I think I'd better get going back to the ranch," she said. "Miah needs me."

Shaina turned and walked toward the door.

"There's no need. One of the hands who is immune to the pox fever is taking care of Miah. She'll be fine without you."

"Ohhh!" Shaina backed up until she came up hard against the wall. "How can you speak so callously of your mistress? She has come back to you, to the one she loves."

"That's not the way it is." Placing a hand on either side of her, he explained with a hot, passionate look in his eyes. "Miah became my mistress, true. Miah bore my child, true. And yes, Miah is sick right now, but she is in capable hands. Last, Shaina dear, Miah loves every man who has it in him to become her lover — short, fat, tall, skinny, she'll open her legs to any man. Now, does all this make me callous?"

"Travis!" Shaina felt her face color hotly. "Let me go . . . I don't want to be here alone with you!"

"Don't be a fool, Shaina!" Travis caught and pinned her wrists against the wall, moving his flushed face closer to her beautiful tormented one. "Tell me you

135

find me tempting and attractive, Shaina. I know you do. It shows in those beautiful blue eyes."

"Damn you!" Shaina heaved herself against him, but it was to no avail—trying to move his body was just like struggling against a huge boulder weighing tons. "Travis, get away from me. . . . you have no right to hold me here against my will and try to make love to me!"

With gentle movements, Travis soon had taken hold of her chin and, using a little force, brought her face against his throat. Hugging her close, Travis's mouth brushed the top of her head and he held her like that, doing nothing more alarming than just being sweetly, intimately close and caressing the back of her head with a gentle hand.

"Be still," he said.

"Oh, Travis, sex is all you want from me."

"Not true, Shaina. Hush now, and let me hold you."

Shaina allowed Travis to hold her, and his manly odor assailed her delicate sense of smell and her pulse quickened from his masculinity so close, so tempting. With a twist of suspicion curving up one side of her mouth, Shaina looked up at Travis. With her azure eyes tilted at the corners, Shaina lowered his hand that had been fondling her. She said, "*No,* Travis. No."

She walked away from him then, flipping her hair over her shoulder defiantly.

Travis went after her, catching up with her at the door she was just about to step through. He pulled her back against his hard, inflamed body. "You don't seem to understand. I want you." He growled. "Not tomorrow. Not next week. *Tonight.*" The pressure of his lips against her nape explained his anguish to her,

136

and the fiery sensations in her body flamed up in answer to his manly body's calling.

"Travis, if I let you do this, make love to me, I know you will be cold to me in the morning light. I know you. You will find an excuse to cast me aside. You, too, are afraid to love," she ended on a breathless note.

"*You* — afraid, Shaina?"

"Truthfully — yes. I've already told you that."

"Let me teach you how to be a woman, Shaina."

"Travis . . . !" She moaned just as his mouth crushed her trembling lips once again.

Trembling in apprehension, with her back to him now, Shaina could feel the long hardness of Travis's thighs where her firm buttocks was pressed against him. Possessively his arms encircled her waist, drawing her against the rock wall of his massive chest.

Desire was renewed in Shaina and tingled delicately along her flushed skin in the wake of Travis's expert hands and lips.

Passion stirred bold in Travis, too, and he felt a strong pull in his loins. "Shaina," he murmured into her hair, "I won't let you go!"

"You are a devil, Travis Cordell," Shaina hissed, beginning to love what he was making happen to her. He was so insistent that there didn't seem to be a way out. In a breathless whisper she said, "I'm not afraid of *you*, Travis, I'm afraid of what you do to me. Afraid you'll not want me again after you've had me once."

"You're crazy, Schoolteacher. But I still want you."

Gently Travis popped the buttons of her bodice with one hand while the other stayed at her waist keeping her imprisoned with her back to his chest.

137

When he had freed one swollen breast, his fingers began to do their magic and Shaina could feel that secret place in her swelling, blossoming until she was trapped in an enchanted web of sensual desire.

Travis stroked and teased a milky breast as he pressed his lips to the curve of her shoulder, biting gently, making Shaina feel a deep response from within, as though Travis was the master musician strumming invisible chords that connected all parts of her body to its erotic center.

Shaina's shimmering red-gold hair fell away from her as she put her head to one side while Travis created a firestorm of rapture exploring her virgin body. Kissing and nibbling the one earlobe turned to him and then the nape of her neck, he slid his large hand down to her waist, then to her belly where his hand lay heavily.

"Travis!" Shaina moaned with exquisite pleasure. "Please—"

"Yes, Shaina," Travis said hoarsely against her bare shoulder. Against her creamy flesh, his hands were as dark as saddle leather. He nibbled and sucked the tender flesh there, always moving his hand lower, lower.

With her back still to him, Shaina relaxed and her pink mouth opened on a big sigh of pleasure. With her heart pounding wildly, Shaina swam in a torment of delicious anticipation as Travis rolled her skirts into one hand and then bunched them with the other. Now Shaina could feel the cool air coming against her legs. Suddenly he was touching her between the legs and, almost unconscious of her movements, Shaina felt with a shock her thighs moving instinctively apart for his better access.

Shaina licked her dry lips, moaning softly, "Travis . . . Travis . . ." Her fingers clung fiercely to the nape of his neck.

Delighted groanings tore from Shaina's throat as Travis began to knead her most tender flesh. Then, when he became more bold with his caresses, Shaina had to bite down on her lips to keep the scream of pleasure from erupting.

Her total abandonment to sensuality thrilled Travis, and as she drove her hips upward against his carefully exploring fingers, Travis moved deeper and came up against the barrier he had fully expected to find in his tender probings.

"Please, Travis . . . don't make me wait!"

Naturally yielding to her most sensual, hidden nature, Shaina undulated her hips to derive the most pleasure from his gentle thrustings. Travis was going wild with her soft bumpings against his already flaming manhood and the blood was pounding madly through his body. The knot of bittersweet pleasure caught her on the first spin downward. "Travis," she cried. "Oh my *God*, Travis!" Urgently she twisted while his probings became swifter and swifter, bolder and bolder. Just when she thought she'd go totally mad with the desire for the ultimate unknown she was seeking, Travis unleashed a storm in her that carried Shaina on wave after wave of exploring pleasure that reached to the ends of her being.

There followed a moment of beautiful golden silence when all movement had ceased — even Travis's heart, it seemed to him.

"Jesus," Travis muttered softly, feeling Shaina's fulfillment like a soft unfolding flower of velvet against his flesh. When she came to rest, Travis gave her a moment before turning her in the circle of his arms. "Shaina," he said, cupping her chin, "Shaina, why won't you look at me? Don't be embarrassed, love, it was the most natural thing that ever happened to you."

With a blurred look in her eyes, Shaina turned her wondering gaze on Travis's desire-darkened face. Shyly her lashes fluttered downward until she could only stare at the deep V in his tan shirt where her fingertip had naturally come to rest.

Travis gasped when Shaina moved against him. "Be careful how you move now, dear heart, I'm very close to, ah, ravishing your body wholly." A dry chuckle escaped his throat.

They stood there quietly, Travis's chin resting lightly upon Shaina's head, his hand caressing the small of her back with movements as gentle as an artist's brush stroke on fine canvas. The pleasures and torments of newly budding love claimed both their thoughts, and they reveled in the pure sensations, so golden and full of splendor.

Shaina had never known such feelings existed, and she could only anticipate what would happen next. But why did Travis restrain himself? She knew that there was more to making love than this encounter, but how much more exciting and pleasurable could the real joining be?

"Travis?" she asked, suddenly impatient to find the answers to all her questions.

"Uhmm?"

"When are you going to make love to me?" Her eyes

skittered from the intent gaze he'd turned on her. "I mean — really make love to me?"

Throwing back his head, Travis loosed a deep shout of laughter. Then he gazed down tenderly once again. "Shaina, Shaina. You constantly amaze me. And what's this? Only a short time ago you wanted to run away from me. Now you want me to make love to you . . . Are you entirely certain of what you want, Shaina?"

With a blush staining her cheeks, she pushed away from him. "I didn't mean it like it sounded, Travis."

"Oh?" Green eyes narrowed. "What did you mean?"

"Nothing." She turned her back on him, heat stealing into her face. She must be as red as a tomato!

"Do you or do you not want me, Shaina?" He came around and forced her to face him fully this time as he gripped her firmly by the shoulders.

"Yes — I *do!*"

Without another word Travis scooped her into his arms and walked across the room. Pulling her beneath him, he bent over and kissed her sweet pink mouth and Shaina ran her sensitive hands over the broad, tanned shoulders and strongly muscled arms. His firm, flat abdomen pressed into her and his hardness came between them. Shaina gasped softly as he shifted his weight. He removed his clothes swiftly, then she felt his hands easing her skirt down her waist, her hips . . .

Moonlight spilled into the room and languidly cast shadows across the bed, the trees outside blowing softly in night breezes creating shifting patterns across the erotic movements of the lovers' bodies. Travis kissed Shaina, caressed her. With passion. Leading her into a stunning world of sensual desire, a rapture

141

from which there was no escape. He tempted and beguiled, no fumbling schoolboy wet behind the ears! She was lost in the abandonment to which she had surrendered herself.

Then he was probing her inner flesh, and again Shaina sucked in her breath as a stunning ecstasy washed over her. As if from afar, she heard him telling her he would hurt her for a moment and then she would experience nothing but the most intense pleasure.

Trustingly Shaina gazed up into Travis's shadowed eyes. His finger slid softly in and out for a few strokes, and then he mounted her, nudging her thighs apart slowly. His searching mouth came down on hers sweetly, tenderly, as his knees spread her wider and Travis settled his body between. Every inch of Shaina's untried body was on fire, and when she instinctively arched toward Travis's hardness, he smiled triumphantly. Then he was sliding inside her tight sheath.

There was a burning fullness, hurting her for but an instant. When the burning sensation left, Shaina was filled with a rapturous feeling as he began to slowly glide in, out, in, out. Deeper and deeper he moved within her. Wild thunder filled Shaina's heart as he played her like an instrument and rode her heartstrings to ecstasy's heaven.

Travis softly moaned her name. "Shaina." His lips moved over hers then, in a divine ecstasy of movement, his tongue thrust in, out, keeping in time with the thrusting of his hips. His hands slipped up her arms, taking them overhead and lacing her fingers with his own. He whispered into her ear, and the erotic words made Shaina writhe beneath him in frenzied, urgent appeal and buck up harder to try to bring him deeper still.

"Shaina . . ." Travis said in a husky tone, "bring your legs up and wrap them around me."

The higher she brought them, the deeper Travis plunged, and then Shaina was crying out for release. He was indefatigible, ceaseless, wonderful.

"Yes, little love, yes . . . it's coming."

They stood at the tip of their mountain of pleasure, straining, and then Shaina lifted and soared, her ecstasy taking flight, winging her way toward a star that grew larger and larger the closer she approached.

"Oh . . . *Travis!*" She ran her hands through the thick dampness of his hair. "Oh God, yes, yes . . . *yes!*"

There was a wild cry. Hers. A million starbursts shattered inside her then, and she gave in to the golden rays of wild ecstasy that flooded her. She had reached the shooting star of rapture.

It was glorious. It was splendor.

With the sheer pleasure of his release tearing through him, Travis lowered his mouth and kissed Shaina at the very moment their senses stood still gazing at ecstasy's blazing star.

Then together they rode their precious star down to earth and peace, and deep contentment flowed tenderly between the lovers. Shaina threw her arm over Travis's chest, still panting in ecstatic repletion and staring around the misty moonlit room as she tried to truly believe what had just taken place.

They slept happily in each other's arms while the moon and stars spun out the remainder of the night;

it was dawn when they awoke. With his arms across her slender waist, Travis murmured in her ear. "Uhmm, let's make love again."

"Travis?"

Before Travis could find out what Shaina was about to ask, there was a call from below. It was then, too, that Shaina and Travis looked collectively to the window to see that the first glimmerings of a golden dawn were creeping across the land.

When the voice was heard reality began to set in for the lovers.

Chapter Fifteen

"Only *eighteen!*"

As the sun peeped through green, towering pines and gilded mountain ranges, Shaina glared at Giles. He had revealed her secret! What a *traitor!* And Travis. She was right about him; all he'd wanted was to make love to her. *Sex.* Nothing more. Her age was only an excuse to be over and done with her!

Shaina and Travis had dressed and come downstairs quickly, believing the worst—that Miah had taken a bad turn or that Roux was sick, too. She couldn't look at Travis now, not since he had learned the truth of her age and looked at her so accusingly. How she wished Giles Wilson hadn't come along just then . . . and how asinine of him to remark angrily that she was "only eighteen" and shouldn't be alone with a man at that time of morning. Hadn't she been alone with Giles at the very same time of day? And she'd even spent a night with Giles here at the sawmill. But, of course, it wasn't the same as it had been with Travis. Somehow Giles seemed to know that, too.

Giles was having his own thoughts, vicious ones to be sure. He'd come along the trail just as the first glimmerings of dawn were appearing in the eastern section of sky and had spotted the pale light burning in the many-paned window of the sawmill's apartment loft. He had given a shout, and minutes later, first Travis Cordell had appeared in the opening, and then Shaina had followed him. Disgustedly he had stared at one and then the other, coming to his own conclusions. Anger and resentment that Cordell should score another victory—especially in the area where he had been expecting to score—had gone to Giles's head and he'd lashed out at the young woman standing there looking not as she should—not embarrassed, not anything but a little surprised at seeing him there.

"Shaina," Giles began smoothly, "I'll take you home, wherever that might be these days."

"There's a smallpox epidemic, Giles, didn't you know?" Travis bit out, not even looking at Shaina now.

"I know. I've had it, so I can't get it again. Shaina, are you coming?" Giles asked gruffly, holding out his hand as if he fully expected her to take it.

Tiredly Shaina regarded both men. Giles was taking over, being possessive, and Travis was doing nothing—his manner was tepid at best, as if he didn't care at all. Well, if he was just going to stand there looking surly and saying nothing, she might as well go with the man who'd offered to escort her.

Travis avoided meeting Giles's sour gaze.

"I'm staying at the ranch," Shaina said, glancing at Travis out of the corner of her eye.

"The ranch?" Giles almost choked.

"That's right," Travis put in. "Got any objection, Wilson?"

"I — no," Giles got out, his pale-brown eyes darkening with passionate anger.

"Yoo-hoo!"

"What's that?" Shaina looked around, trying to find where the musical voice was coming from.

"Is that you, Travis?"

Then Shaina saw her, the loveliest, shapeliest blonde she'd ever seen, coming down from a spur of hill, the Indian pony she was riding eating the distance at an energetic trot.

Giles, after giving the blonde with the alluringly lush curves a thorough perusal, asked, "Who is she?" And Giles wondered to himself where this tempting morsel had been hiding herself. And then, looking at Travis Cordell, he thought he knew and was angry all over again.

"Deanna," Travis began, about to give the young woman a stern reprimand for not staying at home. Instead he asked, "What are you doing here?"

Painfully aware of the silver-haired young woman's striking good looks, Shaina felt her daintiness pale in comparison to the other woman's lush contours. But Deanna only smiled at Shaina warmly as she came down from her horse, and held the thick leather reins loosely in her long-fingered hand.

"All is clear back at home, the fever has broke." Deanna first let Travis know, then she faced Shaina, holding out a hand that was smooth despite all the housework and washing she did; Shaina noticed at once.

"Hello, Shaina," Deanna Kingswell softly spoke, "or

would you rather I'd call you Miss Hill?"

Liking Deanna at once, Shaina said, "Whichever you prefer."

Deanna laughed, a deep, throaty sound like the purring of an elegant cat. "Shaina, I'm so happy we're going to be friends."

"Deanna is my housekeeper," Travis remarked, scrutinizing Giles's reaction to the beautiful woman. He had sensed more than a spark of attraction.

"Yes—" Giles's eyes glittered with a strange light. "Yes, I know."

Damn, Giles thought to himself, if Deanna Kingswell hasn't grown into something quite delicious.

The three riders rode into the Lazy C slowly. Roux exploded from the door like a round ball of cannon shot as they were nearing the porch to tie up before someone came to take the tired, hungry horses to the barn.

"Miah is better!" was the first thing that burst from Roux's mouth. "She is sitting up and taking soup."

Shaina smiled at the girl, thrilled to see that her gay spirits had returned.

"You better get in there and give the rest to her then," Travis ordered, cupping her shoulder with his big hand.

For a moment Roux stared at her father's calloused fingers, and then grabbed two in her dainty hand and held on while she swung his arm back and forth.

"I am happy you are back, Father. But I do not have to feed Miah, Sam is in there doing that." She smiled at the housekeeper and greeted her with a "Hello, Deanna." Then she heaved a deep sigh as her bright eyes skittered to Shaina and her smile grew wider. But to Giles Wilson she said nothing, only drew into her stoic-faced Indian silence as she looked over at the thin man with the fine-boned face and large, powerful-looking hands.

"Are you staying, Wilson?" Travis said in a low, casual tone of voice.

"Sure," Giles said, "why not."

Deanna smiled at Giles Wilson, but missed the look he gave her rounded backside as she led the way inside. Shaina, glancing at Travis, had the terrible feeling something was wrong . . . Did it have to do with what Giles had leaked concerning her age? She couldn't know . . . she'd have to wait. And she didn't have to wait long, she was soon to discover.

Later, they all sat down to dinner at the long, rough-hewn table beginning the savory meal Deanna had hustled about to prepare. Travis reached for a fluffy Texas-size biscuit Deanna had learned to make while living in that part of the country before her family had gravitated upward into Washington Territory.

Miah, gaining strength by the hour, shouted from the bedroom she occupied nearest the long dining room and demanded every now and then that Deanna bring her something to eat. At her third demand, Travis himself rose, snatching yet another buttered biscuit from the large platter.

"Woman eats like a damn horse," he muttered as he

149

passed Shaina's chair, brushing the upper part of her arm softly in the motion.

"Travis!" Miah shouted as soon as he'd resumed his seat. "I want *meat!*"

"No!" he boomed, making the utensils on the table almost bounce. "You'll get meat tomorrow, today is too soon. Your digestive system is too weak to handle meat. Damn," he muttered to himself. "I hate shouting."

Shaina frowned to herself. Travis was awfully surly. What could be wrong? she wondered with growing apprehension and dread.

When the others had gone into the large, spacious living room after dinner, Roux politely offering to help Deanna clean up, Travis called Shaina into his book-lined, leather-scented study.

He sat in a massive leather chair, motioning for Shaina to sit in the smaller chair in front of the desk. Shaina remembered having dusted the room the other day, loving the feel of all the books, neatly stacked papers, pens, pencils, and the oversized pieces of furniture she'd polished to a rich dark gleam.

Shaina gave a long draw-out stare in the direction of the inkwell, feeling a chill of foreboding race up her legs and her spine.

"Yes?" she said, wondering if this was the same loving man who'd made her senses reel just the night before. What could be on his mind that was so urgent? She knew there was something from the way he'd looked her way all during the meal . . . as if she didn't fit in here at the Lazy C, — or anywhere in the valley, for that matter.

Now it was coming. She could feel it, as if Travis

was reaching for a gun to kill her.

"Shaina, I'm going to have to ask you to leave Wild Mountain."

"You—you are firing me?" Shaina breathed the words out in anguish. But she tried not to let him see what a strain he was putting on her already taut emotions.

"Right. You are only eighteen, Shaina. What will the parents think when they discover I've allowed a child to teach their children?"

Humiliation, mortification, pain—pain like she'd never imagined—twisted in and out of her until Shaina could hardly draw another breath. "Oh, of course, I see." Shaina's eyes glowed like heated sapphires. "I am too young to teach, but old enough to make love to. Is that it?"

"Shaina, I'd rather not get into that." He shrugged weakly. "I made a mistake."

Shaina breathed the words "I see."

"Giles Wilson can take you back to—" he waved his hand"—to where you came from."

Oh . . . oh God . . . she had asked this man to marry her this morning. Unable to even look at him, Shaina held out her hand, saying, "Just give me what you owe me. I'll be gone before you even miss me."

Travis's panther-black eyebrows rose as he muttered, "Miss you?"

Taking refuge in fury, Shaina hissed, "Forget my pay, Mr. Cordell, I'll get along somehow. I really don't need you or your money."

"I will have to send it to you, Shaina, I haven't figured it out yet." Travis sat back in his chair, looking at her with a strange light in his eyes.

151

"I—I don't know where I'll be staying." *Maybe with my nasty-minded relatives,* she thought with growing despair.

"Well, then, write to me as soon as you are settled."

"I've told you I don't need your money!" Shaina blurted.

Suddenly she could not take the strain any longer and broke, rising swiftly and, running her arm along the highly polished, beloved desk, she swiped everything, even his inkwell, off onto the carpeted floor.

"Shaina!" Travis shot to his feet as the furious little hellcat rushed to his bookshelves and began to snatch volumes and toss them heedlessly onto the floor. "Have you gone crazy! Damn it, stop!"

Like a spitting tigress, Shaina faced the man she was coming to hate—the first real hatred she'd ever known—and spat at him. "You are a user, Travis Cordell! You've used everyone you have come in contact with in life! You used that beautiful Indian woman—"

"Not true, Shaina." He came around the desk slowly, his hands deep in his pockets, posing no threat to her.

"You used me! You even abused your daughter!" She tossed a book at his head and he ducked just in time.

"Half the time your daughter doesn't even call you 'Father.' What is it, Travis, is she afraid to claim you as her parent?"

He stood stock-still. "You are trying to get back at me."

"Yes."

"It won't work, Shaina."

152

"Yes it will, Travis Cordell."

"What, may I ask, are you planning to do?"

She threw a book at him, this time striking him at the knee, watching him flinch and loving every moment of any pain she could give back to him. She narrowed feverish blue eyes and poked her delicate chin in the air. "Perhaps I will marry Giles Wilson."

"Oh, come on." Even as he said this, there was a strange light in his eyes. "I don't think you mean that." He smiled mockingly.

"You just watch me, Travis Cordell!"

With that Shaina Hill walked calmly to the double doors, halted, then she opened them quietly, and shut them in the face of the man she loved.

Shaina couldn't know his tormented thought. *I'm falling in love with you . . . and I can't allow that to happen.*

Chapter Sixteen

Travis watched the moon rise as he rode Dice at a slow, easy trot across the valley. He surmised that only minutes had passed when, after looking away from the climbing silver orb, he once again saw it. The moon seemed to push suddenly above the crest of Big Blue and stared down upon him moodily. A night like a summer's night, filled with moonbeams and stardust . . .

In the distant past when she'd been in a good mood, his mother had sung songs of moonbeams and stardust, romantic tunes she'd hummed, sometimes sang them out loud in her sweet, lilting voice, a voice that had a western twang in it . . .

Dorinda Evans Cordell. Travis had never known her very well. He'd been too young to be interested in where she'd come from or what *her* parents had been like . . . nor did he much care after he'd come to realize what a slut she was.

Dorinda had possessed a full-blown figure — too big on top, he'd always thought as a young boy. She'd had

154

plenty of admirers, though, he remembered that. Mostly they'd been *male* admirers. Haughtily, with their noses in the air and wanting nothing to do with her, that's how the women had treated Dorinda, but she didn't seem to mind one bit for she had no lack of male company. His father had been too busy with the struggling ranch to notice Dorinda's lack of morals — or kindness to others, for that matter.

Travis flinched as he reflected back to Dorinda's attitude toward her only son. A melancholy frown changed his rough handsomeness into a mask of weary sadness. His life, from five onward, had become a bitter battle as he'd tried to extract some measure of kindness from his mother, but always she'd had eyes and words of caring for only the ranchhands — or any other man, even the drifter, who happened to pass their way. It was as if he had ceased to exist for her. All he'd wanted was a little attention . . . maybe a pat or two on the head once in a while. But Dorinda had hardly ever touched him or allowed him to touch anything else.

Travis had learned to say to her, "Yes, ma'am. No, ma'am." When he had arrived at the impressionable age of fifteen he'd come to think of her as a loose woman. Many facets of their relationship had been as sour grapes thrown at young Travis. For one thing, Dorinda had rarely been home for her son. He had gone hungry, physically and emotionally. He had grown terribly lonely. By the time he was twenty he'd sampled every tainted bit of goods up and down the river towns either side of Seattle. He thought of Dorinda now and then, but without joy in his heart.

Then the Indian girl had come along. Miah had

155

been so beautiful . . . just like Dorinda. In fact, now he could hardly separate the two personalities but for their differences in coloring. With a sigh, Travis recalled that Miah had not always been that way.

Then a charming and lovely woman had come into his life . . . again he felt that agonizing despair just thinking of her, her red-gold hair, her heartbreaker-blue eyes. How could he trust her? Women were not to be trusted. Dorinda and Miah had already shown him that.

Only his daughter deserved his love. He had to try to learn to treat Roux with a little more respect. She was only a child, and he mustn't be so ruthless and continue to take his bitterness out on her; *that* would have to cease.

A bitter smile curved Travis's mouth. Somewhere in the world there was a place for Shaina Hill. But it wasn't here in Wild Mountain. She would be leaving first light in the morning with Giles Wilson. Travis's mouth quirked. She would be gone from his life. It was for the better. He could resume his life once again and get on with what he had to do. And that was to build himself the biggest ranch in the world. He'd rename it the King Bird Ranch, after the magnificent eagles that soared far above and made nests every year not far from his house. Yes, he would do that. It was better than being lonely.

Sunk to her chest in the bathtub, Shaina's lovely face soured again as she thought of Travis and his callousness. Her eyes were misty as she stared down into the water and saw her pale limbs. Was he so beastly to everyone? About the only ones she knew of that he treated with some kindness were Deanna and his tough, rangy ranchhands. Roux, well, he seemed to just tolerate the girl.

Punching the water, Shaina made it slosh over onto the floor; then she picked up the hand mirror on a chair beside the tub and stared at her foggy reflection. *I am changing.* Was it for the better? That was the question. Shaina continued to look at herself, wiping the fogged mirror with an end of the dry towel. Am I childish? Am I silly? Or am I really becoming a woman? A mature woman. A woman who knew how to handle a man in this seemingly impossible situation, that's what she wanted to be. Travis had not seemed to be bothered very much when she'd told him she would marry Giles. *Perhaps,* she'd said. Had he taken it to heart? Could he actually believe she would do that after making love with *him?* Giles did not interest her in the least — Travis was the one she was in love with. Shaina thought of something else then. Maybe Travis didn't believe she'd really marry Giles. Maybe he thought she'd just been saying it to hurt him. The conceited bastard!

Forgetting that that was, in fact, exactly why she had said it, Shaina determined to beard the lion in his den once more and make sure he understood what he was losing. Just as soon as she finished her bath.

Her bronze-gold hair clung in damp tendrils to her forehead and around her neck where the mass had come loose from its pins. She drew a deep breath, rose from the tub, snatched a fluffy towel, and, while

157

shivering from head to foot, she got out of the tub. Wrapping the towel around her goosebumpy body, trying to ward off the morning chill by moving briskly, Shaina was too busy trying to keep warm, to see the man standing just inside her door.

Travis sucked in his breath at the splendor of the naked beauty rising from the tub she had ordered be brought to her room. The final time she would bathe in Wild Mountain! He stood, watching, in the shadowed place between the door and the wood frame. He felt like a peeping Tom, but he couldn't stop himself from staring.

Running a careless, shaking hand through his black hair, Travis decided he couldn't take any more. Besides, he was trespassing where only a man who had it in mind to take Shaina and someday make her his wife should trespass. And he wasn't that man.

Muted sunshine slanted across the floors from the windows on the eastern side of the ranch house as Shaina, fresh as a daisy and full of spunk after her bath, made her way to Travis's "den" — where the lion awaited her. But he had no idea she was coming just yet.

Drawing a deep breath, Shaina ordered herself to be strong as she stood before the doors and knocked, first timidly, then so hard that she was afraid if she didn't let up she'd crack her knuckles if not the door.

"Damn it anyway!" thundered from within.

Travis, looking like murder, wrenched open the door almost tearing it from the hinges, then became very still. He had been about to bring the house down on the head of the intruder who dared bother him at this time of day in his office/study.

"Shaina," he growled softly. As it had been doing for the last half hour, the gorgeous vision of her in the altogether came back to visit him, but this time, with her standing so near, looking so pure and lovely and tempting, a desire so strong to sweep her to his bed at once gripped him and wouldn't let go.

Telling herself that one who hesitates too long was lost, Shaina brushed past him and entered the study. They faced each other at the same moment, like two opponents squaring off for a fight.

Crossing his arms over his wide chest, Travis said coldly, "What can I help you with now?"

"I am not going," Shaina announced, her chin held squarely, her flashing blue eyes defiant.

Feeling his body drain of some emotion, Travis wondered if it was tension. And now another was filling the empty spaces. Was it relief? Not ready for this brand-new assertive Shaina, Travis sarcastically drawled, "It's your funeral, Miss Hill."

"I don't think so," she returned, her long lashes sweeping her flushed cheeks. "What I mean is — I'm not leaving Wild Mountain," Shaina revised, watching Travis closely. He looked so vital, so strong, handsome and masculine. "And there is one more thing . . ."

Going around to seat himself at his desk, Travis totally surprised her with something she'd never seen him do . . . He lit up a foul-smelling cigar and rudely blew smoke in the air before her face. Shaina stared at the ugly brown thing and grimaced.

"When did you start smoking . . . those?" She

pointed with one hand while pinching her nose with the other.

"Just now." Travis leaned back, struggling not to cough. "I've had them in my drawer for a long time. I need something to get me through this day." His eyes narrowed at her through the blue cloud of smoke; he could barely see her clearly. "Might even break out a bottle—or two—later."

"You drink a lot, too?"

"No." He grinned for the first time. "I drink a *little*. Especially when something is bothering me."

"Oh."

Suddenly Travis busied himself straightening his desk, cigar clenched in the side of his teeth, one eye squinting from the thick smoke. He looked just like a handsome cardsharp, it came to Shaina.

"Well, let's have it, Miss Hill. What are you planning to do . . . besides remain a schoolteacher in Wild Mountain . . . *without pay*."

"I am still going to allow Giles Wilson to court me." Her eyes flashed like blue lighting. "I might even consider becoming his wife. We—we have talked about it once or twice."

"That's nice," he slowly drawled, "but you've already made that point, as I recall."

There! He was making her feel like a child again.

"You think I'm so young. Well, I'll have you know that I'm going to be nineteen soon." Shaina tossed her head, making her red-blond hair sparkle in the afternoon light coming in. "That's plenty old to marry Giles."

"So when are you going to grow up?" was the bored response.

160

Gritting her teeth, Shaina decided she would leave the ranch with Giles, making sure she rode past Travis's study window!

Shaina whirled and exited the study as fast as she could make her limbs move. This time she slammed the door in his grinning, smoke-wreathed face. After she'd gone, he glared at the bitter-tasting cigar and proceeded to stub the nasty thing out in the ashtray that was usually left unused on the desk.

After a while Travis went to stand at the wide window and surveyed his vast holdings from one huge mountain range to the end of the other. Big Blue towered in the center, actually off to the right a little when studied from this angle. It stood as a sentinel to the Lazy C, a symbol of power and splendor to not only Travis Cordell but to all who realized its true meaning.

Travis was lost in his thoughts as he continued to gaze out the window. He didn't know how much time had passed before two riders and their mounts came into view. Shaina. She was indeed a rare jewel. Her skin was flushed a warm pink. Her hair, blowing free, was like shimmering fire laced with spun gold. Gold. He had plenty of that rare substance. Gold. This reminded him of an incident. He had once sat in on a game with a cardsharp who'd come to the valley panning for gold. The man had gone away empty-handed, without the gold and minus his reputation as cardsharp. Only he, Travis Cordell, knew where there was gold. He'd gotten most of it from the cool shallows of Blue's Run, but there was more, and he would discover it someday. He had enough right now. Travis shifted his gaze from Shaina, and his eyes narrowed into slits of cold jade. And there was Giles Wilson, looking smug and haughty, almost evil.

Travis stood with his big hands clenched into fists to restrain himself from running after Shaina, then lowered his head. Lightly his toe touched the ink stain on the carpet, his eyes like polished green jade as he stared at the spot. Looking out the window again he saw the two figures vanish into the forest.

"Travis?"

The sound of the small voice intruded into Travis's troubled thoughts, and he turned around to see his daughter standing tentatively beside the partially opened door. He remembered Shaina's words, and he searched his heart, wondering if he'd truly abused the girl by not paying more attention to her. As she closed the door and walked slowly toward him, it came to Travis in a sickening flash that Shaina was right. He *had* been unkind to little Roux. He had used his innocent daughter, saw her only when he wanted her around, sent her to the Indian village when he wanted her out of his hair.

Slowly, full of remorse and regret, Travis pulled his daughter onto his lap where he sat in his deep leather chair. With tears burning in his eyes, he pulled her, his only child, closer and hugged her tightly. Smoothing her deep mahogany hair with a heavy hand, he spoke to her gently, as if she was still a babe.

Roux was holding her breath, her eyes very big and round. She couldn't remember the last time her father had held her, much less hugged her. When she spoke, her voice was muffled against the soft material of his

162

denim shirt.

"Travis, are you ill?"

"No, darling Roux, I am not ill."

"Are you sad?"

"No, I am not sad."

Roux was puzzled. "What are you then?"

"Happy, dear Roux, I am very happy and content just sitting here with you."

"When I go away and come back will you be the same?"

"Of course. From now on you and I are going to be friends."

Lifting her head, Roux said with some disappointment, "I hear Miah hollering."

"She can wait. Anyway, Sam's in the kitchen, he can hear her and go to see what she wants."

"I sat in Miah's room yesterday."

"Oh?" Travis rested his hand lightly on Roux's shoulder as he asked, "What did she have to say?"

"Get out, Fox Fire!"

Travis laughed, a deep, happy sound.

"Oh!" Roux clapped a hand over her mouth and jumped off her father's lap. "I forgot! I have to go over to the hop ranch and feed Sheba. Jay had to go into Seattle with his mother and—"

"Whoa." Travis halted her flow of excitement. "Who is Jay?"

"Just a friend." Roux colored a little. "His father runs the cotton plantation."

"*Our* cotton plantation?" Travis frowned, trying to recall the name. "Oh, of course, Jay Ridingbow." Serious now, Travis studied his daughter closely. "Hey, isn't Jay a little too old for you to be hanging around?

163

Don't you know any boys your own age?" He chuckled deeply. "Actually, girls would be a better choice."

"White girls are silly." Then she shifted her feet, adding, "All except for Shaina, she is very smart. She taught me how to use grammar better . . . You think I am getting better at talking, Travis?"

"Yes, darling, much better. You are growing more lovely and wonderful by the day . . . soon you will be the most beautiful girl in the valley."

"And the smartest."

"And the smartest," he echoed.

"Travis, did you send Shaina away?" Roux glanced down and then up again, waiting with bated breath.

"I—yes, yes, I did." A chuckle emerged upon seeing her crestfallen look. "But she wanted to leave. Besides, she has to get back to her teaching job."

"Here?" With much excitement she asked the question. "Here in Wild Mountain?"

"Certainly here in Wild Mountain."

"You didn't really send her away then, did you?" Roux grinned.

"I am going to be truthful with you, Roux, I think it's time I started doing that."

Roux canted her head. "You never told me the truth before?"

"I—what I mean, Roux, is—Damn, I don't know what I mean. Listen, Shaina is only eighteen, did you know that?"

"What's wrong with that? Is it too young to teach school or something?"

"Well," Travis drawled, "I'm not sure it's too young an age to teach, but think of what the parents will say when they realize a mere child is teaching their children?"

Roux pouted, saying, "Shaina is *not* a child. She is a woman full growed. She's as big as Miah!"

Travis could feel his face actually blushing as Roux stuck her chest way out and patted her hair in a feminine fashion. Fighting to keep from laughing out loud, Travis reached for Roux's hand and, standing, twirled her around like he did the ladies when there was a local barn dance or party.

Roux stopped, laughing breathlessly. Travis finally broke out in laughter, and together they made quite a commotion, so much so that Miah sat up straighter in her bed to listen and the chickens outside the window stopped their pecking to cant their red-combed heads toward the house.

"Father!" Roux shouted, forgetting herself. "You are so much fun!" She hugged him around the waist, and her little voice carried a unique force all its own. *"Father."*

Chapter Seventeen

There could be no doubt in the man's mind that the young woman he'd just seen was his daughter. Graham's small, dull eyes glowed with happiness. He'd found Shainy at last!

He untied and mounted the sway-backed red he'd purchased down in the valley of Wild Mountain. A tall lad he'd figured was a half-breed, handsome, black-haired, golden-eyed, had sold him the old red mare. He'd been pulling the big red along with a length of rope while the lad himself had been mounted atop a beautiful golden horse.

"Hey there," the lad had called from his lofty position, "You are new here. Need a horse to get you around, mister?"

"Well now, I sure do," Graham had chuckled. "You're just the man I want to see, maybe you can tell me a few more things while we're at our business. I

can't pay you too much, see, I'm looking for a job."
And looking for my daughter . . . but that'll come
soon enough, he thought to himself, not prepared to
launch into that topic just yet.

After they had conducted their business, Graham
giving the lady twenty dollars for the horse — a sum he
thought was exorbitant — Jay Ridingbow began to
mount Sheba once again.

"Wait a minute, lad."

"What is it?" Jay's golden eyes sparked as he looked
over to the man suspiciously.

"I need some information for that money there . . .
I gave you an awful lot for this nag. I'm a bit down
and out, been looking for my daughter. She ran away
from home, see, and I mean to find her."

"Well, what does she look like?"

"She's really pretty."

"That don't tell me a whole lot, mister. There's a
few pretty girls around in the valley." Jay had one
particular young lady in mind. Actually she wasn't a
lady yet, but she would be someday, and Jay was
waiting. He would wait forever for her, he told himself, because Roux Cordell was going to be his
woman.

"She's got red hair — " Graham scratched his bristled
chin. "No, that ain't right. Her hair is . . . kind of a
funny gold."

"Like Sheba's coat?" Jay patted his beloved mare.

"Uhh, no."

"It sounds to me, mister, like you are trying to mix
red and gold together."

"Yeah! Yeah, that's it. Red-gold hair . . . shiny as a
new penny and soft as silk."

167

"Well," Jay began, "I don't know if her hair is soft or not, I never touched it. But that sounds like the new schoolteacher. She's pretty as the long painting Abner Selby keeps in the back of the trading post—" he blushed hotly remembering the curvy nude—"all to himself."

"What painting?"

Jay thought the man looked kind of angry all of a sudden so he quickly revised, "I mean, in the painting . . . it is not the schoolteacher, if that is what you are thinking."

"What is the schoolteacher's name?"

Something about the man struck Jay as odd, and he thought the wisest course would be to avoid telling the stranger anything. You never knew what the riverboat was going to bring upstream nowadays!

"Say! Where you going?" Graham had shouted to the lad, but he and the magnificent mount disappeared faster than a trout slipping off a hook. His swift, lithe movements convinced Graham that boy was part Indian.

Graham had gotten the horse but had lost a whole week of his search because of the pox fever going around. He sure didn't want to be catching that, but when the all-clear was given, he had climbed from the boardinghouse room like a blinky-eyed bear after hibernation. Mounting the big red he'd bought from the wily Indian lad, Graham continued his search for his daughter. Every way he turned he got suspicious peeks, and no one wanted to tell him anything, it was like they were protecting someone. Could that someone be Shainy, he'd begun to wonder.

Then, on his ninth day in Wild Mountain, he came upon two riders on the trail. He pulled off behind some bushes, having decided to do some snooping on his own. He was getting nowhere fast with everyone in this whole blasted valley keeping their mouths zippered!

And his independent sleuthing had paid off!

Like a child, Graham clapped his lips together in delight. The girl had turned her eyes toward the brush, and when Graham caught a good look at her face, he knew it was his Shainy. Lordy, how she'd grown since last he saw her.

Girl? No, his Shainy was a woman!

Remounting the big red, Graham gave the horse a kick in the ribs and set off down the trail after the passing riders. Luck was with him, he thought. Shaina most likely had a place to stay and that meant he could eat normal once again. And, the Indian lad had said there was a new schoolteacher. Shainy had a job! They could save up enough money and go to California. Shainy could go back to work, and he could relax for a while—he'd had a hard time of it the last six months—and then he could go out and try to find himself a job, too . . . or maybe he wouldn't. What did he care, as long as someone could do the work for him. Shainy would do for him, just like Eleanora always fetched for him and the kids, too. All he had to remember was never to tell Shainy the secret—that Eleanora had been allowed two indiscretions in their marriage, two sins that had almost cost her her life. First she had given birth to the beautiful, fiery-haired girl child—one that was not

169

from his own loins — but before that he'd almost killed her himself because of the lad, Ellie's first bastard!

Shaina was becoming increasingly uneasy. They had left the Lazy C Ranch over an hour ago and should be nearing the Kingswell's homestead soon. She felt something was wrong.

"I will be happy to get to the Kingswells'," Shaina remarked, trying not to glance over her shoulder again.

"Why do you keep looking back?" Giles asked, his pale-brown eyes squinting beneath the brim of his cocked hat. "Do you think Cordell will come after you, begging you to return to his ranch? What were you doing there in the first place, if I may ask?"

Giles's tall torso loomed beside Spotted Bird. Shaina shifted uneasily, not from the many questions fired at her since they'd left the Lazy C . . . no, it was something else.

"Giles," Shaina said urgently, "someone is following us."

"I told you not to worry," Giles said after searching the trail behind him. "There's no one back there."

"Yes, I guess you are right, I am acting a little foolish."

"Bad case of the nerves after living in the same house with Travis Cordell, huh, Shaina?"

"No!" She whirled on him, then resumed looking straight ahead. "No," she said more softly this time. "I wish you wouldn't keep reminding me of the man, Giles. The pox epidemic is over and I am returning to the Kingswells'."

170

"Do you like it there?"

"It's all right, a place to sleep and eat."

"How about the Kingswell people. Do you like them?"

"Yes. It's a very large family, and they are all very nice." Shaina laughed, saying, "Any more questions you'd like to ask, Giles?"

Reaching over he took her by the wrist, slowing their mounts a little. "Marry me." He smiled that beguiling smile into her eyes. "Will you?"

"Ah . . ."

"Well?"

"Unhand that woman!" came a voice from behind.

Long-forgotten memories came back to Shaina in full force. She turned and saw her father riding toward them looking like the devil himself.

"What the hell . . ." Giles muttered, seeing the stricken look on Shaina's face. "Who is this?"

"It's my father, but I don't understand what he's doing here . . . or how he even found me."

"Shainy!" Graham shouted, bringing the big red horse to a skidding halt beside Spotted Bird. "Damn if you aren't a sight for sore eyes. Who's this man here? Is he bothering you? I saw him grab a hold of your wrist." He glared over to the man wearing the indifferent, lazy look. "No one dares lay a hand on one of my own, mister!"

"Father, what in heaven's name are you doing here?" Shaina asked in nervous bewilderment, then remembering her manners and Giles at her side, she said, "Father, this is Giles Wilson . . . Giles, my father, Graham Hill."

"Well . . . howdy," Graham relented, still looking

surly.

"Mr. Hill, I was just asking your daughter to—"

"Giles." Shaina looked at him with a warning glint in her brilliant blue eyes. "Ah, Graham," Shaina went on, for some reason feeling more comfortable calling her father by his name, "Giles was just asking me to have lunch with him at the Pine Ridge Hotel. Would you care to come with us?"

"Of course I'm going to come with you! I didn't come all the way to this blasted mountain to eat lunch by myself."

Shaina laughed, trying to hide the sudden uneasiness that had come over her. There was something disturbing about the way he was looking at her, as if he didn't really know her, as if . . . Now her thoughts were really getting silly.

They rode in easy silence for a time before Giles spoke up. For some reason he didn't much like Shaina's father. "I'll take you over to the Kingswells' after lunch, Shaina."

"Thank you, Giles, but I can get there myself. I'm sure you have more important matters to attend to." Although she smiled sweetly at him, she gritted her teeth as she spoke.

"Oh, yes, well, guess I can come to see you later, huh?"

"Of course, Giles, I really wish you'd do that."

Graham lingered over the bottle of whiskey, pouring another glass and gulping it down hastily. He was glad that Giles Wilson had took himself to other parts after they had shared lunch together at the hotel's dining room. Graham smiled to himself—a lunch that Wilson had been so generous as to pay for it himself!

Graham looked over to the fuzzy image of his girl, grinning over the rim of his glass. "Shainy girl, you sure do look good, yessir!"

"And you're looking well yourself, Father."

Shaina looked up in time to see Jack Nolan saunter in, tip his dusty hat to her, and walk to the back of the room with the other wranglers with him. Nervously she smiled at Jack and then pulled her gaze back to Graham. "I have to get back to the Kingswells' and prepare my things for school. I am going to reopen tomorrow and there is much work to be done before the morning comes."

With narrowed eyes, Jack Nolan watched as the stranger with Shaina Hill sat back stiffly in his chair as if surprised by what she'd just said to him. The man leaned forward, talking loudly while pouring himself another glass of the tavern's most potent whiskey. When John Ridingbow strode into the room, Jack's interest was taken up by the news big John had from Seattle.

"I need a place to stay, Shainy. You know where I can get a room? Maybe I can stay where you're staying—" At the strange look in her eye, he changed that to: "Maybe I can stay there for a few days?" he hopefully asked.

"I don't think so, Graham," Shaina said, insisting on calling him that so that word wouldn't get around that her father was a drunk come to mooch off her. Still, Shaina couldn't help but feel sorry for this pathetic man who'd lost his wife, his home, and his children.

Shaina placed her hand over his almost tenderly and was shocked to find that, as he turned it over to grip hers lovingly, his fingers were still smooth . . . as if he hadn't done a day's work in ages. Oh God, he must be still living off others! Now that he was here, what was she going to do? She barely made enough to care for herself and purchase all the supplies she needed for the classroom. Travis Cordell never saw to it that the children were well supplied with books and such, the scrooge!

Completely unaware they were being watched by a pair of dark eyes from the table at the back, Shaina and Graham continued to converse on the subject most dear to Graham—money.

Tipping his chair back while sipping his sarsaparilla, Jack frowned when the stranger took Shaina's fingers in a firm grip and stared into her pretty face as if he was going to gobble her up. Jack's chair came down and for a time he sat there, observing the two. Then he rose, shoved back his chair, and walked briskly to the front door, tipping his sombrero once again to Shaina Hill.

"Who is that now?" Graham growled against Shaina's heated face.

"Jack Nolan, he works for Travis Cordell." Shaina ended on a sigh.

"What's that for? This Cordell fellow someone special?" Graham's colorless eyes narrowed in speculation.

"Oh, yes, Travis is the pillar of the community." Graham's eye gleamed. "Rich, huh?"

"Very. He owns most of the valley," Shaina spoke freely, unaware of the schemes ticking in Graham's brain.

Rubbing his bristled chin, Graham asked, "You got something, ah, going with this wealthy fellow?"

Shaina missed the hopeful gleam in his eye, and said a little forlornly, "No. Not any longer."

"Oh. I see."

"No you don't," Shaina said. "No one does."

"You and this Travis fellow aren't getting along too well, I take it?"

"I already told you *no*." Shaina gazed at the intricate knot in the pine wall. "We don't . . . get along. I am the schoolteacher. He's the boss." Looking into her father's bloodshot eyes, she shrugged. "He wants me out of here, and I am not ready to leave Wild Mountain . . . not for anyone." She looked at Graham pointedly. "Do you understand?"

Graham stuttered, "Oh, 'course, Shainy, anything you say. Whatever you want is all right with me."

Shaina blinked. This was Graham Hill, bowing and scraping? In the past it had been the other way around, everyone bowed and scraped and did for him. She knew now that there was something devious on his mind. She should not really be too surprised. Why should he have changed?

"It's time to put the bottle down, Graham. We have to go."

Shaina stood and Graham took one more gulp. "Where we going?"

"I am going to the Kingswells'. You are going to school."

"What?" Graham gaped.

Shaina broke her own pent-up tension by laughing. "For a while you are going to *live* there."

Outside, Jack Nolan was just coming out of the

general store and walking to his mount. As he watched the schoolteacher and the stranger coming out of the hotel dining room, Bill Cooper, another wrangler from the Lazy C, sidled over, nudging Jack.

"What do you make of it?"

"Them?" Jack tipped his head almost imperceptibly, but the other man caught the movement.

"Yeah. Who is that dude anyway?"

"Never saw him before." Jack gave his bundle a jerk to see if it would hold to the saddle.

"She seems to know him pretty well. Wonder what they're cookin' up?"

"Why do you think anything's up?"

"I don't know, Jack. She shows up, brews a storm at the ranch —"

"Whoa," Jack said. "What is that supposed to mean?"

Cooper shrugged. "Well, seems to me like she's sure done something. The boss ain't the same man he was before that pretty redhead showed up in the valley. He used to chew my butt out once in a while, but now he bites off a big chunk. I know it's all cuz of that woman. She's big trouble, I saw it comin' first time I laid eyes on that pretty little thing. I think Travis's got the hots for her. I been at the ranch a long time, Jack, even before you come along, and he never looked at Miah like he looks at the white woman Shaina."

"So?" Jack watched Shaina and the stranger ride toward the green ridge outside of town. Everything was greening up, it was going to be a pretty summer. "I look at a lot of women myself."

"Ahh." He poked Jack in the ribs. "You're full of it, the only gal got your eye is Deanna Kingswell."

176

Just the name Deanna made Jack go shivery all over. Someday he was going to let her know just what it was she did to him. Or did she already know? he wondered.

"Think I'll report this to the boss, he's goin' to want to know what's goin' on with the schoolteacher anyhows."

"Yeah?" Jack said, hurtling himself into the saddle and launching the grulla into a gallop from a shivering standstill. "Not if I don't get there first!"

"Hey, Jack!" Cooper shouted, running to his horse. Chuckling as he mounted, watching the dustdevil Jack's grulla created with its swift gallop, he growled, "It just ain't fair . . . it just *ain't!*"

Chapter Eighteen

Giles rode out of the woods heading back toward the Lazy C, the afternoon sun slanting into his pale-brown eyes, casting sharp shadows beneath the brim of his cream-colored hat. His smile was devilish as he thought of his desire to get something he badly needed, hoping that Travis was not around. Just the thought of bumping into him on his own grounds gave Giles pause, but, usually at this time of day the boss would be out riding the range, checking on fences, his men, of all kinds of ranch related business.

Giles inhaled deeply and stuck his chest out like a banty rooster. It was a beautiful, lazy day and summer was just around the corner. Birds were singing, flowers were blooming, and things were surely warming up — made a man want to go out, flex his muscles and get a little . . . maybe a lot. Giles thought he knew just where to look.

Since Giles had met Deanna, he hadn't been able to get her luscious smile or delicious body out of his mind. He should be applying all his energy toward trying to get Shaina to warm up, he knew, but he also knew, that she was the kind who would insist on waiting until after they were married. Who could it hurt if he fooled around a little more before taking Shaina as his wife? Not himself, that was for sure!

Dismounting in front of the long ranch house, Giles walked up to the door, glancing over his shoulder once or twice before he knocked softly.

"Hello, anyone home?" he called. He was just trying to figure out the explanation he would give to Travis if he was the one to answer the door instead of the beauteous Deanna, when there was a sound from within. "Can I come in?" he asked.

"Come! Come!" was the return shout in a feminine voice.

Ah, Giles said to himself, his eyes villainous. *That would be the squaw Miah. Maybe she can tell me where I can find that luscious Deanna.*

"Ayyy-ayyy," exclaimed Miah when she emerged from the bedroom doing up the laces of her doeskin dress. "So, Mister Giles, this is what you look like. I think you are handsome and very nice."

Giles whistled under his breath when the Indian woman moved into the sunny living room. Blue-black glints came alive in the thick hair she hadn't bothered to braid yet this day. Her body was slender and she was shapely in all the right places . . . he just might not need to look for Deanna after all. Miah didn't look any worse for the pox fever he knew she was recovering from; in fact she was the most beautiful dark-haired witch he'd ever laid his lusty eyes on.

"I just get up." Miah slanted her dark eyes up at him, her look sexy and inviting. "No one is home.

179

You are looking for who?"

"I—ah, I left something here this morning."

"Oooh, but you stay out in the bunkhouse, Mister Giles. What could you have leave in the house?"

"My pipe. During dinner yesterday." He grinned with straight white teeth that gleamed and flattered his handsome face. He laughed. "Yeah, I left my pipe here. You haven't seen it, have you?"

With her hips swaying and her eyes sending out unmistakable signals, the Indian woman murmured, "You come back for something, Mister Giles. I think it is not your pipe. There is something you want maybe Miah can help you with?"

Beads of sweat were beginning to pop out on Giles's forehead and throat. This woman was some looker, so why was it he'd never noticed her before? Then he remembered. The last time he'd seen her she had been pregnant. Women in that condition always turned him off, their bodies all swollen and ugly.

"I know." Miah ran her long, coppery fingers through her glorious hair and shook it out in a provocative invitation. "You look for the housekeeper Deanna. It is true, I know. All men look at that one. She has very big ones, eh?"

Now Giles had to wipe the sweat off his brow with the back of his sleeve, and he smiled wickedly knocking the tawny wave loose to fall over his eye. It always worked. Miah began to purr. Giles loosened his shirt one button.

Miah, licking her lips, tossed her head. "Giles, you come with me."

Following close behind, Giles tossed a glance over his shoulder, then reached out to pinch Miah on her

180

taut little rear.

With a laugh, Miah tossed over her shoulder, "Mister Giles is in a very big hurry." She reached back, became bold, and Giles sucked in his breath. "Nice big man. You will like Miah very much, white man."

"Jesus," Giles gulped. "Hurry!"

Miah slipped into a dark room off the kitchen, and when Giles paused outside to survey the area nervously, Miah reached out and pulled him inside the small room.

At the touch of Miah's lips against his, Giles groaned and swiftly pressed the warm, eager shape against his own. Their tongues did a wild dance, twirling, testing, and a savage light soon began to flicker in Miah's dark eyes.

Discarding his shirt swiftly, Giles pulled her against him again. Finding the dark, secret place he was so eager for, Giles flexed his wrist and soon had Miah writhing against his inflamed body.

"Now," she cried. "Now!"

On the bare wood floor they began the savage ritual of mating. Not one sweet word of love was exchanged, no lovely sighs and cries of bliss, only grunts and groans much like animals seeking gratification.

When they were finished, they both lay back, breathing heavily still, their ecstasy spent in the blink of an eye, no golden afterglow to share with each other. Only stark, cold emptiness. They would hunger for empty release again, and yet again, never to be satisfied in their greedy lust. Two of a kind, neither Miah nor Giles could ever give their love to only one person.

Jack Nolan had finished his important business with Travis. He'd found his boss out riding the westernmost section of land, the one Travis had tagged number seven. The man had not seemed overly interested in the news of the schoolteacher and the raggedy stranger — not until he related the part where the middle-aged man had gripped Shaina's hand and looked as if he meant to gobble her up.

"What does he look like?" Travis had wanted to know.

"About medium build, kind of sandy-brown hair with a few strands of gray here and there. Got something about him I don't trust, Travis."

"Like what?"

"Uh, can't put my finger on it, Travis."

"Did it seem like he was hurting her?"

Jack thought for a moment, then said, "Not really. Looked to me like they were having an argument of some sort, though."

"You couldn't hear what they were saying?"

"Not really, but I heard him call her 'Shainy' often enough." Shaking his head, Jack laughed softly as if he'd just remembered something.

"What is it?" Travis asked, eyeing the other man closely. He had known Jack Nolan a long time and would trust him with his life.

"Oh, maybe it's nothing." Jack shrugged, stuffing his tanned fingers into the pockets of his tight-fitting jeans.

Travis lifted an eyebrow, saying, "Let's have it anyway. It might give a clue to his reason for being in

182

the valley."

"Seemed to me the man was after something, something he needs to get real bad."

"Like Shaina?" Travis said.

"Could be."

Travis looked out across the green meadow. "I'm going to have a look into this." He booted his horse into motion, saying over his shoulder, "You watch out for things here at the ranch. I'll be back later, much later. Don't wait up for me."

Deanna was just slipping into the barn to gather the eggs of a few recalcitrant chickens that chose to scatter some of their eggs outside instead of in the chicken coop. That New Hampshire rooster, always leading the "ladies" astray was the cause of all the trouble, Deanna thought as she caught the rougish fellow skittering out of her path as she was just about to close the door.

"I'll get you one of these days, you nasty old cluck," Deanna warned, knowing he needed more than a roof and wire-netting walls to keep him penned in.

Deanna worked at her task diligently, then, pleased with a job well done, returned to the house. She paused, wondering at the strange quiet . . . usually Miah would holler as soon as she heard the screen door slam.

Gazing out the window to the main road, Deanna's golden-tanned face looked mildly surprised to see Miah riding out on her pony with the fellow named Giles Wilson not far behind. They looked to be in a great hurry, rushing in the direction of the sheltering woods.

Jack Nolan lifted his hand to knock on the screen door but hesitated for a moment when he saw Deanna standing at the big front window. He could see Deanna clear as day, but she hadn't detected his presence just yet. Not wanting her to think he was spying on her through the screen door, Jack knocked as loud as he could and almost jumped when Deanna jumped.

Seeing Jack on the other side of the screen, Deanna smiled. A delicious shudder coursed through his body as he watched her come slowly toward him, her seductive young body drawing a special response from his own.

"Hello, Jack," she said warmly. "Would you like to come in?"

Jack grinned softly. "Anyone home?"

"No," she said, eyeing his amused features.

"Then I'll come in."

Deanna saw that Jack shared her appreciation of the spacious room. Big leather sofas faced each other and exotic plants in huge clay pots were set into corners and beside doorways. A large stone fireplace dominated space on one wall while on the others hung majestic paintings of Big Blue.

"Travis really loves the mountains," Deanna remarked, watching Jack nod in agreement before she asked him into the kitchen for some coffee.

"Sounds good," he told her, "haven't had my fill yet today."

With a laugh, Deanna said over her shoulder, "I

believe I don't know of another man who drinks as much coffee as you do, Jack."

Watching Deanna's hips sway softly, Jack felt completely mesmerized, and without thinking, blurted out, "Hope you don't, Deanna."

Deanna's amethyst eyes became a smoky violet and her walk suddenly became lighter. As they neared the kitchen, she called up memories of when she'd first come to the Lazy C to work for Travis Cordell. He had heard about her expert cooking and housekeeping abilities and she had heard about his being king cock of the valley and his volatile temper. She'd been scared silly, but Travis had proved to be a nice man to work for, his manner pleasant and easygoing. Only on occasion had she witnessed that renowned temper flare up when he'd have a set-to with one of the ranchhands. A few know-it-alls had received the boot, and Deanna was glad she was not a man working at the Lazy C. He was kinder to women, it was rumored—some women.

One day she'd come around the corner of the chicken coop in too much of a haste, and collided with a rangy, dark-eyed man. He'd stared at her as if he couldn't believe she was quite real. Nice and easy, smiling as if in approval of what he saw, Jack Nolan had introduced himself as the top foreman of the Lazy C. It was as if she had only come alive at the instant her eyes met those of Jack's.

When Jack left the ranch to go to Seattle to pick up supplies that he couldn't find at the trading post or the general store, Deanna felt a tremendous sense of emptiness. When he walked into the yard for something, she was instantly at the window. When he came to talk over business with Travis Cordell, usually ensconced in the office, Deanna made certain she was somewhere nearby doing some chore that wouldn't take her far from the office. When she was hanging out the wash, her eyes constantly sought him. When he started having coffee with her just two weeks before, most times while she was alone, her stomach would clench tight and her pulses would behave erratically. These feelings were becoming more uncomfortable as Jack seemed to be getting closer to her.

Taking a deep breath to steady her wildly disturbed nerves, Deanna calmly set about making the strong black coffee she knew Jack liked.

Jack had never found himself in this position before. He'd always been cool and collected around women, able to take them or leave them. Usually he left them . . . cold. With Deanna Kingswell around he might as well be a bowl full of quivering jelly!

Deanna was carrying the steaming speckled-blue coffeepot to the table and Jack forced himself not to stare too blatantly at her luscious body. She was almost there when a fallen potholder caused her to trip. The steaming hot liquid sloshed all over her hand causing her to cry out.

In an instant Jack was at her side. Once a rodeo performer, Nolan was known to be fast as greased lightning with his body, could rope a calf, bring it down and brand it with a Lazy C in thirty seconds flat. Calves be damned, though. This woman — *his* woman — needed help.

"Here . . . I got it!"

Deanna stepped back in time just as Jack lunged forward to smoothly take the fiery pot from her. In a few more seconds he had returned to Deanna after placing the thing back on the stove.

"No, no, don't blow on your hand!"

Before Deanna knew what was happening — and the burn was killing her by now — Jack was leading her over to the sink and was pumping fresh cool water over her stinging fingers. Then her palm. Now the back of her hand. Back to her fingers.

Deanna watched Jack. Her heart pounding, she gazed wordlessly up into his rugged face. It wasn't a handsome face, though some women she'd overheard discussing Jack in town obviously thought so. She herself thought his face powerfully virile and his body tough and lean and rangy. His full black hair waved back from his forehead, almost as if he was facing a strong wind.

Jack's eyes flashed as he said, "I'll go fetch some salve for you now. Do you know where it's kept?"

Deanna raised her eyes to find him watching her. "Yes Jack," she murmured, mesmerized by his presence so close to her.

His smile was as tender as a caress. "The . . . salve?"

"I—" she said with a gulp—"I don't need it. Not now."

Moving closer, slipping one arm about her slim waist, he muttered her name huskily.

"Oh . . . Jack." Her body was aching madly for his touch.

He pulled her against him, being careful of her burned hand. "May I ask the lady for a kiss?"

He leaned over her and she gave her moist, willing lips up in answer to his ardent request.

Jack's first kiss was surprisingly gentle. As his lips moved to slant across hers, Deanna reeled dizzily and was forced to bring her hand up to grasp him by the shoulder.

Feeling Deanna's fingers running along his arm caused Jack to begin to shiver in stunning desire he'd never felt for any other woman before. His ardent lips moved along her jawline, along her neck, and behind her ear.

Deanna's head was flung back in delicious ecstasy as the mastery of Jack's mouth and tongue continued to learn every curve and hollow of her heated flesh. She began to breathe hard between parted lips, and Jack, hearing her passion, feeling it as well, moved his mouth back to covers hers once again.

"Deanna," Jack groaned, lifting his dark head. "I want you, honey, want you so much I feel like eating you up."

"Jack—" Deanna swallowed hard. "I've never . . ." She couldn't finish the words.

"I know, honey, it's all right. I'm not going to take you here on the floor," he chuckled low, "though I'd like to. But I wouldn't do that to you. When we make love I want us to be in a real bed."

For a moment they were wrapped in silence but for the passionate beating of their hearts. Deanna felt as if she was standing on a big wispy cloud . . . If only they were alone. They couldn't . . . not here in Travis's house.

"Deanna." Jack cupped her flushed face in his calloused hands. "There's a cabin up in the hills, stuck way back where no one can find it. The place," he said with a thrilling smile, "is mine."

"Oh, Jack," Deanna said ecstatically, "when can we go there?"

Kissing her wrist, he gazed lovingly into her eyes murmuring, "Soon as your hand is healed."

Mischeviously her eyes sparkled. "It's already better—"

Deanna waited breathlessly.

"Honest?"

"Honest to God!"

Deanna laughed as Jack lifted her to twirl her around in his arms.

Chapter Nineteen

"Shainy—who's this handsome dude tearing down the road?"

Walking to the window in front of the schoolhouse, Shaina came to stand beside her father, still holding the book she'd been studying. Her breath caught in the tunnel of her throat.

"Travis," she murmured.

Graham's eyes grew as he excitedly asked, "The rich one? What's he doing here?"

Shaina gave a nod to his first question and an unconscious shrug to the second. "I wouldn't have the slighest. But . . . will you please go back to the room we fixed up for you to stay in?"

"Why should I?" Graham stuck his thumbs authoritatively beneath his suspenders.

"Because you look a sight! You haven't shaved—in fact you haven't done much of anything except put up that bed in the storeroom we cleaned out. It was a mistake for us to borrow all these things from the Kingswells—Travis Cordell no doubt has had wind of all our activities by now."

Graham looked at Shaina in arrogant puzzlement. "Sounds like you think settling your poor old pa up nice and comfy is a mistake?" His voice lifted unpleasantly.

"Yes," Shaina said with a sigh. "Yes I do, in fact."

"Shainy—I can't believe you're saying this. Why, we were getting along like two peas in a pod—"

"I can't," she began in exasperation, "I can't believe you stole that jug of whiskey from the Kingswells!"

"Well . . . it was just one little bitty jug."

Shaina shook her head incredulously.

"Don't be looking at me like that, Shainy, I'm not off my nut, you know. And don't be prodding your pointing stick at me again like you done this morning."

"Go on," she said while giving Graham a shove into the back room. "In there with you, I don't want Travis Cordell getting the wrong idea about us."

"Shoot, girl, all you gotta do is tell him I'm your pa. Besides I'd like to meet this Cordell fellow. You never know—"

"Get in there, damn it!"

"Shainy, I never—!"

"Be quiet, will you?"

"Ah . . . Christ!"

"Don't swear!"

"*You* did!"

"Go *on!*"

Shaina went to answer the door on legs that suddenly trembled violently. What was Travis meaning to do now? Bodily remove her from the school, from the valley?

191

Cracking the door, Graham peeped out to watch Shaina exchange words with the tall, dark-haired man and then step aside to allow him to enter the schoolhouse.

"As you can see, Travis, there is no one here but me, myself, and I." Shaina gulped down the hot knot of fear that had stuck in her throat when Travis had been questioning her and laughed nervously. "Wh — what are you doing?" she asked as she followed him around the room.

"Looking," Travis said. He seemed to be sniffing and rooting around like a clever bloodhound hot on the trail of scent.

Shaina's eyes flew to the door which had carefully closed only moments before. Dear God, she hoped Graham would know to hide behind the old blackboard that had books stacked in neat rows on either side of it. All he had to do was slip behind and keep his big mouth shut!

"What's in here?"

Travis paused in front of the offending door and Shaina's breath ceased to come.

"That? Oh, that's just an old storeroom." She laughed nervously. "There's nothing in there but old books — and such."

Travis turned, leaning against the door jamb, his arms crossed over his wonderfully massive chest. "What do you find so funny about me coming here, Shaina? Why are you so nervous? Hiding something from me?"

"Why would I do that?" Shaina caught herself. *Why am I hiding Graham as if he was nothing but a thief?* she asked herself. She knew why. Travis wouldn't believe Graham was her father. In fact, she recalled many an

192

occasion when a neighbor would joke that Shaina looked nothing like her sisters and brothers—that is, all but for Will. She and Will looked *somewhat* alike. In Shaina there was nothing that even slightly resembled Graham.

As Travis continued to study her suspiciously, Shaina continued to ask herself troubling questions, but she did find some sound reasons for not letting Travis in on her secret: Graham was a *moocher*, for one. It was very plain to see that Graham had some nasty old plan ticking in his head, something to do with Travis's wealth, and that was something Shaina could not allow him to get away with. She was already on Travis's "hate list"—and she hadn't even done much of anything wrong to get put there except be what she was—an eighteen-year-old woman trying to make a success of her life.

"Shaina, talk to me," Travis ordered sternly. "Jack Nolan saw you in town talking to a stranger. In fact, he said you were having lunch with him . . . if brown liquid can be called 'lunch'."

Sticking her pert nose in the air, Shaina said defensively, "We had already eaten, so it wasn't like he was having it for lu—"

"Ah ha!"

"Oh . . . damn you, Travis Cordell!" She realized he'd just baited her—and had caught her! "*I* wasn't drinking. I never touch the foul stuff!"

"Good for you, Miss Hill. Now, who was the stranger you were having a 'meal' with?"

This man was just too much! Shaina thought angrily. "It's none of your business. How dare you pry into my affairs."

Shaina's eyes flashed with outrage as she stood with arms crossed below her heaving breasts.

Travis took hold of Shaina's stiff shoulders and shook her once, twice, glaring into her brilliant blue eyes.

"Are you forgetting who you work for?"

"How could I?" Her voice held a rasp of frustration. "You are Mr. Big Shot Travis Cordell, the man who thinks he can own just about anything and anybody, that's who *you* are!"

"I wish you wouldn't say those things about me, Shaina."

"Why not? They're true. But you'll never own me, Travis."

"Shaina—why do we fight so much? Better time could be spent making love."

Travis reached out and pulled her into his arms. Shaina's flesh tingled and she dizzily stared up into his face, her lips moist and fresh.

"Oh, Shaina, Shaina, what am I going to do with you?" he groaned right before he lowered his head and, with hungry ardor, parted her lips with his own.

Travis hugged her fiercely tight as his lips moved over hers in an earth-shattering kiss. Then his tongue was slipping in and out in a sweet rhythm as old as time.

Peeping out of the door, Graham's eyebrows rose, higher and higher as the kiss deepened and deepened. To Graham, a stranger to passion, the kiss seemed angry, punishing. But to Shaina, it was a paradise of ecstasy and she gave herself up to its dreamy intimacy. Every nerve in her body was on fire and her senses rose like a floodtide.

Lightly Travis opened his hand over one of Shaina's breasts—but in an instant was halted by the barking of a loud voice from behind his shoulder.

"That will be enough, sir!"

"Oh," Shaina muttered, shattered by the sound of Graham's stern voice. The back of her hand flew to a flushed scarlet cheek.

"What the hell—" Travis ground out, releasing Shaina so abruptly that she stumbled backward, her equilibrium lost after the torrid kiss.

Graham cleared his throat loudly.

With a tight white line about his lips, Travis casually said, "Well, speak of the devil."

"Who are you calling the devil?" Graham demanded, bristling.

Shaina quickly interceded. "Travis, this is my father, Graham Hill."

Travis raised his eyebrows. "If he's your father, Shaina, I'll eat my 'six-guns'."

Shaina said, "You'd better start eating them."

The three of them stood in a little knot staring at one another, each one daring the other to speak next. At that moment Giles Wilson walked into the schoolroom, and, feeling the tension like a tangible thing in the air, he closed the door softly and then turned to face the three tense individuals.

Giles asked, "Something I can help you all with?" as he walked toward them slowly, a hard-cored mischief glittering in his pale-brown eyes.

Chapter Twenty

Travis's jade-green eyes narrowed as he contemplated Giles Wilson intently. A protective urge gripped him. He didn't much like Wilson, and he knew the feeling was mutual, but he'd come here to find out the stranger's identity, and he needed some answers. It was possible Wilson could supply some. Shaina had said the man was her father, but he could see no family resemblance at all. "What do you know about this, Wilson? Have you heard that this man is Shaina Hill's father?"

Shaina interrupted before Giles could answer. "I've already given you the answer, Travis. Graham is—"

"Let Giles answer, Shaina," Travis cut across her words.

"Saw him at the hotel dining room." Stuffing his fingers into his deep trouser pockets, Giles said, "He was bothering Shaina, trying to mooch off her. Off me, too. Too bad, 'cause looks like she's taken him in like some scruffy alley cat."

"Giles . . ." Shaina gritted her teeth and gave him a

furious look.

Travis felt keen outrage toward Shaina, for he believed she had again lied to him, first about her age—now this. "Hellfire," Travis cursed low. "I can see this conversation is getting us nowhere. Excuse me, but I've got some *important* things to do at the ranch in section twenty!"

"Section *twenty?*" Graham gaped at the tall frame moving toward the door. "How many does he have?"

One side of Giles's mouth lifted shrewdly as he said, "About one hundred twenty sections, each six hundred and forty acres."

Numbers ticked and tumbled about in Graham's head until he was dizzy from trying to calculate how many that really was. "Holy cattle-prod, that's like a big city—the man must be a cattle baron!"

Shaina had her back to Graham and Giles, and she stared out the window wearing a look of disappointment that neither of them could see. She had hoped that Travis's visit here was merely to see her, but she was terribly wrong, for he had come to the schoolhouse in order to do some snooping about her lunch companion. That and nothing more. Certainly no desire to be with her. He got what he came for, only he hadn't believed for one minute that Graham Hill was her father. He'd stolen some kisses, too. But it was clear . . . Travis just didn't want her—not as his wife anyway.

Shaina had seemed strangely quiet for some time and Mrs. Kingswell had noticed that the schoolteacher wasn't herself in many ways. Something was troubling her, but it hadn't been Sarah's place to question her, and so she had let it go.

Wearing one of several pastel-colored dresses, her coppery-blond hair shining, Shaina would go off to school with the Kingswell children, riding her spotted horse beside the wagon that transported the children. On Saturdays and Sundays Shaina would spend even more time at the school, but when she returned this Sunday evening, she looked even more frustrated and wan-looking than usual. Sarah Kingswell finally felt compelled to voice her concern. "How have you been feeling?" she asked bluntly.

"I'll be all right, Sarah." Shaina had become close to the middle-aged woman who insisted that they converse on a first-name basis. "Miss Hill and Mrs. Kingswell all the time just sounds too cold and starchy to me," she'd told Shaina.

"There is something bothering you, Shaina." Sarah had meant to keep to her own business, but it bothered her to see the young pretty woman looking so dejected all the time. Sarah went on. "Would you like to talk about it? I'm a pretty good listener, so Pa always says. 'You get things out in the open and take a good look at what's good and bad, Sary,' that's what Marvin tells me all the time."

Shaina's voice was quiet and soft as she began, telling Sarah first about how she'd come to be in Wild Mountain right up to the day two weeks ago . . . when she'd last seen Travis Cordell. She left nothing out except the more intimate scenes with Travis. But Sarah, gentle and wise, could read between the lines.

"I'll have to tell you I'm something of a romantic, Shaina." Sarah set her empty coffee cup down on the table, and when she looked up again her gray eyes twinkled across the space with an amused, mischievous look. "What you want to do with that gorgeous hunk of man, honey, is put a ball and chain onto him."

With surprised amusement, Shaina gaped at gentle Sarah and said in a whisper, "Travis Cordell? Are you sure we're talking about the same man?"

Sarah stared out at the rising yellow slice of moon before she returned her gaze to Shaina. "You love him, honey. I'm sure of it, so don't be afraid to go and tell him. You'll be missing the chance of a lifetime if you let King Cordell get away."

"But he has a mistress already."

"Now you know that isn't true at all, you're just looking for excuses, Shaina dear."

"But I want to be a schoolteacher—a husband and a child would tie me down."

"You can still be a schoolteacher," Sarah said.

At least I'd always be in Wild Mountain that way, Shaina told herself. Would that be so bad?

"Well, get going and ask that man to marry you, girl!" Sarah stood, beginning to gather the coffee cups, spoons, creamer, and sugar bowl she had left on the table.

"M-marry me?" Shaina gasped, her hand in midair reaching to help Sarah. "Me . . . ask him?" Shaina looked thoughtful and bewildered for a moment, then said, "That's unthinkable."

"No, it's not. You just thought on it, didn't you? Right. After a little bit you came to the conclusion it was a crazy thing to do. Unthinkable, you said. Change *your* thinking, Shainy, and you'll see what you're desiring and should be deserving."

Shaina shook her head in confusion, and Sarah turned to face her. "No need to look so perplexed, girl. All of us need love, right?"

"Well . . . I . . . I'm not sure I *deserve* love."

Sarah chuckled. "Honey, those of us who deserve love the least need it the most. And just what makes you so sure you don't?"

"Oh, Sarah. It's Graham. Sometimes I treat him unkindly and that isn't right. He's my father."

"If he's your father, then how come you look so confused and frightened when you talk about him? Has he done something to hurt you?"

"He wasn't a very good father. I mean he never knew how to provide very well, and he was always promising what he couldn't deliver."

Sarah shrugged, saying, "Maybe he didn't want to . . . there's men like that. They'd rather be laying about like slugs in bed. "Honey," Sarah smiled in kindness, "the past you can't do nothing about. It's over."

"I know." Shaina still looked troubled.

"Right, honey. But the future is still in your power."

Chapter Twenty-one

Like one with the stallion, Travis rode a good clip across the fully greened prairie. After a time he slowed Dice and rode easy, his hand riding on one slim hip as he surveyed all that was his.

The prairie foothills were wild, beautiful, open, with something nameless that gave the heart a twist of nostalgia, the soul a oneness with the mountain country. But the only pleasant memories he held inside were ones of his love for this land, the work he'd done on it, and the birth of his daughter.

Aching loneliness washed over Travis all of a sudden. He didn't know what he was lonely for. This was not something new. He'd felt this wrenching emotion often, but recently the loneliness did not come so often, not since, he had to admit, the pretty schoolteacher had come to the valley.

Why, then, was he trying to force Shaina away?

Travis sighed with deep-felt emotion. He needed someone besides little Roux to share all this with him, and the child needed someone to care for her, really care for her. Roux needed a mother's tender love. Miah might as well have never been the girl's mother for all the attention she gave her.

Again the loneliness swept him as Travis came to a

complete standstill. He watched the strong-bodied grullas running across his land and smiled. One, a big stallion feeling his oats, kicked up his heels as he chased after a spirited filly. And the mare led him a merry chase over hill and dale, her full golden mane spinning in the wind, her tail a magnificent golden arc. Again Travis smiled, but this time that frisky little filly reminded him somehow of Shaina, and his full-lipped mouth continued to curl upward.

Travis set Dice off at a full gallop and soon they were racing alongside the grullas. He urged his spotted stallion to his greatest speed, tossing his head and laughing for the sheer joy of the ride. Dear Lord, it was good to be alive!

Shaina riding in the other direction, didn't see Travis acting with enthusiastic abandon as he rode the grullas around in circles and then went plunging after them, and breaking wildly into a full run. She kept her mount's head straight on, heading for the ranch, the sky in the west rosy, slowly, slowly darkening. Finally she reached her destination and Deanna greeted her with a happy smile. "It's good to see you," she said. "Can you come in for a cup of coffee and chat for a while?"

"No, not now, Deanna." She looked at the blond woman through the screen door.

Deanna came out onto the porch and closed it slowly, saying, "What's wrong?"

Nervously Shaina said, "Nothing. I—I'm just looking for Travis Cordell. I would have coffee, but—" She glanced over her shoulder at the setting sun—"it's going to be dark soon, and I'd better find Travis, say what I have to say and get going." She shivered, thinking about having to ride back through the inky woods.

"Maybe I can give him your message. But, Shaina, why don't you stay the night and give it to him yourself? You won't make it back to my parents' house before dark. You can stay right down the hall from me." Deanna grinned. "You'll be safe, not to worry."

"Oh . . . I'm not afraid of Travis, if that's what you're thinking."

"Miah is not here." Deanna lifted a blond eyebrow, wondering if that could be bothering Shaina.

"I am not afraid of *her*, either!" Shaina said with a laugh, and Deanna joined in.

"If it's Travis you're after," Deanna said, "you might find him with Silvanus."

"The cook?"

"Well, he's not really the cook. I do most of the cooking. Silvanus usually does it for Travis when I'm gone. No, Silvanus is the cowboy. You'll find him, just follow," Deanna simply shrugged, "the cows."

"What does this Silvanus look like?" Shaina asked. "In case I can't find him with the cows."

"Well," Deanna began matter-of-factly, "he's rangy and lean and hard from life in the saddle — and kind of still-faced, with keen blue eyes . . . well, you can see for yourself, for there he is, just going into the feed barn with Sam's little boy. If you hurry you might be able to catch him."

The silver-blond woman watched her friend the schoolteacher head toward the barn, and then her violet eyes went skittering off as she wondered what was keeping Jack. He'd gone up to his cabin several days before to bring some things up there. Then he was supposed to come back for her. He said when he returned he would bring the preacher . . . And that's how Jack Nolan had asked Deanna to marry him. She, of course, had said yes.

Shaina stopped dead in her tracks, mesmerized by a deep, soothing voice. A blush crept up her neck . . . The man was describing the sex and age of cattle to someone, probably the little boy she'd seen the tall, rangy man come in here with. Was she ever glad they couldn't see her! She turned and put her back against the stacks of sweet-smelling hay and waited, hoping that Travis would come in before long. She would wait and ask the cowboy where Travis could be.

Before long, the boy confused at Silvanus's patient and discreet anatomical descriptions of bulls and cows, glanced over his shoulder and then back to Silvanus.

"Someone's here to see you, Sil." His voice lowered to a whisper. "I saw the lady come in a few minutes ago."

"Oh? What could she want with me?" Silvanus's eyes twinkled.

Spotting Roux just then out the window riding to the green hills, Sonny took off like a shot and went to fetch his big pony.

Silvanus shook his graying head and chuckled. Then he remembered something about a "lady" being there.

"Howdy there, miss." He watched as the young woman came closer. "What can I help you wi—" His smile faded.

Shaina blinked in surprised shock. Why the man

204

startled her so she couldn't say. There was something about him —

Silvanus stared. This young woman . . . Dear Lord, so much like his Ellie. He knew he was being rude, but he couldn't help staring at her.

Shaina continued staring, too, mesmerized by eyes so much like her own. Who is this man? she wondered with a feeling of utter bewilderment. Was she supposed to remember him from somewhere? What was this strange emotion she felt?

The seasoned cowboy felt himself being transported back about nineteen years. Him and his ladylove had been lying in a field of summer clover and wild-flowers. Kansas. The sun was hot, shining through the tall grass that hid them from prying eyes. They had just finished making love and Ellie turned to him with worshipful love shining in her beautiful eyes, blue, deep blue just like his own . . . and this here young woman's. Dear God, this was like being with Ellie. Looking into her face all over again.

Tears smarted Silvanus's eyes. "God in heaven," he groaned. "Who the hell are you? Where did you come from?"

For several more moments Shaina couldn't find her voice to answer him. Softly she finally said, "I — I'm Shaina Hill." Her voice almost cracked, "The school-teacher." She licked dry lips. "You must be Silvanus?"

"Hill?"

With a hand to her hot cheek, Shaina backed slowly away. "Yes . . . Hill."

The man's eyes turned to blue fire as he heard the name and he put his back to Shaina and snarled, "This can't be. Go from here . . . *Go on!"*

"I —"

"Go on!!" he shouted.

What was wrong? Shaina stumbled backward a step. Then she whirled about and ran, ran as fast as she could to where she'd tied up Spotted Bird. Swiftly she mounted Spotted Bird and spun the alarmed mare out of the big yard. With thunder beneath the pony's hooves, the wind tearing at Shaina's long hair, the two flew with total abandon.

At the hard, insistent driving, the Indian pony gave it all her heart had, her slender legs a fast white blur against the green beneath her pounding hooves. She was unaware of the human tears splashing against her spotted hide.

Travis rode slowly through the misted moonlit night. He had watched the sky growing gray and purple and then dark. The black mountain range, which had looked close enough to ride to before dark, was three miles distant. But he rode toward it anyway, for all his work was done and he hadn't anything to do for the weekend. He had ceased his visits to Seattle during the weekend to take one of the several "Scarlets" there to bed. Besides, Deanna had said Shaina was looking for him and he wondered what she wanted to see him about.

Shaina had reached the foot of the mountain; she had ridden forever, it seemed. Moonlight found her and Spotted Bird where they rested, and Shaina dismounted, walking slowly until the tight muscles in

206

her legs relaxed. Spotted Bird wandered at her will, not going far from her mistress.

How beautiful is the night here, Shaina thought, feeling free from all care. She wouldn't think of anything, just enjoy the moonlit night, she decided.

Soon, though, she became restless and decided to start her return to the ranch house. As she was about to mount Spotted Bird she saw a rider coming toward her. The easy way he rode, everything about him, told her the rider was Travis Cordell. She waited until he came up to her, and then she mounted the mare so that she was almost eye level to him.

He tipped his Stetson, saying, "Nice night for a moonlit ride."

"Yes," she answered shakily. "It is."

"I'm going to Thunder Falls, want to come along?"

Wistfully Shaina smiled. "Yes," she said. "I do."

Shaina chose not to mention Silvanus, for she didn't want to spoil the enchanted evening by discussing the disturbing scene in the barn. She would, however, speak to him about it at a later date.

The two horses rode side by side in silence, and with the moon a round yellow disk behind them they rode across the prairie, through the woods, and then, finally, two hours later, they came to Thunder Falls.

As before, Shaina was awed by the beauty of the falls, but even more so this moonlit night. The mood was heightened by the mere presence of Travis.

"It's beautiful," she said as she had when she'd first seen the falls with Giles. "It simply takes my breath away."

"I know what you mean," he said.

"I'd like to rename this river," she said cryptically.

207

"What would you name it?" He canted his head sideways.

"Paradise River."

"I like that." He smiled warmly, the moon reflected yellow-green in his eyes. "Would you like to go below?"

"Oh yes, I've never been down there."

"Well, come on, you're in for the time of your life."

Shaina knew it was true, for with the thundering roar of the waterfall becoming louder as they made their descent, her excitement grew apace with the force of the pounding and spewing of the falls. When they reached the rocky basin below, she held her breath as the force of the falls beat the water and raised billows of foam which blew upward into a soft moonlit-hued mist.

They left the tangled trail and were suddenly at the bottom of the falls. Travis dismounted at once, letting Dice go, and Shaina did the same with Spotted Bird. Both stood quietly as the horses roamed at their will.

Shaina walked around the small area, delighting in the early summer night and Travis's presence. There was a misty, moonlit rainbow that spanned the area, arcing from one grouping of boulders to another. She bent down, scooping water into her palm and smiling when the moonlight and starlight touched the water in her hand and made it sparkle like precious gemstones.

"It's like diamonds—or gold," Shaina remarked, letting the water trickle between her slim fingers.

He took her hand and kissed it, murmuring, "Like moondust spilling from the hand of Venus."

"The water feels good."

"It's warm enough for a swim." His voice was cool

208

and clear. His eyes, luminous and bright, caught hers and held them. A long, searching exchange built tension until they both trembled from the intensity of the look. "Would you like to?" He smiled, then said, "Swim, I mean."

Shaina hesitated only a moment before she touched her hand to her dress's bodice and merely nodded.

His eyes were glowing in the moonlight, as he murmured, "Take everything off then."

Shaina's eyes glowed as she walked around a huge boulder to do as he asked. When her silken skin was exposed, Shaina shivered at the delicious feel of the cooler air wrapping around her exposed flesh. It wasn't long before her blood began to warm, however, as she anticipated the scene to come.

By the time Shaina had all her clothes off, Travis was already in the water. Shyly, she walked into the bubbles of frothy white and waded up to her waist. Moonlight from the star-fired heavens glistened on her glorious nakedness, and Travis knew he'd never seen a vision as beautiful and golden as Shaina. His glance dropped to her mouth, and he knew, too, he'd never felt so tumultuous a feeling for anyone.

Travis moved closer, his eyes shining as they devoured her lovely breasts, her tapering torso, her legs long and shapely. As Shaina watched Travis approach, thunderbolts of emotion shot across her nerves and settled in her stomach. She wanted him, desperately.

When he took her in his arms, Shaina melted against him desiring to get as close as she could. In a deep, hungry kiss, Travis's mouth moved over Shaina's, and when he lifted his head, Shaina pulled back and surprised him by diving into the water.

Travis grinned, watching his glorious mermaid slip away. He plunged into the moonlit water after her, and they swam about in the rocky cove where the gentlest captured water flowed about them, keeping out of the dangerous area that could sweep them into the river's strong current without a moment's notice.

"Ohhh!" Shaina screeched when Travis caught at her leg and began to yank downward. "Travis, let go, I'll drown!"

"No, you won't." He scissored his legs in the water, moving closer to her wonderfully slippery body. "I'll never let anything happen to you, Shaina."

"Oh Travis," she moaned, feeling his fingers sliding along her rib cage and then capturing the whole of a full, rounded breast in his palm.

The sensation was totally erotic, sending currents of desire shooting through her. The strong fingers massaged the slippery bud, and before Shaina knew what would come next, Travis bent his water-slicked head and took the taut peak into his mouth and rolled it between his tongue and lips. The universe spun! Shaina's head was flung back as Travis did his magic to her quivering flesh, until the flame licking at her became a raging fire.

Travis felt the heat of her desire pulling him and his eyes darkened with amorous emotion. The warm breeze skipped enticingly across the water and tangled Shaina's red-gold hair. Travis looked at her, thinking he had never seen anything quite so beautiful and tempting.

"Shaina," Travis said huskily in her ear, lifting her from the water so that only her toes were skimming the surface as he carried her to the bank and laid her upon the soft, wet moss that grew there at the water's edge.

Lying on her back, Shaina gazed dreamily into Travis's hard, rugged face. "Travis, I want . . ." she began in a throaty purr, but could not finish her question. She wanted him to marry her! How was she going to say it?

"You want—*what,* Shaina?"

"I don't know where to begin, Travis."

"You were looking for me this afternoon, weren't you?"

"Yes." Her voice was small and soft.

Caressing her hip now, Travis asked, *"Why,* Shaina, why were you looking for me?"

She couldn't do it! She couldn't just ask Travis Gordell to marry her. He might turn her down! How humiliated she would be if that happened.

Shaina had to think of something—and fast! It might sound silly, but she had to do it in order to save some part of her dignity. It would kill her if he replied that all he wanted was her body. For a space she just gazed up into his ruggedly handsome face, and then his eyebrows rose inquiringly.

"I do believe you were about to ask me something?" he said.

A smile that was sensuously sweet broke out on Shaina's moon-gilded face. "I wanted you to help get me something . . ."

"Shaina, don't let it hang like that. Tell me, lady, what is it you want from me."

"I—I've always wanted a red . . . dress." *Oh what a coward she was!*

With a chuckle, Travis echoed, "A red dress." he

211

smiled tenderly. He didn't believe her for a moment, that this was the question she'd been about to ask. He went along with her, though, saying, "I'll get you one then."

"Well then," Shaina began tentatively, "what would you want in return, Travis Cordell?"

"You, Shaina, you in it." His hand tangled in her hair. "Marry me!"

Shaina stared at him, her mouth agape. Had she heard him correctly? "Travis?"

"Damn it, I said, Will you marry me?"

Shaina looked around in a daze, trying to catch her breath, but before she could do it Travis snatched it away again.

"You can say Yes, or you can say No. But, lady, if you were just going to let me go all the way with you again, you'd better have been ready to say *Yes!*" he growled. "I'm a bit old-fangled, and the woman I marry has to be high-principled as well."

A slow, disbelieving smile broke out on her face. "You had planned to ask me to marry you this night?"

"Yes," he said, smoothing the hair back from her temple with a wet hand that was gentle in its caress.

She gazed into his handsome face as if she couldn't get enough of looking at him. He bent to get closer to her. An ever-tightening knot was growing in her belly as his musky, sensual odor assailed her senses. She heard her own voice, and it was a sultry whisper. "Travis, I have to tell you the truth. I—I was going to ask *you* to marry me. But I was a coward, and that's why I asked you for the red dress."

"I have to confess that I became aware of that, Shaina."

Shaina's flushed face turned the same bright shade as her hair and Travis at once saw her distress, attempting to ease it somewhat by bantering with her.

"Have you changed your mind?"

"No. I still want you to marry me!"

"You'll wear the red dress on our wedding night — only for me, lady."

Delicious shock flew through her, and this time she could only stare, wordlessly, wondrously happy as his face lowered to claim her lips in a delicious kiss full of fire. Her lips were the color of bloodred roses, fully blossomed and dew-kissed, when at length he finally released her from the firm pressure of his mouth and thrusting tongue. Her glorious mane of hair was spread all around her as he gazed down, captivated by her womanly splendor. With his hand spread beneath her buttocks, he lifted her body to press its soft contours against his harder ones.

There was a fine mist hanging over their paradise river, giving enchantment to the moonlit night and a pearly luminescence to the lovers themselves.

Sweetly tortured by his erotic movements, Shaina emboldened herself to reach around his hips and, cupping the rippling, muscled flesh, she pulled him into a strong embrace. His back arched above her, Travis bent down to take a shell-pink nipple into his mouth which he swirled his tongue about, teasing, lapping, and then sucking like a bee takes sweet nectar from a tempting bud.

The indigo shadows of night deepened. The moon ripened like a melon ready to burst, reflected in the waters which softly made wistful, enchanting music for the lovers. Their hidden love nest was transformed

213

into rapture's haven. Their hands drifted and glided over each other's dew-kissed bodies. There was only one part of Travis Shaina had yet to explore, and when her slim fingers closed shamelessly around his swollen manhood, Travis groaned and sucked in his breath. He could feel the blood pounding in his ears, and the heat surging through his hard, wet body.

"I am going to die of pleasure before I ever make love to you," he said, sliding his fingers to the apex of her thighs where he tenderly probed after parting the soft auburn curls. He found Shaina's glorious paradise wet in readiness for the entry of his swollen shaft of desire. For a moment he gazed into her love-flushed face as he ran his palm along her flat stomach. He murmured his delight when she curled a hand at the nape of his neck and pulled his face to hers.

The flick of her small tongue inside his lips was more than he could take, and he rose above her, poised for a moment as he gently spread her legs and eased between. Sweat-slick bodies merged into one. The sexual tension had been building for many days, and within moments of coming together they exploded into a stunning ecstasy that seemed to go on and on, whirling them together to the farthest reaches of bliss.

Contented and pleasured beyond words, Travis lay beside his love, knowing what had been missing all these years. He had been searching for *Shaina*. She was his shining star. She was the completion of Travis Cordell.

Chapter Twenty-two

Travis and Shaina were married on the fifth of June. Shaina wore a mauve wedding gown with blue-gray seed pearls sewn into the bodice, and after the ceremony she unconventionally donned a floppy, white straw hat with a small veil attached. Later that evening she planned to don the pretty red dress Travis had gone especially to South Prairie to purchase for their wedding night. And Shaina could hardly wait to put it on!

It was a double wedding, for Deanna and Jack became man and wife at the same altar in the First Christian Church at the edge of the woods.

The whole valley had turned out for the double occasion: The Kingswells and their children were at the church, of course; Little Roux in a brand-new yellow dress Deanna had taken from her precious time to stitch for the girl; Jay Ridingbow and his family; many of the ranchhands and their families that lived in the valley. And then there was Graham Hill, sitting with his third cup of spiked punch resting on his knee at the reception at Lazy C.

After an hour or so, Miah came to pick Roux up

and take her to the Indian camp. It was summer vacation for the schoolchildren and the teacher so Travis had promised Roux she could go to the Indian camp to visit her friends. But he didn't like it much when he saw that Miah was riding with three braves, one of them a man he had no liking for. His name was Moon Dog.

The one who stole my horse, Jay Ridingbow was thinking as he watched them ride off with Roux. He turned suddenly to Travis Cordell's profile, saying quite boldly, "I wish to ride with them."

Travis, handsome in dress-black and white shirt, slowly turned to face the tall lad. "Go ahead. Roux would like your company. She speaks of you often."

"She does?" Jay's eyes were a brighter gold, if that could be possible.

"Yeah. But remember, she's just a little girl."

"You don't trust me," Jay said.

"I don't know you very well."

"Well, I am saying you can trust me."

"I'm glad," was all Travis said as he went back inside to his wedding reception.

What a strange man, Jay was thinking as he ran to the barn and dug out the change of clothing he'd earlier hidden there. Just in case there was the chance he and Roux would go for a ride. He had been disappointed to see her go, but now he could join her, that is, if her mother didn't mind. Roux's mother was not very nice; he had seen the look of interest in her eyes as she had looked him over. But he wanted to be with his little friend Roux, no one else.

Inside the house, Deanna contemplated her friend from across the room, "What's wrong, Shaina?" she asked as she went to sit on the mohair sofa beside Shaina. "You look sad, as if someone's missing."

"I'm all right."

Shaina smiled then as across the huge living room, her new husband, between a tall potted plant and a chatting couple, lifted his glass in a second salute to her. Then she gave her full attention to Deanna as Travis turned to speak with Abner Selby and his rotund wife, who was wearing a black dress and a red hat with many red and green feathers. Shaina almost giggled.

"Well, Mrs. Selby got a laugh anyhow," Deanna said, setting her glass down next to Shaina's half-empty one.

"She's—cute," Shaina said, trying to keep her gaze from roaming around the room in· search of one person in particular.

"We haven't had much time to talk, what with all the wedding preparations these last two weeks." Deanna broke into Shaina's musings. "But something does seem to be bothering you, dear friend."

"Yes," Shaina sighed, "I guess there is."

Again Shaina's and Deanna's conversation was interrupted as Shaina caught Graham grinning at her from the huge punch bowl and she was forced to smile even though she didn't feel like it. She thought how nice he looked in the new gray suit Travis had picked up for him. That had been so kind of him. Travis had finally come to like Graham. Well, at least *tolerate* his presence, for Graham was like a pesky fly in the kitchen . . . he wouldn't go away no matter how much you shooed him. She guessed Graham was here to stay. Travis had promised he'd find something for

217

Graham to do, and Graham had looked none too happy at the prospect.

"Shaina, don't keep me waiting," Deanna pressed. "What is bothering you enough to keep you from enjoying your own wedding day?"

"I—Oh, Deanna. It's that man Silvanus."

"Silvanus? What does he have to do with anything?"

"He—he disturbs me somehow. I've been too busy and excited to think much about the man, but he's been in a corner of my mind nonetheless, ever since that day I went out to the barn in search of Travis."

Deanna blinked uncomprehendingly for a moment, then said, "Of course, I remember that day now. That was the first time you met Silvanus Hart?"

"Hart?" Shaina's pulse skipped a beat.

"Yes, that's his last name. Why, does it bother you or something?"

"It just—Oh, it just makes me feel strange, that's all. Like I've heard it before somewhere."

Deanna placed a hand over her chest, saying, "You could be thinking of 'heart,' honey." She winked over to her smiling husband. "We've sure been doing a lot of thinking about love lately, Lordy!"

A few minutes before Deanna had begun to joke about the matter, Graham had come to stand at the back of the sofa, still nursing a hefty cup of "juice" in hand while most of the guests had already set theirs down. He stiffened at what he heard, but no one was the wiser. That is, except for Travis who'd witnessed Graham Hill's switch from gaiety to red-faced annoyance.

Travis, however, displayed no emotion as he contemplated Graham Hill, but wondered to himself why he kept staring at Shaina like that. There was definitely something about Hill he still didn't trust, and Shaina had been awfully nervous when he gifted the man with the gray suit. He had acted as if it was his due! That must have been what made Shaina nervous, he'd thought at the time. But now, what was on Shaina's mind? Something preoccupied her thoughts. Maybe she was only anticipating "later" as he was . . . It had been too long!

Aware she was being watched by several people in the crowded room, Shaina lowered her voice. "Silvanus stared at me as if he'd seen a ghost," she went on to tell Deanna. "I don't understand it, Deanna, he shouted at me to get away from him. It was as if he couldn't stand the sight of me. I ran from the barn and was so distraught that I rode blind for hours."

Shaina smiled wistfully next. "That's when Travis rode out of the moonlight . . . and swept me off my feet. Whew! That day I'll never forget as long as I live, it holds so many conflicting memories for me, so . . . bittersweet."

"Well, honey, I hope you find out what's troubling Silvanus someday." Deanna patted Shaina's arm, and began to rise from the sofa. "It's time to go, Jack's taking me up to the cabin. I've never been there before." Deanna's crystal eyes twinkled merrily as she shrugged. "He made *me* wait . . . imagine that."

Silvanus Hart watched from the stand of tall, redolent cedars as the happy wedding party and its followers, tossing handfuls of rice, had burst from the tall doors of the little ivy-covered church.

With all his might Silvanus resisted going over there to wish the newlyweds well.

Silvanus could hear the taller blond, Deanna, laughing, but Silvanus's misted eyes were all for the daintier bride Shaina. His eyes burned and his throat contracted. His heartstrings were pulled to the breaking point.

Ducking beneath a branch, Silvanus gave his grulla a boot in the side and rode swiftly through the forest, meaning to make it back to the Lazy C before anyone else. He rode fast to the high country and, once there, he swung down off his grulla, his spurs jangling, and picked up his gear and took off for the hills.

Silvanus Hart wanted to be alone with his memories.

Shaina and Travis were alone in the house finally— *almost* alone, for Graham had fallen sound asleep on the sofa—and Shaina hurriedly stepped out of the wedding gown, took a quick bath, then slipped into the sexy little red dress. Travis had made sure all their guests lingering outside in the yard had departed and was now himself in the kitchen having coffee, giving Shaina time to prepare herself for him.

Her hair she swept up from her face in a fat, charming topknot and left a few tendrils hugging either side of her delightfully pink face. Her strawberry blond hair contrasted delightfully with the slinky dress, exactly the effect she'd been seeking. Eleanora used to say red would make Shaina's hair appear more alive and stunning. She was correct, if

Travis's reaction was any proof when he stepped into the bedroom a moment later. With admiration and delight on his face he said with a low whistle, "You are a temptress in that red dress." He motioned for her to come sit on his lap. "The color is very becoming on you, love. But don't go getting any ideas about wearing this little number anywhere except when we're alone in the house, or our bedroom. This is *our* dress."

"Oh?" Shaina lifted a silky eyebrow. "Are you going to wear it, too, my darling husband?"

Travis smiled. "Red, huh?" he said. "Is there a little bit of a 'scarlet' in you somewhere, honey?"

"Oh, really, Travis!" she said indignantly, then, playing with the coarse curls that made a black clover leaf on his chest, she asked, "Have you been with many women, Travis?"

He gave her a rouguish look. "A few. But not any since you came into my life. And that's the honest to God truth."

Without notice, Travis shot up from the deep armchair, making Shaina think he was dropping her, but then his arm reached out to scoop her up. One arm was supporting her back, the other hand went to cup her saucy buttocks. Shaina sighed languidly, already tearing his shirt-sleeve from one broad shoulder to feel the corded muscle there.

Once he had placed her in the middle of his huge mahogany-poster bed, he reached for a slim hand and, guiding her fingers, he brought her to him. Shaina sucked in her breath at his eagerness. Travis groaned deeply when Shaina met his husbandly demand, her slim fingers learning the long, hard shape

221

of him.

Shaina couldn't speak. She was enthralled with the male power she held in one small hand. Bending over, she tentatively touched her pink tongue to him until he halted her motions so that he could remove the precious red dress, then after scattering their clothes about the bed, he brought his lips to her hair.

He touched her everywhere and she tingled in each of those places, responding every time with a quick intake of breath. Travis's heart was beating furiously as he moved to fondle her full, tempting breasts once again. He cupped one in each hand and caught the lustrous curls of her hair in between, driving Shaina mad with want.

Travis's eager hands clutched Shaina's trim waist and he rhythmically pulled her to him then away. And then he was bending over her to suck on one taut breast peak and then the other, while his hand began to guide her legs apart. As his finger moved within her, Shaina cried out that she could not bear this torture anymore.

A small gasp escaped Shaina as Travis's hips settled against hers. "Love me, Travis—love me!"

In moments he was slipping inside her, joining them as man and wife for the first time. From that moment on, their wedding night became irradiated with a kind of magic, sparkling and tangible as motes glittering in a shaft of sunlight.

Travis made love to Shaina very tenderly at first, and then passionately, wildly, ecstatically suspended in love's rapturous joining. In every touch, every caress, embrace, thrust, rhythm, Shaina let him know exactly what she wanted. The excitement built higher and higher, filling each with the fiery splendor of passion as their bodies met in a soul-seizing message that was a sweetly urgent mating.

Again and yet again their bodies shuddered and quaked in ecstasy's sweetest release as the pale, mellow light of moon climbed and flooded the room along with the sprinkled stardust of thousands of huge, twinkling stars.

At last Shaina rose above him, riding with the power in her slender thighs this time. And Travis, he loved every moment of wedded ecstasy . . . there was nothing in the world to compare with this greatest of love's treasures. Her lips parted and his moved over them. They sighed deeply, pressing their slick foreheads together as the sensual oblivion subsided. The velvet-soft night breathed over them, cooling their feverish bodies.

Afterward they lay together, catching their breath, blissfully complete. In the silence of the wondrous night Shaina could feel the strong, steady beat of his heart against her back, and the secure rise and fall of his breathing. A comforting warmth spread slowly through her exhausted body. He was no longer a stranger, she thought, he was her husband, her lover.

Chapter Twenty-three

The hoof marks of three horses showed in the dewy, morning grass. Up ahead sat the riders on those three piebald horses. They were gazing toward the high country, looking across the wildflower-dotted valley up the vast forest with its ridgy steps.

"Reckon we'll find him?" Vinny Sloan asked his sidekick. From his thin, hard face he spat a stream of brown juice, then swiped the back of his arm across his chin.

The sun struck across a broad, dumbstruck face. "Wal . . . I cain't be sure. Could be his daughter's—"

Sloan cut across B.J.'s words, and he shifted in his saddle to look at the third man beside B.J., Joe Creek. This latter was the dangerous one, no man to mess with. Sloan knew it, even though Sloan was spokesman of their threesome.

Joe Creek looked like the devil himself as he drawled, "I hate the sight of your face, Sloan. All I want to do is get that bastard Hill, so me and B.J. can get back to Redmount."

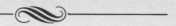

ACCEPT YOUR **FREE GIFT** AND EXPERIENCE MORE OF THE PASSION AND ADVENTURE YOU LIKE IN A HISTORICAL ROMANCE

Zebra Romances are the finest novels of their kind and are written with the adult woman in mind. All of our books are written by authors who really know how to weave tales of romantic adventure in the historical settings you love.

Because our readers tell us these books sell out very fast in the stores, Zebra has made arrangements for you to receive at home the four newest titles published each month. You'll never miss a title and home delivery is so convenient. With your first shipment we'll even send you a FREE Zebra Historical Romance as our gift just for trying our home subscription service. No obligation.

BIG SAVINGS AND **FREE** HOME DELIVERY

Each month, the Zebra Home Subscription Service will send you the four newest titles as soon as they are published. (We ship these books to our subscribers even before we send them to the stores.) You may preview them *Free* for 10 days. If you like them as much as we think you will, you'll pay just $3.50 each and *save $1.80 each month* off the cover price. *AND you'll also get FREE HOME DELIVERY.* There is never a charge for shipping, handling or postage and there is no minimum you must buy. If you decide not to keep any shipment, simply return it within 10 days, no questions asked, and owe nothing.

"I told you he's got a daughter." Sloan's voice rose to a higher pitch. "You can take your revenge out on her. He was diddlin' your wife, and me and B.J. got robbed blind by him. We all want a piece. So what the hell you got against me?"

Snarling through compressed teeth and lips, Joe Creek said, "That bastard's gonna pay for screwing around with Carolyn. What I got against you is you was trying to do the same."

Sloan narrowed his bright blue eyes. "You sure of that?"

"Dead sure."

"Well, I gotta admit Carolyn's a looker. But I never done more than look, Joe. Christ, ain't I been your friend a long time?"

Joe Creek made a gesture before his face as he brushed away a fly, but he refrained from looking at Sloan as he said, "We been at this too long. I'm going to be doing the leading from now on. You—" he turned to glare at Sloan—"keep your mouth shut."

"Why," giggled B.J., "don't you both shut up!"

Vinny Sloan looked over at Joe Creek and relaxed when the dangerously intense Joe cracked a crooked smile and slapped his oafish cousin on the back.

"You're always good for a laugh," Joe said to B.J., "that is why I always take you with when there's some revenge to be taken out on someone's hide—someone whose been messing around with my wife!"

Sloan frowned as he inquired, "You gone after dudes before who done that?"

"Uh huh," B.J. answered for his darker-complected cousin.

"I never knew that," said Sloan.

225

"Now you know."

"Uh huh," B.J. said, nodding at Sloan, "an' you better never mess around with Caro because Joey'll mess your face up." B.J. choked up with laughter, slobbering all over himself. "You should've seen what he done with the last dude who smiled at Caro while she was waiting on him at the Little Big Horn. You wouldn't've like to a seen it, though. Haw-haw, an' then Joey raped that dude's daughter—" But B.J. frowned darkly at his own words.

Joe Creek glowered at his stupid cousin, snarling low, "B.J.! Shut your friggin' mouth."

Silvanus Hart came riding down from the hills, his saddlebags clanking with his gear. He'd been gone the whole weekend, trying to sort things out in his mind. He didn't regret his decision to not join the well-wishers at the reception, though part of him thought maybe he was a fool for not having done so. He'd tried dismissing the memories from his mind, too, but he'd known from the first moment he'd seen the mountains in flower, reminding him of that day with Ellie in the meadow, how little good it would do. Then his frustration and loneliness had festered his insides.

Now Silvanus knew what he must do. He had to face matters head-on. But to tell Shaina Cordell the truth would take the most courage he'd ever had to rustle up in his life. He wasn't all that sure he could do it just yet.

Ah, Shaina must hate me, Silvanus decided, or, if not that, she must really be afraid of me and my temper.

Silvanus did have a temper, and just about every-one at the Lazy C knew it and refrained from goading him. He could joke a lot himself, but he refused to join in when some of the men told dirty ones about women. He had a fair amount of respect for women, and there had been one who'd taught him all about it. His Ellie. He had never married because no one else could fill the empty place in his heart like Ellie had. And—tears smarted his eyes—she'd been another man's wife. He wondered if God could ever forgive him and bless him with happiness once again, for he sure had been miserable all these years.

"Howdy."

Silvanus was not surprised very easily, but this time, with the seriousness of his thoughts, he jumped a little when the friendly voice reached him. He tipped up the brim of his hat and saw three riders coming toward him.

"Can I help you?" Silvanus said with utter calm.

"Sure can," the one with the thin, smiling face answered. "Me and my friends here," Vinny Sloan began, "we're looking for some work. Your boss hiring?"

B.J. loosed a chuckle while the cowboy contem-plated them in silence. "Mebbee he's the boss hisself."

"No," Silvanus said, his keen eyes appraising the threesome. "I'm not the boss." He smiled then, re-lieved to have something other to do than worry himself sick. "But I do the hiring."

"When do we start?" Joe Creek butted in, wedging his mount in between Sloan's and the cowboy's.

Silvanus was a little taken aback with this one's effrontery. "As soon as you see Travis Cordell." He gave the man a look out of the corner of his eye.

"Wal," B.J. snorted, leaning over his mount in order to see the cowboy. "Who's he?"

"The boss."

B.J. fell back as the three rode on ahead of him, and he scratched his head beneath his scruffy hat. "He ain't the boss, but he does the hirin', but we gotta see the boss now. Uh huh . . . I guess that's right," he said to himself, then lit out after the others.

Travis leaned back in his chair as he gave a hard appraisal to the three rough dudes standing before his desk. He rose and came around to the side of his desk, then walked over to the window, then back to his chair again. He stood beside it.

"You boys better not have any manure on your boots." His eyes narrowed. "If you do, you'll get thrown out by the worn part of your pants."

"That'd be right here," B.J. blurted, directing a finger around to the baggy section of his blue jeans.

"For a big man, ah, Billy Joe, was it?"

"Yeah," B.J. said, frowning at his cousin for disclosing his secret.

"For a big man," Travis went on, "you sure don't fill the seat of your pants out very well."

"His brain's empty, too," Vinny Sloan drawled, his bright eyes lit with sarcastic humor.

B.J. held up one stubby finger, opened his mouth to say something, and then zipped it up again.

In the following silence, B.J. looked from Joe Creek to Vinny Sloan and then back again to Joe.

Travis measured the drifters with a cool, appraising

look as he said, "You got horses, all three of you?"

"Uh-huh," B.J. answered quickly. "We brought 'em in with us by riverboat, all the way from — *Oof!*" He looked at his cousin, about to ask him why he went and kicked him when the dark warning zipped up his mouth again.

Travis's eyes shifted from one man to the other. "We got men working here at the Lazy C from as far away as Texas. But I'll warn each of you, if you are running from anything, and I get wind of it, I'll take you in myself. No wanted men working here, understand?" He said this emphatically.

"Yeah."

"Yup."

"Uh-huh."

"Good. Now get your asses to work."

"Keep workin'," Sloan ordered B.J., "that's the boss-man making rounds this time."

"Shoot," B.J. huffed, "I ain't lightnin', ya know."

"Yeah," Joe drawled, pausing to look up for only a moment. "What's he got us shoveling this crap out of the barn for?"

"Yeah, how come?" said B.J. "I don't like shovelin' turds."

"It's a start," Sloan muttered out of the side of his mouth. We'll be moving up, and then we can get a better look around and find Graham."

"I saw him."

Sloan went still, looking steadily at Joe Creek. "You *what?* Why didn't you tell us?"

"Didn't have the chance till now, not with all those

cowpushers rubbing elbows with us in the bunkhouse. Hell, they're all watching us like we're criminals or something. Don't look now, but there's one of them now."

"He's with the boss," hissed B.J. as he leaned into his smelly task. "Sheesh, he's an old coot, ain't he?"

"Shut your mouth, lump-head," Sloan ordered B.J., and then his body received a jolt as a beautiful woman rode into view.

B.J. glanced up. "Holy ba—"

"No," Joe said, impaling his rotund cousin with his dark eyes. "Don't say a word."

But Joe, as he shoveled toward the dung heap, kept the image of the fiery blonde. It was as if his mind had taken a picture of her in that fleeting space of time when he'd feasted his gaze on her. The memory of Carolyn was fast dimming for Joe.

Shaina reined Spotted Bird up alongside her husband's mount, greeting Noah Starr cheerfully first and then pressing Travis's arm lightly. Her smoky blue eyes were shining, for she remembered the night before, and the night before, and the night before . . . She was so full of love for Travis she was bursting with it!

"Morning, blue eyes," murmured Travis, leaning over to buss her on the nose and entwine his fingers with her slim ones.

Color crept into old Noah's face and his glance fell away from the lovers. "Sunny mornin', ain't it," he muttered to himself, looking out of the corner of his eye to see the couple still rubbing noses and holding hands. From the distant blacksmith shed there came the sound of the ringing anvil. "Guess I'll mosey along. See you later, folks."

"Oh." Shaina glanced up. "Oh yes, Noah, see you later, dear."

Again Noah's face turned red, and as he turned he muttered, "Awww," and went trotting away on Quawpaw.

As Noah rode toward the blacksmith shed, he passed Silvanus going in the opposite direction.

"Mornin,' Sil," said Noah, tipping his scruffy hat.

"Morning."

Then Silvanus almost pulled up, for he had spied Shaina on the other side of Travis. He hadn't seen her at first, and he'd been avoiding her for as long as he could, but now it looked as though he'd have to face her—the boss had seen him already.

"Morning, Travis," Silvanus tipped his hat. "Missus."

Shaina went absolutely rigid and her heart pounded up in her throat, but when Travis spun back to her, she only smiled up into his eyes.

"Travis," Silvanus began, not looking at Shaina, "one of the cowpokes got stepped on, and Doc's not here."

"Is it bad?"

"Foot's crushed."

"Oh." Shaina felt embarrassed for her soft exclamation and turned away to stare at the three new hired hands shoveling out the red barn. She started to frown.

"I'll see you later," Travis said, his voice deeply husky. "At the house."

To Silvanus, Travis said, "Let's ride!"

Watching them go, Shaina felt riddled with conflict-

231

ing emotions, and a chill rippled through her. Who *is* that man? There had been a wealth of meaning in his deep blue eyes—but what was it all about? Why did he always affect her in such a strange way? She'd felt she had also affected him quite strongly both times they'd met.

"Shainy!"

Shaken from her troubled musings, Shaina turned to see Graham sauntering toward her. Then all at once her eyes flew to the three new men. The strangest look, in that instant, had come over all four men's faces, even Graham's.

The stares they all gave each other made Shaina go stone cold from head to foot. Especially when the three turned collectively to look at her.

Chapter Twenty-four

They had made love several times, and Shaina thought each time more wonderful than the last.

Travis rolled his head on the pillow, fastening his smoldering green eyes on hers. He murmured huskily, "You always let your feelings show in your whole body, Shaina. You did it when we first became aquainted, you do it especially when we make love, and this morning you were feeling something you were powerless to control. Your body went stiff all over. I felt it."

"Travis please," Shaina rolled away from him, part of her not wanting to talk about what was bothering her — another part begging for release.

Travis stared for a moment at the shifting red rays of lowering sun moving across their bed, then took hold of her shoulder.

"Shaina, I know something is wrong."

"It's Silvanus," she finally blurted, trying to hug her shoulders and move away from Travis.

"Silvanus? My best man?" Travis shook his head. "I've always trusted him. What is it? He hasn't said or done anything I'd be angry about, has he?"

"He . . . he doesn't like me, Travis," Shaina said ever so softly.

Travis's eyes flickered over Shaina's naked back, and then he found himself frowning. "Shaina," he said and pulled her around to face him. "He said something to you, didn't he?"

"Yes."

"What was it?"

"I can't tell you."

"Of course you can. We're married now, and you can trust me to do the right thing."

"You won't fire Silvanus?"

"No." He contemplated the curves of her naked breasts, his eyes feasting hungrily once again. "It depends," he said with a change of mind.

Shaina's heart fluttered and she swallowed hard. Oh, why did she have to allow Travis to read her emotions so well? He saw everything there was to see in her face. It was because they were so close, she told herself.

Travis brought her arms up high, above her head, and bend to suckle the tip of a rosy breast. Shaina squirmed, the thrust of her chest filling his mouth with a little more of the delicious treat.

He kept up the torment, murmuring, "M—m—m, this is good. I could eat these little red cherries forever."

Shaina could feel the pulse fluttering in her throat as he slid his tongue down her rib cage, her waist, paused at her navel to look up at her.

"What are you doing?" she rasped lightly.

A black wave fell over Travis's forehead and he tossed it back with a jerk of his head as he said in a deeply husky voice, "Something I haven't done to you yet."

Naive though she was, Shaina had a pretty good idea where his travels would take him. "You wouldn't."

"Yes," he laughed warningly. "I would."

"I'll be embarrassed," she blurted, trying not to look into his burning green eyes.

"Let's give it a try."

"No!" Mortified, Shaina bent the pillow over to hide her red face. *"Oh Travis!"* she giggled "No, no, don't do that!"

Shaina gaped wide-eyed at the ceiling while Travis had his way with her body. His fingers were sliding up her belly, but at the moment his tongue made forbidden contact, a knife of hot fire shot through her and sent coils of burning sweetness throughout her body. As he worked his magic, Shaina's fingers went automatically into his hair and grasped him closer. He moved with rhythmic caresses and soon Shaina was spinning far from earth into a galaxy where only ecstasy reigned. Then it all came to an abrupt halt as he moved away from her and released her suddenly. She experienced a deep disappointment.

"Travis?"

He was seated on the edge of the bed, his back to her. His hair was dark, burnished fire in the sunset which had intruded on the privacy of their bedroom.

Shaina's hair spilled gloriously over one shoulder as she moved onto her knees and came up behind Travis on the bed. "It was wonderful, Travis, why did you stop?" Her voice was shaky, but she couldn't control it.

"Don't ever keep anything from me, Shaina."

"Is that why you stopped loving me, because you were angry suddenly?"

"That's right."

"That's mean, Travis."

"Ah, Shaina." He turned to pull her into his rough embrace. "I meant to use it as a lever, but I see now that it was a mistake. Quitting what I was doing was a hell of a lot harder than I'd imagined. I just can't seem to get enough of you, love, and I love the way your soft arms twine about my neck." His voice hardened as he held her away from him. "Shaina, you have got to tell me what is bothering you. Jesus, love, I won't be able to sleep at night. Are you sure it's only Silvanus?"

"No, I'm not sure."

"What is it then?"

"I have a feeling . . . of danger surrounding us."

"What do you mean?"

"For one thing, it's those three men you hired yesterday."

"What about them?"

"I don't like their looks."

Travis snorted through his nose. "That would be a helluva way to run a ranch, Shaina, if every time you don't like the looks of one of my men, I run them off. Is that what's bothering you about Silvanus, you don't like his looks?"

Travis had pulled Shaina against his chest, and now he was stroking her velvety head and toying with the thick, rich curls that lay temptingly along the curves of her breasts.

"Tell me, blue eyes, is that all, so we can get on where we left off?"

"Well . . . then there's Graham."

"What? Don't tell me you don't like your own

father's looks?"

"Graham and I never did get along very well, Travis."

"Lord, woman! You sure do have your problems with the everyday characteristics of men. So, tell me, what bothers you about me? Any character flaws that you can see?"

"Oh!" She punched his chest playfully. "You're making fun of me." Shaina didn't know how she could get Travis to understand that there was just something very strange lurking about, something she couldn't put her finger on, but before she could try any further, he shocked her to the core by asking, "Is Graham Hill really your father?"

"I should—hope so."

"You say that as if you aren't all that sure, Shaina."

"Why wouldn't he be my father?" Shaina frowned as she went on, "He's always been my father."

"Something just doesn't seem right! I never hear you and he share moments together like daughter and parent usually do. You two are more like, uh, old friends, and not very good ones at that. Where's your mother, Shaina, what happened to her?"

"She died."

"When?"

"Several years ago."

"How?"

"Travis!" Shaina gasped, rolling her eyes. "What is this, an interrogation?"

"Tell me."

"I don't remember." Shaina shrugged. "She just died, that's all."

"Parents don't 'just die,' Shaina, without your know-

237

ing how and why. My father died climbing mountains. My mother—" He shrugged sadly. "She just went away."

"My mother did that, too."

"What, Shaina?" Travis was surprised. "Your mother 'went away?' "

"Yes."

"I thought you said she died?"

"She did, and then they took her away . . . I guess. I wasn't there when it happened, I was visiting some friends who had some school books they wanted to get rid of. We weren't very close, I only went there because of the books." With a sigh, Shaina paused, then went on, "When I returned home, Eleanora was . . . gone."

"Simply gone. Vanished?"

"Yes." Shaina felt a chill gallop across her back. "Graham said she died. They buried her. That was it." She gulped as she read the seriousness in Travis's rugged countenance. "You don't think she's dead? Eleanora could be—"

"I don't know for sure, Shaina, but the story you just told me is very strange. Seriously strange. A woman doesn't just up and die while her daughter is gone visiting. I suppose it could happen, but somehow something doesn't ring true. Maybe she left, I mean *really* left, of her own accord."

"Walked away from Graham Hill?" No, Shaina thought, Eleanor had loved Graham . . . hadn't she? She'd always thought so. But now Shaina couldn't be certain. What children thought and saw was not always the way it appeared. Graham had always been Eleanora's silver knight, hadn't he?

"Travis, I want to go back."

A warning chill raced along Travis's spine, and he said, "Go back, Shaina, to where?"

"To Mountain Lake. I want to see if Eleanora could have returned there. I, too, believe Graham is holding something from me. Oh, Travis, I mean I won't go right away, maybe in a couple of weeks, if it's all right with you."

"Oh, Jesus, what did I have to go and open my big mouth for."

"Travis?"

"What?" His features tightened and his jade-green eyes narrowed.

"Don't look so funny!" Shaina bounced on her knees. "I think you've hit on something."

Growling, Travis reached for Shaina and pulled her beneath his body. "I'm going to hit on something. We got some unfinished business here, honey."

"Should I get the red dress?" Shaina said with a low giggle.

"No! We won't need it." He slid along her beautifully splendid nakedness, huskily murmuring, "I like you just the way you are."

Her body began to swim in liquid fire as Travis took up where he'd left off, drawing out every measure of passion until, at last, the flame of their hottest desires had been slaked . . . satisfied only until their separate bodies would again cry out for the meeting of their other half to make them whole.

Outside, the moon was well up as the bushes next to the couple's window trembled, and out stepped the fat shape of a man. His eyes grew round as he saw someone else standing there.

"Holy cow, Creek," B.J. hissed, "What the hell you doin' here?"

The dark, evil eyes narrowed as Joe snarled low, "I could ask you the same thing, fat head! Come on," he hissed, "let's get out of here before one of Cordell's watchdogs finds us!"

B.J. grumbled as he followed behind Joe. " I was only lookin' for Roux's kitty cat."

Chapter Twenty-five

The summer thunderstorm moved on and the afternoon was beautiful, the sky bright blue above the big mountain, which toward majestically over the smaller mountains.

After a delicious lunch prepared by Deanna, Shaina seated herself in the big window recess of the living room. She wore a topaz-colored dress, muslin, with eyelet inserts in the bodice. Her shoes were new, too, thanks to her husband's generosity — white and daintily feminine, with tiny buckles.

Shaina and Travis had made the trip to Mountain Lake. The sun had been sinking low in the sky as she looked about the blackened, rubblestrewn clearing where once the Hill house had stood. It hadn't been much of a home, but it had been theirs — Shaina's, Eleanora's, Graham's, and the kids'.

As she had stood there in the orangey ray of sunset, she'd said poignantly to Travis, "There's still no white picket fence."

He had taken her hand and softly asked, "What do you mean?"

"Oh someday I'll tell you. For now I want to remember . . . and to forget." She had known Travis had been eyeing her strangely. "What I mean is, nothing has really changed. Graham is still the same.

241

I am still the same."

"Something has changed," Travis had told her. "Your mother can't be found, and that is something you have to face."

"There's not even a grave," she said, sniffing. "Graham lied, he said they gave her a decent burial. Where is she then, Travis? If she's not buried in the churchyard where *is* she?"

"Well, the pastor did say she could be buried in the unmarked grave, the one we saw at the back of the cemetery."

"But he didn't think so. He didn't even remember anyone by the name of Hill being buried there."

"Shaina, leave it be. If your mother wanted to go away, then you should—"

"Should what?"

"I don't know." Travis shrugged, still holding on to her hand. He smiled and said, "Maybe she was in love with someone else and went to find him. Don't look at me like that, Shaina, that's what could have happened."

"Like your mother went away, you're saying?"

Sighing, Travis said, "Let's forget we ever had this conversation, Shaina. I don't want to talk about the past and my mother."

"But your mother might have been in love with someone else, too, Travis. Did you ever stop and think of it that way?"

"Shaina, let's go home."

And so they had. Two weeks had passed. In that time, Jay Ridingbow had escorted Roux back home. The girl had been full of chatter about her visit to the Songish tribe and their camp. Jay had been welcomed

242

because Roux had said he was her good friend, and even Miah had made the lad feel at home, going so far as to prepare him several delicious meals, but Roux hadn't been very happy when Miah had hugged her friend all the time, saying he was so handsome and big and strong.

For the first time since coming to live at the Lazy C, Shaina was becoming bored and listless, but mostly depressed that there had been no encouraging news of Eleanora in Mountain Lake.

While she gazed out the window, Shaina saw Roux riding by on a fat grulla she'd trained, one that had been wild only three weeks before. She saw Deanna go out to the chicken coop, a new one that Jack had fashioned because his wife had been forever complaining about the rooster leading the hens astray.

And then Shaina spotted Graham and she frowned. For some reason she'd been unable to ask him about Eleanora's disappearance again.

"Why?" Travis had said to her two nights before while they lay close in a tender embrace.

"I just don't want to ask him again; Travis. He told me once already that she's dead."

"Ask him again, love?" he insisted, kissing her forehead, and smoothing back her hair.

"I can't. I think he should come to me about it and be truthful for once in his life. Until then I'll never be able to believe anything he tells me. He told me she died, but he's a liar, Travis, always has been and always will be. He promised my mother a white picket fence, and instead of spending the money for it when he had it, he went out and bought all kinds of foolish contraptions. He liked to play inventor."

243

Shaina was obviously deep in disconcerting thought but finally said, "Graham has become friends with those three strange men you hired several weeks ago. I thought they were only going to work here for a while and then move on."

"One of them did leave for a week."

"Oh? Where did he go? Which one are you talking about?"

"Creek. First he went to fetch his wife Carolyn and bring her—guess he couldn't trust her alone at home."

"Are they going to live here?"

Travis laughed, then said, "Naturally. For a while, anyway, and then maybe they'll move on. Many of the men have their wives living here at the ranch. Most of them build their own cabins with what they earn here, and some of them move on and others take the cabins over. It's like a little community, our Lazy C."

"I know that, Travis."

"What is bothering you then?"

She sighed jaggedly. "I still don't trust those three, Travis. There's something about them . . . even that big fellow B.J. He's always grinning stupidly at me when I go out to meet you on the range."

"So?" he grinned himself. "He's friendly."

Putting her back to him, Shaina snapped, "I don't like them. I wish they'd go away."

"Shaina, for chrissake, I can't let the men go just because of some silly notions you're having about them."

"I'm going back to teach school then, Travis, so I won't have to bear their obnoxious ogling all year long."

244

"And we've been through this before, too. I've already told you, you are not going back to teaching school. Besides, the folks want an older teacher."

"No one said so. And, besides, I'll be nineteen next week." She pouted where he couldn't see her.

He kissed her bare shoulder, murmuring, "Would you like a big birthday party, blue eyes?"

"I don't think so."

"Why?"

"You treat me like a child, Travis Cordell. I'm a full-grown woman and I want to do something besides look pretty as the wealthy rancher's wife. I want to work, too."

"All right, love. I'll send you out to the barn with a pitchfork. After that, you can brand the calves, and then—"

"Travis!" Shaina squeezed her pillow over her head. "I want to be useful!"

Snatching the pillow from her, he leaned over and, kissing the tip of her pert nose, he said, "How much more useful can you get than that?"

"Shoveling dung? You've got to be crazy, Travis. And—and I don't know how to brand calves. But you could teach me."

"Oh," Travis groaned. "I got myself into it again. Tell you what, love, we'll go up to my cabin in the mountains. You've never been there, it's like almost being on top of Big Blue. The boys keep the trail cut through the woods. We'll ride slowly through forests and brush, up and down narrow twisting mountain trails. The cabin is stocked with all we'll need for a week, and we'll bring some more food if you like . . . I know you like to have your midnight snacks. We'll have a good time, and I'll have you all to myself. You'll love it."

Before his last words were out, Shaina was bouncing onto her knees. "When do we go!?"

"Tomorrow, right after branding."

By the time Shaina and Travis arrived at the cabin, the afternoon was well gone. The sun was setting behind the timbered landscape and the magnificent rays shot up through the tallest trees.

The cabin was much larger than Shaina had expected, and it was set into a sizable clearing surrounded by immense trees forming a shelter of awesome splendor. Fragrant flowers dotted the shorter grass around the cabin and everywhere was the delicious odor of pine.

"The trees," Shaina breathed in awe. "So tall." Slowly she gazed up, up, up, and then grew dizzy when she looked down again.

Travis loosed a chuckle.

Shaina was busy with looking around inside the cabin and putting things away while Travis went to take care of the horses and bring them to the sturdy shelter she'd seen outside.

As she worked, Shaina walked in and out of the four rooms, feeling quite at home here. There was the largest room that served as the main living space, a nice size kitchen, a large bedroom with a fireplace made out of the same pink rock as the one in the living area. The room off the kitchen was sizable, too, serving as a pantry.

Travis entered the room just as Shaina screamed.

He saw the object of her distress scurrying across the floor as Shaina watched the tiny brown mouse disappear under the cupboard. As she stared in horror, Travis slowly chuckled.

"That poor mouse," he said. "He must be frightened to death from all the noise we're making."

"Serves him right," Shaina said, her face flushed, her eyes a wildly pretty blue.

Stepping forward, Travis spoke her name under his breath and then everything ceased to exist except their great need of each other. Shaina's arms soon were around him clinging with almost desperate compulsion. She felt the muscles of Travis's back tighten under her caress, heard the mighty beat of his heart and the husky endearments in her ear. The caressing fingers wound in Shaina's hair. He cupped her head and tilted her face up to his and then the voracious hunger in both of them took over.

It was a long time before Shaina broke away from the embrace, but she breathlessly voiced her desire, murmuring, "Oh, Travis, make love to me . . . now." She bent her head and pressed eager lips to the base of Travis's throat above the open collar of his blue shirt.

Travis kissed her back in the same place with such electrifying effect that the breath was crushed out of Shaina and her head automatically fell back on his shoulder.

Travis carried Shaina outside and laid her among the wildflowers and soft grass in front of the house, where no one could see them from the trail even if they stood at the edge of the clearing.

The delicious heat of the sun found them, and

Shaina delighted in the pressure of Travis's body, the deep-green demanding intensity of his eyes burning her senses.

All gentleness was gone, and there was only the fierce, primitive emotion Travis and Shaina shared, making them oblivious of everything but their driving, instinctive need for each other.

Shaina was keenly aware of her power over her man and an exultant feeling gripped her. She gazed up at Travis provocatively between thick tawny lashes as he entered her and began loving her in slow, heavy strokes.

As if through a haze Shaina saw the strength of his throat tense and his eyes fall into a stormy sea of violent desire in passionate response to the graceful liftings of her hips and twinings of her legs.

Later, after they had made love amongst the wildflowers and soft grass at the edge of the clearing, they ate a supper of savory beans and salt pork and apple-flavored muffins that Shaina had prepared. They splashed together, taking turns in and out of a copper hip tub, washing each other and playing with soap like happy children. Then they lazed on the sofa, watching a small fire growing in the fireplace. It was cool up here so high in the mountains, and it felt so good to be warm as toast and cozy.

"Let's make love again," Travis murmured huskily into Shaina's ear. "I want you."

"Oh, God," Shaina blushed, giggling, "I'll have bruises on top of bruises."

"Love bruises," Travis purred like a huge male cat.

Shaina melted into Travis, and returned kiss for kiss, moving in time with the sensual quest of his fingers until she was quivering with the wondrous first release.

"Let's go onto the rug in front of the fireplace." He lifted her, still moist and trembling, and gooseflesh rose as Shaina's bare back came in contact with the hairs of the rug. But her skin soon smoothed out as Travis warmed and caressed her. Travis's hand worshipped the lovely body of his wife, burnished by firelight and flushed with the heat of her passion. With feline grace, Shaina lifted and arched her back, giving over the rosy nipple into Travis's mouth and pushing her fingers into the blue-black shadows of his thick hair. Shaina arched then as he buried himself within her silken sheath with his swollen, thrusting manhood.

A glorious passion shot up through Shaina as his body joined fully with hers and she raised to meet his powerful thrust.

"Travis!"

"Shaina, love!"

She arched up against him then and together they were consumed by the wild rapture that engulfed them as they fused into one joyful being.

The lovers tumbled into a golden afterglow which put them to sleep with the most potent of passion's wines. In the early morning hours they awoke and stumbled with arms wrapped about each other into the big bedroom and slept like two worn-out soldiers dead to the world.

Roseate fingers of dawn crept into the room and awoke Shaina. She could smell coffee brewing and she stretched deliciously, then grimaced as she felt the soreness from lovemaking all over her body.

Travis chuckled from where he stood leaning against the doorjamb. "Sore in places you didn't even know you had, huh, blue eyes?"

Shaina rolled over and peeked at him. "I didn't know love could be so uncomfortable at times."

"Well," Travis grinned, "when you make love as often as we have in the last several days, you're bound to feel some discomfort. It will go away"—he chuckled—"after we do it again."

Shaina gathered the pillow in both hands and tossed it at Travis's head. His laugh turned to a frown as he put his finger to her love-bruised lips. Shaina tilted her head, studying his eyes that were flickering with something that caused a chill to prickle her scalp. Very quickly he said to her, "Go get dressed, Shaina."

"I don't under—"

"Do *as* I say. And dress quickly."

"Is—" she gulped, her eyes big in her head. "Is something wrong?"

"I'm not sure, love. I heard something, and the boys wouldn't be coming up here because they know we wanted to spend some time alone."

"Indians?"

"Don't look so scared. It might be nothing." He gave her a pat on her rump, growling, "Go get dressed. Now."

Backing up almost all the way across the room, Shaina whirled about when she bumped into a table and, clutching the clay pot with its arrangement of dried flowers, she set it aright and hurried to do as he'd asked.

As Travis listened at the front door, all he could hear was the murmuring of the stream on its slow fall from the mountain reaches. He squinted as a small bird landed on a porch chair, nervously twitching its bright blue feathers and looked from the bird to the edge of the clearing, scanning the circle of fragrant pines.

Nothing.

"Travis?"

He jumped and spun on her, swearing, "Shaina, don't ever come up behind me like that again!"

"Well!" Shaina put a shoulder to him and whirled to go back inside. "You're a bear this morning."

Travis followed Shaina back to the bedroom where she'd gone to pout, flouncing on the bed. She kept her face averted.

Then, Shaina frowned, looking alarmed.

"What's wrong with you now?" Travis threw his arms wide as tension swept over him for no good reason he could name.

"Travis—" Shaina stood up, her pupils dilated. "I smell smoke!"

Travis stiffened. "Smoke?" Then he relaxed. "Of course you do. I put some wood in the stove to cook you breakfast, love." Chucking her under the chin, he smiled tenderly and shook his head.

"Travis . . . "

Then he caught the terror in her eyes and he grabbed her shoulders, grinding out, "Now what the hell is wrong? Did you see an Indian outside the window? Shaina, for Godsake, say something."

"T-Tr—" This time Shaina couldn't speak; she only pointed to something behind him.

251

The overpowering odor of smoke reached them both then.

He spun about on his heel, swearing. "The house is on fire!"

Grabbing Shaina's hand, Travis pulled her from the bedroom and out into the living room where tall flames were already lapping at the structure and beginning to consume the place.

The mountain cabin was going fast, and Travis stood for a moment shaking his head at the waste. "I'll never get this fire out, Shaina. The stream is too far and we'd need an army to put it out!"

"Travis, don't stand around! Let's get out of here!"

Travis grabbed Shaina's hand again, and the two of them ran outside.

Four shots rang out in rapid succession striking the edge of the door, smashing windows and dancing from he porch floor into the main room.

"Travis!"

Shaina screamed, yanking him back at the same time he was pushing her back into the room. They fell onto the floor and Travis winced from the burning pain in his leg, realizing he'd been hit.

Shaina covered her mouth, choking back another scream as she saw the blood stream from Travis's leg. With her arms flung out, she sprang into action throwing herself upon him just as two more shots rang out.

"How did you know?" Travis said, grimacing from the bullet wound.

"I could feel it coming," Shaina returned softly, stretching and kicking the door shut with her foot.

"Smart girl." Travis sat up grabbing his leg. "But we

can't stay in here much longer, we'll burn to death."

Shaina went around with a heavy rag rug, beating at the flames, coughing and holding one hand over her mouth. She felt as though she were choking with almost every breath she took. She had struggled only a short distance into the murky smoke when she chanced to glance back to make sure Travis was all right. She felt as though her heart had stopped beating. Where was Travis?! Then she saw him trying to pull himself aright and she breathed a sigh of relief.

"I'm trying to put it out, Travis!"

"No, Shaina. Save your strength. That won't help any, you're only making it worse."

"We have to get out!" she yelled.

"We'll have to go out a back window."

"Look, Travis! We can't!"

Travis swore. The flames were worse at the back of the cabin now, eating away voraciously at the lighter, knotty pine.

Shaina coughed, choking on the acrid smoke surrounding them like dark, evil spirits. "The flames," she cried. "They're all over!"

Travis said, gritting his teeth, "Here, put this rag over your face, . . . it won't help much, but it's better than choking to death."

"Look . . . back there!"

Travis saw stark terror in Shaina's dark blue eyes.

"I know, love, I know." Grunting, Travis came to his knees, ripping off his kerchief and tying it tightly around his wound. "Get my gun, Shaina!"

Shaina looked this way and that, then ran to the bedpost where Travis's gun hung in its holster. "Oh! It's hot," she cried.

She ran back into the main room coughing and holding the gun out by her fingertips.

Travis grabbed it and strapped it on.

Only several minutes had passed since the fire had begun, but it seemed like they'd been in the smoke-filled house for hours.

"Shaina! Wake up! Don't stand there in a trance. You'll never make it if you do that! We've got only the one chance," he shouted. "I'll go first."

She nodded.

"Then I'll draw their gun fire! When I open the door, I'll run to the left, you run to the right and try to get behind the cabin, but not too close to it!" As he gazed into his wife's lovely blue eyes, he asked, "Ready?"

"Travis," she muttered, "I love you"

"And I love you, Mrs. Cordell."

With a new strength born of love and shared determination, Shaina looked at Travis. "We'll make it," she said, squeezing his arm.

Travis stood then, testing his leg. Pain surged through the limb but he knew he had to fight it back.

"Shaina — *Now!*"

Flames seemed to fill the room completely as Travis gave the door a yank and threw it wide. He did as planned, running to the left, laying down a volley of shots as he went.

Shaina went to the right, and, spotting a big woodpile, she made it her destination, ducking behind as she careened around it.

She spotted Travis then, going down for a second time, rolling on the ground as he laid himself flat and out of sight of their attackers.

Silence reigned.

No one had returned Travis's fire.

From the woodpile, Shaina trained her eyes on her beloved and her heart filled her throat as she saw him lying on his side, gun still smoldering. He must be hurting very bad. She drew the back of her arm across her dirty face and coughed, horrified to see a puff of smoke coming from her mouth.

From their separate hiding places, Shaina and Travis scanned the woods. It was then that Shaina spotted two riders filing up into a tree-dotted mountain. "Bastards," she hissed, gritting her teeth.

Leaving the safety of the woodpile, Shaina ran to Travis's side, and gasped as he pulled her roughly to the ground.

"You fool! Are you trying to get yourself killed?"

"You didn't see them? They've gone, up into the hills."

Travis caught the hurt in her sparkling blue eyes, realizing she'd only run to protect him, to be by his side. "You say they're gone, but they might return. We'll go back. I don't want to see you hurt, too."

"*Me?*" Shaina looked stunned. "You need a doctor, Travis Cordell. Don't worry about me."

Shaina gave her husband a hand up and then she left his side to go fetch the horses. They were nervous, their ears twitching one moment and cocked the next. "Shh. Shh," Shaina calmed them, stroking first Dice and then Spotted Bird.

By the time Shaina had helped Travis to mount Dice, the cabin was roaring in flames, being consumed from timber to timber.

"Come on, Shaina, let's go. There's nothing we can

do now but try to get back before I bleed to death."

Shaina took a deep breath and followed on Spotted Bird. But worry never left her face.

The sun was high in the shining blue sky by the time the Cordells came down from the big mountains and emerged from the trail which had been expertly cut through the dense forest.

"Look," Shaina said, drawing an arm across her dirty face.

Riders were coming fast toward them, and seven of Travis's men reined up before the couple, horses churning up clods of grass and bits of rock. One of the horses lost its footing, throwing both horse and rider to the ground.

"Sheesh!" exclaimed the laughing cowboy, dusting himself off with his hat as the horse leapt to its feet.

"What the hell's going on up there?"

"We saw smoke."

"Uh huh," said B.J., nodding, gaping at the bandaged leg.

But Shaina wasn't looking at the other six men. Her gaze was trained on the seventh. He was angry, his dark blue eyes wild and crazy. She held her breath at the intensity of the loving concern riding the cowboy's features hard as he looked her over from head to toe. In his eyes were tears.

The cowboy was Silvanus Hart.

Chapter Twenty-six

Shaina stirred uneasily on the vanity bench. With a pang she realized someone truly had tried to kill Travis—or them both!

But who? Who wanted to see Travis dead . . . and why?

Shaina paused in brushing her hair at the dressing table, the long strands fiery gold reflecting the light of morning sun streaming in. She adjusted the bodice of her dark-blue calico dress and rose from the vanity bench to face the beautiful sunrise. How she wished the sun's rays could blot out the fear and anger inside her. Sighing, she followed the delicious odor of coffee to the kitchen. Deanna was there, a steaming cup in her hand. She smiled warmly as Shaina entered and bade her friend a good morning, her voice as cheerful as the sun itself. "I hope you're feeling better this morning, Shaina. You look a lot better, but you still must be horribly shaken after what happened up there on the mountain."

Deanna meant well, but this morning Shaina wished she had broached a different subject. She had been trying to forget their mountain ordeal for a while. Travis had vowed to find his would-be assassins, and the tension was high on the ranch, for he was foul-tempered since they'd come down off the mountain.

"I'll never forget, Deanna. Travis was almost killed."

Shaina poured herself a cup of coffee, then sat down at the kitchen table, and asked Deanna, "Did Travis say where he was going this morning before he left?"

Deanna offered Shaina a biscuit, but Shaina shook her head. Her stomach was queasy again this morning as it had been for the last several mornings. She hadn't told Travis yet that she suspected she was pregnant. The subject of children had never come up and she didn't know how he would feel about this, especially considering his mood lately.

"He went up" — Deanna took a deep breath" — to the mountain."

Shaina swallowed too hard and too fast, burning her throat with the fiery brew. *"What?"* She stood abruptly, shoving her chair back with her heels.

"I knew that's how you'd react," Deanna said, watching Shaina almost run to the door. To herself she murmured, "I couldn't lie, though, could I?"

Shaina rode fast and hard, her hair flung out behind her like a red-gold banner that kept time with Spotted Bird's furious pace.

As she flew past the bunkhouses, she saw Noah Starr on one of the porches, holding up his hand in a greeting of half pleasure and half puzzlement.

"Where do you suppose she's goin' like the wind's pushing her?" Noah asked Jack Nolan who happened to come out and squint up at the sun. Noah gave his old head a jerk and then Jaw saw Shaina.

"You go find that out. Go get her, Jack, and bring her back home!"

"Right!"

Shaina felt as if her heart was made of thunder. She flashed across the prairie, and her hair, wild in the wind, was like a whipping red flame, and every line of Spotted Bird had again become instinct with wildness.

Jack now turned to the dangerous business of his pursuit. Spotted Bird had run for a mile or so, and was now just slowing down, but Jack was still far behind.

Jack knew where Shaina was headed, and it was his job to keep her from getting too close to Big Blue. In fact, Travis said she was to stick close to home. And so she would, if Jack had anything to do about it!

Still moving fast, but not as fast as before, Shaina started when the shrill, air-splitting whistle reached her. Glancing Jack Nolan over her shoulder, Shaina gave her heels to Spotted Bird and once again they were flying across the savage prairie.

"Heyyy!" Jack whooped wildly and waved his hat when she shot a look over her shoulder the second time. "Missus Cordell! You're not supposed to go that way . . . turn back!"

"I can't hear you!" Shaina shouted back, angry that the man should be chasing after her and giving orders. "I don't care what you say, Mr. Nolan, I am going to keep going . . . *Hiyaa!*"

"Travis says to keep the woman from going up the

mountain," Jack said with hard determination in his dark eyes, "and that is just what I'm going to do!"

The chase was in earnest now.

Everytime Jack was about to catch up, Shaina pulled Spotted Bird sharply to one side, cutting him off.

"You want to kill me?!" Shaina screamed. When she heard no reply, she went on, "Back off!!"

"Damn it, woman, you're going to kill that horse! Slow down! Want to talk to you . . . that's all!"

"I don't believe you!"

Jack let loose with a string of curses.

"If you're going to act like a wild lady, you will get treated like one . . . or a wild grulla, no less."

Shaking out the coil of rope he now held in his hands, Jack kneed his grulla and lit out after her, grim determination riding his cowboy's face as he expertly twirled the long rope with the running noose at one end above his head.

And the grulla stretched out, giving his strong heart a good work out, his sturdy front legs passing between his hind legs, his velvety pink nose flaring wide.

Gliding to the left; gliding to the right. Jack's grulla tracked the magnificent Indian pony that was holding its own and living up to its reputation for stamina on long runs across the prairie.

But Spotted Bird had been running too long and was beginning to foam at the mouth.

Jack was damn angry. When she began to slow the pony, Jack saw an opening and shot forward just as she was coming to the right.

"Got ya!"

The lasso made a hissing sound as it slipped down over Shaina's head, and before she could lift her hand, the thing was down and being pulled tight, making her a prisoner inside the circle of biting rope.

It was a glum-faced man that came around to face his captive, taking up the slack in the rope as he kneed his grulla next to hers.

Jack only shook his head, meaning to tell her he'd once thought she was a nice lady, not one who would purposely ride a horse to death.

"I've got a lot of respect for horses" was all Jack said, trying not to frown into her face as he got closer and began to loosen the knot in order to pull the rope upward.

Then Jack had a second thought and he said gruffly, "If I let you go and you try that again, lady, I'm going to have to do this all over again. What's it going to be?"

Shaina was becoming alarmed. She didn't know too much about horses, but she'd learned how to ride quite well since she'd become the rancher's wife.

As best she could, Shaina reached out to pat Spotted Bird. "I'm sorry if I hurt you, girl." Tears began to roll down her cheeks, and she looked over to Jack with a miserable face. "I only" — she sniffed loudly — "wanted to go to my husband."

Jack's voice softened. "Can't let you do that, missus. Travis is my friend, and my boss, as you know, and he give me and a bunch of the other boys orders to keep you at home."

Shaina's tear-streaked face lifted to the mountain and she said, "Will he be all right up there?"

"Can't say. He's looking for the ones that tried to

261

kill him."

"I thought so," Shaina said, looking up at Jack Nolan with reproachful eyes.

"Hey, lady, don't look at me like that. I was only doing my duty. Travis says to keep his woman at home and that's just what I aim to do."

"I'm sorry." Shaina lifted her arms feebly. "Would you remove the rope now?" Her voice was softer now.

"Sure you're going to behave?"

Shrugging her shoulders, Shaina lifted a hand, saying, "Promise." While he was removing the lasso, Shaina watched him, plans for later ticking in her brain . . . that is, if Travis didn't return by nightfall. She would get herself two horses this time . . . she knew the way.

With his face close to Shaina's, Jack felt a frisson of excitement — and imminent danger — coming from the woman.

"You're a bundle of nerves, ain't you?"

Nervously Shaina laughed. "Not really. Ah, will Spotted Bird be all right?" She rubbed her arms as Jack took the lasso away and sat quietly rolling it into a thick coil.

"She's OK, Mrs. Cordell. I'll take her when we get back to the house and have one of the boys see to her real good. We'll take it slow on the way back," he said, his voice indicating he would accept no more foolishness on her part. "And you *are* coming back with me, Mrs. Cordell."

"Call me Shaina." She shook her head, curling her wild hair all about her flushed cheeks. "We're friends, remember? We had a double wedding."

"I respect you, missus, and I'l just call you that if

you don't mind — for now."

"Oh."

Shaina breathed slowly, patting Spotted Bird as they went in the opposite direction now, back to the ranch.

"Are you going to be . . . around later?" Shaina asked.

"Why?"

"Oh." She shrugged. "Just wondering. Sometimes you and Deanna stay at the house for a while and have cake and coffee with us. I made a cake today." She yawned, patting her mouth. "I'm really tired now, so I think I'll go to bed early, but you and Deanna can do whatever you like. You don't have to go to your cabin right away."

"We only stay for cake and coffee when Travis is around, missus. You know that."

Shaina gritted her teeth. Damn. What to do now?

"Well then, you will be going home early?" she asked, hoping to pinpoint a time when he wouldn't be around. Oh, dear . . . what about the other men? She hadn't thought of that. There must be some way around them . . . but not so with Jack Nolan!

Deanna ran out to meet them, breathlessly inquiring as she saw Shaina's weary mount, "What happened? Shaina, you look awful."

"Runaway horse," muttered Jack, hating to lie to Deanna but knowing he had to. The fewer people he told about Shaina's escapade, the less likely it would be that Travis would find out. He would tell Deanna later, after the tension blew away.

"I do feel awful," Shaina drawled, running her fingers through her messed hair. "I need a bath, then

263

I'll curl up with a book and—" She grinned prettily, "go to bed early."

Shaina backed away, then spun into the house.

"Right" was all Jack muttered before he turned leading the horses away, Deanna keeping up alongside.

Shaina, dressed in dark blouse and blue jeans she hadn't broken in yet, feeling stiff in the hind-end, sauntered to the stable, hat pulled low over her forehead, hair tucked up inside real good.

Keeping a low profile, even though most of the men were having their evening meal in the cook house, Shaina slipped into the stable. The first place she headed for was Spotted Bird's stall, to make sure the mare was faring well.

Spotted Bird was half asleep, so Shaina didn't bother her, but made her stealthy way to the other side of the stable where the sturdy grullas were kept.

Working quickly, Shaina had one big boy saddled, and a mare besides. She was leading them out, Indian file, meaning to go the back way, through the pines and, skirting them, she'd come out on the prairie a good distance away from the bunkhouses. And if she was careful, she wouldn't be seen. The horses she chose were black.

She was just creeping along the side of the barn when a voice froze her in midstride.

Oh, Lord, who could that be?

Shaina tried to keep going but she found to her utter chagrin that she was blocked, one man at her head, the other at the black horse taking up the rear.

"Going somewhere?"

Gulping, Shaina peered into the face of Jack Nolan as he lighted a smoke he'd built in the moments she'd been shaking in her boots.

"Ah . . ." Shaina bit her tongue. "Just for a walk."

"Really?" Jack drawled.

"Don't do it, missy."

Shaina whirled at the sound of Silvanus Hart's soothing voice.

"She ain't going nowhere," Jack said.

Shaina almost cried. Heaving a great sigh of disappointment, she said, "I guess I'm not then."

Silvanus took hold of the trailing horse, saying calmly, "I'll help you, missy."

Missy? Shaina stared at him through the bluish darkness, wondering why her whole being seemed to reach toward the soothing sound of his voice. She couldn't understand it, he had been bitterly angry with her the first time they met, and now he was being so nice and polite.

"I'll take care of it from here, Jack."

"OK"

Intense embarassment flooding Shaina, she averted her face when they came into the lantern light. She sagged wearily against the black's huge neck, and with a sad sound she muttered, "I feel like a child caught being naughty." Sniffing noisily in the hay-strewn corridor she added, "All I wanted to do was join Travis. I'm afraid for him."

She looked at Silvanus. He was being strangely quiet. Finally he spoke, his voice mellow and almost sad.

"I understand, missy. I know what it's like to want

to be with someone so bad it hurts. You don't know what to do. You just want to go to him—or her. But you can't in some circumstances."

Shaina rubbed her pinkened nose, looking at the cowboy through her haze of wet eyes. "You know what it's like?" she asked with another loud sniff.

"I sure do. More than you know."

Shaina shrugged. "I don't know what to do. Can't sleep, I know that for a fact. I'd be up all night. Why did he do this to me? He should have at least told me he was going."

A gentle smile moved on Silvanus's mouth. "A man sometimes has to do that. Get goin' while the goin's good."

"It's not fair."

"Nothing is fair in this life, honey."

Honey? Missy? Shaina felt an odd quiver.

"Who are you?" Shaina said.

Silvanus tore his gaze from the young woman's bright blue eyes. "Just a cowboy."

He led the horses back to their stalls, and Shaina went into the house and wondered . . . and all night long she wondered.

Chapter Twenty-seven

Moving against the timbered, mountainous landscape two riders reached the vicinity of the burnt-out cabin and, coming to a halt, dismounted.

"This is the place where it happened?" Jay Ridingbow asked his boss.

"Yeah."

Jay looked down, seeing that Travis's leg was bleeding again. "Boss . . . look."

Travis looked where the lad pointed and saw the red splotch of blood staining his pants. "I know I'm up too soon on it . . . Shaina's going to kill me anyway." He loosed a dry chuckle, hoping when she discovered his absence she didn't try anything foolish like try to follow him up into the mountain.

"Your woman is kindness itself," remarked the grinning half-breed.

"Oh, yeah? Would you like to be around when we get back and I face her woman's wrath? She'll be kind all right . . . kind of furious."

Jay chuckled, his bright eyes lit with a golden glow.

He was glad he'd asked Travis Cordell if he could come along. It hadn't been easy, for the man had wanted to travel by himself, but Jay had talked him into it. The lad was eager to assist in the search for those who had tried murdering Travis and Shaina Cordell. He liked them both, very much, but he liked Travis's daughter Roux even more. Someday Roux was going to be his wife, that he had decided the first time he had seen the girl by the riverbank.

Walking with a limp, Travis went to the spot where the fire originated and cast about for any clue that might help reveal who had set the fire. *They*, Shaina had said—there had been two of them as far as she could see.

Travis surveyed the area, kicking around in the rubble with the toe of his boot, now looking into the pile of burned ash. Here was a stocking, a woman's, Shaina's, there an iron skillet, and over where the bedroom had been a blackened iron bedpost. Bits of Shaina's chemise and drawers . . . Travis recalled with pleasure those splendorous moments as Shaina lay in his arms . . .

Jay tilted his dark head, looking at Boss Cordell and wondering at his secret expression.

"I will look in the wooded area over there," Jay said, gently nudging his golden Sheba toward the place indicated.

"I'll come with you."

Travis walked slow after Jay and Sheba, his gaze scanning the ground from left to right as he stepped carefully so as not to disturb any sign that might have been left behind.

"Stop, Jay! Don't go into the area just yet. I want to

get a closer look."

"I can see if there are any prints from here, Mr. Cordell."

"I think I found something," Travis said, warning Jay to go no farther.

"I see them now!" Jay exclaimed, squinting his eyes as he studied the boot prints in the soft earth.

Travis hunkered down studying the same, and somehow just looking at the prints, knowing who'd made them, he was drawn closer to their would-be assassin. He felt a funny twinge in his leg thinking he could have lost his love . . . and his life, too.

"Ah! Look there!" Jay cried softly, pointing to a clearer print up ahead of where Travis was looking.

"I see what you mean, Jay," said Travis, noticing the curious heel imprint . . . Strange, there was an X carved into it.

"A strange marking for one to have on the bottom of his boot," Jay remarked, his thin fingers tensing in anger.

Travis lifted his eyes to the tree-dotted hills and winced. "Damn leg is giving me trouble," he ground out, his green eyes suffused with a savage light.

"We should go back," Jay said. "We will get to the ranch a little after dark. It is better if the doc sees that leg." Jay pointed to the leg that Travis had had wrapped before setting out to the mountain. "You need a fresh bandage."

"Yeah, you're right. But let's have one more look up ahead."

Travis straightened and walked to his horse, his eyes still scanning the hills with anger growing as the minutes went by. Together Jay and Travis swung their mounts in the direction where he'd spotted the foot-prints leading into the woods. They started tracking the odd heel print.

"Look," Jay said, pulling his horse up. "This is where the devil mounted."

"Yes, I see that," Travis said with a sneer, then realizing none of this was Jay's fault, gave the lad a half smile.

The two trackers now rode toward the wooded area where the high-binders had gone two days before. Once there, Jay cautiously pointed to a second set of prints moving deeper into the trees.

"What have we got here?"

Travis had spotted something that had caught on the low branch of a evergreen. He urged Dice faster, then halted suddenly at the branch where the curious object hung.

"A scarf," he said.

"A woman's scarf," Jay said more accurately.

"Damn."

Jay looked at Travis with a sneer, then gave the man a cocky smile. Travis chuckled as he brought the scarf to his face, detecting the scent of cheap perfume.

"Ugh!" Jay wrinkled his nose. Then he frowned . . . Where had he smelled that same scent before? The perfume was familiar; the scarf was not.

"Something else?" asked Jay as he saw Travis star-ing at something on the ground shining like metal.

"I'll get it," Jay offered, sliding down off Sheba in a flash.

Travis took the objects that Jay handed to him, and he said, "Brass cartridges."

"Two of them," Jay said, looking at them and then

at his boss.

"Yeah." Travis squeezed them in a tight fist for a few seconds, then jammed them into his shirt pocket. "Let's go, Jay."

The riders swung back toward the ranch, moving at a faster pace as the sun sank slowly into the western piece of sky. The clouds had turned a bright orange and Travis imagined he had not seen such a beautiful sunset in all the times he'd come up by himself to Big Blue. It was because of Shaina everything stood out more brightly in his life now.

Travis hurried now, eager to be back to the Lazy C and the woman who waited for him there.

Back at the ranch, Jay led the horses to the stable for a good brushing down, while Travis made his way to the house.

"Hello," a lilting voice addressed Jay.

"Oh . . . Roux."

Jay looked over his shoulder as Travis's daughter entered the stable, her dark-fire braids shining in the light of mellow lantern.

"Have you seen Shaina?"

"No." He led Dice into his stall and then turned to Sheba, beginning to rub her down. "We have just returned."

"Did you find the evil bastards that shot at Father and Shainy?"

Shaking his head, Jay paused looking down at Roux. He smiled into her lovely, pale bronze face. "Your father's leg is . . . it is bleeding. We saw Sam on the way in and he's getting Doc . . . Roux," Jay

271

began again, stiffly this time, "I thought you quit swearing."

"Oh, yes, I forgot." She laughed uncomfortably.

Jay loved it when she pouted. He loved it when she smiled. He loved Roux any way she was, but he told himself he had no business feeling this way toward her. She was still so young, and as if she'd read his thoughts, Roux broke the silence.

"I am going to be eleven next week. Shainy is having a birthday, too. Are you coming to my and Shainy's birthday party?"

Jay forced himself to concentrate on what she had said, instead of her lovely pink-gold mouth.

"Of course, little fox."

"Fox Fire!" she corrected, then laughing tinklingly she laid a soft hand on his forearm as he continued to methodically stroke the golden hide of Sheba.

"Your Indian name," he said.

"What is yours?"

Jay shrugged. "I do not have one. Remember, Roux, I am only half Indian and have not lived with savages."

"Oh."

Catching her dejected look, he said, "But you can give me one." He stared at her soft bronze hand laying so delicately along his arm and wished fervently she could suddenly be much older. Jay clenched his teeth. He would just have to gain control of himself. All he wanted to do was take precious Roux and hold her against his heart . . . but she might become alarmed and so he checked himself from doing anything to frighten her. "Do not touch my arm when I am working, Roux."

Roux shrugged and took her hand away, then began tapping her lips like she'd seen her father do when he was trying to decide on something.

"Riding Bow!" she cried, dimpling.

Jay chuckled, saying, "But that *is* my name, Fox Fire."

"Say it slower. Riding . . . Bow." She threw her arms wide. "See. Like Indian name. Fox Fire and Riding Bow."

"Ah"—Jay took a deep shuddering breath"—I like that very much."

"Good. I am going to bed after I see Father." She grinned like a bronze imp. "Tomorrow, Riding Bow."

Jay held up his hand and said with deep-felt emotion, "Tomorrow . . . Fox Fire."

With shocked though pleasured astonishment, Shaina felt the arms go around her waist, the kiss being planted at her nape.

"Did I scare you?" Travis murmured along the side of Shaina's neck.

Shaina could not contain her joy at seeing Travis, and she could laugh at herself now. She had been feeling so sorry for herself after Jack Nolan had treated her like a prisoner. But now her love was here, and she felt joyfully liberated.

Pressing herself against her husband, Shaina purred, "I can't believe you're here, darling. When I found out you had gone up onto Big Blue I was so frightened for you."

Travis looked at his wife with adoration, but then suddenly noticed her attire and growled, "Blue jeans!

What are you wearing those for?" His eyes narrowed as he spun her about with the tips of his fingers. "Were you about to go somewhere?"

"No." Well, that *was* the truth.

Just then they heard the doctor's voice in the hallway and a flurry of activity ensued as Shaina, the doctor, Deanna, and Jack all saw to Travis's comfort. After the doctor had rebandaged the leg, he and the wounded man's company departed, leaving Shaina alone with Travis once again.

"Father . . . are you in the bedroom?" came Roux's voice only minutes after the trio had filed out.

"Hello, Roux," Shaina said, motioning that she was going into the dressing room and left her husband to have some private time with his daughter.

Changing into something more feminine, Shaina stood framed in the door as Roux gave a little wave as she went out the door closing it softly behind her.

Her eyes locked with Travis's and his narrowed, turning a deep jade-green. "Come here," he growled huskily.

"My pleasure."

"And mine," he returned, his eyes making love to her as she came.

Shaina's bare feet seemed to glide across the floor toward the heaven only her beloved could take her to.

Half a dozen smoky figures of men gathered at the table and took their seats readying to play cards. There was Graham Hill, Vinny Sloan, Joe Creek, B.J., and two other cowboys.

Graham had been knocked flat when he first found

out that the three were planning to stay on at Lazy C. They talked about the weather, were civil to one another, but Graham felt an underlying tension whenever he was around these men. At first, too, he hadn't recognized them, but when Joe Creek brought his wife Carolyn to the ranch, the past came rushing up to slap him in the face. She was the woman he'd diddled with . . . Creek's wife.

Joe's laughter made a hissing sound as he glanced over at Graham and then down at his cards again. A seventh person joined the group, hanging over Joe's shoulder. It was Creek's wife, Graham saw with a shudder as she looked him over lightly and then moved on to the next man.

After a while the two older men got up. "We're gonna turn in," said the tallest of them.

"Good enough," said Vinny Sloan, kicking the chair out for Carolyn to be seated. She slid into the chair lazily and Sloan had to drag his eyes away from her plump rear.

"Watch your eyes," warned Joe as he flipped a card onto the table.

"Hey," Sloan said as he laid his cards down and leaned forward, "we can talk now."

Graham's eyes traveled around the table as the others made a tighter circle. "We'll all talk," Joe said, motioning for Graham to move closer, too. "He likes us well enough. I can tell by the way he looks at us."

Graham frowned, not understanding.

"Maybe he wants to do it to me again," Carolyn said with astonishing boldness.

Joe reached over and slapped her face lightly and Graham made to rise, but the hand on his arm stopped him. "Hey, what's your hurry?" Joe said, pulling Graham back down. "We ain't mad at you."

"Uh uh," said B.J., shaking his big head.

"What happened before, all of that, it don't matter anymore, does it?" Joe looked around the table at his friends and wife.

"Not a bit," Sloan said, nodding with B.J. and Carolyn.

"Now," Joe began seriously, "we all been making plans, see. Now—" He spread his hands wide. "All we gotta do is include our new friend in our plans. Right?" he asked around the table and received more nods of approval.

"What do you want from me?" Graham's voice was shaky.

"We want you to cooperate, that's all. But we don't want no trouble, see."

"Uh huh." B.J. leaned back, twiddling his thumbs over his fat stomach.

Now the cold bore of a pistol was jammed into Graham's ribs and the equally cold voice hissed into his ear. "We gotta make plans about them people," he snarled.

"What people?" Graham stammered.

"It makes a great deal of difference on which end of a gun a face appears. Mine is on this end, Hill, and yours is on that end. Savvy?"

"Yes, but I still don't understand—"

"You will."

B.J. nodded furiously, saying, "Tell him, Joey, tell him!"

"Yeah . . ." drawled the sloppy-tongued Carolyn.

"We need to make some money, Hill. Remember,

you robbed my friends here—and I didn't exactly like what you took from my Carolyn neither."

"What do you want?" Graham was really getting scared now.

"That Missus Cordell, the one they call Shaina, she your daughter?"

Graham gulped, feeling the gun caressing his ribs none too gently. "N-not really."

"What do you mean, not really!" Joe almost shouted.

"She is just not my daughter. I'm telling you the truth."

"So, Mr. Hill, your wife went diddlin' with some other fellow, you're saying?" Sloan this time.

With a wounded look, Graham said, "She did, yup, my Eleanora did just that."

"So who's the lucky feller?" B.J. snorted and guffawed.

Now Graham clenched his fists, making to rise, but the cold steel pressed against his heart. He blanched.

"Cool it, B.J." Joe said. "All right?"

"Uh huh."

"Now, we don't really give a damn whose daughter Shaina Cordell is, all we want you to do is get her out of here. Take her somewhere for us."

"Why?" Graham blinked uncomprehendingly.

"Sheesh," exclaimed Carolyn. "This guy's a real dummy."

"Shut up, Carolyn. No one asked you to put in."

"Sure, Joe."

Graham smacked his head, then, as the truth of the matter came to him, said, "You want ransom money!"

"Oh, Mr. Hill, now you're gettin' smart," said

Vinny Sloan.

"Lots of cash." Joe nodded. "Gold if he has it."

"Yeah, we'll ask 'im for gold!" Carolyn blurted, then catching Joe's murderous look, she shut up.

"Think she's worth it?" Joe asked Graham.

"Oh, Shainy's worth it."

"What you worried about then?"

"Boss Cordell. He's one man you shouldn't cross."

"We'll worry about that later." Holding Graham by the shirt collar, he spat, "You do as I say, and you and my baby here will get along. Hear?"

Graham's eyes rolled down over the gun and he nodded.

Chapter Twenty-eight

The moon climbed high over the Lazy C and the dual birthday party was in full swing. It was a warm summer night, and some of the folks from the valley had brought their wagons fully equipped with everything a body would need for staying overnight. Some would sleep out under the stars and others would pull up some hay in the barn. Like the younger folk, they would remain awake half the night anyway in their excitement over the big Cordell bash.

In the distance there was the lowing of sleepy cattle and many a cowpusher had come in to have a nip or two of Cordell's special punch and to visit awhile with the folks from the valley.

Silvanus Hart stood back, surveying the goings-on from a quiet spot he'd chosen where he could watch but not get too involved with the folks' conversation. He'd rather have it that way. Besides, he was not much for having fun. His fun was nature . . . and just plain "remembering."

Shaina looked delicious in a rose-pink off-the-shoulder blouse, and creamy white skirt that flared around her slim ankles, showing off a bit of them now and then as she sashayed about the place greeting the guests.

"Don't she look just gorgeous," Abner Selby remarked of the beautiful rancher's wife. "She just come into her own marrying up with you," he said to Travis.

"She is a honey, isn't she?" Travis said. He took a deep breath of the mountain air, smiling as his wife flitted about like a colorful, happy butterfly. He couldn't wait to hold her later on and give her one of her special birthday gifts — a gorgeous, expensive wedding ring to replace the plain band she was wearing now. He had been saving this and other precious items since his trip to Seattle several weeks ago, made as a shopping expedition specifically for this special occasion.

Travis sipped his punch slowly as he milled around, talking and laughing with the guests, but he seemed preoccupied. For the most part, Travis ignored the colorful lanterns strung across the yard, the tables groaning with roasted beef and pork and barbecued chicken, crusty bread, jellies, all kinds of vegetables, and early fruits from the Cordell orchards. Deanna's family had come in to help with all the foodstuff, and Silvanus showed his special skill in cooking the meats.

Roux was a doll come to life in a white western-style dress, her skirt fringed around the waist, deep-auburn braids gleaming down to her waist, and on her dainty feet her favorite silver-beaded moccasins. Her happy face was a portrait in pink and bronze and Travis had often stopped what he was doing to swing her into the air and give her yet another birthday hug.

And Shaina, too, received her share of those. Kisses, too.

Travis himself wore a white outfit with black scarf knotted at his throat, ends trailing over one shoulder. Shaina remarked that he looked just like a Texas Ranger all dressed up and rearing to dance.

Only one thing had disappointed Shaina. There would be no dancing, for the musicians from the valley couldn't make it that night. But there was singing and mountain-style yodeling and a lot of knee slapping and pot banging.

Once in a while Travis would catch Shaina searching the crowd for him, and he had seen the worry in her eyes until she found him.

Nothing had been the same since that day up in the mountain.

"Who has the secret in his eyes?" Travis said under his breath, casually searching the ground for a boot heel with an X carved into it. He couldn't just go around asking people to lift their feet. Would he dare come here? Would she? And why would a woman want to kill him? Or had she only been dragged along as an innocent bystander?

"Why the stony face?" Deanna said. She sat on the bench across from him. "Something wrong with the food?"

"Food's fine, Deanna." Travis looked out over the crowd with a keenly observant eye. "I never found your meals lacking."

"Oh, Silvanus did a lot of it—"

Deanna stopped what she was about to say, for Travis had stiffened visibly, turning to her sharply. She sat back in alarm.

"Is something wrong?"

"Are you wearing perfume?" he ground out. His green eyes drilled into her.

"Why, I never wear perfume, Mr. Cordell. You should know that by now." She peered at him, saying, "There's lots of women here at the party. Most of them can't afford perfume, though, so that narrows it down to . . . let me see. Jenny Wheatley. Mary Johnson. Sara Travers." Deanna shrugged. "I don't know who else. Are you looking for a special brand of perfume for Shaina?"

"Yes . . . I am." Travis stood abruptly. "Excuse me, Deanna. I see someone I want to talk to."

The moon was well up as Travis winked across the tables to Shaina and made his way to the area where the wagons were parked. He walked slowly, trying to calm down his nerves. He had gotten a whiff of the same perfume that was on the scarf now, resting in his trouser pocket right at the moment.

He pulled out the purple scarf and held it up to his nose.

Shaina's gaze followed Travis, and she thought she'd detected a troubled look on his face. He had changed, she decided. Ever since the ambush up at the cabin, Travis was a different man. The magic of their love seemed to have died a little. Maybe she was only imagining it, but the night before he'd seemed to have his mind elsewhere than on their lovemaking. Could he be dreaming of another woman? What about his trips to Seattle? She was being ridiculous, she told herself. Travis would never cheat on her.

Deciding to follow him and give him a surprise hug like he'd often done to her, Shaina stepped off the grass and followed him into the press of wagons.

It was slightly darker between the many wagons, with so many canvasses erected over the frames.

There he was. Shaina put out her toe, meaning to walk stealthily over to where he was standing alone and surprise him as he'd done to her so many times when the flash of something in his hand caught her eye.

Two shiny objects! He was just in the process of putting them back into his pocket . . .

Earrings? Was Travis giving her these for her birthday? It could be a ring, as her wish was to have one, but there would not be two of them if that were the case.

Now Shaina sucked in her breath, watching her husband lift a light purple scarf to his face and as she stared, openmouthed, he breathed in the scent. Travis was holding another woman's scarf, as if he was remembering a time they had together.

A raw grief took hold of Shaina and shook her to the very core. She felt desolate. Travis . . . with another woman? It was unthinkable. Yet lately she'd seen a secret in his eyes. A man as virile as her husband could easily love two women, she thought with rising dismay. Seeing him lift his head, Shaina fell back against the wagon, clutching her breast with a shaking hand.

"Well, well," a voice drawled close to Shaina. It would have startled her but for the fact there was no emotion at all left in her . . . she seemed drained. "The birthday girl is all alone. How fortunate for me."

"Giles," Shaina said. "You surprised me."

"Here." He handed her a brown package with a

ribbon around it. "Open it, my dear."

Shaina could hardly catch her breath after what she'd just witnessed behind the wagon. I'm sick, she wanted to sob, I can't stay . . . I have to go lie down. Nausea threatened her throat. Her palms were clammy. Giles's voice seemed to come from far away.

"Shaina? You look awfully pale. You aren't going to . . ."

Giles caught first his birthday present for her, and then he grabbed Shaina as she keeled over in a faint.

The next thing Shaina was conscious of was Travis bending over her. Then he was sweeping her up into his arms.

Mary Johnson put in, "She's with child, I just know it. Look at her face. I tell you she's pregnant. I've known it all evening. I was just wondering when she was going to swoon after all this excitement and activity."

"How do you know she's going to have a baby?" Roux pushed the tall woman aside. "Baby? I am going to have a baby sister or brother?"

Travis blinked. Shaina . . . having a baby. His baby? Why hadn't she told him?

Giles's mouth dropped open as he watched Travis carry Shaina into the house, kicking the door shut after he was alone inside with her.

With a strange look in his eyes, Giles lingered beside one of the wagons while the chattering females took themselves back to the tables and the great big birthday cakes being sliced there. Now.

"*Psst!*" came a sudden sound, distracting all.

Giles pushed away from the wagon, searching out the source of the sound. Then he saw someone

284

heading toward the call, that Graham fellow who claimed to be Shaina's father making his way to the shadows outside the lanternlight. Giles watched as Graham crept that way, looking over his shoulder as he went.

Deciding to follow, Giles went cautiously into the dark, looking this way and that. Then he heard the voices, coming from somewhere close by.

"What did you learn?" one voice said.

Graham answered, "Nothing much. But maybe Shainy's going to have a baby."

The voice was a loud whisper. "That's even better. Now there'll be two of them."

Giles stepped back as he heard the rats emerging from their hole, and he stroked his chin with two fingers. Thoughtfully. Then he went to find his horse and rode off for the deepest part of the woods where he knew someone would be waiting anxiously for him to come.

Travis arched one eyebrow and with hands on hips, said, "How long have you known?"

Shaina thought he was referring to his act of indiscretion she had discovered and replied with a catch in her voice, "I just found out." She put her back to him coldly, snapping, "I don't want to talk about it." Her voice rose angrily. "So please take yourself somewhere else."

"This doesn't only concern you, you know!"

"Really!" Shaina returned. "Get out, Travis Cordell, the sight of you sickens me."

"Fine," he muttered. Then he turned to her stiffly

held back once more, beginning, "Do all women act this way when"—He waved his hand, searching for the right words"—when this happens?"

"I wouldn't know!" Shaina gritted her teeth. "It has never happened to me before . . . naturally."

Disturbed by her distant, sarcastic attitude, Travis asked her, "Shaina, what is happening to us? We've become strangers."

Shaina's eyes narrowed as she wondered what woman could have caught Travis's attention . . . and how long had this been going on? Had it been right under her nose all along, even before they married?

"I'm not angry, Shaina."

"Well, I am!" She whirled around, looking him up and down with contempt.

"Have you seen the doctor?" Travis stuck his hands in his pocket.

"What can the doctor do about it?"

"Well, one usually sees a doctor when one is pregnant." Travis heaved a sigh of frustration. She was really being exasperating.

"Oh, that. Well, I hope I am not, because I don't want your baby, Travis Cordell!"

"Hellfire!"

With that Travis quit the room, banging doors as he went out the front way. He was going to go and get good and drunk!

Shaina hadn't even touched her birthday presents. They lay in the corner the next morning as Mary Johnson popped in to see how the little lady was faring.

286

Patting Shaina's pale hand, Mary chirped, "You have got to put some weight on, child. That baby's going to be a skinny runt if you don't fatten yourself up. All my kids weighed well over eight pounds, some almost nine and a half. Can you beat that?"

I hope not, Shaina wanted to blurt. But she didn't really care much about anything. Life seemed to have ended for her. Her mountain paradise was no more.

"Here now, don't be looking so sad, missus." Mary said. Her eyes were full of sympathy for what she thought was a pathetic-looking creature. "You're so frail . . . don't know how you could have taught all those kids. Didn't it take a lot out of you, Shainy dear?"

"No. Not really." The woman meant well, but Shaina wished she would just go home like the rest of the folks had.

"Well, all the valley thought you was too young to have been taking on all those kids. We're getting a new schoolteacher, did you hear?"

"No, I didn't." Shaina wasn't really interested, but asked nonetheless "What's he like?"

"Well," Mary's voice lowered, "I hear it ain't a 'him.'" Mary straightened and nodded knowledgeably.

"It—it's a 'her'? Travis had said this one was going to be a man." Shaina swallowed hard. "Is she . . . pretty? How old is she?"

"Well, that knucklehead husband of mine said he saw her in Seattle same time your husband was there."

A squeezing pain clutched Shaina's heart and wouldn't let go.

"That's where she's from?" Shaina could hardly get out.

"Yes, but she's not all that young, you know. Not young like you, leastways. Who knows. Herb acts like a know-all, but she could be old and gray for all we know."

"I . . . don't think so."

Mary peered at the big rancher's wife oddly, then said, "We'll soon see, won't we?"

When Mary had departed Shaina answered the question. "Yes, we will see."

Chapter Twenty-nine

Carolyn Creek was getting bored. Each and every day she had put on the same dress—a sexy red one. But it was old, getting worn out and soiled under the arms, and, besides, Carolyn thought as she walked along the boardwalk of the bunkhouse, it was high time her husband got her a new one. She came to the end of the porch and stood there hugging the railing post.

With a sigh of intense boredom, Carolyn listlessly gazed out over the ranch grounds and then over the prairie and hills beyond, all the while muttering grouchily to herself, "I'm gettin' tired of this hole. One day it rains like all hell's cut loose, and the next it's another hot, still one. There ain't nothin' to do and nobody to gossip with." She yawned hugely, snorting, "Shoot!"

Carolyn was not a bad-looking woman, and Joe had told her all she needed was to take some flesh off her rear and she'd be a real looker. Damn. If only she was the most important thing in Joe's life and money was second. But Joe had a lust for gold.

Now Joe wanted to take Shaina Cordell away and

hold her for ransom. That Graham fellow was supposed to get her out of here first, then Joe had other plans. Carolyn wondered resentfully if Joe had other things besides money in mind for Shaina Cordell!

Carolyn had seen Shaina Cordell and she was a real pretty lady, Carolyn decided. Maybe a bit too thin a body but pretty nonetheless.

"Howdy, ma'am." A voice interrupted her thoughts.

"Howdy," Carolyn said to the passing cowboy who tipped his hat. Wasn't his name Silvanus something or other?

"What you doing out here, Carolyn?"

Still holding the post, the woman turned to her husband who was walking toward her. She hadn't even seen or heard where he'd come from . . . Joe was like that—quiet as a pussycat.

"I'm out here bein' bored all to hell, that's what."

"Poor Caro," Joe purred deeply. "You long to be where there's some action, huh, baby?"

"Yeah."

"Well, babe, you're gonna see some any day now."

"Any day now," Carolyn whined. "We been here too long now, Joe." She rubbed herself against him. "I want a new dress, Joe, a red one. You gonna get me one pretty soon, hon?"

"Yeah, I'll get you one. Maybe we can get Graham to press the lady to bring some of her own clothes with her when we take her out of here." Joe rubbed his hand along Carolyn's backside, but he was imagining the feel of another woman, a slimmer one. "She's maybe got something you can take your pick out of." He winked.

Mischievousness lit up Carolyn's eyes as she ran her

hand up and down Joe's chest and growled in his ear, "Let's go inside for a time, Joe."

"What do you want, Caro?"

"Shoot, Joe, what'd'ya think?" Her hand glided over the broad expanse of his chest.

When her hand lowered and boldly caressed him, Joe thrust into it and then pulled her away from the post to lead her back inside the empty room . . .

Travis had been climbing the walls for the entire week following Shaina's birthday party. He had been spending his nights all alone on the sofa in his office . . . and it was a lumpy damn hard one at that. His already ill temper had worsened into downright surliness.

Travis was just tipping his chair back and stretching his long legs when Shaina chose that moment to enter the kitchen. Her hair was softly tousled from sleep and her cheeks were pale, but it was the dark circles Travis noticed under her eyes.

Travis said nothing, and Shaina just walked around his outstretched legs without even bothering to ask him to tuck them in. And Travis didn't bother to show her any courtesy.

"Good morning," Deanna said brightly. She received the same glum greeting from Shaina as she had from Travis.

With a shrug Deanna set about making the two their usual breakfast. Shaina took her unbuttered toast into the dining room and Travis wolfed down his four eggs and grits in three minutes flat. Then he went out to his horse, already saddled and waiting at the kitchen door, and rode off to his work. Shaina moped around and did little all the day long.

After Travis had gone out, Jack came in for his third cup of coffee that morning. This one, when time permitted, was usually taken with his wife.

"Morning, sweet," Jack said. He planted a kiss on Deanna's cheek and she turned to brush his lips with hers.

Deanna smiled lovingly and said, "You always say so many sweet 'Good mornings' to me. You make me very happy, Jack." Then Deanna heaved a deep sigh.

Jack gathered that nothing had changed with the Cordells. "Same as the last seven mornings, huh?"

"Yes. What happened to them, Jack? They started out like us, so happy." She shrugged. "Why?"

Slowly she sank to the edge of a chair and Jack took her hands in his big, calloused ones.

"Can't rightly say just yet, Dee, but I think there's more to this than meets the eye."

"What do you mean?" Deanna looked alarmed.

"Something's in the wind. Ever since someone tried to kill Travis up at the cabin, there's been trouble."

"Do you think someone right here on the ranch is trying to make trouble?"

Jack thought about that for a moment, then he nodded. "Yes—and I think there's more than one."

Deanna paled a little. "Are you going to try to find out who they are?"

Smoothing Deanna's forearm with his work-roughened hand, Jack murmured, "I'm going to try my damnedest. I owe it to Travis."

Travis was doing some checking of his own, for he couldn't wait until events forced him to a conclusion. It could be a deadly weight if he just let things ride and get worse.

His gun was stuck in its sheath. He had cunning eyes and his hands were like lightning with the gun. There had always been a certainty of success about him. Always in the ranching and planting he'd done exactly the right thing to get ahead . . . and now he wasn't about to let his marriage fall apart because of the tension he was living under. Someone was out to kill him and by finding the killer he wouldn't only be saving his life but the woman he loved and their marriage.

From the very first, the way was hard. Everyone he questioned seemed to know nothing, and all of them appeared innocent. Even the new men he'd hired were good workers and never gave a soul any trouble. There was even a bit of humor in the day, for he'd come upon Joe Creek and his wife Carolyn coupling lustily in the bunk and they had rolled onto the floor in surprise when he'd stepped inside without bothering to knock . . .

Travis tipped his hat, feeling his face grow hot.

"Nice day for that, Creek," Travis growled, and turning his back on the stark-naked lovers, he went out calling, "but you better get to work . . . day's wasting."

Travis had shook his head, and with his glorious Shaina in mind he'd thought, Oh, what a way to waste a day!

* * *

"Silvanus . . . you in there?"

"Sure am, boss."

Travis entered the barn where Silvanus was caring for one of the sickly calves, feeding it from a baby bottle he'd made up especially for this purpose.

"How's she doing?" Travis asked Silvanus, reaching to stroke the calf's velvety ear.

"Better and better. This one's going to make it. The last one wasn't so lucky."

"You sure do have a way with animals."

"Well, thank you, boss."

"Wish you'd call me Travis . . . or Sonny, or whatever you like. Sure do respect you, Sil."

"Well now, Sonny—" Silvanus grinned—"the feeling is mutual."

"Now that we got that sentimentality out of the way, I'd like to ask you a few questions, Sil."

"I know just what's on your mind."

"Do you?"

"You're wondering who took a shot at you."

"Right."

"And you're looking to see if he works here on the ranch."

"Right again."

"Do you have any idea who *he* is—or *they?*"

"You're right about that last one—I think 'it's' a 'they.' "

Silvanus set the calf down gently in its bed of hay, then he turned back to Travis. Travis was staring down thoughtfully at the calf, not really seeing the cute little thing.

Leaning on the rough-hewn partition, Silvanus asked, "What do you make of the new wranglers you hired on not long ago? Are they to be trusted?"

"What would they be after? My land?" Travis laughed. "They're welcome to it, if they can find a way to cart it off."

"I really can't think of who'd want to kill you," Silvanus said. "You been fair to every man jack comes this way. You're a square shooter, Travis Cordell. I'm proud to be working for you and the Lazy C."

"You're a man among men yourself, Sil." Travis bent to give the calf another pat and then he rose. "Let me know if you hear anything suspect."

"Who hired you thugs?" Giles asked Graham, one boot on the lower rung of the fence they were repairing.

"No one hired me," Graham snorted with disdain for the other fellow.

"Shut up, cowpusher."

"How can I shut up if you ask me a question."

"Just don't get smart, that's all." Giles's eyes narrowed dangerously.

"What do you want to know?" Graham went on, lazing against the fence for the hundredth time that morning. "I work here, sure, but no one hired me or those other fellows to do anything what you're suggesting, young fellow. I'm Shainy's pa, and I come here to Wild Mountain looking for my gal. What's wrong with that? All the others in our family are gone away."

"Where's your wife? Why isn't she here with you?"

"Eleanora left me a long time ago."

Giles curled his upper lip. "It's no wonder."

"Why're you snooping around here, young fellow?"

"My name is Wilson, not young fellow!"

"And I ain't no cowpusher neither!"

"All right." Giles nodded. "All right. Just tell me how those other three came along not long after you showed up?"

"You mean Creek, Sloan, and B.J.?"

"That's them."

"They was looking for me."

"What did you do to make them want to 'look' for you?"

"You're mighty nosy, ain't you?"

"Giles stepped closer, snarling low, "I just want to know what's going down. You tell me, and I might be able to give a hand."

"No."

Now Giles yanked the man up by his shirt front and brought his face close. "I heard part of your conversation the other night . . . the night of the birthday parties in fact. You know what I heard?" He waited for the other man to shake his head. "What I heard, was someone saying it was even better for your plans that Shaina was pregnant. What did that mean, can you tell me? Or do I have to go and give this bit of information to the boss?"

Graham gulped, stammering, "I'll tell you . . . if you don't tell anyone else."

Smoothing Graham's shirt front gently, Giles said, "Now, why would I want to go and do that?"

Giles's eyes narrowed as he caught a flash of a white object around the side of the barn. "We'll talk about this later."

Splayed against the side of the building, Roux listened to what the two men were saying. The man with the pale-brown eyes was saying something about Shaina. What did it all mean? Roux wondered.

Before she could step away from the wall, a hand snaked out and clamped over her mouth. With wild eyes Roux looked up, trying to see who had a hold of her.

Her father had taught her just what to do if she was being attacked by a man, and Roux did just that now. With bent knee, she lifted her leg and shoved with all her might into the man's crotch.

Giles howled in pain, automatically releasing the girl and reaching for his lower half.

"Little bitch," he hissed.

As Giles held himself, he watched his prey escaping, and he cursed his stupidity. Now he'd have to stay away. Damn. He should have kept his hands off the stupid half-breed girl.

Roux went immediately to her father with what she had heard and what had happened to her.

She found him just mounting his horse, and she ran up to him. "Father, I have to talk to you. It's important."

"Not now, Roux." He kneed his horse into motion. "You'll have to save it until later."

Heaving a deep sigh, Roux walked away from the spot where he'd mounted up. He was always in such a hurry lately and he had no time for her, and not for Shaina, either.

Roux brightened. Shaina. She would go and tell

her . . . No, she couldn't do that, either. Her father and Deanna had warned her not to do or say anything that would get Shaina too excited.

Hunching her shoulders, Roux thought to herself maybe it wasn't all that important. Then she saw B.J. across the yard. He had been awfully nice to her and he made her laugh at times. Maybe he would know what to make of it all.

How Roux wished Jay hadn't gone to Seattle with his father. As she pondered on this she made her way across the yard to where B.J. was working.

"Hi there, Fire Fox!" B.J. boomed.

"Fox Fire."

"Oh, yeah." B.J. pulled her long braid from behind her back and gave it a tug. "You look like you could use someone to talk to."

"Yes. Will you walk to the stable with me? I am going to get my pony and go for a ride."

"Sure. But then I gotta get back to work."

"You have to work all day?"

"Uh huh."

Roux giggled, asking, "Why do you always say uh huh. What language is that?"

After scratching under his hat thoughtfully for a moment, B.J. said, "Dunno."

With a laugh Roux said, "You sure talk funny."

"So, what'd'ya want to talk about?" Walking beside the lovely girl, B.J. swiped a meaty arm across his forehead to wipe off the sweat of labor.

"I wanted to ask you something."

"Shoot."

"Shoot? You want me to shoot you?" Roux dimpled.

"You wanted to shoot the breeze, so go ahead, little girl."

"I am not little, and I don't want to 'shoot the breeze.' I was going to tell you something."

"I'm listenin'."

"Well . . ." she began hesitantly. "I heard Shainy's father talking to that Wilson guy. They were talking about Shainy, I am sure of it. First that Wilson guy said he wanted to know 'what was going down' and then he said he heard someone talking. They said it was better for their plans that Shainy was pregnant."

"Oh yeah?" B.J. was startled, but he tried not to convey his surprise to the girl. "Come over here, kid." He led her to the barn wall where the sun did not shine. "Listen, kid."

"You can call me Roux or Fox Fire. I do not like 'kid.' "

"Uh huh, OK, Foxy." He patted the silky head. "Don't be spreadin' that around what you heard. OK? See, maybe someone's plannin' a real big party for your Shainy. Know what I mean?"

"A party!" Roux clapped her hands together. How she loved parties.

"Now what's wrong?" He noticed the little face change from happiness to anger.

"That Wilson guy." Roux pouted. "He grabbed me and he was not going to let go."

B.J. hissed a curse under his breath, one she could not understand the meaning of.

"I ain't never seen this guy, little Roux. What's he look like, can you tell me?"

Roux thought for a moment then said, "He is this tall." She tried to reach above B.J.'s head.

"Down, girl. I get the message. This guy's taller than me. What else does he look like?"

"His eyes are the same as yours, only his are more . . . more, uh, shiny."

"Hey kid, don't make him sound like a god or something. I ain't so bad-looking myself, you know."

"Yes." Roux wanted to giggle but she held back. She shrugged. "His face is skinny and he is mean. And I seen him with my mother many times. They go in the woods and meet there. I know what they are doing, and it is not nice. My mother is a whore."

B.J. lurched forward as if someone had given him a sound whack on his back. Roux looked up at him with concern in her deep green eyes.

"Is something wrong?"

"Uh . . . no, but you shouldn't say things like that about yer own ma. My own ma was like that but I ain't never called her bad names."

"I'm sorry . . . I guess." Roux looked down and then up again. "But she is what I said."

"You just let me take care of this Wilson guy."

"Promise?"

"Uh huh. He won't be comin' around here botherin' you anymore. B.J.' ll take care of that now I know what he looks like."

Chapter Thirty

Pale moonlight fell on Shaina as she stepped out-side for a peaceful walk. She had waited patiently for night to come so that she could go outside and not encounter Travis out there somewhere. But she sensed the presence of another close by and was about to turn and go back inside when the voice reached her.

"Shaina—" Silvanus began and then corrected, "Missus Cordell."

"Hello, Silvanus." She smiled. "You can call me Shaina."

"I hope I'm not intruding, but I wanted to bring you something I made for you today."

"Oh?" Shaina was interested in what this strange man could have made for her. "What is it? For some reason she was feeling like a little girl anticipating a present from her parent.

He thrust the checkered napkin with something in it into her hands saying, "Here. I hope you like it."

Shaina looked down, feeling a strong urge to gig-gle. "It's—bread."

"Yep. Made it myself back at the cookhouse. It's my special bread, takes a lot of doing to make it up."

"Mmm," Shaina sighed as she held it up to her nose. "Smells delicious—and it's still warm. I smell raisins, nuts, and—is that apple?"

"Sure is. Travis told me how you was big on all those things, so I thought of my special bread and—"

Leaning with one hand braced on Silvanus's shoulder, Shaina gave him a soft kiss on his cheek. She straightened and looked into his eyes so like her own, murmuring, "Thank you, Silvanus."

With that she whirled and, clutching her loaf of 'special bread' close she ran back across the lawn and into the house, letting the screen door bang shut.

"Oh . . . Lord!"

Such sweet emotion tore at Silvanus's insides. He turned and made his way quickly to the bunkhouse way out back, brushing moisture off his rugged face as he went.

Giles stepped out from the shadows, his eyes narrowed as he watched the last of Silvanus's heel disappear into the night. Now Giles strode quickly to the porch. After a thorough look around, he slipped into the silent house where he knew Shaina was now alone, for he had seen the luscious housekeeper Deanna go to her own place and Travis ride into the forest.

Taking the precious loaf into the kitchen, Shaina sliced off a few pieces and stood slowly munching as tears rolled from her cheeks and onto the bread.

Swallowing the last bite of the second piece, she

302

contemplated the remaining loaf and then shrugged a why not? She took it to the table with her, and sliced off another piece, this one a most substantial chunk.

With her cheeks bulging, the tears still coming, she muttered incoherently, "Might as well make a pig out of myself. Who cares anyway?" She munched away. "No one," she answered herself.

Halfway through the loaf, Shaina was still talking to herself, waving her arms slowly as if she was speaking her piece to someone in the empty chair across from her.

"Well, he doesn't care . . . all he does is go off to Seattle or wherever it is he meets his worldly lady of the school." She'd imagined all sorts of things about the new schoolteacher Travis was hiring including her great beauty. "But Travis *did* get me a ring." *Sniff*.

Talking through mouthfuls, Shaina went on to herself. "He probably even bought *her* a red dress. Maybe she fills hers out better than I do." She stuffed in another bite. "Maybe she's got more meat on her bones . . . but I always thought he liked me just the way I am. He never told me, though, so how am I supposed to know how he wants me to look? He said I was beautiful. He makes love to me like he really enjoys it . . . but he hasn't made love to me for so long."

Shaina was moaning when Giles stepped into the kitchen and rushed to her side. "Shaina! What's wrong?" He truly sounded alarmed.

"Why . . . Giles." She hiccuped. "I was just getting pickled on fruit and nut bread. Care to have a slice?" She shoved the now repugnant loaf aside, saying, "Ugh!"

303

Giles shook his head and exclaimed, "What a way to get foxed! On a loaf of bread. Are you sure you aren't just eating for two?"

Shaina glared up at him, her eyes shining in the glow of the kerosene lamps. "Damn it, I don't want to talk about it . . . it's enough that I'm as depressed as I am."

Shaina stood up, put the sharp knife on the counter behind Giles, and then, absentmindedly leaving the bread on the table, sat down again as if she was quite weary of everything.

"All right." He pulled up a chair beside hers. "What should we talk about? The weather? The cows?"

"Please, Giles—"

But he went on nevertheless, "Birds and bees?"

"Don't be—" Shaina cocked her head at Giles. "How did you get in here? I don't remember letting you in."

"You were too busy getting foxed on that!" Giles indicated the remaining quarter of bread.

"Giles," she said impatiently, "what are you doing in the house while Travis is away?"

"Seeing my favorite girl." He tried to capture her wrist, but she pulled her hand away.

"I am not your girl, Giles, let alone your 'favorite' one. You should go now. I'll be fine . . . after I go to bed and sleep this off." She peered at the nutty loaf and shook her head. "I don't know what made me do it."

"Lonely people overindulge, Shaina. Lonely and unhappy."

"I don't think my emotions are any of your business, Giles. Now I wish you would go. Travis might

304

return at any moment."

What did it matter if Travis came home or not? The only place he haunted lately was that damn office of his . . . and maybe the beds of those Seattle "ladies"—or one schoolteacher lady, in particular. Well, she would have no philandering husband sharing *her* bed!

As Shaina continued to feel sorry for herself, Giles reached over to the counter and picked up a sharp knife.

"So," he said, lifting his boot to his knee and beginning to pick out tiny stones and such that had become lodged in the sole of his heel, "what are you going to do now?"

"What do you mean?" Shaina saw Giles in her side vision. She didn't turn to face him, but just kept gazing about with a down-in-the-mouth look on her face.

"Anyone can tell you aren't getting along with your husband . . ."

Giles let his words hang as he finished cleaning out the X carved into the heel of his boot.

"Giles, I told you, I don't want to talk about *anything* this evening. Especially not a *thing* concerning my husband. Do you hear? Or do I have to shout?"

Shaina turned and had to hold her breath at the strange light emanating from Giles's pale-brown eyes. Only they weren't so pale now, but dark with a disturbing incandescence.

"Giles? What's wrong? Why are you staring at me like that?"

"I'm looking at someone who can help me get up in the world. Maybe like on top of a mountain almost."

"Giles . . . I don't understand you. You aren't making any sense."

"No?" He peered at her strangely.

Giles waved the sharp knife in front of Shaina's eyes and she stared helplessly at it, unable to draw her eyes away.

"Put that thing down," she ordered him, "before you hurt yourself."

With a deep chuckle, Giles made a swift movement and with a downward stroke he stuck the tip into the table.

"What are you doing?" Shaina cried in dismay. "You are making holes in Deanna's table . . . Travis won't like slivers in the food."

"You think I care what Travis likes or dislikes?"

Shaina made to rise from the chair, but Giles held her down and, pulling her across to him, he sat her down hard onto his lap.

"There," he said. "This is where you belong!"

Tossing the knife aside, Giles forced his hand through Shaina's hair and yanked her face close to his. He breathed against her mouth, "I've never kissed you, Shaina."

"Giles . . . *no!*"

Shaina's heart pounded violently against her ribs as Giles opened his mouth over hers and completely covered her quivering lips. Her eyes were wide open and staring with unconcealed shock at his closed ones and she struggled helplessly as his fingers bit into the softness of her upper arms.

Giles's fingers pinched her chin as he kept her from wrenching her jaw away. Over and over he kissed her and thrust his tongue into her mouth. Then, tearing

306

his mouth from hers, he rasped, "Shaina, I want you. Come away with me. Make this easy for me."

She was afraid of the strange look in the eyes that had altered to a silvery brown. "Giles, stop this nonsense. I'm a married woman, remember." She gasped as Giles stared hungrily at her breasts where her robe had come loose. Before she could realize his intent, Giles was lowering his head toward the gleaming whiteness of her flesh.

"No!" Shaina lurched back from his repugnant touch.

She went rigid as his lips brushed a nipple and her hands, which had been shoving at his upper arms, now curled around the back of his head trying to shove him back. His strength, however, was far greater than hers, which had been diminished anyhow by her earlier overindulgence of the bread.

"Your breasts are beautiful, Shaina," Giles ground out huskily, taking one of the pale globes in his hand.

"Oh!" Shaina reached her hand out and succeeded in grasping his wrist . . .

And it was then that Travis walked in. The scene looked most intimately revealing to him, with Shaina holding on to Giles's wrist while he fondled her. And it just happened that at that moment Giles had been leaning into Shaina to capture her lips once again . . . and opening his mouth to speak passionate words.

"Oh, Shaina, I knew you'd want me. It's going to be just you and me from now on."

About to knee Giles where it counted, Shaina lifted her head and encountered a pair of smouldering green eyes.

Her mouth flew open and Giles filled the space with

his tongue.

Shaina bit down hard and Giles drew back, then grasped her shoulders in both of his long, thin hands.

Horrified, Shaina saw her husband's grim face. While her eyes grew even larger and her heart beat even faster, Travis turned and left the room.

Alone now with Giles again, Shaina's eyes rested on his face. She felt nausea rising within her.

"What's wrong with you?" Giles asked, watching her face turn colors.

Without answering, Shaina lurched forward and threw up all over Giles's new trousers.

Giles didn't let her finish soiling him, but jumped from the chair and ran to the door. Once there, he snarled over to her bent form, "I'll be back in a few days . . . and you better be cleaned up and waiting!" With smug satisfaction he went on, "You and I got lots of business to take care of! So be waiting, Shaina—"

Splashing the cold water onto her face in the basin, Shaina lifted her head and hissed, "Bastard." She coughed. "Never!"

Travis lay on the hard sofa with his hands behind his head as he stared up at the ceiling with glittering eyes. He could hardly give credence to the scene he'd just witnessed.

That bastard Giles!

Travis shot up off the sofa and glared across the room. Shaina and Giles . . . of course. He had had a notion for a long time that she had been keeping something from him, pretending it was the new men

308

on the ranch who were making her nervous instead of the deception of her infidelity.

He ran his fingers through his hair and almost tore some out by the roots. "What a sucker!" he said of and to himself.

That woman had led him a merry chase ever since she'd arrived in Wild Mountain. And now she had her part in the Lazy C—or so she thought!

Travis sighed deeply and gazed out at the rising yellow slice of moon, experiencing an aloneness he'd never felt so strongly before. Pushing his tanned fingers through the black luxuriant strands of his hair, he tried to think this out. It wasn't in his wife's loyal nature to be unfaithful. It was Giles who was at fault, not Shaina. He should have gone to her defense in the kitchen, instead of just glaring at her and leaving her in Giles's wicked clutches.

Travis felt the heat of wanting her in his loins. He longed to recapture the splendor of their lovemaking . . . before that ill-fated trip they'd made to the cabin.

Again he lay on the lumpy sofa. Tired as he was, sleep would not come and he let his clenched hands fall loosely to his sides as he once more pondered the situation. It was that damn Wilson who'd tried blotting him out . . . but Giles had not seemed to care that Shaina was in the cabin with him. That was the one thing that didn't make any sense. If Giles was after Shaina, he certainly would not try to kill her! Travis stood in one sharp moment and swiftly moved out of the room, promising himself he'd never again have to occupy the lumpy sofa in his office.

Shaina got into bed, staring wistfully over at the empty pillow. Travis's pillow. They'd been too long estranged from each other. She longed to feel again the velvet warmth of his kiss. His kisses were always gentle, never punishing and angry as Giles's had been. True, her husband's mouth could be hard and passionate, but never brutal. Enticing, stimulating, his tongue would thrust deep and make her knees tremble and she would match his own urgency. Her body would arch and she would draw herself closer to him. He would touch her intimately. She would cry out with joy.

Within the blue pools of her eyes tears welled, tears of past happiness and present loneliness. She hung her head, her voice coming soft and low. "Oh Travis. I need you now . . . so badly." She hugged herself, but found no consolation in the solitary gesture. "I'm afraid. I'm alone. God, how I want to remove that bastard's vile touch!"

The bedroom door opened just then and a voice with a strength of purpose carried to her, "You won't be alone tonight, Mrs. Cordell."

Shaina felt a flush run to the roots of her glorious red-gold hair and tingle all the way down to her toes. Travis!

He shut the door firmly and moved slowly toward her, his voice cold-edged. "Wilson's face is going to be nonexistent around here. I don't know why he was touching you, but I'll promise you this much, he'll never again get even a mile within your presence, sweet."

Shaina heaved a deep sigh, relieved to have Travis's protection and to know he was not angry with her.

There were still so many unanswered riddles, though. One she intended to clear up immediately.

"Travis." She looked down, and then up again quickly. "Why didn't you come to my defense in the kitchen?"

"Shaina, Shaina," he groaned softly. "Don't you know? Giles was practically making love to you in my house, and you wonder why I didn't come to your defense. You looked to be enjoying yourself."

"I wasn't!" She shook her head vehemently. *He almost raped me right there!* she wanted to scream. But then Travis would leave her to go search for Giles, and she wanted him here with her right now. She needed his love, needed to wash Giles's repulsive touch from her flesh and have her husband's healing intimacy.

"I can only say that I was insanely jealous, Shaina. If I'd stayed, Giles would be a dead man now. But enough of Giles. Let's leave the talk for later." Travis pushed her robe off her shoulders. "For now, there's only this, more important business to take care of."

"Travis . . ."

Gazing up at her husband, her eyes feasting at every angle, plane, and yes, even wrinkle, Shaina thought again how amazingly good-looking he had become in her eyes. He wasn't the most conventionally handsome man in the world, she knew, but he was all man and she loved him so!

As her hands came up to either side of his beloved face, Travis caught hold of her wrists and, turning her hands palms up he planted kisses there.

"We have one more problem between us, love . . . that nightgown. It has to come off."

Shaina laughed, a happy, lilting sound.

311

"Lift your arms." He leaned forward and kissed the nape of her neck.

Soon they were on the bed, Travis's weight crushing Shaina's. She loved the feel of him, his hands moving over her, his lips sliding over hers. "I love you, Travis," Shaina murmured over and over. "No matter what happens, always remember that."

"Hey, blue eyes, nothing will ever happen to separate us again. I'll make damn sure of that!"

Travis's lips were soft as he slanted them across his wife's, his hips thrusting against her inflaming Shaina's senses, her body. She moved to meet him, begging, "Travis . . . your pants . . . take them off."

When that was done, he returned swiftly. Shaina made a wanton sound, and when he would have kissed and touched her more, she parted her legs, wanting him.

He shuddered, feeling her pleasure as he entered the quivering softness of her. As they moved together like graceful dancers, they caressed, embraced, nibbled, kissed, and quivered together in the first tumblings of release. Travis lovingly drained all her doubts and fears, over and over murmuring his love for her — even when at last she lay with him still inside when it was all over.

Travis lay looking up at the ceiling. His voice was breathlessly soft. "I couldn't bear another moment away from you, Shaina."

"One more moment and I would have died, Travis." She planted a kiss on his shoulder, begging him, "Don't ever leave me again."

"If you don't go away, I won't."

"Promise, Travis? You'll never have to go anywhere

else for—for . . ."

"For what?" He bussed the top of her head.

"Oh—" Shaina slanted her lashes away from him. "For nothing, I guess."

"I've got everything I need—" He snuggled against her breast"—right here."

God, Shaina thought, *I hope so!*

Silence reigned for several minutes, then pushing her body against the intimate spoon of Travis's body, Shaina whispered, "Later?"

"Now," he breathed into her ear as he began to move.

Chapter Thirty-one

Noting the play of muscle and sinew beneath the tan shirt Travis pulled taut as he buttoned the front, Shaina purred and burrowed deeper into the rumpled bed, memories of the splendorous night just past still fresh in her mind and heart. Sleepily she observed him from the bed and asked, "Where are you going so early in the morning?".

Travis gave Shaina a brilliant smile as he wished his blue-eyed love a good morning. He turned from the mirror after giving his hair a thorough brushing to hopefully keep the thick black strands in place for the day.

Shaina counted herself very fortunate to be married to Travis Cordell, but there were still some things about him she couldn't understand. Like now. Why hadn't he answered her question? And why did he appear to be in such a hurry? She could sense him holding his impatience to be away in check.

"You look good enough to eat," he said. He leaned over and gave her a delicious morning kiss on her

314

love-bruised mouth.

Shaina couldn't contain herself and blurted out, "Travis, where are you going?" Her voice stopped him at the door as he was opening it. "You aren't just going to walk out and not tell me where you're going . . . and what's on your mind?

Travis returned to the bed and looked down at her, his green eyes reaching deep into her blue ones.

"I won't lie, Shaina."

"What do you mean?" There was a touch of alarm on her face. Had their night together all been a farce? Was he going to meet the schoolteacher, so soon from their bed?

"What I witnessed in the kitchen last night, Shaina. I can't just let that pass, I have to go and find Wilson and do something about that." He picked up her hand, and Shaina searched his eyes. "Just be damn sure he doesn't come around you again."

Shaina had nearly forgotten the repugnant scene the night before . . . she had recovered just fine with Travis's help. It was apparent *he* hadn't forgotten, however.

But Shaina could breathe easier, knowing Travis was not going out to meet someone else. She should have more trust in him, yet it was hard to feel this way when he'd been practically fondling that scarf the night of her birthday party.

Suddenly Shaina was afraid for Travis, and it was not because she thought Giles the stronger of the two, but more that Giles seemed a little crazy. Last night his desire for her had seemed almost desperate. And desperate, impassioned people could fly out of control and do just about anything. Like kill.

"Travis, I wish you would let it go." Now she could not tell him that Giles had promised to come back for her. If she did that, Travis might become even more obsessed with finding the man. "I—Don't hurt him, Travis."

Slowly he removed his fingers from her arm where he'd been lightly caressing her, and he stared hard at her.

"What are you trying to protect Wilson for, Shaina?"

"He didn't really do anything to hurt me, Travis."

"No—but it hurt *me* plenty seeing him fondling you." He looked at her softly revealed breasts looking like white half moons above her lace nightgown. "It made me think things that I don't like to think."

She reached out and took his hand.

"He won't be bothering me anymore." If Giles Wilson came to the house again she would threaten him with the word that her husband was out to kill him. That would keep him away!

"You can't be sure. I can't be sure." Travis patted the six-gun slung low on his lean hip. "For now he'll have to be peppered a few times in the rear to realize I mean business. Like the mangy dog he is, he just might return—and then I might just have to take sterner measures, love."

He kissed her gently and she watched him go out the door, afraid for him, but powerless to stop him. His stubbornness would lead him to do just as he intended.

Later, as he mounted Dice to ride to his mission,

he paused and caught Shaina around the waist, kissing her almost violently. Into her ear he murmured: "Be wearing the red dress when I get home."

But, Shaina thought as she watched him ride toward the forest, when will that be? She kept him in her sight, staring until he was long gone.

The sun was going down slowly, and glinted on the porch along the right side. This was where Shaina stood, wearing the red dress, unaware that someone had caught the stunning flash of scarlet from one of the bunkhouse porches.

"Well, well," Carolyn Creek drawled. "The uppity Shaina gots a red dress." Carolyn licked her lips. "Just what I been wantin', too 'cause mine is old and worn out."

Coming to stand beside Carolyn, Joe Creek had serious thoughts of dumping his wife as he watched, mesmerized by the beautiful sight set afire by the blazing sunset. Shaina Cordell. The strawberry blonde made his loins burn and his heart slam against his chest. He had to have her. Not just for ransom. No. He had to make Shaina Cordell his own. Once he had the money, gold to be exact—and he'd found out there was some of that, for he'd wheedled the fact out of that old geezer Noah Starr—he would light out of Wild Mountain with his beautiful captive. First he had to make sure Giles Wilson got rid of Travis Cordell, as planned, but then he in turn would put Wilson's lights out. There was only one problem. Carolyn. She was a damn jealous woman and she might try to hurt Shaina Cordell. He had to find a way to divert her attention.

Joe slanted his eyes at Carolyn. "Still want that red dress, Caro?"

Carolyn's face was pinched, angry and white around the eyes as she hissed, "Yeah, you know I do, Joe Creek. But do you know what *I* know? I know you got the hots for that rancher's slut. I been watchin' you, Joe Creek."

Joe turned on Carolyn, hurtfully grabbing her on either side of her soft shoulders, snarling, "I saw you run out and meet that no-good Injun the other night when you thought I wasn't looking. You don't fool me none, Caro, he was diddlin' with you." He gave her a hard shake. "Wasn't he?" he ground out.

"Yes! Yes! I'm bored to hell with this place!"

Shoving her back, he slapped her face from side to side. "No-good Injun lover . . . slut!" He spat in her face, adding, "I divorce you right here, and don't ever darken my bedroom door."

"Awww, Joe." She leaned into him, trying to run her hand up over his chest. "You don't mean that." She peered up into his fierce, dark eyes, asking, "Do you?"

He shoved her away like she was repulsive to him. "Keep your hands off me, dirty Injun lover. I told you if you ever diddled with one again, that was it. And you did."

Drawing herself up to her full height, Carolyn slammed her fists onto her hips. "You're just saying that, Joe, 'cause you want that rancher's wife. You want to get her away so's you can diddle her. I won't let you, Joe, I aim to tell that Travis Cordell what you

318

got in mind."

Joe didn't let his alarm show in his face, but he moved closer to her, speaking in a calm, low voice now. "Hey, Caro, what are we fighting for, huh?" He wrapped his arm around her waist, feeling the thrill of arousal when the gorgeous woman in the red dress came to mind. Shaina was the woman he wanted, and have her he would. "Let's go inside and make up, huh?" he cajoled. His desire was great after seeing Shaina posed so beautiful and forlorn on the porch and he needed a woman. Even his silly wife would do. He gritted his teeth as he led Carolyn inside, thinking *No wonder that Giles Wilson wanted Shaina Cordell.* Any hot-blooded male would.

At the same time Joe Creek entered Carolyn's body his mind was already devising a way to get rid of her without having to kill her. And when he made believe this woman, his wife, beneath him was Shaina and found his shattering release, the vision of Moon Dog leading Carolyn away came to mind.

Weary of waiting, Shaina lay down and fell asleep in the red dress, not even caring if she rumpled it. She entered a vivid dream where many tangled hands were reaching out to grab her. She broke away finally and ran. Over her shoulder as she saw *them* — men — as they hurried after her, reaching out and tearing at the red dress like mad dogs in pursuit of their terrified prey. They were naked. And ravenous. They all wanted her, she could tell and she gasped over and over, her breath coming hard and fast as she ran seemingly

319

without going anywhere. Now they were tearing at her dress, ripping pieces off from her running legs . . . But up ahead suddenly loomed an even more horrible and grisly sight. It was a monster . . . with dark fur all over it. Like a huge monster-dog. The thing turned and when it saw her, sniffing and licking its chops, it stood on its hind legs and became even bigger. The jaws snapped close to her face, the fangs long and sharp, the wickedly glowing eyes finding her. It was just about to clamp its powerful jaws into her when she woke up screaming . . .

"Shaina, Shaina." Travis rocked her in his arms. "You were having a nightmare. It's all right. I'm home now."

The dream was still in her mind vividly.

"Oh, Travis . . . it was horrible!"

She clutched the front of his shirt in both hands, trembling from head to foot. For a while Travis just held her, and then he gently began removing the red dress, murmuring to her as he would a frightened child . . . like he'd done with Roux when she had had a nightmare. When the dress and her petticoat and chemise were off, he just as tenderly dressed her in the softest nightgown he could find in the drawer.

When they were in bed and he held her against him like she was the most fragile doll, his body embracing hers, he quietly asked her about the dream.

"It helps to talk about it some, so it won't return," he explained.

"There were horrible men chasing me, Travis." She peeked up into his eyes, then down again to his chest where the lamplight burnished the curly mat there.

320

"Then there was a terrible monster . . . a bear I think it was. Oh, Travis, it was so real. All of them were out to get me."

"But *I'm* the one who has you in reality, love, and I'll never hurt you, only protect you with my life. You will never have to be afraid as long as I'm around."

"But the dream came when you were gone, Travis."

"And it was just that, love, only a dream. Nightmares can't hurt you, neither can the dead."

"Eleanora always said that, Travis, but she added, 'It is the living that hurt, the real people.' "

"Don't be afraid." Travis snuggled her closer, stroking her red-honey hair from her face.

"I'm not," Shaina said, "not now."

Moonlight streamed through the window as Carolyn slowly and cautiously climbed over the sill and dropped to the ground below. She walked a little ways, tossing a glance over her shoulder every few moments to see if anyone was visible in the window. Once away from the spindly trees backing the yard, she began to move swiftly.

Up ahead a figure stepped out from behind an outcropping of rocks. He was gilded by the moon, long braids, bare chest, fringed leggings, even the moccasins became visible as Carolyn neared the statuelike Indian.

Carolyn's face was one deep, happy smile.

"Moon Dog," she breathed, already excited by his mere presence.

Moon Dog smiled to himself as suddenly she stood

there before him.

"Car-o," he said in a rough whisper. He spoke clipped English and that further excited the passion-filled woman. "You will be all my woman soon."

Carolyn fell against him and delighted in the instant hardness of his body. Joe Creek had a few soft places on his body, but this man, this Indian, was all hard—heavenly stonelike . . . and he could stay like that for hours. Carolyn had also enticed the lad Jay Ridingbow into her bed one day when Joe had ridden into the hills. The lad had seemed nervous and had kept popping up to scour the grounds outside the window. He, too, had been built so very hard just like Moon Dog, and it was too bad he couldn't have stayed longer. But Jay was too young for her. Besides, he had only wanted her for the one time, and then he had avoided her like the plague. But she had taken care of the hankering that had bothered the lad.

Joe Creek left the spot in the shadows where he had concealed himself to watch as Carolyn went out to meet Moon Dog. As he returned to his still-warm bunk, he smiled, telling himself he would not wait up for his wife. He dreamed erotic dreams about Shain Cordell and the day he would make her his. That day was coming soon, he would see to that or burst from wanting her.

Graham Hill had finally found a time when he could speak to Silvanus Hart alone without anyone overhearing them. He followed the cowboy into the barn and closed the door softly behind them.

Silvanus turned and his questioning gaze encountered the demon Hill. "What can I do for you?" he asked with disdain, and smelled the lingering stench of whiskey on the other man.

"How long you been working here?" Graham said, his words blurring together.

"If you're looking for someone to be your arguing companion, Graham, you've come to the wrong place."

"Don't want to argue," Graham said flatly.

"What do you want then?"

"I want to know if you have any idea where my Eleanora is."

"Why do you ask?" Silvanus said. He hunkered down to pet the sick calf.

"You know where she is, don't you?" Graham wavered slightly where he stood.

"If that was true, then how come I'm being questioned as to her whereabouts?" he asked Graham.

"What *do* you know about it? She went away, she was mad at me. Christ, Eleanora never got that way with me, but something made her hopping mad and she took off. Maybe it was because I slapped her around a little, but she never went away before." Graham missed the intense look of anger on the other man's face. "I had to send the kids down to Texas with my arrogant sisters. I'd like to get them back, but first want to find my Eleanora."

Silvanus stood; he was slightly taller than Graham and the other man looked suddenly much smaller in his pathetic state of inebriation.

"I think you better go," Silvanus said, feeling sick from the conversation and the strong smell of liquor.

"No," Graham said promptly. "Not until I've had my say."

"Well," Silvanus growled. "*Say*. Then get the hell out of my barn."

"Your barn?" Graham laughed at that. "Now it's *your* barn? Since when do *you* own things around here? Just 'cause you think Shainy's your daughter, don't give you no special privilishes around here."

"You're drunk, you can't even talk straight. Get out, Graham, before I throw you out. I can't stand the smell of your stench."

Graham stepped forward and poked Silvanus on his chest. "You diddled with my Eleanora . . . and don't think I didn't figure out where Shainy came from and that *Will's your kid, too*."

"Shut up!" Silvanus clenched his hands into tight fists at his sides.

" 'Fraid Shainy's going to hear, that it?"

"No," Silvanus said calmly. "But I don't think you would be wanting her to know the truth, Graham."

Graham peered at the cowboy, his voice cracking as he said, "How come Eleanora was in love with you and not me? Oh sure —" He waved his arm in the air. "she told me she loved me in front of the kids, just for them to hear, but later, in bed, she never said those words, not even one time. You got her pregnant the first time, why didn't you marry her? Why did you send back her to me? for chrissake."

Silvanus shook his head in pity. "Eleanora felt sorr

for you, Hill, and I must say you are indeed a sorry excuse for a man."

Graham stood aghast. "She felt sorry for me? My Eleanora?"

"She was never yours, Graham. Eleanora was in love with me, yes, and I treated her poorly. Now I wish to God she was here so I could make it all up to her." He gritted his teeth, snarling, "And I'd make up for all the years I left her with such as you, Hill. Eleanora was a real lady."

Graham snorted. "Hah, and you just a cowboy. The cowboy and the lady."

"That's right, Graham. We were a pair . . . I realized that too late." He gave the man a look of disgust. "Better a cowboy for Ellie than a yellow belly mouse."

"She give me more kids than she ever gave you, Silvanus Hart. And none of them bastards!"

Before Graham could act, Silvanus's fist shot forward and he laid a good one on Graham's jaw. Graham staggered back against the wall, blood instantly welling from his cut face. Dazedly he pushed himself away from the wall and shook his head to clear it.

"Now, hear me," Silvanus said in a hard voice. "Don't ever come around Eleanora again."

Graham, even in his befuddled state, asked abruptly, "What do you mean? Have you seen Eleanora? You know where she is, don't you?"

"No. Not yet. But I aim to find her." He didn't think Ellie was dead, no, he had a feeling she was looking for him. After he'd heard that the Cordells took a visit to Mountain Lake, he did some investigating on his own his last visit to Seattle, only he didn't stay there long, he went on to Mountain Lake immediately, and there he discovered what Shaina had discovered, which wasn't much to go on. But it was something. And he'd left a message with the minister as to where he could be reached . . . just in case the lady in question was looking for him . . . and her daughter.

Wiping his cut nose and lip on his sleeve, Graham staggered to the door, throwing a taunt over his shoulder.

"You'll never find her. She don't want to be found. Me, she don't want nothing to do with, and you, even less."

Under his breath Silvanus muttered, "We'll see." He looked out to the lonely starlit heavens and soon his tears blurred his vision so that all the stars seemed to slide down the world and cry with him. "By God, Ellie, we'll see."

Graham was spitting mad, ready to kill.

He was going to fix that Silvanus Hart real good this time. He'd get Shaina away from Silvanus and Travis Cordell, and together he and Shaina would go away to California. Maybe Ellie was there. Yes. She could be. He had talked about California enough to her. He had told her a lot of things, one of them being that Silvanus Hart had found himself a real nice looking woman and had gone away with her, that Silvanus wanted nothing to do with Ellie again

Maybe she believed him. Maybe she didn't. But not long after that she took off. Well . . . it was probably all his own fault, he had beat her up because she was always mooning over Silvanus Hart like a sick female calf. Now he had a chance to lure Ellie back to him. Shaina had always been Ellie's favorite. He'd use her as bait. He'd do that, just like him and the others had planned. There'd only be one change: *He'd* be taking Shaina, not Joe Creek, not that Wilson fellow. He would fool them all. Even Shainy.

Chapter Thirty-two

B.J. didn't like it. His cousin Joe was making plans
with the "Wilson guy"—that's what little Roux called
him, B.J. recalled with tender affection. On his
stealthy way out of the kitchen, B.J. stopped to swipe
a boiled potato from the pot, glancing around, and
then took another. As he munched in the corner by
the stove, he mused on what to do as he stared out to the
wall hung with well-scoured utensils. Beyond that he
could see the dining table laid out with knives, forks,
tinware, where the men drank their coffee now as they
lolled in their chairs. Wiping his fingertips on his blue
shirt, B.J. glanced around to see if anyone was watching, then with a shrug he stole yet another potato. He
wiped his fingers again, decided he had better beat it
before Cooky came in and found him stealing some of
the precious dinner. He eyed just one more potato
and, lifting it with two fingers, deposited it in his
mouth.

"Heyy!" Cooky was just walking in as B.J. was
walking out munching away. Cooky gave the rotund

B.J. a swat with his spatula, saying, "You eat when you're supposed to, fatso, and not before!" But Cooky smiled and shook his head as the big man with the skinny rear hightailed it out of the dining hall.

As B.J. was crossing the way from the barn to the corral, he spotted Shaina Cordell, and she saw him and waved. B.J. grinned happily. She was getting used to him, and he really liked her now. At first he'd thought she was nothing but a rancher's snooty wife, but the more he saw her about the ranch the more he thought seriously about abandoning the crazy scheme to have her kidnapped and hold her for ransom. Joe was crazy! It would never work, he knew it, because Travis Cordell could be one mean sonofagun if crossed.

No sir, B.J. didn't want to have anything to do with firing that dude's wrath.

B.J. blushed and lifted his shoulders in a shy shrug as Shaina Cordell waved and smiled again before she bent to care for the flowers nodding in the sun beside the porch.

Boy, she sure is beautiful. Like one flash of glorious beauty. He couldn't hurt her. He didn't want to. She seemed so pure, so shining, and, as time had passed, strangely close to his heart. Just like the Fox Fire had come to be.

Joe walked up to him, and said, "She's a sight, ain't she?" He smiled, licking his lips as she displayed a view that made his thighs tingle. "Can't wait to have her in my clutches."

"Oh, shut up, Joe," said B.J., then left his dark-visaged cousin to stare after him with a blank look.

Joe merely shrugged. "Must be having a bad day."

329

After he leered at Shaina Cordell for a few moments more, Joe took himself and his fevered body elsewhere.

From the place where he had concealed himself in the woods, Giles watched all that went on at the ranch. He had seen the big oaf B.J. walk away in a huff, while Joe Creek looked after him and hardly batted a lash. Then a frown gathered his black brows.

Giles smiled. Good. There was tension between the men. That meant Travis would feel it, too, and more would be created between him and Shaina. Nervous men made mistakes, and Travis had already made a big one . . . he had left Shaina unprotected. Giles's smile was smug. And he wouldn't have to lift a finger, not yet. That candy-assed Graham was going to do all the dirty work.

Travis arrived home late that night. Shaina was already asleep, so he went into the kitchen to fix himself a bite to eat, and sat alone at the table. He remembered the scene he'd witnessed and his anger grew all over again. Where could Giles be? He'd searched the whole damn valley and forested hills for him. The Senior Wilson, the riverboat captain he'd gone to see at the landing told him that as far as he knew, Giles, this captain's son, had not been around in quite a while, and had not taken the riverboat back to Seattle. There had been a time or two when the captain had let one of the other crewmembers take the *Clementine*. The other riverboat captains? They hadn't seen Wilson, either. So where *had* he hid out? Lord. How stupid. Wilson could come to the ranch any time while he was away . . . he would have to leave someone in charge of the protection of his wife. Damn. What a time for Jack Nolan and Deanna to be away visiting relatives in South Prairie. He could have used Jack right now. He smiled and remembered what Jack had told him just last week, that Shaina had tried to follow him up into the mountain that day he had gone searching for his would-be assassins. He chuckled. The brave schoolteacher. His wife . . . his love.

Travis set his coffee cup down and stared into the low flame of the lamp he'd lighted a short time ago. The question he'd been asking himself for some time now besieged his weary brain. Who had tried to kill him? More questions: What did Wilson want with his wife? Did he just want a 'time' or two with Shaina? Oh, yes, and the one that troubled him the most, though he'd tried time and again to set it from his mind:

Shaina yelled at him again as she had the night of her birthday party, *"I hope I'm not pregnant, because I don't want your baby, Travis Cordell."*

Why?

That hurt.

More than anything, that hurt.

He had withheld nothing of himself as they loved. He had thought she loved him for himself, just the way he was, without reservation. Too, he had thought Miah loved him. He hadn't been enough for her, though, it seemed, for she'd had to go and seek one lover after the other. Why did both women seem to love him before they married, then afterward turn against him? Did marriage turn all women against their husbands? No, he'd witnessed some happy couples in the valley, so that couldn't be the case. He could make the ranch thrive. He could plant just about anything and make it grow and his cattle and horses flourished. Why then was his marriage to his beautiful, precious Shaina withering?

Travis slammed down his coffee cup. Was she pregnant or wasn't she? They hadn't talked any more of it . . . He'd like a son to carry his name. Or a pretty little girl who looked just like Shaina, a glorious beauty with dark-blue eyes, strawberry blond hair.

"Father?"

At the sound of Roux's sleepy voice, Travis turned in his chair and held out his arms to her. "Why isn't my girl asleep? The hour is late, baby."

"I could not sleep." Roux slid into his lap and her legs dangled over his closed knees. "The dreams bothered me."

Travis thought of Shaina's dream the other night and asked, "Were you having a nightmare?"

Roux nodded. "A bad one." She reached out and took a sip of her father's coffee. She grimaced and set down the cup.

Travis's frown was thoughtful, a deep line set between his well-shaped eyebrows. He smoothed the deep auburn hair away from the girl's face and she looked up at him in adoration.

"Tell me about it," he said. His voice was soft and gentle.

"Someone chased me. No. Many chased me. They were ugly and they tied me up to something. Like a tree. Then a big thing, I think it was a bear, came after me." Roux jumped down from his lap and gave her impersonation of the "thing" in her nightmare, and she curled her fingers over her head and bared her tiny teeth in what was supposed to be a ferocious growl. She made a show of it as she lumbered about the kitchen and slapped at things in her way. "Arrrghhh!" Her voice went deep and low and scary as she could make it.

Travis began to laugh, and he slapped his knee, saying, "I'm shaking in my boots . . . that must have been some scary dream."

He looked up and saw Shaina standing there, her hands crossed over her chest. She seemed paralyzed by Roux's actions, and as Travis looked from one to the other, his smile faded and his face went still.

"That —" Shaina said, and she pointed at Roux who'd stopped her act only a moment before. "Just like that." Her finger shook as she reached it out. "My . . . my dream."

"You had the same bad dream?" Roux said, her expression was astonished.

"Yes." Shaina seemed to be staring back into the nightmare. "The thing was . . . horrible."

Roux nodded slowly and said, "I know. Mine was, too."

Suddenly Roux ran to Shaina and grabbed her arms to wrap them around her. Shaina tightened the embrace and held the girl securely against her.

"I do not want to be alone!" Roux stared up into Shaina's still dazed face. "Can I sleep with you?"

"Of course," Shaina said. Her eyes found Travis's and they said, "I'm sorry."

"I — I'll just go in the study and make myself comfortable." He sighed. "I'm getting used to it, anyway."

Shaina frowned at his slouched back as he went out

of the kitchen. What was wrong with him? Why did he sound so dejected and alone?

Shaina mumbled to herself as a sleepy Roux trailed her into the bedroom, "It's his own fault, he should stay home where he belongs. What is he out chasing Giles Wilson for anyway?" She tucked Roux into one side of the bed, kissed her forehead, said good night, and before long the girl was sound asleep. "He didn't even kiss me," she continued muttering, "maybe he is not looking for Giles at all. What a flimsy excuse. And I'm a fool for believing him in the first place. He went out to meet that new schoolteacher from Seattle. I wonder when he's going to present his mistress to his wife?" She fumed as she stalked her shadow cast on the bedroom walls, then tore off her robe and lay down, not even bothering to turn down the lamp. She stared at the ceiling until her eyes grew drowsy.

Finally she was sound asleep. But her dreams were not pleasant, she kept seeing the tall, hairy creature loom up before her. Over and over she dreamed the same horrifying dream . . .

The oil lantern in Miah's hand swayed as she helped Giles move brush away from a pair of old cellar storm doors that led to their underground hideaway. The place was situated halfway between the forest and the ranch house, and had not been in use for years because of the new one that had been constructed, closer to the house.

Down in the hole there were a few rickety chairs and a bulky table, besides some other odds and ends, like Miah's Indian blankets and the remains from the day before of their tortillas and beans.

Giles let himself down slowly and easy onto the blanket spread on the earthen floor, rubbing his backsides as if he'd been riding long and hard.

He groaned, "Cordell is like a bloodhound, I swear. He was on my tail all day. Got close to me so many times I thought for sure he had me."

"You should have come here to hide." Miah said over her shoulder as she pulled shut the flimsy door that had long ago fallen into disrepair from neglect. She backed down the creaking ladder, flinging her shiny black braid over her shoulder as she faced Giles with hands on hips.

"I can't stay holed in this dugout all day, Miah. A man could go crazy."

Sidling up to him, Miah rolled her dark eyes, murmuring, "Not if he has beautiful woman for company. I will make you happy, Giles Wilson."

As she moved closer to suggestively brush his knees, Giles pulled back as if she'd burned him. "Not now, Miah. We have business to take care of."

Miah pouted. "All you think of is Woman with Fire in Hair."

"Shaina?" Giles laughed. "You're just jealous, Miah. Remember, when all this is over and we've got the gold, it'll be just you and me."

"I think you lie."

"Come here, and listen. Stop being so suspicious of everything I do. We're in this together."

Heaving a deep sigh, Miah said, "I will listen." She sat on the blanket next to him, her bare legs close to his knees.

"Now, what we'll do tonight is get Roux while she's

sleeping. Have you got those herbs and powders in your pouch like I asked you to get?"

"Sleeping powder."

"One whiff and it'll keep her asleep for a while? Are you sure?"

"I know my medicine, Giles Wilson. Very powerful stuff will knock out child when you put cloth over her face. I have made it wet."

"Liquid. Good." He watched her rise gracefully and get the vial in the pouch which she showed to him. "Can't tell much by looking at it, but I'll take your word for it."

"Very powerful stuff. White man call it knock-out powder." Putting the concoction aside, Miah turned her liquid-black eyes back on Giles's wild pale-brown ones. "You are very excited. We will take Woman with Fire in Hair, too?"

"No. That will never work. We're going to lure her with with the child, like I said."

"Travis will come, too." Miah squatted in front of Giles, studying his eyes intently. She toyed with the heel of his boot, plucking small stones from the carved X.

"You could be right. But if I know Shaina, she'll try to look for Roux on her own at first while Travis is rounding up his men. I don't know for sure. If they both come—" Giles shrugged"—so much the better."

"How will she know where to look?"

"I think Graham will take care of that," Giles cryptically said. "He's got his own plans, and I know just where he's heading. After he's liquored himself up real good, Graham talks in his sleep. See?"

"Ah," Miah said. Then she frowned, asking, "Why

do we take Roux then?"

"For insurance. We still need her for bait if all else fails."

What Giles didn't tell Miah was he had plans for himself and Shaina—after he got rid of Travis Cordell.

"Let's get moving. It's getting late."

Once they were outside and walking to their mounts that had been concealed in the bushes, Giles spoke very little.

"You get in the window. Open the back door for me."

This was all he said and then they mounted their horses, the pony trailing behind on a length of rope.

Like Indians sneaking about in the night, Miah and Giles crept stealthily up to the house. They paused there in the blue-black shadows. Then Miah, the smaller of the two, opened the window and Giles put his hand to her rump and gave her a boost inside.

"Meet you at the back. Open the door for me, and, Miah—find me a weapon. Something to use as a club," he whispered, "and don't take all night."

All was silent inside the house. Miah moved through the room and down the hall like a wraith in the night. Looking this way and that, she reached the kitchen after several minutes. Going directly to a lower cupboard, she bent down and slid something out—the candlestick holders she had stolen from Shaina. A birthday present from Travis, one that Shaina had not even opened yet because Miah had seen to it the Woman with Fire in her Hair never got a chance to enjoy them.

The moon was climbing and Miah hurried now to let Giles in the back door. "I have the weapon." She held out the silver candlestick holder and Giles snatched her hand down as the elegant object caught a glint of illumination from the moon.

"No one awake in house. Not to worry," Miah said, her white teeth gleaming as she grinned with mischievousness alight in her eyes.

Giles hissed low, "We might not have to use it. But I'm not going to chance leaving it behind. Do you have the pouch?"

Miah brought the pouch up after she'd dug in the low pocket of her doeskin shift. "Here."

"Let's go."

They crept through the sleeping house, unaware until Miah bumped against a table and knocked a china vase to the floor, that Travis was moving restlessly on the lumpy sofa. The vase clattered. Then all was still. Only a moment of silence reigned, however, before the intruders heard the movements inside the room, telling that someone had just arisen from bed.

In truth, Travis had been half asleep when he heard the slight commotion outside in the hall. Sleepily he arose from the sofa, cursing its lumpiness. He had delicious visions of Shaina walking to meet him for a midnight tryst. Believing that the sound had come from the living room, he headed in that direction raking his long fingers through his hair and slicking i back from his forehead.

He was unaware that someone was sneaking up on him until he felt the blow come crashing down on hi head. After that there was nothing. He was out cold

Above Travis stood Giles with the candlestick holder held loosely in his fingers. Miah stood beside him, tugging for him to come away and stop staring gleefully at their victim who was laid out cold.

"Help me tie him up," Giles ordered, removing the rope he'd earlier fastened about his waist in case something like this happened to warrant its use.

When that was done, Giles coldly gave one last look to the trussed-up man, then crept back along the hall toward the bedroom where he hoped to find little Roux.

"She is not here," Miah hissed in the darkened room, stuffing her pouch back into her shift.

"Where is she?" Giles snapped. When Miah bumped against the table, knocking yet another object to the floor, Giles cursed. "You are the clumsiest Indian I've ever known. C'mon, let's try the next bedroom."

Once out in the hall they both froze and Giles flattened himself and Miah against the wall as a woman with long, flowing hair, tousled and moonlit bright, stepped out from a bedroom.

Chapter Thirty-three

Over and over Shaina had dreamed the same horrifying dream until at last she was wrenched awake.

There, that is what had awakened her, Shaina had thought. Not the dream at all, but a sound coming from somewhere in the house. Quietly, so as not to waken Roux who slept peacefully beside her, Shaina had thrown her legs over the side of the bed and grasped her robe in front of her after throwing it on.

At the bedroom door, she had paused with fast-beating heart before she ran down the hall, meaning to wake Travis so that he could investigate the sound she'd heard. For all she knew, Travis could be up and about. As she stopped at Travis's door, she wondered in a frantic moment why there was no light in his room. That could only mean that he was still asleep.

"Travis . . . wake up!" she cried, then gasped as she looked down at the empty bed. She whirled and exited the room, hurrying down the hall toward the living room, her heart in her throat.

It seemed an eternity before she reached the living

room . . . and then she saw him, bound hand and foot on the floor.

There was blood at his temple!

"Travis!" She rushed toward him and fell to her knees. "Oh, dear God, what has happened!"

No response from Travis.

"Oh, please, Travis, wake up!" Shaina cried with great shivers passing through her body as she clutched his shoulders trying to rouse him. The blood! "Oh Travis, darling, please be alive." She wept as she reached for the sharp letter opener on the table and carefully sliced the binds around his wrists and ankles.

He didn't move . . . not even his eyes. They were closed. His beloved face was pale. As in death.

Shaina continued to stare down at Travis, wishing to God he would open his eyes, move a finger, an eyelash — anything!

She was so afraid for him. He might still be alive. She had to do something in case the villains returned . . . she had to get his gun. Her eyes flew to the door as she scrambled to her feet, and, moving faster now even in her benumbed state, she ran to the door, flung it open, and screamed. "Help! . . . Silvanus . . . help!"

Whirling about, she ran down the hall, into the study, searching frantically for Travis's six-gun.

It had to be here, had to be . . . somewhere!

There!

Her heart almost stopped then as she ran back into the hall and saw across the way that a window had been carelessly left open. The curtain was blowing in and out, eerily, giving her the creepy feeling that someone stood right behind her. She whirled about, sticking the gun straight out in front with her unsteady hand. Hairy fingers of apprehension ran up her spine as she looked about in frightened anticipation. But there was no one there.

Breathing a sigh of relief, she sped back to the living room and Travis's side. Again she pointed the gun, this time at the door . . . waiting. Still holding the gun, she bent over Travis and laid her ear against his chest, praying that she would hear a heartbeat.

There . . . there it was!

"Oh, God—" she sobbed. "Your heart is beating. Oh, Travis . . . thank God . . . *thank God.*"

Just then a man stepped into the shadowy room, startling a scream from Shaina. She quailed inwardly but managed to hold the gun out in front of her, if not too steadily.

Silvanus saw the fear in Shaina's wide blue eyes change to utmost relief and she jumped to her feet, crying, "Silvanus! I was scared stiff. I—I didn't know what to do. I'm so happy you're here . . . so damn happy. Oh, please, please look at Travis . . . I'm afraid he's hurt bad."

"Slow down, honey," Silvanus said, bending over and checking Travis. Holding the wrist trying for a pulse, his shoulders relaxed when he found one. "His pulse is strong, Shaina. He's not as bad as you think." He wanted desperately to ask what had happened but this was not the best time. "Give me a hand and we'll get him into the bedroom."

Shaina sat with Travis while Silvanus took the gun from Shaina's cold fingers, thoroughly searched the house and grounds, and then hurried to fetch the doctor. It was during this time that Travis opened his brilliant green eyes and looked up at her. A hand reached for her shoulder and she cried out as she turned, looking into his face. "Are you all right? I—I was so afraid, Travis, afraid you were going to leave me."

"Leave you?" He turned his face into her luxurious hair as she laid her cheek softly against his. "Where would I be going, love?"

Frantically her eyes flew across his face, her smiling mouth trembling, her hand smoothing the hair back from his forehead. He winced.

"Ouch!"

"Oh, damn, I forgot." Shaina lifted her hand and he captured it, pressing a dry kiss into her palm. "Do you hurt anywhere else? Can you move?"

"I'm fine."

"Fine? How can you say that . . . you look terrible!"

"I'll take a look." Travis indicated the mirror and began to rise from the bed.

"No you don't." She pushed him back down upon the pillows the same time he reached for his head and groaned.

"There," he said, directing a finger at something lying on the floor.

"What is it?" She bent to pick up the heavy object, turning it over in her hands, saying, "It's a candlestick holder. Is this what hit you?"

With narrowed eyes, Travis said, "*Silver* candlestick holder, to be exact . . . and it didn't hit me by itself."

Shaina stared into eyes hard as cold emeralds and felt her heart pound thickly. Anger thinned Travis's lips.

343

"You think — ?" Shaina hefted the candlestick holder, then set it down hard onto the bedside table. "Travis, you have got to be kidding — ?"

"I see you found a use for your birthday present . . . finally."

"Travis, if you think . . ." She pointed at what must be genuine silver and had cost him no little money. "Why would I?"

"You tell me. Why would you, Shaina? *Love.*"

Shaina shook her head. Her wild tresses fanned out over her shoulders like flaming gold, her wide blue eyes troubled. She pushed herself up from the side of the bed, unspoken pain alive in her eyes.

"I — " She indicated the silver "— I never did open that birthday present, Travis, so how could I know to use it on you, as you seem to be accusing."

Sitting up in bed now, Travis said, "What do you mean you never opened them?"

"*Them?* There are two then?"

"Of course — two."

"Someone else must have found them, Travis — whoever struck you over the head."

Raking a hand through his hair and wincing, Travis held out his hand to her, saying, "God, Shaina, I'm sorry. Come here."

"No!" The angry whisper burst out of her and she ran from the room, heartbroken to think that her husband would accuse her of trying to harm him.

"Damn," Travis swore at her fleeing form. *"Damn!"* Things would never be right with his beloved Shaina again.

Travis was up in a flash. He was still wearing his blue jeans . . . he had slipped into them when he'd gotten up from the sofa after hearing a noise. When he turned to reach for his shirt someone had whacked him a good one on the skull.

As Travis's fingers were flying over the buttons he forced through the holes, he collided with old Doc as he was going out the door.

"Where do you think you're going?" Doc boomed, his silver hair sticking out every which way.

"I'm going to get to the bottom of this mess—" He stuck his surly frown into the doc's face"—if I have to ride ten horses to death in getting down to it!" He called over his shoulder in slamming out the door, "if I have to ride into hell itself to drag them out!"

"Wait a minute, son," the doc yelled, "We got to bandage that head."

Shaina appeared in the hall, wringing her hands, crying, "Where's Travis now?"

"Calm down, honey," Silvanus said, curling an arm about her shoulder and pulling her close to his side.

"I *can't* calm down!"

The doc looked exasperated as he asked, "Why not?"

She ignored him and turned to Silvanus, sobbing, "Roux is gone!"

Grabbing on either side of her shoulder, Silvanus turned her to face him. "Maybe she got up early," he said, feeling helpless looking at his darling Shaina.

"She *never* gets up this early. I've searched everywhere . . . she's gone!"

"C'mon, honey." Silvanus took her by the hand.

Shaina shook her head, as if she had a headache. "I've already been to the barn . . . Roux's horse is still there." Her hand was held in a firm grip as she was led out of the house. "Where are we going?" she asked tiredly, feeling ready to drop . . . and she had that nausea again.

"To find Travis . . . where else."

Travis, Shaina thought, he didn't care about anyone. All he ever did was ride around in a black mood. Where had the thrilling first days of their marriage gone? The terror at the cabin had changed them. He thought she hated him. Maybe she did. She just didn't know anymore. God, she wished her head would stop pounding and the nausea would vanish.

Shaina tugged feebly at Silvanus's hand. "Silvanus, I feel . . . feel so . . . so funny. I think —"

"There he is," Silvanus said. "Just mounting Dice."

Everything would just be easier if she slipped to the ground right here. And she did just that . . .

Chapter Thirty-four

Travis started to ride, to go immediately in search of the person who had clubbed him over the head with the candlestick. Looking down at the ground, searching for clues, he found to his immense surprise he'd come across one with fortunate ease. The fool had left a clue right in Travis's own yard!

"Glory!" Dismounting Dice, he bent to trace the X with his finger, and it was at this point that Silvanus called to him from across the yard.

"Travis, come quickly!"

Travis looked over to Silvanus, saw him bent over the figure lying on the ground . . . Shaina!

Travis ran. He reached Shaina and Silvanus, bent down, and scooped his wife up in his arms.

"What happened to her?" he asked, having a pretty good idea already.

With great concern in his eyes, Silvanus told him and then followed Travis into the house and stopped outside their bedroom door.

The doc chose that moment to walk out of the

kitchen, and when he saw through the open door Travis just laying Shaina down on the bed, he tossed the half-eaten blueberry muffin he'd been munching onto a nearby table and rushed into the bedroom.

"What happened?"

"She fainted again, twice now in the past two weeks."

"She's more than likely with child," Doc said. "Can't rightly tell without examining her, though, but more than likely." He bent to feel her forehead and Shaina opened her eyes just then and looked from one man to the other.

"More than likely?" Travis's voice was deceptively soft. "Haven't you examined her like I told you to do after the night of the party?"

Weakly Shaina broke in, "I told him it wasn't necessary."

Doc looked at Travis and shrugged helplessly while he nodded in confirmation of her statement.

"I'll say if it's necessary or not, Shaina." Travis stood before the bed, hands buried in his jeans' pockets. "And I say it is. I'm going out, Shaina, and when I return I better have some answers." He turned to the doc, saying, "Examine her this time — and thoroughly."

"No!" Shaina shouted. More softly she said, "I don't like doctors and I've never had to have one look in on me before. Nothing against you, Doc."

Travis nodded to the doc. "She's just being defiant. I'll be back later, I'm not going far."

Doc put in, "Right. But I'll need to see your wound, too, Travis. So make yourself available *later*."

After Travis had gone out to further inspect the

yard, Silvanus told the doc he'd wait outside the door.

"You don't have to wait, Silvanus," Shaina said, narrowing her blue eyes at the doctor. "He's going, aren't you, Doc?"

"Well —" he muttered, not liking the hard way she was staring holes right through him. "Come on, now, Shaina, be a good girl. This won't take long . . . Silvanus, hand me my black bag out there, will you? Then you can shut the door."

"No, Silvanus. Don't bring in Doc's bag. Don't shut the door. In fact, you can come in and visit if you like . . . I'm feeling much better now." She eyed the doc, sustaining her defiance.

Doc's face crossed with worry. "You ain't being very nice, Missus Cordell. You know what Travis will do if this examination isn't done?"

"He'll probably fire you."

"That ain't nice. I thought you were a real sweet lady —"

"Not today. Oh, Silvanus . . . I forgot! Did you tell Travis that Roux is missing?" She began to rise from the bed, but the doc determinedly pushed her back. "Please, we have to tell him about Roux . . . I have to find her!"

"No." The doc was very strong, and he kept her from rising, telling himself his job was much too important to lose over some silly disagreement she was having with Travis. "You're staying right where you are, lady, we're going to find out for certain if you're with child . . . just as Travis ordered."

"Ohhh," Shaina moaned. "Silvanus, go tell Travis about Roux for me, will you?"

"I'm sure she's about somewhere, honey."

"I don't think so."

"I'll go," he said, reaching for the doc's bag, walking into the room with it, "only if you let the doc examine you, honey." He set the bag onto the table, smiling tenderly into Shaina's impudent face. "You be good now," he said in a hoarse voice, reaching out to cup her chin. *Lord, how he loved this girl!*

Shaina nodded her head slowly, mesmerized by the tender expression on Silvanus's rugged face. She murmured, "Who are you . . . really?"

As before, he answered her, "Just a cowboy . . ."

He was going to say, "Nothing more," but she wouldn't let him, and as he hovered over her, she pleaded, "Tell me . . . please."

"Why?"

"I know you are someone special. There's a feeling I have . . . here." She placed a hand over her heart.

If Silvanus's face revealed the intense emotion she had wrought, so did Shaina's. Their expressions were as similar as their eyes.

"I do have something to tell you, honey."

"What is it?" She looked over at Doc, who appeared a little embarrassed at the tender scene, and then back at Silvanus who had a curious mist in his eyes. "Can't you tell me?" she pleaded, reaching for his hand as he flinched and stepped back. "What's wrong? You can tell me . . . please!"

Silvanus patted Shaina's hand, saying, "You'll be all right . . . *my* little girl is going to be just fine."

When the significance of what Silvanus was implying sank in, she was conscious of a wonderful burst of tranquil relief. Perhaps in her heart she had always suspected.

Blue eyes stared into blue eyes for one suspended moment . . . and then the misty-eyed man stepped back out into the hall, closing the door softly behind him.

Shaina stared at the closed door. *My God, Silvanus Hart is my father.*

When Shaina again passed out, Doc grabbed his chance and set to work on examining her.

Before Doc even approached Travis, he was aware of a tremendous excitement racing through his blood. He was going to become a father again! This time with the woman he loved more than life itself. Their children would be strong and proud to carry on the Cordell name.

After her pregnancy was confirmed, Silvanus and Travis visited with a more tractable Shaina for a time until she became drowsy, unaware Doc had given her a mild sedative in some Indian herb tea he'd had his wife Maria come over to prepare.

As Shaina grew sleepy, her eyes kept moving over Travis as Doc cared for his wound, and then they found the man Silvanus lounging in a deep chair watching her closely . . . and lovingly. Her father . . .

"I have to go," Travis said, giving his wife a chaste kiss on the forehead. "Roux is still missing."

"Oh, no."

"We'll find her. She might have gone riding off with Jay Ridingbow, but—" He shook his head.

"But you don't really think so." No, of course not, Shaina told herself, how silly of anyone to think that, for Roux had disappeared shortly before dawn and just following the intruder's attack. "They took Roux, didn't they."

It wasn't even a question.

Silvanus stood, confirming out loud his resolve, "We'll find her. They can't have gone far. Travis found the imprint of the heel marked X in the yard. He's the one we're looking for."

"Oh." Shaina sat up, holding her head. "I just thought of something."

"What, Shaina?" Travis frowned intensely.

"Giles was removing stones from the heel of his boot the night he —" She could hardly mention that night again. "When he came upon me in the kitchen. He was picking something out from the flat of the heel of his boot. At the time I didn't think it was strange, but now it surely strikes me as being so."

Travis moved quickly, spoke tersely. "That's our man."

"Let's go get him." Silvanus stood, walked over to give Shaina's hand a squeeze — while Travis rushed out unaware of Silvanus's gesture — and then followed Travis.

Outside they were greeted by Jack Nolan and his smiling wife Deanna. Her smile faded when she caught the looks on both men's countenances.

"What's happened?"

Briefly the happenings of the last three hours were sketched out, while Silvanus and Jack made ready their horses for long-distance traveling. Deanna rushed inside the house to go to Shaina's side after she'd exchanged a kiss and a few words with her husband.

The way Travis saw it, the villain, no doubt Giles, with someone to aid him in the kidnapping, had sneaked in to take Roux and, finding him awake, had stealthily come up behind him and struck him on the head from behind. As far as he could remember he'd been in the living room. Shaina told him she'd gone to the door and yelled as loud as she could for Silvanus. While all this had been going on, the villain (or villains) had carried Roux off.

Before they rode out, Travis put a few men in charge of guarding the women. He had a strong feeling that Roux was being used as bait. The question was: to lure whom?

"What does that bastard Wilson want?" Jack Nolan put his question to the quiet, grim man riding beside him.

"Wants Shaina," Travis ground out.

Silvanus cleared his throat, saying, "I think he wants a whole helluva lot more than that, son."

Travis blinked out of his trance, both from Silvanus's statement and his calling him "son" again. But he hadn't the time to question the man's words, for at that moment Jay Ridingbow appeared in the road up ahead, a handsome spectacle astride his mount as the rising sun splashed between the trees and bathed them like shining knight and golden charger. They could see the bear necklace adorning Jay's bronze and naked chest. Anyone who knew the story remembered how Jay at thirteen had been attacked by a female grizzly and had slain the bear with only the one blade he carried in a sheath fastened at his ankle. His back was scarred but he lived to see an old Salish man make him a nice necklace out of the bear's sharp claws.

Travis had never seen the lad look so intense as he rode up to him at the forest's entrance, unaware that visions of his beloved Roux had come to Jay in the darkest hour before dawn.

Tight-lipped, Jay confronted Travis. "Something is wrong. I have felt it. This feeling has to do with Roux, am I right?"

Travis shook his head to clear it, snapping, "How in hell did you know that? She's only been gone a few hours."

"That's when the feelings began," Jay said. "Have you looked up on Big Blue?"

"Why?" Travis squinted from the sun's beaming rays.

"I was just going there. When the mind pictures came to me, I saw Roux being taken up there."

Even as he spoke, Travis whirled his mount in the direction of Thunder Mountain range. What Jay had to report next almost caused his heart to stop beating.

"That is where the grizzly attacked me," Jay said softly. He lifted the necklace and slowly fed it from his long fingers back to his glistening bronze chest.

"Grizzly!" Travis bit out. "The damn nightmare."

Jay gaped at Travis's back. "She has dreamed of the grizzly?" He gulped down the fear in his throat.

"Both her and Shaina." Travis began to ride faster.

Jay caught up. "That is bad. Have you left men in

charge of your wife's safety?"

"Yes." The word came out like a snarl.

"We have to get to them," Jack Nolan said. As he was part Indian he knew the import placed on revealing dreams that came to one in times of impending disaster. "Who did you leave in charge?" Jack wanted to know, looking over at Travis.

"Shaina's father. He will give my orders to the others." Travis jerked his head around after hearing what sounded like an angry shout. "Sil, was that you?"

Silvanus nodded when Travis looked over at him. Oh Lord, here it comes. Would Travis believe him? Would anybody? Especially Shaina . . . God, what was she going to think of him after he'd told everyone she was his daughter?

Following a deep breath, Silvanus said, "Graham is not Shaina's father."

Travis pulled up his reins, almost making Dice rear. "Well then, just who the hell is he?"

"He is Shaina's stepfather."

"What do you mean by that?" Travis was growing impatient and alarmed.

"Shaina and her brother William—" Silvanus pulled another deep breath from his chest"—are mine."

Travis made a sound lift from his wide chest that was like wind rushing between canyon walls.

"That isn't all," Silvanus said as Travis continued to regard him curiously.

"Go on."

Silvanus's face positively glowed as he announced, Eleanora and Will are coming here. They'll be here next week sometime. Just got a letter last night,

355

brought aboard the *Clementine.*"

"My God," Travis exclaimed. Then, "I thought Shaina's brother went off on his own to California. At least that's what I remember her telling me. And we couldn't find Eleanora, or any trace of her."

"They are both alive and well," Silvanus said with misty eyes.

Travis smiled. "This is all a shock to me, but I'm happy for you, Sil. Now," he said, getting down to business, "what are we going to do about this Graham character?"

Silvanus shrugged. "He's harmless. I think he only wants to convince Shaina to go away with him and make her work, like he made Eleanor and the kids always slave for him. He's a lazy no-good, and he knows Shaina would work damn hard for a living."

His lovely Shaina . . . she'd no doubt slaved like a work horse most of her life. He was going to make damn certain the rest of her days would be taken up with rearing his kids and taking care of him as only she knew how. She would be that schoolteacher she'd always wanted to be . . . for the Cordell brood!

"You're not all that concerned then?" Travis asked Silvanus.

"Like I said, I think he's harmless, and Shaina can take care of herself."

Travis smiled grimly. "That's what I'm afraid of. Shaina's so independent. For now, I think the most urgent thing is to find Roux." He spoke calmly, not wanting to reveal to the others how worried he was. "And we have only one man to deal with — Giles Wilson!"

Jay's young face lined with worry and fear. If that man Wilson touched Roux, just touched her body where he wasn't supposed to, Jay would be the first one to gut the man. He said out loud, "He won't hurt Roux?"

"He won't until after we get his message, and that depends," Jack put in. The others turned to him and Jack explained, "Wilson covets everything Travis has, and that means Shaina now, too. He don't especially want the girl Roux. What Wilson wants mostly is Shaina. And he'll do anything to get her."

"You're right," snarled Travis. "I've seen that one work, in Seattle. When he couldn't get a woman away from another man he would sulk, just like a kid." Travis gazed upward to the tip of Big Blue reposing in the morning sun. "You're right. Wilson has always wanted what I've got. But my wife is one thing he'll never have. That I swear."

With a faint frown knitting her forehead, Shaina watched as Graham Hill walked toward the porch, looking around furtively. Reaching her, Graham seemed surprised to see the girl seated on the porch rocking the swing gently to and fro.

Indecisively Graham regarded Shaina as he ran a hand across his forehead, then he blurted, "You have to hurry, Shainy! Come on, hurry!"

The swing stopped.

Shaina looked at the man who had been her counterfeit father for so many years. Suddenly she knew why her mother had never really found lasting happiness. Eleanora had not loved this puny man . . . she loved only Silvanus Hart.

Now Shaina felt truly sorry for this weak-kneed man, and she calmly asked, "Why do you want me to hurry, Graham? Where's the fire?"

Graham gasped. He whirled to look at the barn. It was not on fire, no, it couldn't be, not yet — that wasn't supposed to be pulled off until Travis returned.

When Graham turned back to Shaina he found her laughing . . . *laughing* at him. He'd show the uppity Shaina who was boss!

"There ain't no fire, Shainy. But I think you better be coming along with me . . . Travis will be murdered if you don't."

Startled, Shaina could only gape at Graham. Becoming angry, she snapped, "Don't be playing games with me, Graham, I don't appreciate the humor. You see, it has just been confirmed that I am to have a baby."

"All the more why you you should be coming with me, Shainy. Your husband is being held by . . . by Giles Wilson, that's who, yeah, he's the one."

"You're not making sense. Who sent you?" Shaina had stood and began running her shaky hands down her skirts.

"Ah . . . ah, someone who is with Giles."

"You don't sound too sure of what you're telling me yourself, Graham. I don't think I believe you."

Graham's face colored with rage, but he held it inside him as best he could. Shaina noticed that he clenched his hands at his sides, hands untouched by work. But Eleanora's hands had been work-rough

358

ened. Oh yes, Eleanora had been his work-slave, as had his kids.

"You have to, Shainy." His desperation showed in his eyes. Another idea came to him, and he tried. "If you don't believe me, that's your loss. That kid of yours won't have a father. All Giles wants is some of the gold—"

Shaina shot to her feet again. "What do you know about the gold?"

"Travis has lots of it, right in that big safe in his office." His eyes shone with greed. "Lots of the men know about it, they was talking all about his boodle. Joe Creek says he's going to get him some, and so did Giles."

"You mean they are working *together?*"

"Sure, you could say that."

Oh . . . what should she do? If Graham was telling the truth, then her husband would die if she didn't get that gold to whomever was holding him. "Are you sure it's Giles?" Maybe it was Graham himself, fooling her as he'd done in the past when he wanted to get his way. With a combination of wild fear and confusion, Shaina looked at Graham, wishing to God she knew the truth.

Graham remembered something Joe Creek had told him, and his eyes urgently meeting Shaina's, he said, "Bring the red dress. Someone wants to bring it to Travis, then he'll know for sure you're coming."

For only a moment's hesitation, Shaina's eyes flew across Graham's face, and then she turned from him, saying, "All right, I'll get the red dress . . . and the gold."

"Yeah." Graham rubbed his hands together. "Bring as much as you can carry."

Shaina did not wholeheartedly believe anything Graham said. All she knew was a determination to find this out for herself and go along with anything to see Travis and Roux safe.

Graham rushed into the bunkhouse with the bundle under his arm, glad to see that the others were just rising from the table to go out and return to work. He spotted Joe with Carolyn at the back and slowed his steps so as not to draw attention to himself. He had not alerted the others Cordell had ordered him to put on watch. He'd let Joe know only enough so he'd not become suspicious of his actions. Once he had Shaina up in the mountains for a time, hiding from the others, they'd stash that gold and then when all the excitement cooled down, him and Shaina would light out for California.

"Here's the dress." Graham shoved it into Joe's hands, his back turned to the last cowboys dribbling out the door. "This shade's a brighter red," he explained to Carolyn. "Don't get this one mixed up with that old dress you was wearing."

"Don't worry," Carolyn said. "I already threw away the old rag."

"You know what to do?" Joe asked Graham.

"Yeah," Graham said. "I take Shaina into the forest and wait at the three burned pines. Carolyn puts on Shaina's red dress when Cordell returns. She takes off with Moon Doggie —"

"Moon Dog," Carolyn corrected, making her own plans to steal away from everyone with the Indian . . . once she was sure she really had that red dress! She wasn't even going to put it on and take a chance getting it dirty while she rode to Moon Dog's camp.

There was a wicked gleam in Joe's eyes as he said, "Good plan. Wait a minute." He stopped Graham at the door before he could rush out. With a hand on Graham's shoulder, Joe spun him about to peer into his dark face and whispered just in case someone was within earshot, "Did she get the gold?"

"Yeah. But there wasn't much," Graham lied.

"What?" Joe snarled in Graham's face.

Graham shrugged, saying, "There's enough for all of us, don't worry."

Joe let Graham go, and turning to Carolyn, he said, "He's right. There'll be enough . . . when Graham's dead."

"I'm going with Moon Dog, Joe."

Joe's eyes narrowed. "Go ahead, Caro. I know you think he's a better lover than I am. Once you have your red dress, keep going with Moon Dog . . . and don't look back in case Cordell is watching." As Joe showed Carolyn his back in going out the door, he smiled evilly, knowing she wouldn't get far—but far enough to lead the others on a wild-goose chase!

Later that day Joe talked to Vinny. His friend said that Cordell was on his way down from the hills. "Why not change our plans a little, Joe. It occurs to me we could eliminate Cordell faster. Let's try settin' the barn on fire first—with Cordell in it!"

"Good idea, Vinny." He slapped the thin-faced man

on the back. "Carolyn just might be too chicken to wear the red dress, thinking Cordell might come after her. We'll keep Carolyn and Moon Dog around a while longer, and if Cordell gets out of the barn alive, we'll send Carolyn and Moon Dog on their way."

Shaina paced the forest floor beneath the three pines, twisting her hands together. She started as Graham came crashing through the brush leading his horse behind him. "There you are, Shainy, right where I told you to wait." He glared at her slim back as she walked over to Spotted Bird. "You got the gold?"

"Yes." Shaina glanced him over her shoulder. "I have another question, Graham. Does Giles have Roux also?"

"Roux? Is she missing?" He remembered having seen the girl with that Indian woman Miah, and the kid looked to be struggling. He'd thought it odd at the time. It had been awfully early in the morning, too. They had been heading for the mountain. "Maybe she just went off with her mother," Graham suggested.

"I hadn't thought of that." Shaina mounted her horse, staring at the trail up ahead. Then she shook her head, praying she would not become nauseated again. "Did you send the red dress ahead?"

"Yeah. He'll get it, and soon as Giles gets the gold he'll let Travis go."

But Travis won't let him go, Shaina kept to herself. Yes, she thought, Giles Wilson has seen his last day in Washington Territory. Maybe his last day, period.

Travis rode into the Lazy C that night, returning for fresh horses and supplies for going up into the mountain. He checked with Deanna, and the woman told him Shaina had gone to bed early. Travis badly needed a few hours' sleep, but if he slipped into bed with Shaina he'd never get *any* rest.

The sky was just turning dusty gold when Travis entered the barn, brushing from his sleeve strands of hay from the stable where he'd slept. He was still groggy; he'd had a time of it trying to sleep.

"It's here somewhere," he said to himself, looking for a fresh cinch belt, for his other had come apart after several hours of hard riding. He thought it strange, however, that the new belt had busted so easily.

"Sil? You in here?"

No answer. Where had he gone off to?

"Sil?"

Moooo.

Travis started at the cow close by. "Damn, I'm as jittery as a woman."

It was then that the rope came down around him, pinning his arms to his sides holding him prisoner. "What the hell!" He was being pulled off the floor and dangled in midair. Looking up into the loft, he sputtered, "If this is someone's idea of a joke, they better run their ass off when I get loose!" No answer. Travis looked above his head but could not make out the forms. Now he heard the muted shufflings of boots.

"Here it comes, *rancher boy!*"

Before he knew what was coming, a lantern whizzed by him from up above and broke on the floor below, and as if in slow motion, Travis watched the orange flames spread beneath him like the gates of hell had opened up.

Travis shook his fist at his side, shouting upward, "Whoever you are up there, you guys just messed with the wrong person!"

"Hah hah," the voice drawled a laugh. "You ain't gonna live long enough, Cordell. We'll mess with you or anyone we chose . . . like your wife for example."

The taunt made Travis see scarlet fury before his eyes . . . or was that only the flames each moment growing closer to his feet. He struggled in violence to free himself from the ropes that circled his body. He could feel the heat. The smoke was choking him. This was sorely reminiscent of another time.

Shaina. He had to free himself and get to her!

Then it came to him . . . He had a knife in his boot!

Raising his leg with a grunt and a groan, Travis snatched the knife from its sheath, bringing the sharp blade up underneath the rope that was tightening around his chest, cutting off his breath.

Now Travis swung himself on the rope as he sliced through it and fell on the edge of the flames, rolling away as soon as he felt the burn.

Leaping to his feet, Travis ran to the barn door. He expected to find it open, but it had been blocked from the outside.

He turned to seek a way of escape and ran to the

364

ladder leading up into the hayloft. No one in his right mind would still be up there. He coughed and began to scramble up the ladder, pulling himself up and over. He ran for the hayloft doors choking as the smoke curled around him.

He poked his head out, shouting, "Where the hell is everyone?

Travis flung the doors wide. It was at least a fifteen-foot drop to the ground. He grabbed on to the rope that dangled in front of him from the pulley. Down below he spotted the reason the doors hadn't budged. A wagon had been used to blockade the doors!

As he was sliding down the rope, he caught sight of two people riding into the hills and two others heading in the opposite direction.

Coming to a hard landing, Travis could only gape in the direction of the two going in the opposite direction, a distinctive shade of red flowing from the back of the horse . . .

The red dress!

"Shaina!" he shouted. "Where the hell are you going?"

Just then Silvanus and Jack Nolan came running up, and gaped while others began to run to and fro passing water buckets along Indian file to try to douse the fire raging in the barn.

Travis growled, "Where've you two been?"

"Having breakfast," Jack said, looking sheepish as he perused the sad state of Travis's appearance.

Travis slapped a saddle onto his horse, saw the broken cinch he had forgotten to repair and swore. Tossing the saddle onto the ground, he mounted bareback while the other two men stood mutely on the ground, staring at the blackened face of Travis Cordell. They would have had a good chuckle, that is if Travis had not looked like murder.

Then they watched him light out after the two riders, and caught sight of what Travis had seen . . . a flash of red flowing from the horse.

Jack Nolan turned to Silvanus, saying, "That horse is not Spotted Bird."

Already going in the direction of the house, Silvanus said, "I know, Jack. But when is Travis going to notice?"

Jack answered, "He was interested in the red dress and Shaina—not the horse. He saw blond hair, a red dress, and lit out!"

Chapter Thirty-five

Travis galloped his trusty Dice like one possessed until he neared the two riders, then he whipped out his gun, ordering the Indian with the woman to halt. There was stern command in his voice as it rang out across the prairie.

"Draw up!"

Moon Dog turned to look Travis Cordell squarely in the face and the white man saw that there was apprehension in Moon Dog's eyes.

Now he turned to face Shaina . . . but the woman wasn't Shaina. "Carolyn Creek," he said and wearily rubbed his forehead. "What are you doing with my wife's dress?"

"How dare you!" Carolyn hissed, visibly trembling. "This dress is mine. Joe give it to me . . . ah, for a birthday present," she lied.

"Is that right?" Travis eyed the Indian, who merely shrugged. He went on, "That makes it a present twice now."

Carolyn just stared at him and Travis said, "Never

mind. Just please tell me how your husband happened to come by it?"

"Wait a minute." Travis pulled Dice up before Carolyn's horse. "Do you know anything about the fire?"

"What fire?" She smirked as she stared the ruggedly good-looking man in the face. "I don't know what you're talkin' about."

"I think you do." He bent to swipe up the precious dress sticking out from her saddlebag. "No offense to you," Travis said, holding the dress up for Moon Dog to see, "But this dress belongs to my woman."

The Indian shrugged as if it didn't matter one way or the other to him.

"Hey, gimme that back!" Carolyn kicked her mount and rocked in her seat as she tried to grab it. "You ain't got no right taking my dress! Moon Dog, go get it back from him." She sulked when Moon Dog only shrugged again. "Some warrior you are." When he started to ride away, she called him back. "Moon Dog, I didn't mean that!"

"If the dress means more to you, then I go."

She groaned, "Moon Dog."

When she turned back to Travis Cordell, she hissed, "You bastard! I hope you rot in hell!"

Travis tossed the dress back to her. "Here, it's yours. I wouldn't let my wife wear it after your dirty whoring hands have been all over it. I'll buy her twenty more like it."

Travis shot a glance over his shoulder at the moun Carolyn was riding as he made his way quickly bac to the ranch. All he'd seen was red—no wonder he hadn't noticed the horse was not Shaina's. Coming down off his mount, he ran into the stable in search of Spotted Bird.

"Damn." Spotted Bird *was* gone. Now what? he asked himself.

Leading his horse, his expression grim, Silvanus said, "Shaina's not in the house. Deanna doesn't know where she is."

"I gathered that." Travis narrowed his tired green eyes. "Where's Graham Hill?"

"I checked. He's gone, too."

"Joe Creek?"

"Gone," Silvanus said.

"Sloan?"

"Gone."

"How about the fat one—B.J.?"

"Lit out on his horse after he heard Roux was missing or so Sam said."

"Most likely going to meet his sidekicks."

"Yeah," Silvanus said. But he wasn't so sure about that one. He asked, "Should we go now?"

"Wait a minute." Travis stroked his two days' growth of whiskers. "If Giles has Roux up in the hills, who set the barn on fire and tried to do me in?"

"No doubt Joe Creek and Vinny Sloan."

"Yeah." Travis let out a slow breath. "You're right— we've got more than one culprit to contend with."

"Maybe a whole slew of them." Silvanus rushed his prancing black Lucy to the doors.

Travis, already mounted, looked down at him. "Everything ready?"

"Ready," Silvanus answered.

369

They could see Jack Nolan as he rode up before the stable doors. He was ready, too, both six-guns strapped to his lean hips.

"Good." Travis rode like a tempest bursting from the stable doors. "Let's go get them for good this time!"

Up ahead of Travis and his men rode Vinny Sloan and Joe Creek, hightailing it out of there like bats out of hell after they had started the fire.

"I think we done him in," said Sloan.

Joe's look was a dark one indeed as he changed direction on the gradual slope, easing off toward the left. "I could lay money there will be Lazy C riders catching up before long."

"They don't know we started that fire."

"Yeah? They will, when they take roll call. I got a feeling in my gut that Cordell is still alive."

"Graham and Shaina Cordell weren't at the three pines to meet us. Somethin' must've gone wrong."

Joe's eyes went even darker. "Yeah. I know how Graham's mind works. He'll come up here into the mountains with the loot to hide out. He thinks he's going to get it all. But he ain't."

Sloan stared at Joe Creek as they continued to climb up into the mountains. Joe's greed had turned into a frightful, unreasoning hatred and Sloan wasn't sure he wanted to be a part of it anymore—even if they ever got the gold and shared it. Which brought him to his next question.

"Did you get the combination to the safe?"

"Naw," growled Joe. "There wasn't time. Have to get

370

it from Shaina Cordell when we catch up to her and Graham." He wouldn't tell Vinny that Graham had had Shaina grab some of the precious substance before they left. Maybe there would be enough for just him and Shaina to take off and leave the others behind. First he'd have to kill off the others so him and Shaina could have it all.

After a time Joe ground out, "That traitor! My own cousin . . . traitor." His face was a mask of fury.

"You mean B.J.? Yeah, he sure took to the Cordells, like stink on dung, didn't he?"

Suddenly Joe felt very alone. His wife had thrown him over for a stinking Indian, and his own cousin had turned traitor. And he would have to get rid of Sloan after he'd used him for company until they caught up with the others, but that didn't bother him. What did, though, was how he was going to manage getting away from Cordell's Lazy C riders with Shaina. And if Cordell himself had survived the fire, he was going to be in deep crap, up to his neck.

"We're goin' to be in trouble, Joe, if we don't find a place to hole out pretty soon."

"My name is Joe Creek." He suddenly turned to face Sloan with a crazed look in his eyes. "And I was born to trouble."

Vinny Sloan looked away. He didn't doubt it, no, not one bit.

The sun was sinking low on one side of the mountain while the moon's pale face was making an appearance on the other. The air was sweet, smelling of wild mountain flowers, and the wind was crisp and cool even on this summer evening.

Roux, with a light blanket covering her shoulders, stared up at the stars just popping out in the deep velvet sky. Soon the mountain would be held in a starlit embrace and the sun would at last surrender to the full yellow moon.

Now Roux glanced over to where her mother and that Wilson guy were laughing over some joke he'd just told. Roux knew it was a dirty joke. They were different from other jokes. When they were told, people acted nervous and stupid and their faces got all flushed and funny looking. It turned Roux's stomach. Wilson was one of those kinds of men she didn't trust because his eyes went all over her body. Her father had told her to always stay away from such men, men whose eyes went where they should not. This Wilson's eyes weren't only on Miah. He was getting too friendly with her, and Roux cringed every time he happened to brush her shoulder . . . accidentally he said. "Sorry." She knew how sorry he really was. Jay Ridingbow had also warned her to watch out for "those" kinds of men. She would be safe, she *prayed* she would be safe as long as her mother was here. But, actually, Miah was not much help, she'd already seen where Wilson's eyes had touched and had said nothing to the man. She hated Miah. Her mother, her own mother had kidnapped her from her father. She never thought of Miah as her mother any longer. Shaina was her mother now, and gave her the love her mother never truly had. Tears began in Roux's eyes; she missed Shaina now. She wondered what they were going to do to her. *They took me away from home early this morning. When, oh when will they bring me back?* Her father must be worried by now. Maybe they had even hurt him. They were sure planning something. When they looked over the campfire at her, Roux saw the "secret" in their eyes. They were drawing up a dark evil plan. Biting her lip, Roux looked away from her mother and Giles Wilson. They were touching each other in places a man and wife should only dare go. Her spirits sank even lower when they started talking about things in a louder tone of voice.

"We pulled this much off so far."

"We did, Giles Wilson. When the others come with the One with Fire in her Hair we will take the gold from her. Then we will get rid of the others. This is true?"

Wilson stared into the black eyes and saw only deep blue ones. But he answered, "If they pulled it off without mishap. What about your ol' lover Travis burning to death, doesn't that bother you?"

"Be still. The girl will hear."

"I'm talking low."

"You must whisper when you speak of *him*. She is very wise for one so young."

Giles tossed a glance in the girl's direction, and he saw the campfire glowing in the thick strands of her hair, turning it to an even darker fire. Yes, for one so young she was certainly a beauty, one he wouldn't mind sampling . . . someone had to do it someday. He could almost laugh at the thought. Giles Wilson deflowering Cordell's precious daughter, ah, what revenge on that one who he'd always despised for all his arrogance and wealth and rugged good looks. Travis Cordell would walk down the streets of Seattle and all the women's eyes would follow. He'd turn them away with only a look, all but for the women he'd considered classy enough to bed down with—until Shaina came along, that is. Now he never looked at other women, and Giles could see why. He, too, wanted that enchanting morsel for himself. And have her he would one day.

"Where are you, Giles Wilson?" Miah waved her bronze arm in front of his face.

He caught her arm and held it. "Why do you always call me by my full name? Isn't Giles good enough? Why do you Indians have to use a person's full name?"

She laughed, a lilting laugh that had driven Giles wild with desire since the first time he'd heard it. No doubt Cordell had thought the same thing . . . but Giles was tiring of Miah. He cast his pale-brown eyes in Roux's direction—he needed some new meat until he could at last be with Shaina. Shaina was the only woman who truly mattered. The others were only good for one thing, and one thing only.

"Do not know, *Giles*." Miah pronounced his name lazily, sticking a brown finger in his ear. Then she stuck out her pink tongue and licked the lobe. "You like Miah?"

Giles shoved her away, saying, "Miah, love, why don't you go trap us some dinner, huh?" He rubbed his knuckles on her small bottom, leaning over her and gazing at Roux while she was in the process of braiding her long dark-fire hair. "I'll take a few winks while you're gone, and then we'll eat . . . and after dinner . . ." He let it hang. After dinner he'd probably be too pooped to do anything, but he'd let her go along thinking that there'd be some wild lovemaking

374

later.

"Joe Creek will come soon." Miah stood, smoothing the curves of her hips encased in soft doeskin.

"You like Joe, huh?" Maybe this would work out better than he thought. But would she be angry if she knew he'd played around with her daughter? He'd just have to find out for himself, wouldn't he.

"I have *desire* for him," she said, drawing out the word he had taught her.

Giles grinned arrogantly. "You've taken on just about every man on the Lazy C, haven't you, Miah love?"

She laughed. "Maybe one or two." Then she pouted and told Giles she didn't know how it had happened, but that she had somehow managed to lose the pretty purple scarf he had given her a time back, the scarf that Indian Joe had found and given him.

"I'll get you another one." When was she going to leave? She realized he was hungry, so why did she stand around and talk? Ah, he thought he knew, she is afraid I will try to seduce her daughter. She was already jealous, he'd seen it. He didn't think there was any love lost between Miah and her daughter. A thought occurred to him. "How come you hate your own daughter?" he asked her.

Miah spat on the ground, grazing her daughter with a contemptuous look.

"She is of Travis Cordell blood. He is not the savage you are when we make the love. He likes to kiss. Ugh. And like to hold a woman. This takes very long. Too long for Miah. He wants to make the babies. *Ugh!*"

Giles bet Cordell took all night with Shaina. "Shaina's pregnant," he told Miah.

"The paleface woman with child? Ugh. She will grow fat and ugly. She will hate her body. My body will never grow that way again." She smiled evilly. "Miah takes care."

Over the campfire, Roux sighed in boredom. Was she supposed to be afraid? She was not, not a bit. *Father will come for me soon. I just know he will.*

Roux pillowed her head with her hands and soon drifted into a relaxing slumber, never hearing her mother leave the camp.

It was not long before Roux was awakened by a body hovering over her, and she squeaked out a scream right before the hand clamped cruelly over her mouth.

"Be still, little one." Giles breathed close to her face. "I won't hurt you. Just want to get a little friendlier, that's all."

Her green eyes were wide and frightened as Wilson lowered himself onto her, one leg pinning down her coltish legs. He smiled down into her eyes, moving his face ever closer.

"You're twelve now, aren't you?"

"Y-yes." She could barely press the word through his tight fingers enclosing her mouth.

"That's old enough, don't you think, little fox?"

"I want you to let me go, Mister Wilson."

"Mister Wilson?" Giles looked offended. "Why not just Giles, honey?"

"Where is my mother?"

"Gone, hunting. She won't be back for quite some time. Says she's got some other 'things' to do, though I couldn't imagine what they could be, could you?"

"N-no." Roux tried slipping out from beneath the heavy leg, but he only pinned her down harder. "You are hurting me, W-Wilson."

"I thought I told you to call me Giles." His eyes darkened and anxiety ran cold in little Roux. "You'll be calling me more sweeter things than that before I'm done with you, sweetheart."

Not only was Wilson's body weight making Roux sick, but also his calling her all those names only a man should say to his wife when they were alone.

"Now," he said huskily close to her ear, "let's have a little sample, hmm."

Just as he began to get bolder with his intentions, forcing her skirt up her slim thighs, Roux brought up a knee and rammed it between his legs.

"Not again, you little slut." Wilson caught her long hair and gave it a twist, bringing her slamming against his chest while he shoved his face into her small, frightened one. "You're lucky, you didn't get me as bad as you did last time. I'm afraid you're going to pay for that . . ."

Winding the dark-fire hair around his wrist, Giles violently bruised her delicate mouth with a kiss and slammed her back onto the ground and climbed on top, thrusting in a knee to separate her legs. Into her mouth he stuffed a dirty handkerchief he'd whipped from his pocket, and tied it behind her head in a painful knot.

He growled, "Now we're going to have some fun!"

Roux gnashed her sharp little teeth, but to no avail, and her dark green eyes spat her hatred at him as he bared her thighs and lowered himself onto her, grinding out, "You admit you want me, don't you? Come on, little — "

The shadow moved fast.

There was a loud Indian war cry right before the long-bladed knife buried itself into Wilson's back, causing his hips to thrust backward, his chest to lurch in a violent bow that snapped his neck almost in two. Staggering wildly he reached around and with a loud cry yanked the knife from his back. Screaming like a demented devil, Giles ran from the camp just as a tall, slim form leapt into view, silhouetted by the angry red flames behind him.

To Roux, he was a shining warrior coming out of the darkness. Like the hero Shaina had read to her about.

"Riding Bow!" Roux shouted his name and followed it with a terrified scream. "He hurt me! He hurt me!" She wrapped her arms about his chest, while Jay stared down mesmerized by the sight of her bare thighs and huge bruise marks.

Holding Roux away from him, Jay ground out, "He hurt you. How did he hurt you, Roux, tell me."

"I cannot tell you . . . Jay."

"You must, Roux."

Roux stared up at him while he held her at arm's length, and all she wanted to do was be held close by him. Jay would make the terror of the night go away, he always made her feel better when she was afraid or lonely.

"He tried to do that 'thing' to me, Jay."

Jay laughed weakly in relief, saying, "He did not, though?"

"He only crushed me to the ground, Jay. But that

hurt. He was very heavy."

"That is all?" Jay looked worried.

"Father told me about a man's 'stick.' To run away fast. Or use my knee if I had to. I used my knee on Wilson." Roux rolled her eyes. "But he didn't do *that* to me. Ick. Only big people do that when they get married."

He hugged her to his breast, almost crying as he said, "Yes, Fox Fire, yes."

In spite of the horror of the situation, Jay almost smiled. Someday he would smile again. But not now, damn it. Not now.

Chapter Thirty-six

Eleanora Hill sat alone in the darkened room of the boarding house gazing out the window. The morning moon still hung suspended in a royal-blue sky and cast a pale light across the landscape. From upstairs in the tall building she could see all around. The town was so small she could stretch her vision past it to the outskirting hills.

Her heart turned over when she heard the train in the distance, its lonely whistle calling from the hills to her as it had when she and Silvanus made love in the field of wildflowers. It seemed so long ago now. . .

"I should never have left." Eleanora sighed, looking around the room, smiling when her eyes touched on Will's sea bag lying open on the saggy cot in the corner. The owner of the boardinghouse, a kindly old woman named Sarah, had loaned them the cot for Will's use, for Sarah knew they could not afford two rooms. Sarah knew that Eleanora's coins were few and had said the woman and her son could stay as long as they wished. But they would not be staying much longer. "I should never have left," Eleanora told herself again, thinking she had abandoned poor Graham and her children.

Poor Graham indeed!

But she had gone away because she had been slowing dying inside. As it was she had moved around from town to town, looking like a pale ghost of her former self, she remembered as she stared into the mirror and wondered where the woman had gone who had once been so in love and so pretty. How often had Silvanus told her that she was pretty . . .

"I'm not pretty anymore." She touched her still smooth face. "I feel so old. I should never have left my children. Nor my husband. I have sinned, Lord. Forgive me."

But I loved him so much. Tears of remembrance burned and she tried to blink them away. *I love him, I still love Silvanus Hart. I had to find him . . . to see if he still cared for me, if the splendor of our love yet existed.*

With what little money she'd had, she had set out from her home looking back over her shoulder until well after the train had left. *Should I go back?* But she hadn't. She had caught the train, and another, and another, but no Silvanus Hart. It was as if he had vanished from the face of the earth.

Not any younger, not any younger, the train wheels had kept reminding her over and over as they clattered over the tracks. No, she had not been getting any younger. She couldn't give up now.

She had finally found Will in a small town in California. He had done as he'd promised. He had shipped out on a boat in San Francisco and gotten on as cabin-boy. At his first meeting with his mother he'd explained that a cabin boy he had remained, for he had never been given a chance to work himself up. Will had slung his sea bag over his strong, wide shoulders and gone with Eleanora, if not reluctantly. He had been lonesome for his family, for most of them anyway . . . He never spoke of Graham much.

She wouldn't have left Graham if he hadn't beat her so bad that she'd lost the baby. After all the years of catering to him and subjecting herself to his spineless cruelty, thawt had been the deciding factor. He had taken the life of an unborn child!

Now Eleanora and Will had returned, but not to Mountain Lake, not to stay — not there, not ever again. The house there had burned down anyway, burned down without ever being surrounded by the picket fence of her dreams. They were in a little town outside a place called Wild Mountain. Wild Mountain . . . a little cry caught in Eleanora's throat.

"I am close to finding him, dear Lord, close to my Silvanus at last!" She knew he was working near a town called Wild Mountain, on a ranch, but that's all she knew.

Eleanora sat back and sighed. She knew she had finally come to the right place. And then her thoughts turned to her children. Her sweet, beloved daughter. *Shaina, she would make a grand schoolteacher.* She smiled a little. *And an even better wife to some man.* Was she happy? Would she ever see Shaina again?

William and Shaina, her love children, hers and Silvanus's. One more time, she had told herself that long-ago day, she would see Silvanus once more, and

382

only once. They would not make love, she had told herself . . . but other forces had been at work, beautiful, wonderful ones. She remembered that day as if only yesterday . . . The kiss . . . that had started it all over again. Summer magic filled the air, the flowers were in full bloom and the mountains smiled down on them. Dear God, how wonderful to be alive!

"Ellie!" Silvanus had held out his arms. "I thought you'd never come, darling girl." He lifted her and spun her around in his strong embrace. "My love . . . my ladylove. You are everything in the world to me."

Ellie had put her head on his shoulder as they walked to a spot and sat, spreading her skirts around her, both hidden from view by the tall meadow grass and nodding wildflowers.

It was cooler in the grass, and Ellie and Silvanus gazed adoringly into each other's eyes for an eternity. As if by silent mutual agreement, they moved closer, and soon they were sharing a soul-shattering kiss. The kiss moved on to little touches, then caresses, then strained embraces, holding each other hard and fast, exchanging kiss for kiss, touch for touch, each surrendering to the wild, intoxicating ecstasy of blazing passion.

"I was afraid you wouldn't come," Silvanus breathed into her ear, holding her so tight she could feel the thick pounding of his heart.

"I am here, love, and today is ours." She put her finger to his lips when he would have questioned her. "No. Don't talk, Silvanus. Just love me. Love me."

"I want to marry you, Ellie! Come away with me."

"It's too late, darling. Please—" she put her cheek on his chest "—please don't break the spell. We may never find it again. Let us have this last time together."

"Oh God, Ellie, I'll want you again and again."

"Someday, darling, maybe someday. But for now, just love me."

And so they had abandoned themselves to the exquisite pleasure of the love their hearts could never escape. Pleasure radiated from one to the other as they kissed as if they had forever. She caressed the length of his back as they became one, as they had only once before. They made up for all the lost times, all the nights of longing, all the lonely, spent tears. As they reached paradise together, there was a moment suspended in time as their souls blended and gazed at each other in splendor while Eleanora conceived what was to be their second love child—Shaina, the beautiful, golden one . . .

"Mother!"

Startled out of her dream state, Eleanora stirred in the chair and turned to face her excited son who had just burst into the room.

"Silvanus Hart sent a message." Will was all smiles, but he didn't yet know that the man was his father. "I don't know where you know this man from, Mother, but he says to come ahead. He even paid for our fare on the *Clementine*. We're going to a ranch up in the foothills of the mountain, a place named Lazy C. Think they'll give us work there? It's a big ranch. I been asking around town, and they say it's owned by a rich, powerful man by the name of Travis Cordell. One of the dudes in town says he used to work there, and Cordell is always hiring new men. Do you think he'll hire me? Maybe he even has work you can do. I

384

mean something easy, like sewing or something, Ma."

"Slow down, son." She smoothed back the red-gold hair and stared into eyes a smidgen darker than her own turquoise ones. "If he's as kind as he sounds, I don't think we'll have any trouble." Eleanora's hands flew to her face. Would Silvanus still find her pretty even though so many years, hard years, had passed?

"I'm so darn excited, Ma, I know I won't be able to sleep tonight." Will ran a strong-fingered hand through his curly locks. Suddenly his face fell into a mask of sadness. "I sure wish we could find Shainy. I looked around and asked about her everywhere I've been but no one ever heard of a schoolteacher named Shaina Hill."

Shaina Hill. Eleanora gazed off into the distant hills, wondering where her sweet daughter was at this minute. Her name should rightfully be Shaina Hart, not—Oh, Lord, if only Silvanus should love her as before, then they could go together in search of Shaina. Will would come along. If only . . . if only everything turned out that they could all be together and happy.

Eleanora held her arm for her son and he came, kneeling beside the chair, his curly red head resting beneath her bosom. Holding her hand, Will softly asked, "Did you ever love Graham, Mother?"

She didn't even stiffen as she replied, "At first. Graham was such a child, he needed me."

"Did *you* ever need him, I'm asking."

"I suppose I did. At first."

"You say 'At first.' What happened later?"

"We—" she smiled"—we got to know each other better."

"Was that bad?"

"In some ways. We were young." And I was already pregnant with another man's child. But that wonderful man had gone away, to find work, and he had not returned quickly enough. She had been so afraid to tell her parents, and so she had married Graham Hill. How ironic it had turned out to be that she had displeased them by marrying Graham. She'd often wondered if they would have liked Silvanus better, the real father to her unborn child. Silvanus had come looking for her and had found her. But too late. How could she ever tell her son all this, even though he had never been close with his "father"? But perhaps she should have told him a long time ago, perhaps she hadn't been fair to Will. Oh Lord, she thought, as she placed a tender hand on the curly head and looked up into the brightening sky, how, after all this time, am I ever to tell him that his name, his full name, is Silvanus William Hart?

Chapter Thirty-seven

Thunder Mountain Range was bathed in white moonlight, creating deep blue shadows along its chain of alternating high and low peaks. And below this, in the forested foothills, where sparkling waterfalls and towering timber existed, Shaina lay on a blanket beneath the redwood sentinel. It was growing chilly, despite the summer month, and Shaina snuggled and drew the blanket about her in search of warmth.

About ten feet away from Shaina lay Graham Hill, snoring like he could saw down ten of the giant timbers surrounding their campsite.

Shaina could hear the strange sounds of the night creatures stirring. The glowing embers and the gray smoke curling upward into the tall trees lent little in the way of easing her tension. She was as tight as a coiled spring and every time she closed her eyes and began to drift, she would come suddenly awake, her eyes staring wide from over her blanket.

So far, the animals she'd seen on their dangerous journey consisted of every conceivable mountain animal, it seemed, except for the bear. And, thank God for that!

Shaina was tired from worry and the fear that they would not get to Travis in time. It was taking so long! Her eyes went to Graham rolled up on the ground and sleeping comfortable and cozy. How could he sleep so easily, she wondered. He didn't seem to have a care in the world.

She was worried for Roux and worried for Travis. From time to time the horrible feeling that she'd never see them alive again washed over her.

From across the way came a loud snore from Graham, and then, smacking his lips, he shifted to a more comfortable position and resumed sawing logs.

Shaina stared up at the moon that was high in the black sky, surrounded by millions of brilliant stars. The night was alive with shadows that seemed to be ever-shifting, and if she stared long enough in one spot she could almost imagine she was looking at the frightening shape of some huge monstrous beast with long, thick hairs sticking out all over it.

There . . . over there. She bolted to her elbows, staring. Wasn't that bush moving over there? She could have sworn there was something—

Dear God . . . *there was!*

Detaching itself from the bush, the shadowy figure moved closer and closer. Clearing her throat shakily, Shaina tried calling out valiantly, but her voice emerged like a hoarse croak.

"Graham."

Shaina scurried over to where Graham slept, pushing and tugging at his shoulder to rouse him. Graham came awake, slowly, and stared around groggily. Then

388

his eyes came to rest on Shaina.

"Wh — what is it?" he mumbled, shaking his head to clear it of drugging slumber. "What you doing, Shainy?"

She pointed, stuttering, "There . . . over there. Graham, where's your gun?"

"Huh?" He blinked up at her, asking, "What gun?"

Now Graham, too, could see that indeed something was walking — or stumbling — toward them. Something — or someone — that was wounded.

Graham choked on a nervous laugh. "Shainy . . . do something."

She stared at him like he was crazy.

"I asked you where your gun was." Fear and anger knotted her stomach.

"I didn't bring one."

"You *what?*"

"I didn't —"

"Never mind." Graham could be so infuriating! Shaina eyed her horse hobbled on the other side of the campfire, and her saddle resting on the ground near a tree. She had a gun in her saddlebag . . . if only she could get to it.

Graham sent her a brief look that told her he was scared to death. Graham was still in a state of shock, staring at the "thing" that walked slowly into the circle of low firelight. A gasp caught in Shaina's throat as she recognized who the creature was . . . no beast at all. Then again, he *could* be called just that.

Shaina's face was one deep bitter mask of hatred.

"Giles Wilson."

Now Graham blinked out of his daze, but he was tossed right back into another form of emotion, this

389

one just as unpleasant.

Shaina stared from one to the other, and in a flash of awareness, knew! She immediately whirled and looked at him. Graham had never intended to bring her to her husband at all, and now she realized what he had been doing. Graham's idea was to draw her away from the Lazy C, just as Giles had once tried. Graham had succeeded in one thing—bringing her to the one person who would never let her go. That is, if she didn't act fast. Giles was hurt, she could see that much. But could she just let him die?

Turning on Graham, Shaina asked, "Where is Travis?" She knew by the look on his face he'd been deceiving her. "And you'd better explain what this is all about."

"Think you're pretty smart, don't you, Shainy? Well, you ain't. Not this time. You know it all, don't you? Yes, I can see that you do know I'm not really your father. Think you really knew it all along, but you never said nothing."

Without hesitation, she said, "I knew in my heart, yes." Shaina carefully let her eyes skim her saddlebag, judging the distance and time it would take to reach it, her calculating completely escaping the other's notice.

Giles, wiping sweat from his forehead, settled onto a rotted log away from the fire, grimacing at the same time he listened to what the other two were arguing about. Very interesting, he was thinking shrewdly all the while they thought he was in pain and unable to follow their conversation. He was in pain, that was true enough, but still he could hear . . .

After Giles had been wounded by Jay's knife, he set

out into the woods feeling dizzy from the loss of blood and too weak to return to the campsite and fight the young man. He had wandered for the remainder of the night, almost delirious. After bathing his face in a mountain stream, resting by it for as long as he needed to renew his strength, and waiting for the bleeding to stop, he set out heading back in the direction of the campsite. But, as he'd thought might happen, no one was there—only a thin trickle of smoke curled into the cold blue morning sky. He'd tried tracking them all day, but he'd soon lost their trail. Miah was gone, too. She must have returned to find everyone had vanished and gotten frightened. Deep inside the Indian woman was terrified of Travis, Giles knew, and whenever she felt threatened she ran back to her people and stayed until she got up enough courage to venture out into the world again.

Darkness had settled in again by the time Giles stumbled onto Graham and Shaina's campsite. What luck, he'd thought, for now he didn't have to use Roux to lure them here. But two were better than one. Roux was missing. Shaina was missing. Travis and his riders would be all over the mountains like stink on dung pretty soon . . . and he had the bait right here in his talons. He had been smart enough, too, in searching in the saddlebags over by the tree before walking into the camp. A little treasure had been waiting, waiting just for him!

"Looking for this?"

Giles pointed the gun·at Shaina when she whirled from her saddlebag, where she had been searching futilely for her gun. His laugh carried a nasty ring to it.

Shaina took courage in anger. "Damn you," she hissed, "damn you, Giles Wilson."

Travis, Silvanus, and Jack rode all day, resting only when it became too dark to see. Travis lay awake, staring at the brilliant stars woven between the branches of the tallest spruce making them look like huge Christmas trees. If his deductions were correct, Shaina would give birth sometime in late January of the new year. Shaina, with his baby. Shaina. What a glorious woman!

He sighed deeply. It was a sad sound. How could he ever have thought Shaina didn't love him? How could he have questioned her fidelity? Her love led him on as bright as the shining stars above his head. He knew she must be thinking of him at that very minute; he could feel her love. She was up here somewhere in the forested hills . . . so damn close and yet so far away.

He would never forget the day she came to Wild Mountain. Even as their eyes had made contact for the very first time, a thrill of intense love had run through him, one that he had been powerless to control. With forced courage she had met his probing gaze. Determined blue fire had flashed in those wonderful eyes and she had moved away from him as if he'd tried to bite her . . . She had made his world so content. Holding her in his arms at night was paradise. Shaina was his light. His shining light. He would follow her to the ends of the earth if need be. He did something he hadn't done in a long time; he said a fervent prayer that she would be all right.

How he loved that woman, now and forever. Roux loved her, too, and he would find them, he vowed, find them both safe and whole . . . if God was truly God.

Joe Creek and Vinny Sloan rode slowly. They traveled like creatures of the night, going by the light of the moon and stars. Curving up the hillside, they came to a halt halfway up the slope, for there was a sheer drop down a mossy, rocky cliff and they could go no further until the sky lightened. No campfires were lighted; no food was prepared. They ate dried jerky and drank from a canteen, leaning their tired bodies against the base of one of the thousands of Douglas firs that towered into the star-dotted sky.

Sloan's weary voice was just above a whisper. "Looks like we ain't going to get our gold after all. Graham run out on us, Joe. What do you plan to do now?"

"Keep looking till I find them. What do you think, idiot."

"These hills are too big and deep, Joe. They could e way on the other side of the mountain by now and eading back to the river so's they can take the verboat outa here."

For a moment, in a lusty flash of fantasy Joe's eyes evoured Shaina's alabaster body, the perfect body he wanted to plunge into. "Don't think so. Giles is up ere, too, I'd stake my life on it."

"I think he's gone, Joe. Gone with the wind . . . ith Shaina, too."

"He won't get Shaina Cordell. She's mine. Come

on." Joe stood and stretched out, sheathing the thin-bladed knife he had been caressing all the while he sat against the tree.

The silver of the moonlight was being gilded by the first soft beginnings of dawn. Sloan muttered angrily but came to his feet, just wanting to get this over with so he could return home. He could almost smell Ma's mouthwatering cooking, and he almost turned back down the tree-dotted mountain. Joe was crazy, just as he always thought.

They were headed for tragedy. Sloan could feel it in his bones.

Back at the ranch, in the shade of the porch Deanna sat tensely on the swing, rocking to and fro. She halted suddenly when she thought she saw someone coming down the trail from the mountains. Was it another false alarm?

Where are they? she wondered. What could be happening up there? Was Roux all right. Was Shaina? Travis?

Her Jack? Dear Lord, if Jack got hurt—or worse—Deanna knew she could not go on living. Jack Nolan was her love, her life.

No, he wouldn't die. Jack was strong, he was careful, and he knew how to expertly use his gun and knife. Thank God for that!

Deanna's eyes scanned the grounds thoroughly and methodically, but nearly a whole afternoon of the constant watching went by before she spotted a sign of movement. Coming from the woods. Her eyes flew to the hills. They were not coming in the way she had supposed they would. Then . . . who was this? There were two of them? No, a third rider. One, she recognized now as Abner Selby's eldest son riding the huge black horse that had brought Shaina to the ranch.

As they drew nearer, Deanna could make out the features of the woman. She was lovely, petite, and she rode with a tired grace of movement. There was a boy, no, a young man. He had reddish-gold hair. Deanna swallowed hard. Hair strangely like Shaina's.

"Oh, Lord," Deanna breathed. "Could this possibly be?" There was too strong a resemblance for it not to be, Deanna thought. The woman, she was an older replica of Shaina. There was no doubt in Deanna's mind that these two were Shaina's relatives. But what were they doing here? And hadn't she heard that Shaina's mother had disappeared from her home some time ago?

Tobias Selby drew up before the hitching rail, then dismounted to help the woman down. The young man looked none too sure of the welcome they would receive as he stared across the space from the rail to where Deanna was just coming down off the porch. She smiled and he relaxed with a tired blink of his incredibly large, blue eyes.

"Howdy," he said to the woman walking over to greet them.

"Hello," Deanna said, smiling as she took each one of their hands in hers and shook them. "I'm so happy to meet you." First to the lovely woman, "It can't be otherwise. You must be Shaina's mother."

"I—"

Eleanora exchanged a look with her son, a look of

such intense longing that Deanna couldn't help but put out her hand again and touch the woman gently on the arm.

"Come inside. You must be tired." To Tobias she said, "Thank you, Toby, you can rest the horses in the stable, and if you like you can join the men back in the cookshack, they should be having cherry buckle just about now."

"Yes'm!" Tobias happily led the horses to the stable, his eyes lighting at the thought of the delicious dessert he would receive for payment of his services.

Eleanora bent to lift her carpetbag, but her son beat her to it, and carried his bag and hers into the house. In the enormous living room, Will stared in awe at the sturdy western furnishings and the beautiful paintings of mountains and green hills.

"That sure is pretty," he blurted out, then he blushed as Deanna turned about to see what it was he was specifically complimenting.

"That's Travis Cordell's favorite picture. It's of Big Blue."

"That the biggest mountain we saw coming in?" Will asked the pretty lady who led them into the kitchen.

"Sure is." She smiled as she heated up the big black stove. "Please sit down, Mrs. Hill." Deanna blushed. "I don't know your first name. Or yours either, young man."

Will went to stand beside his mother's chair. "This is my mother, Eleanor. I'm William Hill."

"I'm so very glad to meet you both. I'm Deanna King—Oh Lord, I almost said Kingswell. That was my name before I married the Lazy C foreman, Jac

Nolan." She laughed softly. "My name's Deanna Nolan now."

"You're very kind, Mrs. Nolan," Eleanora said. She
looked up at her son and heaved a deep sigh before
she spoke to the young woman again. "I'm very
curious, Mrs. Nolan—"

"Oh, please—" Deanna pressed her chest "—please
just call me Deanna."

Eleanora smiled graciously, crinkling the delicate
fan lines about her still-bright eyes and trying to still
her racing heart. "I'm afraid curiosity has gotten the
best of me—uhmm, Deanna." She clutched her son's
big hand for reassurance. He pressed back. "You
mentioned my daughter's name. Shaina."

"Of course." She began to place coffee cups on the
table, and looked up in surprise when the surprisingly
strong hand caught hers. "You *are* Shaina's mother?"
Deanna looked confused.

"Just tell me, is Shaina Hill here?" Eleanora's voice
caught on a little sob, "Is my daughter . . . *here?*"

"She certainly is," Deanna said to the misty-eyed
woman, "but," she added with a smile, "she's Shaina
Cordell now."

Will's throat moved before he spoke. "Our Shainy's
married?"

"Yes, she is." Deanna looked toward the kitchen
window where the gingham curtains blew softly in
and out. "But she's not . . . not here now."

Eleanora stood suddenly to her feet, saying, "Something's wrong. Tell me, young lady, what is it?"

"Well, I think Graham Hill took her away. I
mean—" Deanna shook her head "—I don't know why
she went with him."

397

"Graham Hill here . . . too? *Lord!"*

"My *pa?"*

With a frightened glance in her son's direction, Eleanora asked the young woman, "Has Graham been trouble?"

Will cut in, "You know the answer to that, Ma."

"I wasn't asking you, Son. Let the young lady answer."

"Sorry." He smiled at Deanna, then blurted, "But Graham's always been trouble. That's his middle name."

"I really feel as if I have no choice but to tell you folks," Deanna said, biting her lower lip.

"Go ahead." Eleanora sat again. "Please."

"I think that man took Shainy away."

Will's hands balled into fists. "What do you mean?"

"Shaina wouldn't just go away like she did. She, uh, she's going to have a baby."

"A baby?" the walls tossed back the second voice like a resounding echo.

"Yes," Deanna said. "Travis Cordell's baby."

Eleanora shot up from the chair.

"When?!" *My Shainy is just a baby herself!"*

Deanna shrugged, saying, "I'm not sure, ma'am but she ain't . . . I mean, she isn't too far along. She don't show yet."

Eleanora sat down again. "I would like to ask you something else, Deanna. I—you see—a man by the name of Silvanus sent us tickets to come here. Do—do you know of him?"

"Oh sure. Silvanus's been with Travis for a long time." Deanna poured the hot coffee in the three cups then sat down with them. "He's the kindest, th gentlest man you'd ever want to meet." Deanna sipped her coffee. "You know him, ah, personally?"

All the time Will was watching his mother closely, wondering as he had before about the tender expression that came over her face as the man Silvanus Hart was mentioned. She looked that way again. And she looked a little scared, too.

"I have known Silvanus Hart for a very long time." Eleanora looked down at the table and up again. "Yes, a very long time."

"Mother —" Will asked her softly "— who is this man Silvanus Hart?"

"He's . . . he's —" Her eyes filled and she couldn't keep it in any longer. "He's your *father.*"

Sudden anger flashed in Will's eyes, and he rose from the table, almost upsetting the chair.

"Ma!" He clenched his hands to his sides. "Why didn't you tell me?! Jeez, what a time to tell me!"

"Will!" Eleanora shouted as her son ran out the door. "Will, come back!"

Deanna's eyes followed the young man out the door. She said under her breath, "Lordy. We sure have had us some excitement around here ever since Shaina Hill first showed up."

Eleanora turned to face the young housekeeper. "I heard you. You are right." She shook her head as she returned to the table. "Neither has my life been a quiet one. Not lately. I knew Shaina would be like me. She followed her heart. I've had to, too."

"I understand, and so will your son. He will come back. We sure wouldn't want him missing when your daughter returns. Shaina's going to be so happy. She was looking for you."

"Really?"

"She certainly was. I remember them making a trip to Mountain Lake."

Eleanora shook her head. "So much has happened in so little time."

"Oh, Lord, wait until you catch up with what has been going on around here!"

Eleanora lowered her head wearily, as she said, "I just hope my daughter will not hate me when I tell her Silvanus Hart is her father. Will sure didn't take kindly to my confession."

"You did the right thing." Deanna reached across and patted the work-roughened hand. "Will is going to come around, especially when he meets Silvanus. No one can ignore that man's quiet charm. And you know what else?"

"No."

"You won't have to tell your daughter nothing. Not by yourself, honey. You and Silvanus can do that together."

"Oh . . . I wonder what he'll think of me after all these years."

"Did he love you before?"

Eleanora's blue eyes sparkled mischievously. "Oh, yes!"

"Well, Silvanus hasn't had a woman around him in ages. Not that I could tell, anyhow. It's just him and the cows."

Eleanora's eyes misted over.

"The cowboy."

"Yeah. And I'll just bet that there cowboy still love his lady, too!"

"I—I hope so."

"You got nothing to worry about, Eleanora." Deanna sighed, staring down into her cup. "Now — all we have to is sit and wait and pray for their safe return."

Chapter Thirty-eight

"Jay! Let her go!"

For the hundreth time Jay felt Roux's gentle caress as she touched his arm; it made Jay feel brave just to have his little beloved touch him so trustingly. Now he knew he must truly be courageous, and let Roux know that her mother must be brought to Travis Cordell for trial for her misdeed. She had kidnapped Roux, and could not be allowed to get away with it, even though the girl *was* her daughter.

Mounted together on the golden horse, Jay grimaced and lifted Roux's slender hand from his thigh where it had innocently drifted.

Firmly Jay set her hand aside, saying, "I must not let her go, Fox Fire. She has been bad, you understand. She must be taken to your father so that he might punish her."

"Please, Jay. I do not want her to come around

anymore. She can stay away. Miah will be afraid to come to Lazy C now. It is better this way. Jay? Do you hear me?"

"Yes." Jay sighed. "I hear you."

"Please. Just let her go?"

Jay smoothed the raven-red hair. He adored this girl, he always would. He had loved Roux Cordell from the first moment he'd seen her outside the Indian camp. He only waited for the time he could make her a woman, his woman, forever and evermore. If there was a need, he would wait forever, and no woman would ever come between them—ever.

"It will be as you say, Roux. But mark my words. Miah will be trouble again one day soon."

"Will you do something for me, Jay?"

"If it is possible."

She cleared her throat, then blurted, "Do not tell my father that she stole me away with that Wilson guy." Roux grimaced just saying the terrible man's name.

Jay's strong shoulders lifted and fell. He was being sorely tested.

"That is impossible," he answered.

Roux stared into Jay's golden eyes, asking, "Why? Why is it so impossible?"

Jay stared as Miah disappeared into the hazy pink and gold of dawn light. He blinked wearily, trying to explain, "Now, look I have just let that bitch go. For you, Roux. But I cannot keep what you ask from your father."

Roux continued to twist in her perch, gazing into Jay's troubled eyes. "Oh." Finally she tore her eyes from his face and turned to look down upon Sheba's

403

golden mane.

"Do not keep yourself from me, Fox Fire."

"I will if I want to." She pouted, screwing up the bronze-pink bow of her mouth.

Gritting his fine white teeth, Jay turned Sheba into the tall trees where it was jungle green and dark. He swore deeply.

"That's a bad word, Jay."

"Close your ears then because you are going to hear many more."

"That's not nice, Jay."

"You have made me angry, Roux."

"I can tell. All you call me is Roux when you get that way. You love me when you call me Fox Fire."

"I love you all the time . . . Fox Fire."

"No you don't."

"Yes I do."

"No." She swiveled to look at him out of the corner of her eye. "If you loved me you would not tell Father that Miah kidnapped me with Wilson."

Jay's already broad shoulders lifted and fell in exasperation. But he didn't know the word to use to tell her how he felt, so he simply said, "You make me feel crazy, Roux!"

"Do not yell in my ear, Jay Ridingbow!"

"I'd like to spank you!"

"You better not!"

"Silly Roux. I saved your life. All you do is get mad at me."

"All I want you to do is forget all about my mother." Her face was infused with an even brighter pink than her emotions disclosed as the sun beamed a bright morning ray into the forest of gigantic firs. "Forget her! Forget Miah! I never want to see my mother again!"

"You will. She will be after you again if you let her get away this time. Miah will be back to haunt you . . . always."

Roux held her breath, then let it out in a huff. "She did not die yet, Jay. What are you talking about! The only ones that haunt are dead ones. This is what Silver-White-Fish told me."

"You don't understand, Roux. You are too much a child yet."

"I am not! You are making me mad now and I am going to call you all kinds of names like I do when you don't come to see me, and you go to the city and stay there and don't come back for many days!"

Jay stared at the shining back of Roux's head made even brighter by the yellow sunlight streaming through the trees. "You never told me you were jealous, Roux," he said, his heart beating dangerously fast. *He had to get her away from him and to home!*

"I just bet you were diddlin' with Carolyn Creek, too!"

Jay angrily stiffened against her back, but only for a moment before he realized what he was doing.

"Jeezus, Roux." Jay pulled the horse up and halted out of the sun's rays. "Where did you ever hear that kind of language?"

"B.J."

"Do you know what that word means."

"Kind of."

Jay twisted her around to face him. "Tell me."

"You were kissing and holding hands with Carolyn Creek just like you do when you go to the city and

405

find other girls there."

Jay's countenance was stern as he said, "This is not for you to know about yet, Roux. When the time comes we will discuss this. Not before then."

With a trembling lower lip, Roux gazed up into Jay's dark face, noting that he was growing fuzz on his chin again. Suddenly she was reminded of Noah Starr and his big, long beard. She didn't like to see Jay like this, she liked him much better when he was smiling and happy, not frowning and angry. She said, "You know what Noah Starr said to me the other day when I asked him how old he was?"

With a relaxing of tense shoulders, Jay said, "No, what did he say?" He tried to smile at her, but his emotions were still riding a high crest.

"He said, 'When the Dead Sea was alive I was still a young whippersnapper'." She giggled, saying, "Isn't that funny?"

"Yes, Roux." He pulled her toward him, brushing her forehead with a tender kiss, pushing her disheveled hair back from her face. He stopped to stare into the dark-green eyes. Seriously he said, "I don't think you even know what the Dead Sea is."

"I do." Her chin lifted. "Yes I do. Moses in the Bible parted it when he wanted his good people to get to the other side away from the bad people."

Jay pursed his mouth, saying, "Jeezus, Roux. You are smart. I didn't even know all that. You are growing up."

Sliding from the mount to privately relieve herself in the bushes, Roux said, "You're damn right I am!"

Jay stared after her, his mouth struck wide.

After a few minutes, Jay stroked his bristly chin,

asking himself, "But wasn't that the Red Sea?" He shrugged, flinging black hair over his shoulder. "Close enough, anyway."

Shaina sat watching the four men watching her from across the blackened campfire.

"Where's the gold?" Sloan came right out and asked.

"Shut up, Vinny!" Joe hissed, slapping the other man upside his head.

"Gold?" Giles asked. "You got the gold?"

Greedy-Graham blurted, "There ain't enough for all of us."

"Sure there is," Joe drawled with a nasty gleam in his eyes. "I'm here to make sure it gets passed out evenly between us." Joe used his best English in an attempt to impress Shaina. He stared over at the young woman with hungry ardor lighting his eyes. "Isn't that right, honey?"

Shaina lifted a finely arched eyebrow, saying, "Are you talking to me, slime?"

"Ohhh," three collectively hummed. But Joe just narrowed dark eyes that said, "I'll take care of you later, Shaina baby."

Shaina smiled in mock flirtatiousness at Sloan who gaped back at her, pointing at his chest. Brilliant blue eyes flashed back at Sloan with a come-hither look, and his throat bobbed as he gulped.

"She's trying to start trouble between us," Giles slowly announced, making to rise from the ground.

"Let her."

"What?" Giles stopped and stared at Joe Creek.

"I said—" slowly "—Let her."

It was then that Giles whipped out the gun he'd swiped from Shaina's knapsack and pointed it directly at Joe's heart. Joe's black eyes smoldered with hatred and hot passion.

"I wouldn't do that," Sloan told Giles. "Joe's got a mean temper. He'll get that gun and he'll get you back, hombre."

"Try."

"Take me home, Giles," Shaina said, drawing all eyes to her. "If you do, you will be rewarded for your trouble."

"Think I'm stupid?" Giles asked. "I do that and Travis will be on my tail like stink on horse crap."

While the three were arguing, Graham rose from the rock and cautiously stepped back and eased himself toward his horse whereon lie his rifle in the scabbard.

The men, with their backs turned to Graham as they argued amongst themselves, did not notice as he slowly pulled the rifle and quietly chambered a bullet. As he turned to level the rifle at the three of them, Giles half turned bringing the revolver under his arm and along his side.

A loud roar erupted and flame emerged from the pistol, striking Graham dead center in the chest, throwing him back with the impact against the horse, which reared and whinnied.

Shaina's eyes grew wide as she helplessly watched the scene with horror.

The rifle slowly fell from Graham's hands as he clutched the festering wound in his chest, blood spilling between his clenched fingers. As his legs buckled, he went slowly to his knees with a strange glaze to his eyes. He fell forward, facedown, striking a rock as if adding insult to injury. It split open his head. The gurgling sound came from his mouth along with the blood that spilled from it.

Cradling her head with hands that shook, Shaina screamed.

Graham twitched and lay still in death.

Joe and Sloan immediately stepped back, reaching for their weapons as Giles spun with his weapon pointing toward them now.

Giles hissed through clenched teeth, "Try it and I'll kill you both."

"Stop it!" Shaina yelled. "Stop it now . . . *all of you!*"

The men simply ignored her, and Giles repeated his warning, waving the pistol in their direction. "Got any argument with me?" he asked.

Both men dropped their hands to their sides, then raised arms, one left-handed, one right, as if to salute in unison, saying collectively, "Not us."

Now Joe, with nerves of steel, turned his back to Giles with a sneer on his face. He muttered to himself, "You'll get yours." He then headed in Shaina's direction to try to quiet her down.

Trembling all over, Shaina was standing and gaping at the dead man who'd been more like her enemy than her father in these last few hours. But why couldn't she find hatred in her heart? she wondered as a rough arm grabbed her arm and pulled her over against a small tree.

The bitter hatred in Joe's eyes put wild fear in Shaina's heart and her knees became weak as jelly as he trussed her up to the tree. She watched, mesmerized by the scene that played before her, as Sloan dragged Graham's body over to a green ravine and shoved the body over the edge.

"What is he doing?" Shaina asked Joe, staring in a near trance.

Joe only shook his head and smirked over in Giles's direction.

Dispassionately, Giles had watched Shaina as she witnessed the killing, had taken note of the horror reflected in her beautiful blue eyes, and then, just as unmoved, watched as Sloan disposed of the body.

Shaina's misted eyes studied Giles for several minutes, fear and confusion surfacing in the orbs. Was this was the same man who'd been so kind and caring to her so long ago on the riverboat? Incredulity was added to the other unwelcome emotions, and then she looked aside in disgust. Two men in her life had disappointed her. She couldn't take it if Travis should ever do that to her . . . But had he, had he already? Was he searching for her even now? Or had he gone to the pretty schoolteacher in Seattle as soon as she had disappeared? Did he believe she hadn't left him for Giles? If only he would come to her . . . She had always been a foolish little girl, with knights in shining armor coming to her rescue in her golden dreams. But in the real world there were no such things as real heroes . . . were there?

Giles slowly holstered Shaina's revolver into his own empty holster. He had no weapon of his own; he'd lost everything when Jay Ridingbow had driven him ou of his camp. Now he didn't want to lose what he'd fought so hard to gain. He would have to tread cautiously with Joe Creek around. After all, he wa wounded.

Quite by accident, B.J. wandered upon the scene. He was standing on a mossy cliff overlooking the distant shelf, watching the smoke that spiraled gracefully like a gray snake up through the huge trees. Three figures were seated upon a log. Were there more of them? Did they have little Roux? He nudged his fat mare. Something told him to be extremely cautious . . .

The bacon sizzled over the fire in the heavy iron skillet and the odor of delicious coffee hung thick in the air. Shaina had begun to feel ill immediately following Graham's murder. The sight of blood had always sickened her. Now, the length of leather she was trussed to the tree with bit painfully into her wrists. Every time she moved it seemed Joe's eyes settled on her, like he derived some sadistic pleasure from her discomfort, and she got sicker by the moment.

"Evil bastard," she hissed under her breath, gasping when the leather bit into her throat.

Joe watched Shaina Cordell as he ate, his eyes narrowing into evil, dark slits, his face pinched with lust, his black hair askew on either side of his head, making him look like the devil himself.

Sloan watched Joe watch Shaina. And Giles kept a watchful eye on them all.

"I don't know how much more of this stare-down I can take," Shaina whispered to herself, trying to keep

411

her sanity and forget the horrible scene of a while ago.

After a long silence, Sloan was the first to speak as he stood, and walking to the fire, called over his shoulder, "Hey, lady, want somethin' to eat?"

She was just about to open her mouth to say something when a movement from Joe stopped her.

Lounging on the ground, Joe leaned to his elbow and shot a nasty look at Sloan refilling his tin plate, growling, "Let her be. I asked her already, she don't want anything to eat." He leered at Shaina, adding, "She wants to keep her nice figure, don't you, lady?"

Slowly Shaina blinked her eyes. She'd like to tell Joe Creek she couldn't stand the sight of him, but if she did, he would only give her a rougher treatment than she was already getting. She simply ignored him as best she could.

"Hey, sugar pants, I asked you—"

"What was that?" Sloan had spun about and froze. "Did you hear that?"

The fine brown hairs on the back of Giles's head stood up as out of the corner of his eye he took in two bear cubs lumbering on the perimeter of their camp-site.

"What the—?"

Coming swiftly to his knees, Joe swore. "Where there's cubs there's a mama."

"Yeah. A *big* mama," said Sloan. Already the sweat was beginning to form at the back of his neck. "I once saw a man get torn limb from limb—"

"Hush your mouth!" Joe ordered. He cast a swift look at Shaina, seeing her eyes freeze on the cubs. "Never mind, lady, we'll get rid of them. Sloan, pic up sticks!"

Shaina watched, mesmerized, as the two men flung sticks at the playful cubs chasing them off into the woods. Shaina swallowed, relief going through her.

"Hah!" Sloan crowed. "Easy as chasin' scaredy chickens off."

Just as Sloan's last word dropped, the earth-trembling roar sounded from the brambles and then they saw it, for one horrible instant, the huge head of a bear rising above the bushes and then just as swiftly disappearing.

Shaina's heart almost stopped. She had never seen a bear in real life, only in a picture book and . . . only in her nightmares.

"Please," Shaina whimpered. "Please, will someone untie me and *let me go?*"

Suddenly, terrifying, there was a crashing sound as the huge bear entered the clearing, jaws snapping with a deep, angry growling coming from within its huge fleshy body.

"Grizzly!"

Sloan's eyes bugged. Joe shouted as he ran. Giles stumbled on a log, then spun about to shoot but realized he hadn't reloaded. With the bear at his heels, Giles took off across the clearing and jumped over the side of the mossy shelf, landing on a jutting boulder below as he clung to the slippery vines hanging from a tree. He grimaced; he was bleeding all over again.

"Try and get me now, beast!" Giles taunted and laughed crazily, feeling the sticky blood run down his back.

The terrible grizzly peered down at the man, and

when the sow realized she couldn't get to him, she turned and wheeled in retreat galloping off full tilt toward the other humans.

The cubs had returned and Shaina noticed that they looked so much bigger than when first she'd spotted them. They weren't tiny babies, that was for certain!

Shaina, pressing her body to the tree, swallowed a cry when she heard the grizzly returning with a great scraping and tramping of the sow's feet. Coming upon them quite suddenly as she had, the bear had been surprised, Shaina thought, as if only seeking to protect her babies. She only prayed the sow did not think of her as a threat to them.

But the dream, the warning. *What about the dream?* Now, close to her, Shaina could hear the great snorts and the snuffing of nostrils.

And here she was, dear God, tied to a tree.

"Oh, I am going to die," Shaina cried softly. "Travis . . . Travis, if I never see you again, please believe that I loved you, for I do with all my heart and soul, I do! Oh, God, please let me be with Travis and Roux again, oh please let this child within me know life!"

Shaina's head was flung back so that she could no see the bear lumber past, huge, long claws digging up moist turf and twigs and even rocks to send them flying every which way.

"Where's my rifle?" Joe cried. Then, almost as an afterthought, he thought of the horses and turned to see them rearing up, pulling their reins loose from where they had been carelessly tied.

Shaina had thought of them, too, and prayed that they would get away from the grizzly, especially he

414

Spotted Bird. *Go, go, Spotted Bird!* her heart silently cried.

The huge sow hit Joe with such force it knocked him clean to the ground. The cavernous jaws clamped about his arm as it sank its teeth into the man's flesh sending blood pulsing from the gaping slash. At the same time, the sow had bowled over Sloan, who scrambled to his knees searching for something, anything, to fend it off.

"Damn it!" he sobbed, feeling utter helplessness soar over him.

The sow then raised itself upon her hind feet and stood almost erect, its mouth opening and closing as it growled deeply at the intruders, the humans who had not been here the last time she visited the berry bush with her cubs. It stood there, paws waving in the air as if grabbing at an invisible beehive. The long fur bristled on its back.

"Why is it attacking?" Sloan gasped over to Joe, who was clutching the gaping wound in his arm, blood spilling over his fingers.

Joe could hardly speak, but he could groan the words out. "It's a grizzly, a damned grizzly, stupid. Them and their relatives are likely to attack just cause they feel like it . . . and the sow's got cubs."

"The horses . . . they're going!"

Joe swore. "There goes our rifles along with them." He was laying low to the ground, hidden around the side of a bush from the bear.

"I've got a gun, Joe, a six-gun!"

"Where'd you get it?" Joe grunted out.

"Giles musta dropped it." He checked it, and finding it empty, he slithered on his belly over to Shaina's knapsack, and, finding the bullets, he reloaded.

"It's coming at us again!" Joe shouted.

The grizzly dropped back down to all fours and began to lumber toward them. Sloan lifted the gun and fired, which only seemed to enrage the bear even more.

The bloody mouth of the sow opened and closed, and Sloan stumbled trying to get away. He tripped on a small log, falling backward and dislodging a shot into the air.

B.J. could not see the bear now, but he knew it was attacking those at the camp. His daddy once told him, he who was a sheriff at one time, that, "The grizzly are fierce and untractable (B.J. never knew what that meant) and cannot tolerate the presence of humans. The grizzly and its relatives are more prone to attack without apparent provocation (he didn't know that word, either) than with other kinds of bears." And Billy Joe never doubted Daddy once. Especially at this moment. There was a shot, and B.J. rode faster, thinking that maybe Roux or Shaina was with them. That was his only thought, the one that spurred him on . . .

The sow had found and attacked Joe again. Now was atop the man as Sloan fired point-blank into the bear's face. Simultaneously, the bear swiped the man with her powerful paw, breaking Sloan's neck and almost tearing his head off.

Another bullet ripped through the air followed by

another and yet another from a powerful rifle some sixty feet away.

Dazedly Shaina looked toward the thickest trees, wondering who had fired the rifle. No one was in sight.

The sow collapsed onto Sloan, and the man screamed wildly as the grizzly sank its huge fangs into his skull . . . and then they both lay dead. Or so it seemed.

Shaina stared at the bloody scene, knowing she would never be able to entirely wipe the horror of this morning from her mind. She struggled to keep the strangled sound from emerging as Giles rose, like Lucifer out of the depths, and stumbled toward her. He was all scratched and bleeding, his breathing labored, and Shaina beheld the man as more frightening than the poor sow who had only been trying to protect her cubs.

Stay away from me, her mind screamed at the man.

He bent, found the gun, checked the chambers, and then aimed the thing at Shaina's head.

"Giles . . . *what?*"

Fear, sharp and knifing, leaped to Shaina's eyes. *No, no, Giles.* And then the gun went off.

No more grunts or tramping of huge paws were to be heard. B.J. slowed his barrel-chested mount and cautiously passed into the tangled forest that would lead him to the clearing where he knew the bear had just breathed its last. It was then that he heard the woman scream . . . a terrifying sound that ripped through the silence of the bloody morning.

Another shot broke the stillness. A rifle, he decided as he spurred his horse toward the clearing, praying he wouldn't find any dead women . . . or a child—a special child that he had come to love very much.

They all converged on the scene at almost the same moment. B.J. and Roux and Jay. Then Silvanus, Jack Noland, and Travis. The latter's rifle was still hot and smoking and he didn't look happy at all after what had transpired here.

Travis stared at the body not twenty feet from where Shaina was still tied to the tree. She sagged in great relief upon seeing him standing there . . . the man who had ended Giles's life before the villain could shoot her.

Shaina almost wept. Dreams do come true . . . she had a real-life hero after all.

Shaina would never know what had prompted Giles to try to take her life. It couldn't have been for the gold, for he could have taken both her *and* the gold. Insanity? That she could understand. Giles had always been of unsound mind; he just hid the fact better than most other crazy men.

"Shaina—" Travis started toward her, his eyes full of concern and love.

It was then that the bear rose again, stunned rather than dead, and prepared to attack.

"Watch out!" Silvanus yelled.

The beastly sow swung its head instantaneously in the man's direction, and with a low, wounded growl, as if it was off balance, started not toward Silvanus but Roux, who had come down off her horse intending to run toward Shaina . . . the only woman who had ever really and truly loved her.

"Mother!" Roux was running. "Are you hurt?"

"No!" Shaina screamed. "No! Untie me, someone. *Hurry!*"

But there was no time to untie Shaina, for at that moment the bear went for Roux. Jay lunged, swiping the ready pistol out of Nolan's hands before the man could even think to shoot the sow himself.

"Roux!"

"Fox Fire!"

"Look out!"

"Roux—" It was her father. "Drop!"

At once Roux flung herself to the ground.

Jay's shot rang out. Then another. Travis added one from his rifle, the killing shot that penetrated through the bear's eye and entered her brain.

Shaina sobbed and gasped, trying to catch her breath. She caught sight of the cubs scrambling away into the brush.

The grizzly, with its last ounce of life, surged forward to collapse on the ground, banging its blood-streaming nose into the dirt close to Roux's small, moccasined feet.

Roux gulped, staring down at the big furry head . . . So like the bear in her nightmare . . . Roux trembled with relief when it at last lay still . . . this time for good.

Instinctively Shaina, still bound, had yanked her knees up to her chest, a movement that caused her to pass out.

"Mother!" Roux cried. "Someone help her!"

A gurgle rose from Shaina's throat as the leather

strained and tightened around her neck after she had fainted. Travis flung aside his rifle, drew his long knife, and cut the leather strips that had been strangling her. He cursed the bastard that had bound her like this and held Shaina before him.

She came to to the sight of him, his face close, and felt him cradling her chin in his hands. "Hello, blue eyes," he said.

"Hello, my husband . . . the man I love." Her smile was weak. He had a beard, a real beard.

"Do you mean that?"

"Forever I will love you," she said as her arms held him close to her breast, "and ever and ever."

Then, as Travis drew her up with him, he held out his left arm for Roux, who came running and crashing into them both, hugging them about the waists with loving ferocity.

Shaina looked over to see the tears misting Silvanus's beautiful blue eyes, and her voice was strong and clear as she said, *"Father."*

Just that one wonderful word as she held out her hand to him.

An incredible look entered the cowboy's face, and then he walked over and joined the family circle . . . the circle of love.

Chapter Thirty-nine

A slight breeze whispered through the lace curtains and softly billowed them, causing Shaina to stir beside Travis and come awake. They had only been back home for several hours, but Shaina had found she had a hard time staying asleep. She kept waking up expecting to find a huge grizzly looming over their bed. Not only that. With Travis so close, she was becoming aroused and knew a terrible need to draw him within her. Shaina sucked in her breath suddenly when Travis's hand slipped beneath her hip and, traveling to her buttocks, he caressed the firm round globes. He breathed a question into her ear, his deep, soft voice sensuous and sleepy. In answer, Shaina touched his lips with her soft, parted ones and her hips responded to the calling thrust of his loins. Then she placed her hand upon his shoulder in a tender caress. His lashes lowered as he gazed at his wife silvered in the soft moonlight coming into the room.

Slow, sweet fire came alive in Shaina's body as his hand moved to the soft, round flesh of her breast, his fingers beginning to stroke and tease. Then he tugged the back of her neck, bringing her face close to his for a flaming kiss of rapture, a kiss that melted every last remaining trace of tension from Shaina's body. Now Shaina lost herself in the wonder of Travis's possession and he delighted in the warmth and love of her response. With a sigh of satisfaction she felt him slide down over her, kissing her quivering flesh with tender care as he moved between her thighs and, cupping her hips within large hands he nuzzled her tantalizing velvet secret, seemingly unable to have enough of her sweetness. His tongue stroked through the soft curls and his lips began a deep erotic kiss that sent Shaina's senses spiraling to an ever-heightening rapture that finally shattered into a million shards of sensuous bliss. At once his body moved over her and he merged them into one. Wild with desire, Shaina's body lifted to gracefully sheathe his hard manhood and urged him onward and upward, taking all of his thrust as he melted into her hot, silken core. When the release finally came, it burst upon them at the same frenzied moment in shimmering waves of rapture that flooded their souls and flung them into the far reaches of ecstasy.

Affected deeply by the perfect union, Shaina and Travis wordlessly lingered in love's tender caress, flushed and aglow, facing into the golden ember of the rising sun. They fell asleep in each other's arms with smiles of deep contentment and love.

In another part of the ranch house, Eleanora was just waking up, her lovely face etched with fine wrinkles as the stark morning light found her. There were several strands of silver gray woven throughout her golden hair, and her skin had lost much of its freshness. But she was still the most beautiful woman in the world to the man standing at the foot of the bed.

"Ellie."

The name had been spoken like a loving caress.

Eleanora started at the deep voice, but she knew who it was. Oh yes, she knew . . . she knew!

"Silvanus."

Eleanora sat up in bed, and as their eyes met, the room came instantly alive and it sparkled, how it sparkled and shone.

Silvanus stared, wordlessly, but his growing smile was as intimate as a tender caress. "Hello, Lady."

"Hello, Cowboy."

His frank appraisal as he came around the bed and stood there made Eleanora's gentle sensibilities come alive. Her hands flew to her hair and her sweet face became alarmed.

"Oh, dear, my hair," she said, "it must be a rat's nest."

Silvanus came close and took gentle hold of the trembling hand that had been rushing to smooth back the tendrils of hair, and she succeeded, on one side. The other was left up to him.

"Oh, Silvanus." Shyly her head dipped as he carefully and caressingly arranged her hair on the right side, and then tipped her chin with a forefinger.

"Don't be shy, Ellie." He was frank. "I love you."

Eleanora swallowed hard in relief, saying, "Oh, darling, all these years, you don't know how worried I was."

He bent to kiss her forehead, then straightened. "I'm going to let you sweeten up, Ellie, not that you need any. But I can see that you are embarrassed. Meet me in the kitchen in half an hour?"

She smiled, nodded, and watched him tiptoe to the door and wave. Then he was gone. But not for long, she knew, not this time, this time she could feel that they were going to be together forever.

Eleanora flew through her toilette, washed her face, brushed her hair back into a neat bun, put on a fresh mint-green dress she'd washed only the day before, cleaned her teeth, and put on her shoes.

Silvanus was waiting as he'd promised in the kitchen, cupping a hot mug of coffee in his hands. His muscular arms were bare and tanned, his shirt-sleeves rolled up, his hair combed neatly and slicked back. His fingernails were clean. His eyes were bright and shining as Ellie entered the kitchen.

"Lord above, Ellie, you're just as lovely as the day we met."

Her movements were graceful as she went to take down a cup and pour herself some coffee from the steaming pot Silvanus had prepared for them to share.

"This is different," she said as she took a chair across the table from him.

He wondered what she meant, and then it struck him, too, even before she began to explain.

"We have never sat down to a table together."

"True." He smiled lovingly into her eyes. "But,

darling, we're going to have many more times to share like this, you wait and see."

Biting her lip, Eleanora looked away. Now that she was here, here with the man she loved and adored, she realized she'd been a fool. Even if he still loved her, and she loved him, that did not mean they could jump in with both feet and get married.

"What's wrong, Ellie?" Silvanus matched her worried expression.

"I'm not sure I'm doing the right thing, Sil. I—I'm still married, you know."

"I—" Silvanus paused, wondering how hard she was going to take the news. He decided to give it to her straight, as he'd always done. "You're a widow now, Ellie."

A look of grief—and guilt—crossed Eleanora's countenance, but it was fleeting. She felt sad that her husband was dead, but that meant nothing, nothing at all, could stand in the way of their getting married at last.

Quietly she asked, "How did it happen?"

Staring out the window, Silvanus said, "When our party returned to the Lazy C, I happened to notice that someone was missing."

"Graham."

"Yes. Shaina had told Travis the story and he—" Silvanus looked candidly into her eyes. "I don't know you want to hear the gruesome details, Ellie. I'd tell you if you really wanted to know, but I don't think you should."

"Was it . . . painful?"

"It was quick."

Eleanora gulped and nodded, saying, "That's all I

want to know, Sil."

Wasting no time, for he'd waited too long already, Silvanus reached across the table for Ellie's hand. She paused for only a moment, and then she placed her hand in his.

"My darling," he said. Then he gazed directly into her eyes, and said, "Will you do me the honor of becoming my wife, Miss Eleanora?"

"I will."

His face beamed with pride and joy, but it was short-lived as he watched Ellie turn worried eyes back up to him. His own clouded, and he asked her, "Something else, Ellie?"

"I—we have so many things to talk about, Sil."

"Like?"

"Like . . . Will, for one."

"The boy." Silvanus squared his shoulders, asking "How old is he now, Ellie? I've so lost track of time

"Twenty." She smiled, love for her son shining in he bright blue eyes. Then the smile faded. "He knows But I don't know how to handle it . . . he is ver upset."

"Oh." Silvanus heaved a deep sigh. He took Ellie hands into his. "We'll do that together, love, like we' do everything else from now on."

Eleanora blushed like a shy schoolgirl, dropping he eyes and shifting her feet under the table.

"Don't be shy with me, Ellie."

A soft whimper escaped her as Silvanus leane toward her face and brushed her lips with his. The: feeling the old flame burst alive, he took her by t shoulders and, lifting her at the same time he ros Silvanus came around the table and stood before h

426

"My sweet, sweet Ellie."

Their lips met and Ellie and Silvanus kissed as if there was no tomorrow, a voracious kiss, a kiss that could equal the ardor of any young couple just in the first throbs of passion. Ellie's slender body moved provocatively closer.

"Oh . . . Sil," Ellie said between the breathless, enchanting kisses.

His lips let hers go. He lifted his head and murmured several endearments, ending with, "I love you, Ellie, and I want you. I want you something fierce."

"I want you, too, Sil. Never have I stopped wanting you. I shall love you until my dying day." Her hands, on either side of his face, learned the planes and grooves all over again as they worshipfully touched.

"Ellie?"

She gazed into the happy, glowing eyes of her love. "What, darling, what?"

"Remember the house you used to always dream about, the one with the white picket fence around it? The one you never got?"

"Yes." Her voice was barely above a whisper.

"I'm going to build it for us, darling. Soon as we're married."

Resting her cheek above his broad chest, Eleanor murmured with tears in her eyes, "You make me so happy, Sil, you always have. I feel young and alive once again, and pretty."

"Oh, Lady, you've always been pretty. But now, darling, now you're beautiful."

She laughed, feeling twenty years younger. "And you're the most handsome cowboy in the world."

Silvanus chuckled, "I don't know about that. But

you make me feel ten feet tall, lady!"

Wiping at her eyes, Eleanora reluctantly broke from his arms and, picking up both cups, said "Want more coffee?"

"Sure do, Lady. Might as well empty the pot. We got a lot of talking to catch up on."

Travis was just getting out of bed while Shaina stretched her body in wanton splendor. What a glorious night. What a glorious morning!

"How about some coffee?" Shaina purred, holding her arms high over her tousled head.

"In bed?"

"Why not? Seems like that's where we've been doing everything else ever since we got home."

Travis clucked his tongue. "Shameless hussy. Are you going to stay in bed all day?"

"Why not?"

Travis shook his head. "There's an echo in the room. All it ever says is, Why not?" He made fun of her in a high-pitched voice.

"Oh, Travis, do we have to?"

Wiggling a dark eyebrow in her direction, he asked "Do we have to do what?"

"Get up, silly!"

For a moment Travis stared around the room reflecting back to the night of Shaina's birthday, and he smiled, happy, to say the least, that they had resolved that part of the misunderstanding. "I do want your baby," Shaina had whispered in his ear as she lay beside him in all her naked elegance. "I am going to have your baby." But there still seemed to be some thing bothering her. He had no idea what it could be and wondered if she would ever tell him. Surely, he had thought, she didn't think he'd been seeing another woman. Ever since their first stunning encounter she'd drawn him like the moth to a flame. Another woman in his life? Never! There was no woman on earth who could take the place of his beautiful Shaina, there never *could* be another Shaina.

"Come on, sleepyhead, get your gorgeous rear out of that bed. We've got company."

"Oh?" Shaina tossed her head with reckless abandon.

"Yeah." He pulled on a blue shirt with pearl-glazed buttons and began to do it up. "They arrived while we were off chasing each other in the hills."

"Funny!" She tossed a pillow at his head, at the same time swinging her long legs over the side of the bed. Her rounded breasts bounced as she stood up and walked naked across the room, her long flame-blond hair fanning down over her back and tickling her saucy buttocks. Travis could almost feel the sensual heat she exuded from every corner of her womanly being.

He reached out and slapped her bottom as she went by. "Stay like that," he growled, "and I just might forget about our guests."

Pulling a fresh white chemise and pink-laced pantaloons from the drawer, Shaina bent over to purposely tantalize and torment him. His eyes narrowing into bits of renewed desire, Travis gave her bottom a lusty leer and, unable to control his baser nature, crossed the room in a few eat-'em up strides. He whirled her in the circle of his arms. Clutching handfuls of her

429

small, hard bottom, he kissed her ardently, rubbing his hardened shaft against her velvety flesh while gazing into the mercurial blue eyes. After the wild kiss, he hugged her tight, then blew her a kiss on his way to the door.

"Later, blue eyes."

Shaina retrieved the pillow and flung it at his head again. This time it hit the floor in a plop after he'd deflected its course by closing the door. He opened it once and tossed her a lopsided grin, then once more disappeared from sight. When he was gone to the kitchen — the first place he always headed — Shaina began to wonder just who their visitors might be.

She dressed with care, smiling tenderly when she realized how lovingly her friend Deanna had cared for her clothes and possessions while she'd been gone. " will have to thank her," Shaina said aloud to be sure t remind herself later.

Then she whirled about to face the wardrobe. He face was awash with anxiety. The one thing that ha been a special gift to her from her husband . . . sh had given it over into Graham's care with the belief i would save Travis's life. She had not had time to te Travis about it. Oh, dear. The red dress . . . how wa she going to explain that one! Well, he would unde stand, wouldn't he? Of course. She had no worr there. Travis was always so understanding . . . we almost always.

"Travis . . . are you in here?"

Shaina stepped into the kitchen, looked aroun found three empty coffee cups situated around t table, and decided she might find him outside with Deanna and Jack. He sometimes had coffee with them in the morning and then, as Jack said good-bye to Deanna for the day, Travis and Jack usually lingered for a moment on the porch, looking over the land before they rode out, either together or separately.

"Travis?" Shaina called as she came to the front door, peered out and, seeing Travis and Silvanus standing there, she let the door slam behind her. She cocked her head wondering who the lovely woman was sitting on the glider looking straight ahead.

The woman's profile . . . It was so familiar, so very familiar . . . .

"Oh!" Shaina exclaimed. The she gave another little scream of surprise mingled with untold joy.

The woman had turned to face her and then she stood up as Shaina walked toward her.

"Oh," Shaina said, softer this time. "Oh, oh . . . *Mother!*"

"Shaina!" Eleanora had her arms around her daughter and they held each other close for a long time while neither spoke another word. Happily, Eleanora pushed her daughter out to arm's length then, her voice catching emotionally as she spoke.

"My child . . . How could I have ever left you . . .? Let me have a look at you . . . . Isn't she beautiful, Sil?"

"She sure is," Silvanus said, emotion thick in his deep voice.

"And . . . you're no child. You're a woman, all grown up." Eleanora smiled at the handsome Travis. "I hear congratulations are in order, honey."

"Yes." Shaina's face pinkened.

"I —" Eleanora reached for Silvanus's hand, pulling him closer. "We have something to tell you, Shaina dear."

Shaina's eyes sparkled like sapphires as she looked from one to the other, mischievously saying, "I already know."

"You . . . know?" Eleanora looked from her daughter to Silvanus. "I thought —"

"He didn't have to tell me," Shaina said, hugging Silvanus close to her side. "After I fainted," Shaina smiled, explaining to her mother, "I was put in bed, and he told me there was something he must say to me. He didn't tell me, all he said to the doc was 'my little girl . . . ' And I knew. I think I have always known, deep in my heart that Graham was not my father, and then when I met Silvanus I realized there was something special about this man. He told me he was 'just a cowboy,' but I knew he was so much more than just that. He's my father," she proudly announced.

Silvanus felt all choked up. *The loveliness of this day I will long remember,* he told himself while smiling into his beloved daughter's blue eyes, blue like his own.

Roux came down of her pony and ran up to the porch, breathlessly tumbling words each over the other. "I am so happy for you, Shaina. I have found a mother, and you have found a father."

No one had the heart to tell her that although Shaina had found her *real* father, Roux had only found a *step*mother loving though she might be. They didn't realize that Roux thought love was love, and that was that, and the heck with "flesh and blood is thicker than water." Shaina stared down at the dark-fire head

432

praying that one day the Indian woman would come to realized how very precious her little girl was. Right now Miah was too selfish to even start to appreciate her daughter. And Roux—she thought her mother was rotten to the core.

Shaina's attention swung from Roux to the stand of pines at the corner of the fence, where sat Jay Ridingbow astride his golden horse.

"Why doesn't he come join us?" Shaina questioned Roux.

The girl looked none too happy as she forlornly said, "Jay is going away. His uncle in New York is sending him to school."

"That should make you happy, Roux."

"It don't." Her face was very sad. "He now stays away from me, Father. Why does he do that?" she wanted to know.

Shaina turned to Travis, saying, "I think Jay is—" She wasn't able to finish her sentence, for Travis broke in with, "I know. We'll talk about it later."

Travis was still holding Shaina's hand while the happy group assembled on the porch spoke softly together. But Roux was not as happy, and that troubled him. He let go of Shaina's hand and tipped his daughter's chin up as he tried to explain to her that sometimes people had to go away, but they came back, they always did, if they truly cared.

"I love him, Father. But he does not love me anymore."

"You were good friends, Roux, I can understand that. Let him go, Roux, and if he really cares, he'll come back."

She nodded, and then sniffing loudly, she held her

hand and waved to Jay Ridingbow, her heart crying out for her beloved friend to please return someday.

Jay acknowledged her heartrending permission for him to go, and he lifted his hand to the lovely girl, knowing he would return. For now, he must go. He could not stay around and watch her grow. It was too hard for him to be around her with his whole being so filled with loving images of her.

"I will come back." Jay mouthed the words and then he turned the golden horse and rode from sight.

Roux sniffed again, drawing her arm across her nose, and then she went down off the porch, calling over her shoulder, "I am going to put my pony away, Father. Then I am going to my room."

"Without supper?" Deanna called from the door, smiling happily at all the company that was going to partake of the beautiful feast she and Jack were preparing.

"I'm not hungry."

Travis and Shaina watched her go, and Silvanus gently said, "She'll get over it." He stared for several moments in the direction Jay Ridingbow had taken. "That's a fine boy. He'll return." He tugged on Ellie's hand to get her to stop chatting for a moment. "By the way, honey, where's my boy?"

Just then Will rode up and there was another happy reunion. This one was not quite as easy, but when Will heard that his real name was not just plain old silly Will Hill but the important-sounding Silvanus William Hart, something in him relaxed and he pumped the hand of the man who was supposed to be his father.

"I like that name a heck of a lot better, sir," he said,

and when Silvanus pulled the lad into his arms for a bear hug, William's face turned red from ear to ear. Then, smiling into the man's face, she said, "Father." Turning to his sister, he said, "Damn, Shainy, ain't this something!"

Later that evening, as all were gathered round the dinner table, Roux excused herself, saying she would be right back. Complimenting Deanna on her excellent cooking, Silvanus turned to Travis then and cleared his throat before he spoke. He held on to Eleanora's hand real tight.

"What is it, Sil?" Travis asked, noting that the man was slightly nervous over what he was about to say.

"Ellie and I, ah, we were wondering if the kids could come to stay . . . I mean they would work hard for their keep."

"Kids?" Travis hid a knowing smile. "You two got more you have been hiding?"

Ellie blushed, saying, "No. *We* just have the two—" She smiled across to Shaina and Silvanus William before she went on "just the two we had together."

"You see," Silvanus picked up for her, "her and Graham had more kids."

"You remember," Shaina said to Travis. "I told you about them on our trip to Mountain Lake."

"Oh, yes, now as I recall there are three more down in Texas?"

"Yeah," Silvanus Jr. put in. "The poor kids are in Texas with our oddball relatives. I sure do feel sorry for them. Especially Abbie, she's the quiet one. I don't believe we half know how sad she really must be away from Ma. poor kid."

The tension broke with the lad's remark about the

relatives, and Travis, with an arm about Shaina, decided quickly what must be done. And Shaina squeezed his arm, in complete agreement with what he was saying.

"We'll send for them right off. No use letting poor Abbie—" he chuckled—"be there any longer than she has to. I'll pick up the tickets for their train fare myself and we can all greet them at the train station in about, let's see, four weeks? Does that sound about right, Sil?"

"Yeah, after all is taken care of. Shouldn't be any longer than that."

Roux had been standing in the doorway next to her large friend, and she was all excited over the news that she was going to have other children to play with on the ranch. Still holding B.J.'s hand firmly, she rushed over to Shaina's side.

"Is it true, Mother? Are there going to be kids my age to play with?"

"Yes, honey, Shaina answered, stroking the girl's shoulder where the long, thick braid lay. "Abbie is just about your age, maybe one year older."

"Oh, good! She can help me read when you're busy with the baby."

"The schoolteacher will take care of your schooling, Roux," Travis told her as he set down his coffee cup.

"S-Schoolteacher," Shaina stammered, then averted her face when Travis looked at her strangely.

But Roux's excitement broke the new tension as she turned to face B.J., asking him, "Are you gong to live here, too?"

Travis nodded once his way and B.J., with a huge grin, one tooth missing in front, looked down at his

436

special little friend, and while all looked on, he exclaimed:

"Uh-huh."

That night, after sharing the exquisite rapture of their special lovemaking, Shaina lay close to her husband, one of his hands resting tenderly across a passion-ripened breast, his fingers merely brushing a cherry-red nipple.

"Travis?"

"Yes, love of my life, what is it?"

"I—I have something to tell you."

Travis looked up into her passion-flushed face, telling her to go on and yet dreading what it could be.

"I don't have the red dress," she rushed on. "It's gone."

"I know."

Shaina blinked. As simple as that?

"You . . . know?"

Shaina moved a little away from him, listening eagerly to what he had to say next.

"I gave it to Carolyn Creek."

"Carolyn Creek!"

With her mouth agape, Shaina moved even farther away from him in shock. "You *what?*"

Rising from the bed and going to the window, Travis stood at the full doors, holding out his arm in invitation to her to come and stand beside him.

With her arms crossed over her chest, Shaina said, "No. Absolutely not!"

"Shaina," he said across the room to her. "Think, Shaina. Try to remember."

Shaina only looked at him and he said, "Are you doing that, Shaina, are you thinking back real hard?"

"Yes." She crossed the room to stand beside her husband, her breath catching as she beheld the glorious new moon he was staring at. Quietly, with Travis's arm wound about her waist, she thought back to the day she had gone away with Graham Hill. "Oh, Travis, I'm so embarrassed! I should be wondering if you are going to be angry with me. Instead I'm acting like a shrewish wife."

"What? Say that again. What's a *shrew?* That's a word I've never heard before." He concealed a grin from her, "Maybe I'll have to go back to school."

Shaina recalled there was a time not that long ago when he didn't think much of schoolteachers, now it seemed he couldn't wait for the new one to come. "Uhmm, maybe the new schoolteacher can find room for you in her class."

"Never!" His eyes gazed deeply into hers, seeing the moon reflected there. "Now, tell me, what's a shrew?"

"No, sir. Not until you tell me how in the world Carolyn Creek got my dress when it was supposed to be used to save you!"

He listened then while she told the details of how Graham had said he was going to use the dress and bring Shaina to Travis so that he could be let go.

Then she listened while he told her how he'd seen Carolyn Creek riding off with the red dress, in the company of Moon Dog. All the while Travis had thought it was her, Shaina, until Carolyn had turned to face him.

"How could you mistake that woman for me Travis?"

Travis shrugged. "All I could see was that dress. I was like a bull seeing red and going after it. I was so angry thinking you were running off with another man."

"Oh, Travis, I could never do that. Never in a million years."

"I thought it was all part of a plan, because right before I spotted the dress, I was in the barn fighting for my life. Those men . . . I know who now, but didn't at the time . . . anyway, they put a wagon in front of the door and then set the barn on fire — with me in it and a rope holding me prisoner."

"How terrible for you. Who was it?"

"*They*. Joe Creek and Vinny Sloan."

Shaina sighed. "*They* will never bother us again."

"Now." He caught her to him and tipped her chin so that she was forced to look right into his eyes. "Tell me what else is bothering you."

"Me?"

"That's right, Shaina. It all started the night of the birthday party. What was that all about?"

"I — I was jealous, Travis, jealous and afraid."

"Afraid of what?" His hands closed over her arms, not willing to release her until she told it all.

"That you were seeing another woman."

Travis gaped down a her, saying, "Did you really believe that?"

"If you think back to the conversation it sure sounded that way to me."

"We were talking about you being *pregnant*, love. nothing else." He shook his head, smiling into her eyes. "No wonder you said you didn't want my baby." He chuckled. "I wouldn't blame you if you had "clubbed me over the head."

"Which I didn't."

"Oh," he said, his turn to look embarrassed, "that."

"Yes . . . that."

He shrugged, saying, "Can't a man have his jealousies, too?"

"I suppose." Shaina was quiet for a minute, then said, "What does the schoolteacher look like?"

"Ahha! The schoolteacher, so that's it. Well, I just happen to have a picture of her."

"You . . . have a photo?"

"Yup." He crossed the room to the tall bureau and pulled the small photo from the drawer. "Noah Starr gave it to me, saying you might like to see who was going to take your place in the schoolhouse. Miss Peabody sent it to him, thinking Noah might want Wild Mountain to see what they were getting."

"Miss Peabody?" Shaina walked over to the dresser as he lighted a lamp there. The light flooded the corner, reflecting onto the photo he held.

Shaina took a look, then threw back her head and laughed a full-throated laugh that made Travis laugh, too, just watching her.

"Well?" He stared down at her, his broad grin sparkling with glee. "What do you think? What does Miss Peabody look like?"

One more look and Shaina flipped the photo back into the drawer, holding her sides as she began to giggle uncontrollably. She stopped between gulps to gasp, "A *shrew!*"

"Really? Is that what a shrew looks like?" This time his smile was a sneaky one. "I thought a shrew was a woman with a nasty temper. Miss Peabody doesn't

440

look very mean to me."

All Shaina's giggles stopped and she stared at him, shaking her finger. "you louse! You knew what a shrew was all the time. But," she said flippantly, "that is not the kind of shrew I was referring to."

"Oh? There's another?"

"There is." She nodded, bringing the photo of the woman to mind again, saying, "The other shrew is a tiny creature with a long, sharp snout."

"Oho! My dear love, you are so clever. That describes Miss Peabody to a T."

There was silence for several moments until Shaina broke it once again.

"Travis?"

"Yes?"

"Uhmm, what about the scarf?"

"Scarf?" He looked startled for a moment, then said, "The purple one?"

"Yes. That one."

Travis sighed, then he launched off in an explanation of how he had discovered it up at the cabin site. Shaina at once understood the significance of its discovery — whoever its owner was, that same person, female, had been with Giles Wilson when he'd tried to kill Travis.

Travis now had a pretty good idea of who was the owner of the purple scarf — he just didn't yet know how to deal with her. He guessed Miah had enough demons of her own to wrestle with. Someday maybe he'd know what to do, but for now he'd let it go and pray Miah's heart would trouble her enough that she'd come to him with her confession. If she knew what was good for her, she'd ask his forgiveness

. . . and her daughter's, too.

"Travis? What's on your mind?"

"You, darling. Just you . . . Come on," he said, blowing out the light, "let's go watch that moon of ours rise."

"Oh," Shaina sighed happily. "We are going to be such a happy family here at the Lazy C."

"What do you mean, *We are?*"

"I mean, when all the kids come to stay, and the baby is born, won't it be wonderful? I've always wanted to be surrounded by those I love most. And now I have you, too, my darling."

"I love you, too, blue eyes. *Forever.*"

Shaina's head tilted and lifted to the shimmering night sky. Tonight all the shadows had been erased from her heart. Splendor was on her lovely face and shining in her eyes like stars.

Epilogue

Despite the cooler weather, the pine trees retained their beautiful shade of deep green and the last of the summer flowers still nodded in the redolent beds Deanna had seen to while Shaina took care of her children. It had been a difficult birth, but the children were doing fine, and Travis was a very proud father.

The twins were nine months old and Shaina sat beside Travis near the hearth while he bounced Mark on his knee. Across from them Roux held little Matthew, shaking the rattle Grandpa had fashioned out of cedar wood for the boys, one for each of them.

Matthew's jade-green eyes matched the alertness of Mark's deep-blue ones. Both boys looked to the door as their grandmother and grandfather walked in. Mark went to Eleanora's lap, and Matthew went to Silvanus's. It was a cheerful family circle that Jack and Deanna walked into. All Eleanora's children had been summoned and Abbie was seated next to Roux, Charlie next, and tall Robert stood behind the sofa, his eyes lighting on Roux every now and then. She smiled up at him. He was her new friend, Jay's age, but he could never take the other's special place in her heart.

Deanna and Jack entered the room just then, with Noah Starr and B.J. close behind.

Jack smiled around the room saying, "The population is sure growing on the Lazy C. Sure is cozy."

"Yes, it is." Deanna said, then announced that there was going to be another addition. Congratulations were in order, and Jack grinned, the proud father-to-be.

"Oh," Travis said, "I forgot to tell the news I heard this morning from Miss Peabody. She gets everything firsthand from Captain Wilson."

"What is it, darling?" Shaina said, waving at her sons while Grandma and Grandpa held them across from her.

"Jack was right when he said the population is increasing. It will even more so."

"Why?" This time it was curious Sil Jr.

"It is the Territory's best claim to statehood."

One and all turned to gawk at Travis. "That's right," he said, "Washington just attained statehood."

All gave a cheer, and the twins, watching the merriment around them, lifted chubby hands and smacked them together. Travis proudly leaned toward Shaina, whispering in her ear, "I love you, blue eyes, you're the best there is in the whole state of Washington—" He kissed her tenderly. "In the whole *world!*